Now *and* Always
YOURS

a novel

Now *and* Always YOURS

Anita Stansfield

Covenant Communications, Inc.

To Dennis, my big brother

Cover design copyright © 2016 by Covenant Communications, Inc.

Published by Covenant Communications, Inc.
American Fork, Utah

Printed in the United States of America
First Printing: February 2016

22 21 20 19 18 17 16   10 9 8 7 6 5 4 3 2 1

ISBN-13: 978-1-68047-941-6

Chapter One

The State of New York

GREGORY TURNEY ROLLED OVER IN his narrow bunk and gazed through the nighttime shadows toward the prison bars of his tiny cell. He'd become accustomed to sporadic sleep during his years within the walls of this modern-day fortress, just as he'd become accustomed to not being in charge of his own life in any and every way. He was told when to eat and what to eat. He went to bed when the lights went out, and he got up at the same designated time as every other man who shared his predicament. He'd learned whom to avoid, whom to stand up to, and whom to defend. He'd learned how to show perfect respect to the guards no matter how unsavory their behavior; some of them were decent men, and others thrived on the power associated with their occupation.

The situation among the prisoners wasn't much different; the same culture existed on both sides of the lines drawn in this place. Gregory had found friends among his prison mates, those who were humble and regretful about the crimes they'd committed and their reasons for being here, men who only wanted to avoid trouble and serve their time. And he'd also learned there were many who only wanted to serve their time so they could get back on the streets and continue their criminal activity, men with no remorse and only a delusional perspective of their standing in the world. These were men who believed the injustices they'd suffered somehow gave them the right to mete out injustice to others in a variety of horrible ways. And they were just biding their time. Greg avoided these men, and he'd managed to be tough enough to avoid being hurt by them—for the most part anyway.

For Gregory, prison had changed his life. It had changed *him*. He'd committed no violent offense, and he'd never taken anything that didn't belong to him. But he'd been closely associated with some very bad people, mostly because that's where he could get the drugs he'd become addicted to in order to escape the painful realities of all the inequity he'd endured from the time he'd come into this world. He'd been completely stoned when he was arrested, so he didn't recall details of all that went down. But he hadn't been able to deny that he'd been in possession of an inordinate amount of illegal substances. He'd quickly figured out that his supposed friends had sold him out and had let him take the rap for many of *their* crimes, and Gregory had ended up being sentenced to many more years than he deserved—at least that's what his attorney had told him. But there was nothing to be done about it since Gregory couldn't even remember enough to help piece together a case in his own defense. So he'd entered these prison walls and had turned his life over to the undeviating structure and tedium of doing his time.

Not many weeks into his sentence, Gregory had awakened to the realization that the only thing he had control over was how he conducted himself and whether or not to take advantage of what little good this place had to offer. He started reading more than he ever had, loving the way books could lure him out of the horrors of his surroundings. And then he found out there was a Bible study class held twice a week, and he couldn't help feeling drawn to it. The more he attended, the more drawn to it he felt. He'd also begun attending the church meeting held every Sunday in the prison, and with time, the Bible study and church services started to change him from the inside out. He'd shared these changes in lengthy letters he wrote every week to his sister, Shannon, and he'd shared just a little with his two children in the same way. Now, his only friends on the inside were those who were also genuinely drawn to these spiritual things, and his only friends on the outside were his kids and his sister.

While he'd been serving his time, his sister had obtained legal custody of the children when their wretched mother had proven herself unfit one too many times. Gregory had felt overwhelming relief once he'd known his kids were in Shannon's care. His sister was an amazing woman who had made all the right choices in spite of growing up with the same horrors he'd experienced. She was now married to a wonderful man and had a new family that Gregory only knew from photos and letters. He was happy for her and grateful for all she'd done for him, but he wondered every day if it would ever be possible for him to be a part of her life again. Or that of his children.

A typical day began, drawing Greg away from his sleepless musings. He was glad to be distracted from his thoughts and worries—even if it meant immersing himself in the same old tedious routine. But he did have Bible study to look forward to in the afternoon. During the hours leading up to one of his favorite aspects of life, he mentally counted his blessings, which was something he'd learned to do a long time ago after he'd heard about it in church. He'd found gratitude to be a great remedy for all the things in his life he had no control over and all the things he hated. He was grateful for such a remarkable sister, grateful his children were in her care, grateful she'd found a good life for herself. He was grateful he didn't have to share his tiny cell with anybody; at least while he was there he had privacy and didn't have to put up with the foul language and negative attitude that would have come with the majority of any possible assigned cell mates. He was grateful to have found God in this most unlikely place and for the healing and mighty change that had taken place within him during these years of incarceration. He was grateful for the good people who gave of themselves to come to this place to teach Bible classes and conduct church services every week. He recounted the list over and over while he did his assigned work, went through his daily exercise routine, and endured the barely tolerable meals.

Greg felt a little downhearted after Bible class. He'd enjoyed it thoroughly but hated that it was over, knowing that the time until they would gather again felt so far away. He was on his way out of the class when he received the news that he would be going before the parole board the following week.

"But it's too soon, isn't it?" Greg protested. He was well aware of the length of his sentence, and he hadn't expected this to happen yet.

"Good behavior, apparently," he was told.

That night Greg tried in vain to sleep while the possibility of parole both thrilled and terrified him. As much as he longed to get out of this place and make a fresh start, he knew that beginning life as an ex-convict was no easy road. At least here inside he knew exactly what was expected of him, and he was considered one of the "good guys" among his peers. Given the overall population, he didn't necessarily see that as a positive thing, but perhaps he needed to keep perspective. He was one of the good guys *here*; but he wouldn't be on the outside—at least not among the kind of people he would choose to emulate in a new life. He wanted only to be part of a community, to get a decent job, to become capable of caring for his kids. But his criminal record would follow him wherever he went, and his relationship with his kids was little more than several years' worth of letters and phone calls. They knew he loved them, but they didn't really know him. They'd been so young when he'd separated from their mother, and not much older when he'd gone to prison.

Two days later, Greg had the weekly phone call with his sister and his kids. They had an established day and time; therefore, it was rare that the three of them weren't all available to talk to him for a few minutes. Unfortunately, minutes were all he'd ever been allowed. His son, Neal, was now fifteen; his voice was getting deeper, and Greg knew from photographs that he was growing tall and starting to look more like a man than a boy. Jeanie was thirteen and just beginning to blossom out of childhood. They were both happy and well-adjusted— thanks to his sister. Her husband, Phillip, and his mother, Marj, had also made tremendous contributions to the care of his children, and had made them a part of their family in every way. Greg was grateful beyond words for these people, for their love and generosity, for their genuine Christian attitudes toward him and his kids. He couldn't even imagine where he and his kids would all be without such love and acceptance. Greg was grateful for the letters, the photos, and the phone calls that allowed him to remain as close to them as possible, even though they lived too far away to visit. And he'd insisted from the start that he didn't want his kids coming to this place to visit him, even if it were possible. He preferred the distance. But now there was a possibility that the distance might no longer exist. As much as he ached to see his kids and hug them and be a part of their lives, he was terrified over what the reality of that might entail.

After Greg had talked to both Neal and Jeanie for a few minutes, Shannon came on the phone, and he hurried to say, "I'm going before the parole board next week."

"Seriously?" she said and laughed, as if it was the most wonderful news she'd ever heard. When he didn't comment, she quickly asked, "What's wrong?"

He admitted with only a little hesitance, "I don't know if I'm more afraid of having to stay or of getting out."

Shannon had never been one to dismiss his feelings, and he wasn't disappointed when she said, "I can understand why the prospect of such a big change would be unsettling, but . . . you know we're all here for you, right?"

Greg pondered exactly how to say what he needed to say. "I'm grateful for that, sis; more than I can say. But . . . I wouldn't blame you if you would prefer that I—"

"That you what? Stay in prison? Go somewhere else when you get out? Greg! We've talked about this. How many times have we talked about this? Go back and read the letters we've all sent you."

Greg recalled the many letters from Shannon assuring him that he was welcome to stay in their large home so that he could be with his kids while he became acclimated to society. Legally it would take some time for him to prove that he was capable of having full custody of them, but Shannon was supportive in helping him with that, and since she'd been caring for the children for years, it was understandable that she'd want them to remain close even when he regained custody. Shannon's husband and mother-in-law had also sent him very convincing letters, assuring him that he was completely welcome in their home and in their lives. They were good Christian people, and he had no reason to believe they hadn't been sincere. Still, he had his doubts that everything could work out as well as they all seemed to believe.

"You've all been very kind," he said. "But . . . the reality . . . is . . ."

"Greg, listen to me. If you need me to remind you of all this, I will. You know that none of us will tolerate any bad behavior or anything that would bring difficulty to our family or the community. That's the way it needs to be, whether you were an ex-con or not. You know all of that. But I know you're not that kind of person; we all know it. And we all know that you have a much better chance at succeeding in this transition if you come to a place where you have support and a stable environment. You need your kids, and they need you."

"Do they?" he asked, trying not to sound as cynical as he felt.

"Yes!" she insisted. "You know they do!" He heard her sigh, and her voice became softer. "We love you, Greg. If this works out . . . and you get to come home . . . we will all be thrilled."

"And if it doesn't?" he asked, again wondering which prospect frightened him the most.

"Then we will deal with it the best we can and pray that next time goes better."

"Okay," Greg said and took a deep breath. "I've got to go. Obviously I will let you know, one way or the other."

"There's a room waiting for you if it works out—*when* it works out."

"Thank you," Greg said, trying to be gracious, and trying even harder not to be terrified.

"I'll be there to pick you up . . . whether you get out next week or next year or . . . whenever. You let me know, and I will be there."

"But you're so far away."

"I'm on the other end of the state; I'm not in Siberia. Picking you up when you get out is a moment I've been imagining for years," Shannon said. "I won't let you deprive me of it."

"Okay," he said and blinked back the sting of tears. "I love you, sis. I thank God every day for you."

"And I thank God every day for *you*," she said. "These kids love you, Greg. They talk about you all the time. Whatever happens, just keep being their dad; they need to know they have a dad who loves them, even if he's not physically here. We never had that, you know. And you've given them that. The letters and calls mean more than you could ever know."

With an audible crack in his voice, Greg said, "Thank you. I needed to hear that."

"Okay," she said, sounding emotional herself. "Good luck. Let me know. If you need me to do anything, let me know that as well."

"I think everything is already in order, but I'll let you know."

They said their "I love yous" and "good-byes," and Greg reluctantly hung up the phone. Walking back to where he was expected to be, he considered the letters that he knew had already been written on his behalf in anticipation of this day. His sister and some decent people he associated with from the church services and Bible study classes had all written to the parole board on his behalf, and they were kept updated. His brother-in-law—a man he'd never met but had shared many letters with—had also written a letter on his behalf. And so had his children. He prayed that the hearing would go well and that it might actually be possible to start his life over. Now that he'd heard Shannon's encouraging words, he missed her and his kids so much it hurt, and he wanted this to be over. He knew in his heart he was a different man, that the changes inside of him were real, that he would never again return to his old habits or lifestyle. He only hoped the parole board could believe that it was true.

* * * *

In the days leading up to the parole hearing, Greg prayed more frequently and with more intensity than he had since he'd feared that his children were in danger while he'd been stuck within these prison walls, unable to do anything about it. Shannon had been the instrument in God's hands to answer his prayers. She'd left behind a successful law career and a nice apartment in New York City in order to take on the care of his children and give them a fresh start. Years after that, his fervent prayers had once again been answered when his ex-wife had sued for custody of the children and it had seemed there was a good chance she might win. Greg knew from phone calls and letters how terrified Shannon had been of losing the children to their biological mother. The children had surely been at least as terrified, and Greg knew that Shannon's husband, Phillip, and his mother had felt much the same. He marveled that these people he'd never met had become so involved in the care of his children. He'd had a few moments of being tempted to feel some jealousy toward Phillip over the way he had become a father figure to Neal and Jeanie, filling a role that Greg hadn't been able to fill. But he had always been able to pray away such petty feelings, replacing them quickly with an overwhelming gratitude that a man would be so thoroughly charitable as to take on the care of two troubled children and treat them like his own. Phillip and his mother were certainly evidence of how many times

God had answered Greg's prayers, and all these events combined had strengthened his belief in the power of prayer and the existence of God. And now he was trying desperately to hold on to those beliefs with the hope that God would give him yet another miracle.

The very idea of freedom felt nothing less than miraculous. Greg had become so accustomed to living within prison walls that he could hardly comprehend life outside of them. In fact, during the days since he'd been told that the possibility of parole was before him, he'd come to realize that he'd long ago forced himself to stop thinking about what it might be like to live outside of prison, simply because it had been too painful. It had been easier to just accept his circumstances and get used to them. The theory had been useful to him then because it *had* helped him cope, but now he realized it had perhaps been detrimental. He'd stopped trying to imagine life on the other side, and now the possibility felt as out of reach as it felt terrifying. However, there was one idea that overrode his fears and that was the desire to be reunited with his family. The prospect of being with Shannon and the kids again felt so thrilling that he couldn't think about it without feeling his heart rate increase, and he often had to fight back the urge to cry. He missed them so much! And he could see now that he'd missed them far more than he'd allowed himself to feel, simply because it would have been too difficult. He hadn't seen any point in torturing himself over what he couldn't have. But now the possibility of getting it back was before him, and his fears had quickly become outweighed by hope.

When the time finally came to be interviewed by the parole board, Greg felt more nervous than when he'd gone before a judge to receive his prison sentence. Back then he'd likely been in shock, or perhaps the drugs he'd been using prior to his arrest had still been affecting his brain. Now he was fully aware of his past crimes, his time served, and the deep changes within himself. He could only pray that the words that came out of his mouth would sound as sincere as they felt and that he wouldn't sound like just another criminal trying to say whatever he believed the parole board wanted to hear. Greg felt sure these people had heard it all, and he prayed over and over that the men and women who held his fate in their hands would be able to feel the truth and sincerity of the man he'd become and give him a chance for a fresh start.

* * * *

Shannon Meadows came awake to the annoying beep of her alarm clock. She turned over and smacked it to make it stop before she pressed her face back into the pillow and tried to motivate herself to face another busy day. Gratitude helped feed her motivation. Her life *was* very busy, but it was also very good. The typical challenges of family life came and went. Viruses and cuts and scrapes were almost as common as the constant flow of dishes and laundry that needed to be washed. There were always toys to be picked up, groceries to buy, meals to be made, and little bouts of bickering between the children to be settled. There was homework to be overseen and practices and rehearsals and school that required a significant coordination of schedules, not to mention a great deal of energy. But compared to Shannon's growing-up years, she knew this was a functional home that provided a fairly normal environment for the children being raised here. And she would be amiss to not thank God for *that* every single day.

Shannon rolled over and found her husband watching her, wearing a pleasant expression that made it evident he'd been awake long before the alarm had gone off.

"What *are* you doing?" she asked with a little laugh.

"You're beautiful," Phillip said. "Since I was actually awake while you were asleep, I thought I'd take advantage of the opportunity to just appreciate how beautiful my wife is."

Shannon soaked in the perfect genuine quality of his compliment and snuggled close to him. "How do you do that?" she asked, loving the feel of his arms coming around her.

"Do what?"

"Make me feel so perfectly loved."

"It takes no effort whatsoever," he insisted.

"That's just the point," she said, unable to help comparing his behavior to that of her own father and many foster fathers and all the men she'd been acquainted with prior to meeting Phillip Meadows. He had a way of giving love so naturally that initially she'd had trouble believing he could be real. But time had proven that he was simply the best and kindest man she'd ever known, and marrying him was the smartest thing she'd ever done. The years she'd been married to Phillip were the best she'd ever known, and every day that passed made all of the ugliness of her early life feel more distant and less painful.

Phillip kissed Shannon with all of the tenderness he was known for, and Shannon was reminded even further of all that was good in her life. She was just beginning to really enjoy it when a little voice from the next room alerted them to the fact that their son—not even three years old—was in charge of many facets of the household, including when they had to get up. There would be no lounging about when little Evan needed attention.

Shannon and Phillip both laughed as they got out of bed. "I'll get him," Phillip offered with a pleasant smirk. "And you can deal with Her Majesty. Since she doesn't believe I'm capable of choosing the right clothes for her to wear, it's always better if you do that part."

"I'm not sure she respects my opinion much more," Shannon said as she and Phillip exited their bedroom and went in different directions down the hall. While he went to help Evan get dressed, Shannon entered Grace's room to find her awake but still in her bed. The four-year-old was keenly attuned to the sounds of her little brother, and he was never awake more than a few minutes before Grace woke up too. But Shannon enjoyed the minute or two that Grace was still sleepy enough to not be wiggly and overcome by toddler energy. She sat on the bed and eased Grace onto her lap, snuggling with her in a rare, peaceful moment. The moment didn't last long before Grace was up and running. Once she'd used the potty and washed her hands with Shannon's help, the child was picking out the horribly mismatched clothes she wanted to wear to preschool. Grace attended three days a week for half a day, but she always knew exactly which days those were, and she was strong-willed about what she intended to wear. Sometimes Shannon just had to give in for the sake of getting through the morning routine with her sanity intact, but she tried very hard to not allow her daughter to end up dressed in stripes *and* flowers *and* polka dots. Even trying to purchase less colorful and more coordinated clothing hadn't worked, when Grace had made it clear that anything too plain or subdued would rarely get worn at all. Shannon could only feel grateful that clothes in Grace's size were inexpensive, and she knew a few different mothers who were always thrilled to receive Grace's hand-me-downs for their daughters who were a little younger and smaller.

With the battle of the wardrobe partly conquered, Shannon had to deal with Grace's abundant curls that were as stubborn as the girl and always reluctant to be brushed or put into place. Grace's blonde hair was similar to Shannon's, except that her own had never been quite this curly.

More than an hour after the alarm had gone off, the family was gathered in the kitchen to share a typically simple breakfast. Everyone had the option to choose between toast, frozen waffles, cereal, or yogurt. Or all of the above. Some fresh fruit or juice was mandatory for every child, with the hope that they'd start the day with *something* nutritious. Neal and Jeanie, being typical teenagers, barely managed to be present for the blessing on the food and to grab something on their way out the door when their car pool rides honked outside—even though they attended different schools and left at different times. On the weeks when Shannon drove for Neal's car pool, she had to leave with him and usually ate her own breakfast after she came back, before going in to work. Sometimes they managed to work it out so that Phillip could drive the early car pool on his way to work. On the weeks when Shannon was responsible for Jeanie's car pool, she tried to time it so that she could do the same.

In contrast to the teenagers barely managing to eat anything at all, the toddlers played in their food and usually made a terrible mess. A fight between them over something ridiculous usually broke out sometime during the meal, but Shannon and Phillip had become a proficient team in keeping the chaos to a minimum, and Marj—the children's grandmother—was there to offer support, although she often preferred to just sit back and chuckle over the entertainment value of the children's antics, a privilege she declared every grandmother deserved.

Shannon and Phillip worked together to clean up the children after their meal and also to clean up the kitchen. Once the kids were playing in the baby-proofed family room just off the kitchen, Marj took over watching them so that Shannon and Phillip could get off to work. Phillip usually left an hour or so before Shannon, and during that time she dabbed on a little makeup, put in a load of laundry, made the bed, and straightened the rooms of the younger children. Then she kissed the kids and her mother-in-law and was off to her office, where she did legal work that was usually quite simple and well-suited to the community in which they lived. Marj took care of the children until a part-time nanny arrived late morning to feed the toddlers their lunch and look after them throughout the bulk of the afternoon. Since naps were becoming increasingly rare, the nanny had become invaluable. Marj loved helping with her grandchildren and being involved in their lives, but she didn't have the energy that a college-aged nanny could give to the overcharged toddlers.

Taylor had been helping with the children for more than two years now, which worked out perfectly with her attending night classes at a college in one of the two cities that were about half an hour's drive from the suburb community of Sugar City. She was a wonderful girl they knew from church, and she'd become almost like a member of the family. She'd grown to sincerely love Grace and Evan, as well as the other members of the family. And they'd all grown to love her. The arrangement couldn't be more ideal, and Shannon hoped that by the time Taylor was ready to give up being a nanny, the children would be old enough to be in school, and summer vacation could be mostly handled by their older siblings while she and Phillip got in their hours at work.

Shannon drove the short distance into the middle of town, where a small number of businesses served members of the community, most of whom commuted to one city or another to work. Phillip was a veterinarian whose business had thrived as he'd cared for the pets of people who didn't want to drive half an hour or more to obtain the necessary services. He handled a continual influx of cats and dogs and rabbits, and he even provided a boarding facility so that small animals could be well cared for while their owners went out of town. Phillip also did house calls to care for many horses and even a few pet goats.

Shannon's legal office was in the same building as Phillip's animal clinic. In fact, the waiting rooms were adjacent to each other. The large, old home had been beautifully remodeled into the perfect working space that met all of their needs. The fact that they could often see each other during their breaks and almost always spend lunch together was an added bonus to working in the same building. And since they weren't terribly far from the schools their children attended, one or the other of them could almost always work their appointments around giving the kids rides or dealing with any need that might arise. Since they both had great people working for them, balancing work with parenthood was made easier. And Marj could fill in and give one of the kids a ride if necessary. She always took Grace back and forth to preschool and did the majority of the grocery shopping, insisting that she enjoyed it. They all worked together to prepare meals and keep the house clean and orderly. All in all, life was well arranged and generally went along without too many hiccups. Shannon and Phillip were very busy people, but they were busy for all the right reasons.

Shannon walked into her office only a few minutes late, although she never had appointments scheduled until ten and after, which gave her leeway in case any given morning presented unexpected challenges with the children.

"Good morning," Celia said from behind her desk in the small waiting room. Celia was a head shorter than Shannon, but Shannon was a little taller than average. Celia often called herself chubby but not in a self-deprecating way. Except for occasional moments of feminine insecurity, Celia was comfortable with not being what the world considered an ideal weight. She was active and tried to eat healthy for the most part, and she had an unassuming confidence that Shannon admired. Celia's dark hair was cut short and well styled. She had a unique way of dressing that added class and character to her warm personality. Her smile and sparkling eyes were always there to greet Shannon at the beginning of her workday, but the fact that they were longtime friends added to the comfort of their professional relationship.

Celia had actually been Shannon's assistant years ago in New York City at a prestigious law firm that both of them had left due to its stuffiness and blatant focus on acquiring wealth and prestige. Here in Sugar City they were able to work together to provide common-sense legal assistance to more down-to-earth clients. And they both loved it. Shannon had the law degree and the experience of being a certified attorney, and Celia was a certified paralegal who was brilliant at organization and efficiency. They made a great team.

"Good morning," Shannon replied, heading to her own office.

Celia followed her, spouting off a list of today's appointments and setting files on her desk that had everything that Shannon would need in them. She finished her daily ritual by asking, "What did Grace wear today?" A little spurt of laughter accompanied her question. Celia knew Shannon's children well due to the time she regularly spent in their home, and she found Grace's antics especially humorous. Since Grace had entered this stage of adamantly declaring her wardrobe choices, Celia always wanted to know the daily outcome.

Shannon chuckled and sat down at her desk, looking absently through the files as she gave the report. "Her black shoes with pink bows."

"The ones that squeak when she walks?"

"Those are the ones." Shannon laughed again. "At least I can hear her every step."

"And?"

"And her purple-and-pink-striped tights."

"So far so good," Celia said.

Shannon looked up as if she had grave news. "Orange and lime-green flowered shirt and turquoise skirt."

Celia grimaced and chuckled at the same time.

"But . . ." Shannon drawled, as if there was hope in this dire situation, "she rarely leaves for preschool without changing her clothes at least once, so maybe Marj or Taylor can talk some sense into her."

"Maybe," Celia said as if it were a serious legal matter, "but not likely."

Celia's phone started to ring, and she hurried into the other room to answer it. She came back only seconds later to say, "It's your brother. I put him on hold."

Shannon glanced at the flashing red light on her phone. Her heart immediately began to pound, and her stomach fluttered violently. Ever since she'd last spoken to Greg, the possibility of him finally being free had hovered in her thoughts almost continually. She'd told Phillip and Marj about the possibility but had said nothing to anyone else—especially not Neal and Jeanie. She hadn't wanted to get their hopes up only to have them be disappointed if it didn't work out. But Shannon certainly had her own hopes seriously invested—almost against her will. She began thinking through plans they had discussed for years, adding more detail into how she imagined it would be when they were all reunited. For all that she'd told herself she shouldn't think about it, and she certainly couldn't count on it happening now, she'd figuratively been holding her breath, not knowing when Greg might call or what the news might be.

Shannon took a deep breath and nodded at Celia, who seemed concerned over her reaction but closed the door to offer Shannon some privacy. Shannon picked up the phone on her desk.

"Greg?" she said eagerly.

"It's me," he responded, and she thought of how she always loved to hear his voice. The very idea of being able to hug him and spend time with him increased the fluttering in her stomach, and she had to force herself to stay calm. Then she realized he was sniffling.

"What's wrong?" she demanded, feeling her hopes crash around her. "What happened?"

"Everything's fine," he said, but his voice cracked, and her heart threatened to implode. "Although . . . I need a favor."

"Anything!" she said, thinking back to the day he'd asked her to make certain his children were safe. She'd turned her life inside out to keep that promise, and it was the best decision she'd ever made.

"I'm going to need a ride home," he said, sounding more emotional.

"Oh!" Shannon gasped, then said more loudly. "Oh!" Before she could get out another syllable, she broke down in childlike sobbing, not caring that he could hear her through the phone. Together they had endured an early childhood with abusive, alcoholic parents. They'd been separated throughout their youth while being shuffled in and out of different foster homes. But they'd never lost track of each other. During the years of Greg's imprisonment, Shannon had remained as close to him as it was possible under the circumstances. And now they had come to this enormous milestone. She felt so happy she could hardly breathe.

Chapter Two

FOR SEVERAL MINUTES AFTER SHANNON hung up the phone, she sat at her desk and wept. At first her mind swirled frantically with questions about how they would handle a long list of things that needed to be addressed. But it only took a minute to recall that she had been planning this for a long time. She'd had many conversations about it with Phillip and almost as many with Marj.

She silently thanked God for the millionth time that her husband and mother-in-law were such kind and giving people. Their willingness to share their home with her brother—in spite of his prison record—was more generous and charitable than she could comprehend. Since Phillip and his mother had been sharing a home long before Phillip and Shannon were married and she had moved in, along with the children, she still felt in some ways that the house was more Marj's than her own. In all fairness, however, Marj had never once said or done anything that had even remotely implied that Shannon didn't hold the proper place in her home as Phillip's wife.

In truth, Marj was perfectly skilled at being supportive and helpful while maintaining proper boundaries of not being too intrusive. Shannon loved her for that and for many other reasons. They got along well and managed to work together to care for home and family with only occasional minor challenges that were easily negotiated with straightforward communication. Marj had taught her things about family and motherhood that Shannon had never comprehended, growing up as she had; she was the mother Shannon had never known. Still, Marj didn't know Greg at all—other than through Shannon's talking about him. But she had always been completely encouraging and eager to help Neal and

Jeanie stay close to their father through their limited communication. And Marj had made it unmistakably clear that she looked forward to the day when Greg could come home and be a part of their family. Shannon was so grateful now to not even have to wonder if it would be an imposition for Marj or if she might feel uncomfortable about it. Marj's ability to express her feelings with straightforward sincerity left no room for doubt.

For all of Marj's avid support, Phillip was even more on board and 200 percent willing to open his home and his heart to Shannon's brother. He genuinely wanted to help Greg become a father to Neal and Jeanie again, even though Phillip had been their father figure for years now. With Shannon's history in dealing with many selfish and abusive people throughout much of her early life, she still felt a little in awe over Phillip's goodness. He'd long ago proven he wasn't too good to be true; he was simply the kind of man who strived to live a life of integrity, and he had a genuine compassion for the struggles of other people. He also had enough backbone that Shannon knew he would never tolerate even a hint of bad behavior in his home—and Greg also knew that from letters she'd sent him over the last few years as they'd prepared for this. But Shannon wasn't worried about that, and she wasn't worried about Phillip and Greg both being able to maintain active roles in the children's lives. It might take some effort to iron out the wrinkles, but she felt confident that everything would be fine.

Shannon took a deep breath and managed to stop crying while she thought of the room in the house they had prepared for Greg more than a year ago. It had been Neal's idea to convert a generic guest room into a room that could be specifically prepared for his father's return. Little by little they had decorated it with masculine bedding and curtains. Shannon had kept some of Greg's personal belongings in her possession, and she had put those in his room as well so that he might feel at home.

Now that Shannon had recovered from the shock and regained her composure, she bolted out of her chair and hurried into the waiting room, where she found Celia pacing and completely ignoring any work. "What's wrong?" Celia demanded. She'd been there the day Greg had called from prison with a desperate plea for Shannon to help get his kids away from their drug-abusing, neglectful mother. And she'd been Shannon's best friend during all the years since. Celia had never met Greg, but she knew everything about the situation, and her concern was completely genuine.

"Nothing's wrong," Shannon said and impulsively hugged Celia tightly, as if that might express her gratitude for all the years of Celia's support in these challenging circumstances. While they were still hugging, Shannon said with a faltering voice, "It's over. He's coming home."

Celia let out a delighted gasp that quickly turned to laughter as she looked at Shannon's face to be certain she meant it; then she literally jumped up and down a few times—which was no small feat in the high-heeled pumps she was wearing—and she got tears in her eyes. "So . . . now what?" Celia asked.

"Everything has been planned and planned again," Shannon said. "We just . . . have to go get him. I have all the information of when he'll be released. I need to make arrangements."

"Tell me what to do, and I'll do it," Celia offered eagerly.

"Okay, but . . . first I have to tell Phillip . . ." Shannon laughed. "And I can't wait to tell the kids, and . . . oh, my goodness! I can't believe it!"

Shannon opened the door between her waiting room and that of the animal clinic. Daphne, who managed the front desk and took care of most of the business aspects of the clinic, had become a constant bright spot in Shannon's life during the years she had been married to Phillip and working in the office next door. Daphne was short and endearingly plump, with short, curly hair that was mostly gray with only a hint of the dark color it had once been. She was so prone to being naturally cheerful that Shannon often thought her to be much like Mrs. Santa Claus if only her hair had been white. Daphne was a loyal employee as much as she was a kind and supportive friend to all of them. She'd become close to Celia while they'd each manned their offices, and they often kept the door between the waiting rooms open during less busy times so that they could visit.

Shannon felt anxious to tell Daphne the news, knowing that she too would be pleased, but Phillip needed to hear it first. Daphne smiled when she noted Shannon's countenance, as if she knew there was some good news in the air. Before she could ask, Shannon said, "Can I snag him for just a minute between appointments?" She spoke quietly in order to not be overheard by the woman in the waiting room with a fat black lab sitting at her feet, likely waiting for his yearly shots. A glance at the dog made Shannon smile; he was adorable, but she suspected the doctor might suggest a diet for the sake of improved health.

"Sure," Daphne said. "He's in room three trimming rabbit teeth. You know how those teeth can get out of control. I'm glad *my* teeth don't grow like fingernails."

Shannon chuckled. "Yes, we humans would definitely have a problem with that. I'll just . . . loiter here until he . . ."

They both heard the door open from the nearby hallway, and Shannon headed in that direction, passing a college-aged girl holding one of the silliest-looking rabbits she'd ever seen. She loved the humor and diversity of Phillip's patients, especially when he often talked about them as if they were people.

Shannon moved into the open doorway of exam room three to see Phillip jotting some notes in the patient's file. When he closed the folder and looked up to see her, he immediately smiled.

"How's the rabbit?" she asked.

"Ned is doing great except for the fact that he's one of the few whose teeth won't wear themselves down the way they're supposed to. But that just means I get to have a chat with him on a regular basis."

"And what did Ned have to say today?" Shannon asked, moving closer to her husband, loving the humor that sparkled in his eyes.

"Ned is concerned about the economy but feels confident that his three-room plastic condo in the corner of his owner's living room will not be affected."

Shannon chuckled. "You're a funny man, Dr. Meadows."

"I know." He took her in his arms. "That's why you love me." He kissed her. "To what do I owe this visit?" He glanced at the clock. "It's too early for break time."

"I have some news," she said, and his expression turned inquisitive. She hurried and got to the point, feeling as if it might burst out of her. "Greg is coming home."

If Shannon had felt any need to question whether or not Phillip had reservations over the situation—which she didn't—they would have been immediately dispelled by the way he lifted her feet briefly off the floor and laughed with perfect delight. "Oh, that's wonderful!" he said. "At last. The kids will be . . . ." He laughed again. "I don't think there are words."

"I know what you mean."

"I'm sure glad that Greg and I have already agreed to share them because I couldn't live without them."

"Neither could I. Let's just hope that Sugar City works out for him the way we're hoping."

"Are you worried?" Phillip asked, his brow furrowed.

"There are so many variables," she said, "but nothing we haven't talked about before. I just hope and pray it all goes well . . . that he can feel comfortable here."

"I pray for the same." The delight returned to his voice. "When should we tell the kids?"

"After school," she said. "We can—"

"I don't know if I can wait that long," he said. "Can't we check them out for a while? Take them to an early lunch or something?"

"I think that's a great idea," Shannon said. "I don't have an actual appointment until two; just some paperwork to get through, and it's nothing urgent. Will your schedule allow for that today?"

"Let's find out," he said, and they walked back to where Daphne was just finishing a phone call to verify an appointment. Phillip smiled and waved at the patient waiting, then said to its owner, "I'll be with you in just a few minutes."

"No problem," the woman said. "Unless any cats come in, we're doing fine. Rupert loves to play with cats, but the cats generally aren't agreeable."

Phillip laughed and so did Shannon. "We'll do our best to steer him away from any visiting cats."

Daphne hung up the phone, and Phillip asked her about his schedule for the day, saying he'd like to take an early lunch and perhaps be gone a little longer than usual. They determined that the intern working for him, a young woman who was getting close to finishing her veterinary education, would be able to handle a couple of basic checkups on the schedule, and there was nothing that required his attention between eleven and one.

"I'll see you at eleven," Phillip said to Shannon and kissed her before he turned his attention to Rupert, talking more to the dog than the owner as he said, "Let's see if we can get you taken care of before anyone of the feline variety shows up to distract you."

Shannon watched for a moment as Rupert and his owner followed Phillip down the hall, then she returned to her own waiting room and closed the door, seeing a smile on Celia's face that reflected her own feelings. Shannon sat down, and they talked for a while about how long plans for Greg's return to the real world had been in the making. Shannon could have talked about it all day, even though there was nothing to say that hadn't already been said more than once. But she had work to do. And if she would be taking time off to go and get her brother, she needed to make certain everything was under control.

* * * *

Shannon went to the middle school to check Jeanie out of class while Phillip went to the high school to do the same for Neal. They'd each agreed they would only tell the children they'd decided they should have a nice lunch together without the little ones around, who always created distractions and a certain degree of havoc. They all met at a diner that was one of their favorites. Shannon had brought the children here when they'd first arrived in town, and they had continued to be regular customers. She was glad to note that the children didn't seem at all suspicious over this surprise outing, and once they'd ordered their food, a nod from Phillip let Shannon know that now was the time to spill the good news.

"We have something to tell you," Phillip said, and the children looked momentarily alarmed until they noted that Shannon and Phillip were wearing pleasant expressions.

Phillip nodded again toward Shannon as if to give her a nudge to continue. "Your dad is coming home," she said.

A burst of excited laughter and hugs made Shannon glad they were there early and the place had very few customers who might be disturbed. The children were full of questions, but they enjoyed a leisurely lunch while they talked through all of the plans they'd been discussing for years, along with details of exactly when Shannon and Phillip would be flying to the airport nearest to the prison's location, and renting a car in which to go and get Greg. Even though the prison was less than an eight-hour drive from where they lived, they'd decided the price of the flights would far outweigh the traveling time they would save. They would be flying back the next day. The tickets had already been purchased with Celia's help, and everything was set.

That evening at supper, Shannon noticed that Neal and Jeanie were both unusually quiet. A glance at Phillip and then Marj let her know they had both picked up on the same concern.

"Is everything okay?" Shannon asked, but before anyone could answer, Grace spilled her food. Evan apparently noticed the uproar over the mess and decided to mimic Grace's accident by dumping his own food on the floor. It was nearly an hour later before the kitchen was cleaned up and the little ones had been bathed.

While Neal and Jeanie were sitting at the dining room table doing their homework, Phillip and Shannon joined them, and Shannon asked again, "Is everything okay? You've both been awfully quiet."

Their lack of response only verified that there was a problem. After a reasonable length of silence that would have allowed the kids to speak up, Phillip said, "Do you have concerns about your father coming back? Because if you do, we can talk them through. There's nothing you can't talk to us about."

"We know that," Neal said at the same time Jeanie said, "Yeah."

Shannon allowed several more moments of silence in which the children could respond if they had anything to say. She exchanged a silent, well-practiced cue with Phillip that let her know he was on the same page with her. They'd both gone to counseling sessions with the children during the adjustment period after their mother had gone to jail and Shannon assumed custody of them. Phillip had been there almost from the beginning of her caring for Neal and Jeanie, and they knew well how to pick up on certain cues from the children—and from each other—and how to handle issues when the need arose.

Finally, Phillip interrupted the silence to try and coax the topic into the open. "For years your relationship with your dad has been through letters and phone calls. It must feel strange to think of actually seeing him."

Neal and Jeanie each made a noise to indicate agreement, but still they didn't speak.

Shannon was grateful to have Phillip continue. "Is there something that concerns you? Something you might be afraid of? If there is, we should talk it through. You know that thing we've discussed before . . .

that if you're prepared it will help ease your fear." More silence. "*Is* there something you're afraid of?" he asked.

Neal let out a sigh that indicated he was preparing to speak. He was usually the one to lead the way in such things. He finally said, "I love my dad; I really do. I love talking to him on the phone and getting his letters. But . . ." He hesitated and cleared his throat, and the silence grew long again.

"Just say it," Shannon encouraged. "Your dad isn't here, so you don't have to worry about offending him. If we know about the feelings you're struggling with, then we can help you."

"Yeah, I know," Neal said and assumed an expression of courage. "Okay, well . . . I guess I don't want things to change. I want my dad to be happy, and I know he's been looking forward to this for a long time, and he wants to be our dad again, but . . ." Neal glanced at Phillip. "I've come to see *you* as my dad. I guess that's it. I love both of you, but you're the one who's been here every day for years. You're the one who's taught me right from wrong and all that. I know my dad would be in my life if he could, so it's not his fault; not really, anyway. I mean . . . he did some bad things that got him sent to prison, but I know he's changed, and I know he loves us. I'm just . . ."

"Confused?" Shannon guessed.

"Yeah," Neal said. "And . . . I want to make my father feel welcome in my life, but I don't want things to change. I guess I'm worried that I can't have it both ways."

"Okay," Shannon said. "Those are all really valid feelings. I can certainly understand why this would be difficult to face, because you don't know what to expect. So, let's talk about it." Neal nodded, Jeanie looked keenly interested, and Shannon went on. "You know there are lots of kids who have more than one father, right? When parents divorce and remarry, kids end up with two sets of parents. Even if a parent dies and the other one remarries, the love a child feels for the dead parent doesn't end, so they still have two mothers or two fathers. I know of people who consider foster parents to be very much like second parents because they form loving relationships. I think it's also important to remember that I'm your aunt even if I've been like a mother to you, and Phillip is my husband so he is legally your uncle. I know for a fact that your father doesn't want to disrupt your lives.

He doesn't want to uproot you from school and friends. He's been adamant that he wants to live here in our home—at least for the time being—so he can be a part of your lives without changing your lives. And even when he's able to be more independent, he wants to live in Sugar City so that he can always be around for both of you. More than anything, he wants the two of you to be happy. Does that make sense?"

"Yeah," Neal said. "I know we've talked about all of that before. I guess I just needed to talk about it again. Maybe I'm afraid he'll change his mind. I mean . . . he will have legal custody, right? Can't he legally take us away from here if he chooses to?"

Shannon exchanged a quick glance with Phillip as the root of Neal's fears came closer to the surface. The attorney in Shannon stepped forward to help her answer the question. "Legally, he cannot take full custody of the two of you until he proves to the court that he is capable of doing so. He will be on parole. He will have to live by very strict rules and check in with a parole officer regularly. Until he can stand before a judge and prove that he has a good job and adequate living accommodations for his children, he will not be granted legal custody. Also, you are both old enough now that a judge would want to know your preferences regarding where you want to live and with whom you want to live. But I know your dad; he wouldn't ever put you in a position to have to make such a choice. He's not like your mom."

Jeanie offered a huge clue to her own fears when she blurted, "Can she sue for custody again after dad gets out of prison? Isn't that what the judge said last time? That this was settled until our father got out of prison?"

Shannon put her hand over Jeanie's on the table. "Honey, I want you to think about how that court hearing ended. Your mother made it very clear—both by her words and her actions—the kind of person she is, and that was written down in the court records. Even *if* she has changed enough to be a good mother—which we all know she hasn't—the two of you can speak to a judge and express what *you* want. Given the number of years you have lived with us in a stable environment and that you like your schools and that you have friends here, it is very unlikely a judge would change that. And once you're eighteen, the courts no longer have a say in such things. That's not so many years away for either of you. But right now we just need to focus on what's happening next. Your dad is coming here to live with us. I'm certain it will be an adjustment for all of us, but I think we are well prepared, and I promise you that Phillip and I will communicate openly with him about anything that needs to be addressed. And if either of you has any difficult feelings or issues, come to us, and we will help you talk to him, or we'll talk to him on your behalf. We're all going to work together to make this go as smoothly as possible. And I think," Shannon urged a positive tone into her voice, "that it could be really amazing. I think you might realize that you *can* have two dads and that they both love you and want what's best for you, and we *can* all be a family. We've added babies to the family, and our love for them has strengthened the love we share for each other. Surely we can add an adult to our household and do the same."

Neal and Jeanie both seemed to like that idea, and their expressions seemed more relaxed. But Shannon and Phillip allowed more moments of silence to pass in order to see if either Neal or Jeanie had anything else they might want to bring up. Jeanie's eyes grew distant before she said, "I was little when Dad left and they got a divorce. I know now what my mom is like, and I think he was right to leave her. Sometimes I was angry because I felt like he'd left us with her and she was so mean. But we've talked about that in counseling, and I know he just wasn't capable of doing any better than he did. Most of my memories of my dad before he went to prison are of him arguing with my mom, and it frightened me. I know he's changed, but . . ."

"But?" Phillip encouraged when she hesitated too long.

"But . . . there's a part of me that feels . . . like maybe he hasn't changed as much as we want to think he has. Maybe it's because I heard my mom say so many times that she'd changed but she never did. Can't a person just write in a letter what they know sounds good? Our phone calls have been good, but they're so short. How do we know what he's *really* like?"

Shannon sighed and again shared one of those glances with Phillip. She could see her own concern mirrored in his eyes, and she hurried to come up with a suitable answer. "That's a very good question, Jeanie. I've known your dad all my life, and I really believe that his bad behavior in the past and that the unfortunate choices he made were more a result of his difficult circumstances than they were an indication of the kind of person he really is deep inside. Now he's learned how to behave better and how to handle his life better. I believe the change in him is real and genuine. If I didn't believe that, I wouldn't be opening our home to him. And I've made it clear that if he shows any inappropriate behavior, he will *not* be welcome in our home. He knows that. The thing is . . . we can only know if he's changed by giving him a chance. I think we need to trust him until—or unless—he gives us a reason *not* to trust him. We should give him the benefit of the doubt. Do you know what that means?" The children both nodded, and Shannon asked, "What do *you* think?"

"I think you're right," Neal said. "We need to believe that everything he's said to us all these years is true. We need to forgive him and not judge him by the way he used to be, or by the way our mom is."

Shannon smiled and saw Phillip do the same. All these years of taking the children to church and teaching them to forgive and not judge had actually sunk in. To see Neal and Jeanie actually living by the Christian principles they were being taught was deeply gratifying.

"I believe that is a very mature attitude," Phillip said to Neal. "And it's the right thing to do, even if it's difficult. What do you think, Jeanie?"

"I think he's right. I feel a little scared, but . . . I feel a little excited too."

"Okay," Shannon said. "How about if we do our best to stick to being a little excited, and we'll just see how it goes? We'll do our best to make your dad feel welcome, and we'll take it one day at a time, depending on how he chooses to respond to us. But I want to add that we need to be patient. The transition from prison to living in the real world can be very challenging, and we can't jump to any conclusions if he makes a mistake. That's why we need to be open with each other and communicate. Okay?"

"Deal," Neal said and Jeanie repeated it.

They all talked for a few more minutes about their plans for welcoming Greg back into their lives, then Shannon and Phillip left the kids to do their homework.

"Well," she said to her husband after he'd followed her to the laundry room, "I'm glad we cleared the air on all of *that.*"

"Yeah, me too," Phillip said. "None of it's surprising. I'm just glad they've gotten so good at being able to talk about what they're feeling."

"All that counseling paid off," Shannon said, feeling a renewed gratitude for the remarkable therapist who had guided the children through a great deal of healing. She'd also helped Shannon and Phillip—and even Phillip's mother—learn how to communicate more effectively and to appropriately handle tough issues.

"So," Phillip said, leaning back against the washer while Shannon pulled towels out of the dryer, "are you more afraid or excited?"

"Both, I think," she admitted. "Although I believe I'm more uncertain than afraid, I think I'll feel better once we actually pick Greg up and get him home. Hopefully, the rest will just . . . fall into place."

"I'm sure it will," Phillip said.

Shannon stopped what she was doing and kissed her husband. "What was that for?" he asked and kissed her again. "Not that I'm complaining, but . . ."

"You're just so good to us—all of us. I couldn't ask for a better husband."

"It's the other way around, my love," he said and kissed her once more.

* * * *

Greg's feet suddenly became very heavy and his head very light as he stood and watched the opening of the first set of bars that had kept him separated from the world. Memories of coming to this place quickened his already increased heart rate and took his mind back to the day he'd entered this prison through the same series of electronic doors and bars. He completely zoned out as if he'd briefly been abducted by aliens and taken through some kind of wormhole in space to be able to look at himself through the eyes of the man he had been all those years ago. The barred door clicked loudly into its open position and snapped him back to the present. Prison guards escorted him to the next set of doors, and they waited as the bars closed behind him and the next sentry point opened in front of him. It all felt like a dream or perhaps memories of an episode of *The Twilight Zone* that he might have watched during his early childhood, in which he was the main character about to step into some strange and frightening unknown world. If not for the knowledge that his sister would be waiting outside to take him home—and that he had two children at home waiting for him—he might have preferred to turn around and ask to stay. Not that they'd let him. Prison was a place people wanted to *leave;* not the other way around.

Feeling a little crazy, he forced himself to focus his thoughts only on the positive prospects that lay ahead, drew a deep breath of courage, and hoped Shannon would be here to pick him up as she'd promised. If there had been some mix-up of times, or she'd run into any trouble getting here, he'd probably have a nervous breakdown that would surely get him committed to some psychiatric hospital.

Greg had been so distracted by his irrational thinking that he was a little startled to breathe in fresh air and realize he was free. *Free.* He closed his eyes and breathed the air more fully into his lungs. Surely it didn't actually smell any differently than the air he'd breathed every day while in the prison yard, but in his mind it *did* smell differently. He lifted his face toward the sun, certain that it shone a little brighter on *this* side of the walls and fences and bars he'd just left behind.

"Greg!" he heard and opened his eyes, a little startled to see Shannon running toward him. He'd actually only seen her a few times in the years since she'd rescued his children from their horrible mother and taken them to the other end of the state. And since the time he'd been sentenced for several charges related to drugs, he'd only been able to visit with her through phone handsets with a pane of glass between them. It only occurred to him that he could actually hug her just a moment before she flung herself into his arms with a tearful hug that took him back to a montage of many moments in their lives. Growing up in the foster system where they'd never been placed in the same homes and then living adult lives that had taken dramatically different paths, their relationship as siblings had been full of a series of tumultuous greetings and farewells. But he'd never been so glad to see her as he was now, never so grateful to have a sister who loved him and cared about what happened to him.

Greg dropped the bag he'd been holding and wrapped her more tightly in his arms, lifting her feet off the ground. When he realized she was crying and perhaps even trembling, he gave himself permission to stop fighting his own urge to cry. They held each other and wept for a good minute or two before she pulled back to look at him, touching his face with both hands and laughing through her tears. He returned the gesture, struck with the reality of actually being able to touch her.

"I can't believe it," they both said at the same time, which made them laugh.

"Are you okay?" Shannon asked.

"Better now that I know my sister is here to hold my hand," he admitted. "It's a big bad world out there."

"Worse than the little bad world in there?" she asked, tipping her head toward the prison he'd just left.

"I knew where I stood in there," he said and looked around with trepidation.

"Everything's going to be fine," she insisted. "You need to meet Phillip," she added at the same moment Greg realized a man was leaning against a silver SUV, watching them through the sunglasses he wore, a smile on his face. Even from a distance Greg recognized a familiarity from all the pictures he'd seen of this man who had taken such good care of Shannon—and of Neal and Jeanie too. Greg felt like he owed this man so much already, and now Phillip was willing to take Greg into his home. They had exchanged letters that were open and honest about the situation, and Greg knew exactly where he stood with Phillip. He felt like he knew him already, but without ever having actually met him, that strange sensation of being in a time warp overcame him again.

Greg picked up his bag, and Shannon took his other hand. Together they walked toward Phillip, who stepped forward and held out a hand. Greg let go of Shannon to offer a firm handshake, unprepared for the way that Phillip reached his other arm around Greg with a welcoming embrace, saying with kind resolve, "Welcome home, brother."

Greg fought back the sting of more tears in his eyes over the words *welcome* and *home* and *brother* all put together that way in regard to himself. "Thank you," Greg said, managing a steady voice.

"It's so good to finally meet you," Phillip said, relinquishing the brotherly hug but still shaking Greg's hand. Phillip's smile widened. "Are you hungry? We waited to eat. I told Shannon the food in that place can't be too great. So, what have you been craving? Anything. You name it. Lunch is on me."

"Wow," Greg said and didn't even have to think about it. "Pizza. Real pizza from that place with the—"

"I know the place," Shannon said with a smile. They weren't terribly far from the city where they'd both grown up and lived most of their lives, and he was pleased when she added, "We can be there in less than an hour."

"Okay," Greg said, and Phillip took his bag, chuckling with surprise at how heavy it was.

"What have you got in here?" Phillip asked, opening the back of the SUV.

"Mostly books," Greg said. "My books have kept me sane. There was nothing else worth taking except all the pictures and letters you've all sent me."

"This bag holds great treasure, then," Phillip said, and Greg instantly liked him—not that he hadn't expected to, but it was nice to finally be able to hear the man's voice and interact with him.

Greg sat in the backseat right behind Phillip, where he had a perfect view of Shannon while they drove into the city. He was relieved to hear her telling him about the children and what they'd been doing. She talked about school and church and the neighborhood where they lived. Much of what she said wasn't new, since her letters had always been detailed and full of such information, but hearing her talk about it helped calm his nerves. He mostly listened and asked an occasional question, just wanting her to keep talking.

Shannon guided Phillip to the pizza place that had been in business since Greg and Shannon had been kids. The food was heavenly, and it helped Greg appreciate what a great blessing it was to now be free. His hesitation to leave the comfort zone of prison already felt ridiculous.

Greg asked Phillip questions about his work as a veterinarian, and he made Shannon and Phillip tell him the story of how they'd met and fallen in love. He'd read the details in letters, but he wanted to hear it. Since Shannon had come to the town where Phillip lived and worked while searching for a new place to start over after taking on the care of Greg's children, he felt like the story indirectly included him. Hearing it made him feel like he could comprehend his own place in their family and in their lives. Phillip had been a father to Neal and Jeanie in ways that Greg and Shannon had never comprehended possible. Neither of them had ever known a truly kind and good father figure in their lives. But Phillip was a good man, and he'd been as drawn to Neal and Jeanie as he had been to Shannon. Over the years, Greg had experienced some moments of jealousy as he'd read letters about the things Phillip had done with and for Greg's children. But such feelings were trite and fleeting; what he really felt was gratitude. Phillip had taken an active role in escorting these children from a troubled childhood into their teen years. And while he'd taken on a fatherly role and had been there for the kids since the day he'd met them, he'd always helped Neal and Jeanie remember that Greg was their father. Greg had been afraid of stepping into their well-established lives and trying to somehow share fatherhood with Phillip, but Phillip had written more than one letter expressing his belief and desire to be able to do just that. And now that Greg was actually sitting across a table from Phillip, sharing comfortable conversation with him, he believed it would be possible.

They shared a leisurely afternoon in the city since they would be staying in a motel that night. Shannon insisted that Greg also choose what they ate for supper, and he chose cheeseburgers and fries, which was something else he'd missed and often craved. Shannon told him they could have arranged to travel home the same day as his release, but the flights and the driving would have made it a very long and exhausting day, and she had believed it would be better to take it a little more slowly and have a day to become somewhat acclimated to his newfound freedom before he adjusted to a new home and to being with his children again after all these years apart.

Once he was settled into his own motel room for the night, Greg took a shower and put on a new T-shirt and pajama pants that Shannon had given him. She'd come prepared with a shopping bag that held some new clothes and shoes, and he appreciated her foresight as well as her generosity. He'd crawled into the bed that felt absolutely luxurious, and he sprawled out over the extravagant space of a queen-sized mattress. Looking toward the ceiling, tears leaked from the corners of his eyes into his hair. He recounted the day and all the kindness and generosity that Shannon and Phillip had already offered him. His gratitude increased his tears, and he said aloud, "Thank you, God. Thank you."

Greg had thanked his sister and her husband more times than he could count, and they'd kept insisting what they were doing for him was a pleasure, not a problem. They assured him they were glad to help and were so happy to have him in their lives. He felt in awe, knowing that the majority of people getting out of prison could never hope for so many blessings. It was in prison that he'd come to know God, and that single fact had changed him completely. He wasn't the same man and he knew it. But he was grateful that Shannon and Phillip knew it too. Without them in his corner, he would be utterly terrified to try and start over, and especially to face his children and try to rebuild a relationship with them. As it was, he only felt a little nervous over the prospect and was willing to take it one day at a time.

Silently he expressed his gratitude to God for a long while, recounting his every blessing through prayer. He fell asleep before ever getting to the amen.

Chapter Three

GREG WOKE UP A FEW times in the night, feeling disoriented. But as soon as he realized where he was and recalled the time he'd spent with Shannon and Phillip, he was able to go back to sleep quickly, blanketed with hope and contentment.

When morning came, they went out for a nice breakfast before heading to the airport, where they left the car Phillip had rented. Greg felt strangely nervous when they had to go through the security screening, but he had all the proper paperwork with him, and he had to keep telling himself this was entirely different from being constantly guarded and having every move watched over by strangers. One airport security officer was especially kind to him and eased his nerves. After passing through the checkpoints with no glitches, he walked with Shannon and Phillip the long distance to the appropriate gate. He liked the way Shannon kept smiling at him or sometimes taking his hand. And he liked observing her comfortable companionship with Phillip. He'd never doubted her word when she'd written to him about the good relationship they shared. He'd simply never been a close observer of a good marriage before. He felt fascinated and intrigued, and he wanted to learn how to be the kind of man that Phillip was.

Every few minutes Greg found himself silently thanking God for all he'd been blessed with, simply because not many minutes could go by without thinking of his freedom, his wonderful sister, her good husband, his sweet kids, the fact that he had a place to go home to. The list went on and on and cycled around and around.

The flight was even briefer than Greg had expected, in spite of Shannon telling him it wouldn't be terribly long. They were only flying from one end of the state to the other. Before he could barely process the reality, they were getting into the dark green SUV Shannon and Phillip owned, and they were quickly on their way to Shannon's new hometown—and the place that Greg would now call home. He'd wondered a great deal about what it would be like, and how the people of Sugar City might treat an ex-convict. But he and Shannon had discussed it through letters and their weekly phone calls, and he was as prepared as he could be to take on a new life with all the possible repercussions of his old one. They had both agreed that the important thing was him being a part of the family again. That too made him nervous, but he knew he needed to focus on integrating himself carefully back into the lives of his children before worrying about anything else. Shannon had assured him they had plenty of space in their home for him and he would always be welcome there. Whether or not he ever reached a point where he was able to get a place of his own remained to be seen. It would depend on what kind of work he could find, along with many other variables. What mattered most to Greg was being close enough to his kids to be a part of their lives. He would work everything else around that. Equally important was that he would never move his kids away from Phillip and Shannon. He wanted to be a good father, and he knew a great part of that was respecting all the good that Neal and Jeanie derived from being a part of his sister's family. And he would never take that away from them—which simply meant that Sugar City would become his home whether he liked the place or not, whether he could fit in or not. He would stay there to remain close to his son and daughter. It was as simple as that. Therefore, he had already come to think of it as home, even though he'd never been anywhere near this place and had only a few photographs to give him any idea of what it might be like.

"We're almost there," Shannon said, startling Greg from his thoughts. She reached a hand back toward him as if she sensed his nerves, and he squeezed it. "You okay?" she asked.

"Nervous," he admitted. "But excited too." He resisted the urge to say *thank you* to them again; he'd already said it so many times, and while he didn't want his gratitude to go unspoken, he also didn't want to say it so much that it began to sound trite. Instead he just looked out the window, anxiously watching for his new hometown to appear. He wanted to take in every detail, and he realized that a part of him was having difficulty accepting that this would actually last. He needed to internalize the belief that this place would become comfortable and familiar to him. He really was free. This really was happening. He had no reason to believe it wouldn't last. He needed to remember the counseling he'd gotten while in prison, which had taught him that it was okay to believe that good things could come into his life and that all of the difficulties in his personal history did not have to determine the paths he would take in the future. He also needed to remember the faith he'd gained throughout these years. God was with him in this journey, and that was the source he needed to turn to when things got rough. And he knew things were more likely than not to get rough. The road back from prison wasn't an easy one, but he was as well prepared—and as well cared for—as any person could hope to be. Once again he silently thanked God for *that*.

"Here we are," Shannon announced, and Greg looked out the window to notice a quaint sign that declared "Welcome to Sugar City." He kept his attention focused on the scenery as they passed through a residential area of nicer-than-average homes with beautiful yards. It certainly wasn't like the neighborhoods he'd lived in throughout his life. He felt out of place already, but Shannon reached for his hand again. She had grown up the same way he had, and she had pioneered the path into a different kind of life. She was here by his side to guide him; she'd told him more times than he could count that she would be there every step of the way. He needed to trust her and try to remain calm. Or at the very least he needed to appear calmer than he felt. He'd survived brawls in the prison yard and the constant demeaning scrutiny of arrogant prison guards. Surely he could survive Sugar City.

Phillip drove into the center of town where a variety of businesses were located. Greg knew from letters that Sugar City had thousands of people living there, but most of them drove into one of two larger cities to work and the businesses here were mostly to support those residents or people who came to visit them. Shannon pointed out the motel where she and the kids had stayed when they'd first arrived here and the park where she had taken them to play. And that's where they'd met Phillip when he'd been out walking dogs that had been among the pets being boarded at his clinic at the time. She also pointed out the diner where she and the kids had eaten pancakes while staying at that motel. Eating breakfast or lunch there at least once a week had continued to be a tradition.

Greg looked at each location through a dreamlike haze. He'd heard about them through phone calls and letters. He'd visualized the stories Shannon had told him of how she'd begun a new life here, caring for his children. He'd even seen some photographs. But the reality—and the fact that he was here to see it—hadn't yet sunk in.

Greg became most interested when Shannon pointed out Phillip's veterinarian clinic, which was a large, older home that had been completely renovated. He'd seen pictures of this place as well. He knew that Shannon's legal office was in the same building. He'd spent many lonely hours imagining his kids coming and going from this place, and he looked forward to seeing inside. But they drove past, and Shannon stated, "We'll go there later or tomorrow. I'm sure you're most anxious to see Neal and Jeanie."

"Yes, I sure am," Greg said and almost gasped from the sudden nervousness that assaulted him at the realization they were only minutes away from a moment he'd been imagining for years. The thought of seeing them again—and being able to look them in the eye with the confidence of being a different man—had kept him going through many difficult periods during these years apart. He hoped they would be glad to see him, that they would be willing to accept him back into their lives to some degree. He knew he'd be living under the same roof, but he wasn't naive enough to believe that meant the kids would want any kind of real relationship with him. He'd made some bad choices, and his time away from them was his own doing. They knew all of that, and they'd told him they'd forgiven him and they understood. But he had to earn their trust again; he had to earn the right to have a relationship with both Neal and Jeanie. And he had no idea what to expect. He was grateful for all the photos and letters, but he still felt entirely unprepared.

"This is it," Shannon announced with glee as Phillip turned into the driveway of a very fine, spacious home with a beautiful yard. Pictures of the house had not done it justice. Shannon had told him it was more moderate and practical than many homes in the area, but it still looked awfully big and nice compared to any home he'd ever lived in.

A garage door opened after Phillip pushed the button on the car visor. He pulled the car slowly into the three-car garage, and he noticed two other cars already there. He reasoned that both Phillip and Shannon had their own vehicles, and Phillip's mother, who lived here, also had her own car. Greg was momentarily distracted by the thought of what it would take to get a vehicle of his own. First he'd have to get a job, and he'd need to save some money in order to avoid debt as much as possible. He wondered how long he would have to depend on family to taxi him around. He remembered then that he wouldn't be driving anything anywhere until he got his driver's license renewed. Overwhelmed by the idea that driving a car was only one detail of the life he needed to put back together, he was startled to realize Phillip and Shannon were getting out of the car and he needed to do the same.

Phillip insisted on carrying Greg's bags and motioned for Greg to follow Shannon through a door. He found himself in the most spacious and beautiful kitchen he'd ever seen, and something smelled good; it was a variety of aromas—something hearty and Italian, perhaps. But there was also a hint of cinnamon in the air. Before he even had a chance to wonder where Neal and Jeanie might be, he saw them standing on the other side of the kitchen. He caught his breath and had trouble letting it go. His hand went unconsciously over his heart, as if it could calm the sudden pounding in his chest. He only had to wonder what to do for a couple of seconds before Jeanie ran and threw herself into his arms, exclaiming with perfect joy, "Daddy!"

Greg held her close and let out his breath. She was so much bigger than the little girl he'd left behind. He'd expected that, but her pleasure at seeing him had already soothed his nerves. He found it difficult to hold back tears, then decided it was just too much effort and let them come. When a quick glance showed him that Shannon was also crying, he didn't feel emotionally alone. Following a long, tight embrace, he eased back to get a good look at his daughter, but he was immediately overtaken by an equally tight and welcoming embrace from Neal, who was not much shorter than his father. Greg remembered having to get down on his knees in order to hug his children. That was no longer necessary; so much had changed. But the love and acceptance he felt from his children was still the same. The biggest difference was that he could now truly be there for them; he could promise to help take care of them and know that he was in a position to keep that promise. Their messed-up mother was no longer a barrier between them. Memories of the way she would yell and scream at both him and the children made him a little sick, and he pushed the thoughts away, focusing instead on this moment.

Once the initial embraces were complete, Greg was able to get a good look at both Neal and Jeanie. He saw tears in their eyes that made him less embarrassed by his own. They both looked very much like teenagers should look—well on their way to becoming adults but caught between childhood and adulthood with the promise of everything smoothing out in the next few years.

Their hair color was almost identical and very near his own—somewhere between dark blond and light brown. He saw a vague resemblance to himself, and he could even see a bit of Shannon in each of them. He also saw some resemblance to his ex-wife, but he was quickly able to replace the connection with the comforting fact that Neal and Jeanie were simply two young, wonderful people, individual and unique and beautiful. Their DNA and genetic structure didn't matter in the least—except that he knew he was their father and he'd never felt so happy in his life as he did in that moment, reunited with them, knowing that he could now work toward becoming the kind of father they deserved.

Neal shyly took in the way Greg told him how handsome he was and how grown up he'd become, but a glisten of new tears in the boy's eyes let Greg know that his words had meaning. He told Jeanie what a beautiful young lady she'd become. She too responded with some shyness, but Greg recognized something in his children that he'd never seen before. They were likely as nervous as he was with the present situation, but Neal and Jeanie both had an air of confidence and maturity that he found inspiring. He knew that Shannon and Phillip were responsible for anything good his children had learned, and his gratitude made him want to cry like a baby. For the moment, he wiped away a stray tear and hugged them again, laughing more than crying when Jeanie hugged him again, saying close to his ear, "I love you, Daddy."

"I love you too, sweetheart," he said. He put a hand on Neal's shoulder and added, "And I love you, son."

"Love you too, Dad," Neal said with a genuine smile, and Greg laughed, feeling perfect delight and happiness. This was the moment he'd been most nervous about. Now it was over, and it had gone far better than he'd hoped. He felt like he could face anything.

Greg noticed an older woman standing some distance away, watching the reunion with a certain glow in her countenance. He knew this had to be Phillip's mother, Marj. Thanks to Shannon, he already knew a great deal about her, including her role in helping his children become who they were today. Their eyes met across the room, and she smiled at him.

"Hello," he said, liking the way the kids moved to his sides and each put an arm around him.

He put his arms around their shoulders and gave them a quick squeeze at the same time Jeanie said, "That's Grandma Marj."

"I assumed as much," Greg said, letting go of his children to step forward with an outstretched hand as Marj moved closer. "It's such a great pleasure to finally meet you."

"Oh, that just won't do," Marj said, ignoring his hand and going on her tiptoes to hug him as if he might be her own son whose return truly meant something to her. She pulled back from her hug and looked at him earnestly with a warm sparkle in her eyes. "You can't know how glad we are to have you here with us at last."

"I'm not sure I deserve such a kind welcome," Greg said, "but—"

"You certainly *do,*" Phillip interjected.

"But I am very grateful," Greg finished, finding ample evidence that his presence here was not a burden or a source of awkwardness.

"Come see your room," Jeanie said excitedly and took his hand. Neal picked up Greg's bags from where Phillip had set them down and led the way through a spacious room with comfortable-looking couches, then up the stairs. Shannon, Phillip, and Marj all followed. While Greg was still a little in awe of the house, he still almost couldn't breathe when his daughter pulled him into the room that she declared was all his. It wasn't extravagant or ostentatious in any way, but it was certainly the nicest bedroom he'd ever had in his life. The simple decor was masculine, with plaid curtains that coordinated with the bedspread, which was brown and navy blue. He took in the queen-sized bed flanked by little tables and lamps. There was a large dresser and a simple desk and chair. Memories of the prison cell where he'd lived for many years magnified his gratitude. He was already a little stunned when Jeanie urged him into the private bathroom that she declared would be his very own. It was decorated to match the bedroom, and his eye was drawn to the large bathtub and the big fluffy towels hanging neatly on a nearby rack. The luxury seemed too much to take in.

"Wow," he said, trying to resist the temptation to gush with the dramatic emotions he was feeling. He met Shannon's eyes and said, "There wasn't anything like this in foster care."

"No, there certainly wasn't," Shannon said, and he felt years of painful memories pass silently between them. But she smiled brightly, her delight apparent in being able to offer him such comfortable living quarters. "Hopefully we can make up for that a little bit."

Greg glanced around. "More than a little, I think. It's like a palace."

The whole family laughed as if they shared Greg's pleasure; it almost seemed as if he was doing them some kind of favor to simply be there and accept their hospitality. Shannon had told him that Phillip and his mother had taught her a great deal about how innately good people could really be and how much they had changed *her* life by taking her and the children into their lives with unconditional love and acceptance. He'd certainly believed her. But experiencing their generosity personally felt a little overwhelming.

Overcome as he was, Greg was relieved when Shannon said to the kids, "Okay, I'm sure your dad is tired. It's been a busy couple of days with a lot of changes. Let's give him some time to rest and get unpacked."

Neal and Jeanie both looked a little disappointed, but that too assuaged some part of Greg that was accustomed to feeling and even expecting to be hurt. They each hugged him and told him they were glad to have him back. He returned the hugs and told them with all the sincerity he felt, "I am so glad to be here. We have a lot of catching up to do. Thank you for making me feel so welcome."

Both children smiled at him and left the room, following after Marj and Phillip. Shannon hesitated and said, "You should have everything you need. There are razors and shampoo and . . . well, everything you should need. If there's anything else you require, don't be afraid to say something. Promise me."

"I promise," he said, "but after what I've been getting by on, I'm certain I'll want for nothing."

Shannon hugged him tightly, and he returned the hug with all the fervor he felt. "I'm so glad to have you back," she said earnestly.

"I'm so glad to be back," he said but heard his own self-doubts leaking into his tone. Perhaps it was being alone with his sister that allowed him to let down his guard a little.

"Is something wrong?" she asked, looking into his eyes as if to make it clear she wouldn't allow him to lie to her.

"It's just . . . a lot to take in. You've all been so kind, and . . . the kids are great. I just have a long way to go, and it all feels kind of . . . disconcerting."

"Disconcerting?" she asked with a little laugh. "I find it interesting that your vocabulary has actually *improved* in prison. I suspect that's not usually the case."

"I'll take that as a compliment," he said. "I suppose I enjoyed talking to the people who came there to teach classes and do church meetings. And I did a lot of reading."

"Well, the changes look good on you," she said and reached up to press her hands briefly over his shoulders as if he were still her little brother, even though he was looking down at her.

"Thank you," he said. "Let's hope the rest of the world agrees—or at least someone who can give me a job, for starters."

Shannon spoke with soothing encouragement. "Don't forget; we've talked about this. Just be confident in knowing who you are inside and in the changes you've made. Be honest and up-front with people about the situation. Some will be put off, others will appreciate your integrity—those are the people you can rely on to help you through the transition. No matter what anyone thinks or how they behave, you'll always have a family who loves you." She kissed his cheek. "It will be all right."

Greg nodded with courage, and Shannon headed out the door. "I'll be somewhere in the vicinity of the kitchen if you need anything. We'll have dinner in a couple of hours, and the little ones will be up from their naps by then so you can meet them."

Greg felt embarrassed that he'd forgotten since their arrival that Shannon had two children of her own. He just nodded and said, "I'll look forward to it. Thank you . . . for everything."

"A pleasure," she insisted and closed the door behind her.

Greg spent a good three or four minutes just standing where he was, turning slowly to take in his surroundings and trying to accept this new season of life. His newly acquired freedom washed over him, and he silently thanked God for being given a new chance. He finally moved from that spot to more closely investigate the bathroom before he unloaded the shopping bag of new clothes Shannon had gotten for him and put them away in the drawers. He unpacked the remnants of his prison life that he'd brought with him. He stacked his books on the desk and put his large collection of letters and photos into a drawer. He put a few of his favorite pictures of Shannon and the kids on top of the dresser, thinking he would like to get some frames when he found a way to earn some money.

Realizing he was as unpacked as he was going to get, considering how very little he owned, he had to admit that he likely *was* in need of some rest. He'd not exerted much physical energy since he'd walked out of the prison gates, but it had been emotionally draining. He made himself comfortable on top of his new bed, not wanting to mess it up too much before bedtime. He sighed contentedly over the quality and comfort of such a bed, which was even nicer than the one he'd used in the motel room the previous night. Considering where he was and the fact that Shannon and his children were under the same roof, he allowed tears of gratitude to leak from his eyes into his hair while he stared at the ceiling. He then closed his eyes and quickly drifted into a peaceful nap, unable to recall the last time he'd been able to indulge in such a luxury.

* * * *

As soon as Shannon knew her brother was settled, she went in search of Neal and Jeanie, wanting to make certain they were all right. She found them sitting on one of the couches in the living area just off the kitchen, with Phillip and Marj sitting on the opposite couch. Everyone was completely silent—something that *never* happened.

"Is something wrong?" she asked. Phillip and Marj both said no, while Neal and Jeanie just shrugged but didn't make a sound. Shannon sat down next to her husband and added firmly, "Okay, who is going to talk first? This is a big adjustment for all of us. We're not going to have anyone keeping feelings to themselves with the potential of causing problems." Still no one spoke. "What is wrong?" she asked again.

"Honey," Phillip took her hand, "I'm guessing there isn't anything *wrong*. I think we're all just . . . well . . . perhaps overwhelmed— because it *is* a big adjustment."

That made sense to Shannon, but she looked at the children to see if they agreed with what Phillip had said. Their faces expressed that they did, but she still asked, "Is that true?"

"Yeah," Neal said but shrugged again, as if he weren't entirely certain. "I mean . . . it's just . . . weird. But it's a good weird. It really is good to see him, and I don't feel uncomfortable around him or anything. It's just . . . weird."

"Okay," Shannon said and looked at Jeanie. They had all been through enough counseling to know that communication was mandatory and they all had a responsibility to appropriately speak their feelings and make certain there were no misunderstandings among family members. "Jeanie?" Shannon prodded when the girl didn't speak.

"Yeah, what he said," Jeanie muttered. "I'm fine; really. It's just . . . weird. But I'm glad he's going to be staying here. I'm glad we can get to know each other again without having to live somewhere else. I think it's going to be okay. It's just like you've told us: it's going to take some time. But I'm okay. I really am."

"Okay," Shannon said and looked at Marj and Phillip, silently urging the other adults to offer some input.

Marj spoke up and said, "He's every bit as polite and kind as I expected him to be. I'm glad he's here, which is far better than thinking of him in that dreadful prison." Shannon felt touched by the way Marj had put it; she was admitting that even though she'd not actually met Greg prior to this day, she had learned to care for him and had worried about him. Marj added gently, "I'm certain that given some time, we will all adjust. In fact, I think that in a day or two we will all wonder what we ever did without him here."

Marj's optimism eased Shannon's concerns about the adjustment period ahead. Phillip added his assurance when he kissed her cheek and said, "He's a good man, and he's family. Everything is going to be all right. Even if challenges arise, we've already discussed how to deal with them. You sent him letters about the rules and boundaries of our home, and we have no reason to think he won't respect them. I think he's probably a lot more nervous and uncomfortable than the rest of us combined. Let's just do everything we can to make him feel welcome and enjoy having him here."

"Of course," Shannon said. "Thank you."

"I didn't say anything we haven't said many times before," he said with a smile and another quick kiss.

"I know, but . . . I needed to hear it again." She put her head on his shoulder, and the kids moved to the other couch, squeezing between Phillip and Marj as if they were years younger. They shared what Shannon had come to think of as the family chuckle, when they all let out a little spurt of laughter at the same time, which seemed to indicate they were all thinking the same thoughts, feeling the same feelings, and whatever might be going on, they were in it together.

A few minutes later the kids left to do their homework, and Marj insisted she would start working on dinner while Shannon and Phillip unpacked. They were unloading their suitcases when Grace woke up from her nap, and Evan woke up minutes later. Phillip and Shannon took some time to just be with the children, since they hadn't seen them at all the previous day. Everything felt so normal to Shannon that it was strange to think that Greg was here in the house. She agreed completely with Marj. Whatever challenges they might face, having him back in their lives was so much better than thinking of him in that dreadful prison. In her heart she really did believe that everything was going to be all right.

* * * *

Greg felt a brief moment of panic when he awoke to a strange sound. He quickly took in his pleasing surroundings, which were strangely dreamlike but at the same time too real to be denied. He really was free and living with his family in the kind of home he'd only imagined could be possible for *other* people. It took him several seconds to identify the noise that had awakened him. It was the distant crying of a young child. He considered how many years it had been since he'd been exposed to such a sound. It had been before the divorce, when he and the mother of his children were both very young, before the ugliness of the life they'd been living had blown up in his face and the consequences had landed him in prison. Neal and Jeanie had paid the highest price in all that had happened, but thanks to Shannon and her new family, they were turning out to be great kids.

Greg let go of his memories and focused on the present. The crying in the distance ceased, followed a minute later by laughter. He smiled, wondering what funny thing might have occurred. Realizing that he was a part of this family and he was missing whatever might be going on, he got up and headed to the bathroom, still overcome by the privacy of such lovely living quarters.

Reassured that he looked presentable, Greg went down the stairs, following the sounds of talking and laughter as they grew louder. He paused on the stairs when the large living area in the center of the house came into view. Jeanie was sitting on the floor with a little boy that he knew would be two-and-a-half-year-old Evan. They were stacking blocks and knocking them down, which made Evan giggle. Neal was on the couch with four-year-old Grace, playing some game with her that was a combination of peekaboo and tickling. They were both laughing, and Greg couldn't hold back a chuckle while observing the tender scene. He'd wondered what life was really like for his children. It had been described to him in many letters, but seeing it for himself was entirely different. He felt that swelling of gratitude again but moved on down the stairs before he could get emotional over it.

Coming into the room, he focused more on his sister's young children. They both had their mom's blonde curly hair, and he recognized them from photos she'd sent him. But again, the reality was different. Seeing them as living, breathing, giggling children warmed his heart.

"Hello," he said, alerting the children to his presence.

"Hi, Dad," Jeanie said so naturally that he smiled.

"Hey," Neal said with no apparent discomfort. So far so good, Greg thought.

"These must be your little cousins I've heard so much about."

Neal said to Grace in an animated voice, "That's your Uncle Greg."

Grace immediately muttered some kind of gibberish before she ran down the hall.

"Did I scare her?" Greg asked.

"No," Neal chuckled. "She said something about her dollies. I think she went to the playroom to get them."

Jeanie added, "You must be officially introduced to all of her dollies."

"Well, okay," Greg said and sat down, reminding himself that he didn't need an invitation to make himself comfortable. Shannon and Phillip had both made it inescapably clear that he was to consider this his home. Looking toward his children, he added, "You'd better stick around. I think I might need an interpreter."

This made both Neal and Jeanie chuckle, and the sound made him feel more relaxed. A moment later Evan picked up a toy truck and brought it to Greg, explaining something in a completely different kind of gibberish.

"They aren't shy," Greg said with some delight as he easily got Evan to sit right next to him. They talked about the toy truck, even if Greg couldn't understand most of what the child was saying. Grace returned with three dolls and sat down on the other side of Greg. The children seemed thrilled over having someone new around who was taking an interest in them, and Greg loved it. He could almost believe that being a part of Grace and Evan's lives might help make up for all that he'd lost with Neal and Jeanie—if only a little.

"You're up," he heard Shannon say and looked up to see her entering the room from the nearby kitchen, wiping her hands on a dishtowel. "Did you get any rest?"

"I did, thank you," he said.

Shannon chuckled when Grace and Evan both seemed to be competing for Greg's attention. "Don't let them overwhelm you," she said. "They're like a couple of puppies, thrilled to have anyone show an interest in them."

"Don't worry about *me*," Greg said. He smiled at Neal and then Jeanie before he put his arms around Grace and Evan. "I don't think I've ever been better."

He saw Neal and Jeanie smile at each other, and he pretended not to notice the glimmer of tears in Shannon's eyes. From her smile he assumed they were happy tears, but he was afraid that if he gave them any attention, he would start crying himself. It was true. He had never had life any better than this.

Chapter Four

GREG THOROUGHLY ENJOYED HIS FIRST meal in his sister's home. It only took a few minutes to overcome any awkwardness. No one seemed at all uncomfortable with his being there, and their genuine kindness put him at ease. He loved the antics of Grace and Evan, each in separate highchairs and making a mess of their food. He loved watching his own children and seeing how mature and kind and polite they were. He had to give Shannon most of the credit for that. Phillip and Marj had contributed a great deal to helping them overcome the horrors of their early childhood, as well as teaching them all the good they had learned, but it was Shannon who had given up everything to give Neal and Jeanie a new life. It was Shannon who had been the kind of person to attract a man like Phillip into her life. Greg couldn't imagine anyone having a better sister or being able to love a sibling any more than he loved her. Just being across the dinner table from her and occasionally catching her eye was like a dream come true. It occurred to him that they'd never actually lived under the same roof since they'd been taken away from their abusive, alcoholic parents in their early childhood. After that they'd always been in separate foster homes until their adult lives had led them in drastically different directions. They'd always kept in touch and had managed to remain close in spite of all the difficulties, but it was really great to just be living in the same house and eating at the same table.

After dinner, Greg helped clear the table and insisted on doing his part to clean up the kitchen. Shannon put him to work at the sink rinsing dishes, which she then put into the dishwasher. He noticed that everyone else had left the kitchen, and he was glad for some one-on-one time with her. He told her what he'd been thinking at the dinner table, and she admitted that she'd been thinking the same thing.

After Shannon had loaded and started the dishwasher, she wrapped her arms around Greg and hugged him tightly. He returned her embrace and whispered, "I'm so grateful for you, Shannon, so grateful for everything you've done for me and the kids. And for allowing me to be here now."

"You don't have to keep saying it. I know you are."

"I don't ever want you to have to wonder if I'm taking all of this for granted," he said.

"I'm not worried about that," she said and looked up at him. "If I ever start to feel that way, you'll hear about it. I promise. I've learned a lot about not letting feelings go unspoken."

He smiled at her without letting go. "I've been through a lot of counseling myself," he said.

"Then we have nothing to worry about," she said brightly.

"I don't know about that," Greg said and leaned back against the counter, folding his arms over his chest. "If we're committed to not let feelings go unspoken, I have to admit that I'm nervous, sis. Today has been . . . perfect. I could have never hoped that settling in with all of you would be so easy. I'm very grateful for that. But I feel like I'm still in a little bubble. I have to get a job and earn my keep. I have to try to make a new life for myself and not be mooching off family. But I have a record, and it will follow me wherever I go. Since I have to check in with my parole officer regularly, I'm certain I won't be able to forget where I stand."

"One day at a time," Shannon said. "Giving you room and board isn't a burden on any of us. If it takes you a while to get a job and get some momentum, it's okay. We're not worried about you mooching."

"If I start turning into a couch potato, you'll let me know?"

"Let you know?" She laughed. "You'll never get away with it!"

"Good!" he said and laughed with her. "As long as I have my big sister around to keep me in line, I'll be fine." More seriously he added, "I need you to promise me that you won't let me start feeling sorry for myself, that you won't let me get depressed. I know it's something I tend to struggle with when things get tough. So don't be afraid to call me on it if you see even a little bit of that kind of behavior. Promise me."

"I promise," Shannon said. "It's just like we've taught the kids: everyone is entitled to have a bad day now and then, and everyone gets discouraged and upset sometimes, but we just don't allow anyone to take out their bad moods on anyone else. And no one gets out of their chores or their homework over such things."

"Fair enough," Greg said. "I promise to do my chores and my homework, no matter what."

"Well," she laughed softly, "if you get sick or something, we'll help cover for you. We have that agreement around here too. If someone gets sick, the family pitches in to cover their chores and help take care of them."

"How amazing," he said and heard the sadness in his own voice. But he knew Shannon understood it. "What might our lives have been like if we'd grown up with such concepts in our home?"

"I've often wondered," she admitted. "But we can't change the past. We can, however, change the future. And we can do it by teaching our children to *be* better and *do* better. We didn't know better before, but we do now, and we have to be responsible for what we've learned and pass it on."

"Yes, we do," he said and hugged her again.

Phillip caught them hugging and teased, "It's only because you're her brother that I'll let you get away with that."

"We've missed out on a lot of years' worth of hugs," Shannon declared, putting her head on her brother's shoulder. "We have a lot of catching up to do."

"You do indeed," Phillip said. He smiled at Greg and asked, "You doing okay?"

"Everything is great, thank you," Greg said.

"Okay. You let me know if you need anything." Phillip winked at Shannon and added, "If you need some guy talk or something, I'm around."

"I appreciate that," Greg said lightly.

Shannon said in the same light tone, "Phillip is probably thrilled to have another adult in the house who isn't prone to being overcome by female hormones."

"You have no idea," Phillip said to Greg with exaggerated desperation, and they all laughed.

Greg appreciated the teasing and the laughter more than he could say. Shannon had told Greg that Phillip was easygoing and had a sense of humor, but the evidence that they could laugh together eased him one step closer to truly feeling at home.

* * * *

Greg went to bed after he'd shared an evening prayer with the, and everyone had given him a hug—even Marj, who had taken his face into her hands and told him how glad she was that he'd come to live with them. He slept well but woke very early while it was still dark and the house was very quiet. He prayed according to well-established habits and read from the scriptures, thinking how great it was to be able to turn the lights off and on whenever he wanted.

The next morning when Greg got out of the shower, he could hear muffled noises coming from elsewhere in the house, and he knew the day had officially begun. Breakfast was a combination of delight and chaos while Shannon and Phillip were both preparing to head off to work, with Phillip leaving first. Neal and Jeanie were getting ready for school, and everyone worked together to help keep the little ones under control. Neal hugged Greg before he left with Phillip, who was on car-pool duty this week and would drop the boy off at school before going to his animal clinic. Since Jeanie went to a different school, which started a little later, Shannon would take her and the other children in *that* car pool when she was on her way to work. Marj would look after Grace and Evan until the hired nanny arrived. And Marj would pick Neal and Jeanie up after school while the nanny was still with the little ones. Apparently car pool only applied in the mornings, since the children involved all seemed to have so many different commitments.

When Greg heard all the explanations of how a typical day was going to play out, he wondered what he might do with himself. He realized that discussing how he would use his time until he found a job had not yet come up, and he felt a little out of sorts until Shannon said, "I forgot to mention it last night, but I was thinking you could come in to work with me if you want. I've got a slow day with only one actual appointment, so I'm mostly just doing paperwork at my desk. Then you can see where I work—and of course Phillip works in the same building. You can meet everyone and just hang out. And later we can make some plans. We don't want you to get bored."

Greg felt relieved with the way she had almost read his mind. He wanted to be helpful, but he wasn't sure he was ready to be left at home with Marj and the children and the nanny he hadn't met.

"That sounds great," he said. "Do I need to bring anything?"

"Just yourself," Shannon said. "Although, a book might be a good idea—if you have something you're reading—in case you have time to kill. I know how much you love to read. We can hit the library later or tomorrow if you like."

"I *would* like that," Greg said, thinking how books had been his salvation during his years in prison. But there had been limitations to what was available. The very idea of a real library felt exciting. But not as exciting as seeing where Shannon and Phillip worked and meeting the people he'd heard so much about.

Greg enjoyed being with Shannon while they dropped Jeanie and her friends off at school. Jeanie gave them both some semblance of a hug in the car before she got out and started walking toward the big double doors, along with many other young teenagers. Greg put a hand on Shannon's arm as a silent request to not drive away just yet. He watched his daughter and caught a glimpse of everything he'd missed in his children's lives due to his poor choices. He'd chosen a selfish, abusive woman to be their mother. And he'd chosen to drown his own pain in drugs until he'd completely lost control of his life. He'd spent many hours discussing his past with therapists and spiritual leaders—and his sister. He knew that with the way he'd been raised, he'd found himself incapable of making better choices; he simple hadn't known how. And yet Shannon had been raised in the same circumstances and her choices had always been better. He knew that she too had experienced a great deal of counseling. But she'd always stayed on the right side of the law. She'd worked her way through many years of college and had become a successful attorney in a prestigious law firm—a life she'd left behind to care for his children. They had both acknowledged many times that they couldn't change the past but needed to focus on the future, and they were glad Shannon had ended up in Sugar City with Neal and Jeanie. Now Greg had ended up here too. He was grateful for how far they'd all come, but he still had a long way to go in making a life for himself, and he had to be careful not to get caught up in regret.

"Okay," Greg said to Shannon, and she pulled the car slowly away from the curb and onto the road.

"You all right?" she asked.

"Yeah," he said. "Just . . . a lot to think about."

Shannon took his hand and squeezed it as if she completely understood without his needing to say anything else.

Greg focused his attention on his excitement at seeing where his sister worked. He'd loved imagining her busily handling the simple legal needs of this community in an office that was a part of the same renovated house where Phillip's animal clinic was located. He found it quaint and even romantic to think of them working in the same vicinity, even though their professions were so dramatically different. They'd driven past the location when they'd come into town the previous day, but Greg enjoyed getting a closer look as they got out of the car, which Shannon had parked in a small parking lot to one side of the building. He doubted that Shannon would have taken her ex-convict brother to work if she'd still been working in that enormous, pompous law firm in the heart of New York City. For that and many other reasons, he was glad to have her circumstances more simple and down-to-earth.

Greg followed her up the steps of a large porch, where he saw two doors, one of which was clearly marked as the entrance to the veterinary clinic of Dr. Phillip Meadows. Shannon opened the other door, on which was painted *Shannon Meadows, Attorney at Law, Office Hours by Appointment.* She'd told him that her friend and assistant, Celia, was almost always in the office on weekdays from nine to five, and Shannon usually was as well. They generally alternated lunch hours so the office was usually manned. But Shannon still preferred to avoid being completely obligated to be in the office continually. The challenges and busyness of family life were more easily dealt with when she had more flexibility.

Shannon opened the door and motioned for him to go inside. As she closed the door behind them, he noticed the woman on the phone behind the desk in the waiting room. She had short, dark hair that she wore in a unique and flattering style. From this angle he couldn't see anything else except that she wore a bright-pink, shiny blouse and silver loops in her pierced ears. Still, his heart quickened a little, and he wondered why. Of course, he'd just gotten out of prison; therefore, having a positive reaction to an attractive woman wasn't a surprise. But as Celia turned to acknowledge their entrance, it only took one glance for him to feel far from indifferent. He felt intrigued by her. She wasn't at all what he'd expected, even though he'd never even thought about *what* he'd expected. Shannon had told him a lot about Celia; their working relationship was as warm and comfortable as their friendship. But the only pictures he'd seen of her had been from Shannon's wedding, and he'd barely paid any attention to the short, dark-haired girl whose face he'd barely been able to see in the small photos.

Greg saw Shannon and Celia exchange a casual wave while Celia continued her phone call, which was obviously with a client regarding some forms that needed to be filed with the city. Celia smiled and nodded at Greg, and he felt like a kid with his first crush as he did the same in return. She looked away in order to focus on the phone conversation, but he didn't stop looking at her until he heard Shannon say, "Have a seat and make yourself comfortable. I just need a few minutes to take care of one thing, and then I'll show you around."

"No problem," he said and sat down in one of the comfortable chairs available. The magazines laid out neatly on a nearby table held no interest for him. He preferred to discreetly observe Celia while he nervously tapped his fingers on the arms of the chair. He looked around the room, examining the details far more carefully than he would normally do, if only to keep himself from staring at Celia and possibly getting caught at it.

Greg heard Celia finish her call and hang up before she said, "So, I finally get to meet you, Gregory Turney."

Greg met her gaze and smiled, pleased by the way she smiled back, showing deep dimples in her cheeks. "And I finally get to meet you, Celia . . ." He chuckled. "I don't know the rest. She's only referred to you as Celia."

"Celia Mae Lindley," she declared. "Back home everyone still calls me Celia Mae."

"Well, it's a pleasure to officially meet you, Celia Mae Lindley."

"I'm *very* glad to finally get to meet *you,*" she said. "I don't have to tell you how long Shannon's been telling me all about you."

"No," he said, trying not to feel embarrassed to realize that she knew his entire life history. He attempted to focus on the positive facet of the situation. "I'm *very* glad that I don't have to tell you all of that myself. I'd much rather talk about you." Greg immediately felt awkward, hoping that hadn't sounded like some kind of pickup line. He felt like he was back in high school with no idea what to say to a girl.

"I could bore you to death," she said, coming to her feet. "If you'll excuse me for . . . just a minute. I need to go over a couple of things with Shannon, and please . . . make yourself at home. We won't leave you alone too long . . . I promise."

"Okay," he said, wondering if he made Celia nervous. She hurried into Shannon's office and closed the door, giving him the opportunity to breathe deeply and check his thoughts.

* * * *

Shannon looked up from her desk to see Celia enter the room. She closed the door behind her and leaned against it as if she'd just escaped from something dreadful.

"Whatever is wrong?" Shannon asked, but not too loudly.

Celia crossed the room, pulled a chair close to Shannon's, and sat on it. "Your brother," Celia said in a dramatic whisper.

"Yes," Shannon drawled, wondering if Greg had inadvertently said or done something that had embarrassed or shocked Celia.

"He's *gorgeous*!" Celia said, taking hold of Shannon's arm with a firm grip. "You never told me he was so *gorgeous*!"

Shannon chuckled. "You've seen pictures of him."

"They didn't do him any justice, I can assure you," Celia said, continuing to speak softly. "I know all about how much he went to church and Bible study and all of that while he was in prison, but you didn't tell me that he was *obviously* going to the gym too. I have *never* seen jeans and a T-shirt look that good! Surely you've noticed!"

"He's my *brother*," Shannon said and chuckled again. Never in a million years would she have thought to line up Greg and Celia with the possibility that they might actually want to go out with each other. But Celia was obviously intrigued with Greg. In fact, she looked downright flushed. Just as Shannon noticed this, Celia picked up a file folder from the desk and began to fan herself with it, making Shannon laugh.

"It's not funny!" Celia whispered sharply, which made Shannon laugh more—albeit softly.

"Lucky for you," Shannon said, "you come over every Sunday for dinner anyway, and he'll be there."

"Oh, my!" Celia said then looked alarmed. "Wait. Wait, wait, wait. Just because I'm having . . . a hot flash or something doesn't mean I want you to . . . well, you can't possibly think that . . . I . . ."

"That you what?" Shannon asked.

"He would never be interested in someone like *me,*" Celia muttered, revealing a rarely seen evidence of her own inability to see how remarkable she was. Celia was a beautiful woman with too many good qualities to count, but some of the attitudes she'd dealt with in her upbringing had damaged her self-esteem. Her childhood had been entirely different from Shannon's, but the emotional impact had many similarities, and they'd shared endless conversations about coming to terms with false beliefs and gaining proper self-confidence. But Celia's worst self-judgment always came out in regard to such things.

"And why wouldn't he?" Shannon asked.

"Look at me!" Celia said, moving the folder up and down to imply that Shannon should take a good, long assessment from head to toe, as if she'd never before seen Celia clearly. "You know I've never had the discipline to lose weight like I should, and I—"

"Celia Mae," Shannon said in a scolding tone that always accompanied the use of her middle name, "don't you *dare* make this about your weight. You eat healthy without making a big fuss over your diet. You're active and you take good care of yourself. You are a beautiful, shapely woman. And don't pretend it's the first time I've said so. I have no idea where my brother's head is at; he's pretty overwhelmed right now. I'm not going to play mediator. But you've met him, and he'll be around. So . . . just see what happens. And if you even *hint* to me or him or anyone else that you are not a beautiful woman just because you're not shaped like the magazine models, I will slap your face off."

"Ooh," Celia said lightly, "I've brought out that violent side of you."

"Not funny!" Shannon said, pointing a finger at her, although they both smiled. Celia knew well enough that Shannon's birth parents had both been violent, but Shannon never had been.

Any sarcastic reference to Shannon being violent was more of a compliment to the fact that she'd not allowed her childhood to determine the kind of person she'd become.

Shannon stood up and moved toward the door. "Try to pull yourself together. I promised him a tour."

"I'll try," Celia said with false drama, waving that folder in front of her face again.

Shannon left her office and found Greg sitting in the small waiting room, ignoring the magazines, lost deep in thought.

"You okay?" she asked.

He looked up at her and smiled. "Yeah, I'm good. Everything all right with you?" he asked, nodding toward her office as if it indicated some kind of problem.

"Yes, of course," she said.

Greg chuckled with a hint of suspicion. "I just wondered. It seemed like some kind of emergency meeting was going on in there."

"No, we're good," Shannon said, certain Greg was sharp enough to pick up on Celia's reaction to meeting him.

Greg proved her right when he asked, "I didn't scare her, did I?"

"Of course not. Why would you scare her? Or anyone else?"

"I am an ex-con," he said with self-recrimination.

Shannon longed for him to be free of that label or at least free of the negative way he viewed himself because of it. She hoped that time would ease that. For now they could only take it one day, one conversation, at a time. She was determined not to gush with trying to talk him out of such feelings. But she did say, "I can assure you that Celia is not scared off by your prison record."

"Really?" he asked with a subtle eagerness in the question that made Shannon wonder if he had some degree of the interest in Celia that she had in him. She resisted the urge to smile and reminded herself that Greg had a long way to go before he could even consider getting involved in a romantic relationship. But in the same thought, Shannon recalled how Phillip had shown up in her life when she had believed the same about herself. They'd been cautious and appropriate, and in the long run he had helped her and the children find a better life.

"Really," Shannon said and hurried to add, "You want a tour?"

"I'd love it," he said and stood up. He followed her through a door that adjoined her waiting room to that of the animal clinic. There were no patients waiting, which meant this might be a good time for Phillip to take a break. She introduced Greg to Daphne, who was sitting behind the counter until she stood up and walked around it to give Greg a hug, as if she'd known him all her life.

"It's so good to finally see you here," Daphne said to Greg, holding on to his hand once she'd concluded her long, tight hug. Daphne had many children and grandchildren of her own, but she had always treated Shannon and her loved ones as if they were a part of her own family.

"It's such a pleasure to meet you," Greg said with a genuine smile. Shannon felt warmed to observe him. No one would ever look at him and think *ex-convict*. He was clean-cut and dignified and respectful. He was humble and polite. She knew he had a lot going for him and she hoped that his prison record wouldn't be too difficult to overcome.

Daphne chatted with them for a few minutes while Phillip was finishing up with a patient—a cat named Sirius Black. Daphne asked Greg about Neal and Jeanie and how it had felt to see them again. She engaged him in conversation as if he'd had the opportunity to meet his favorite celebrity and she wanted to hear every detail. Greg humbly admitted that he'd been extremely nervous, but the kids had been great and everything was going well so far.

After Sirius Black had left the clinic with his owner, Phillip greeted Shannon and Greg cheerfully, and he took Greg on a quick tour of the clinic, including the basement where dogs and cats—and sometimes other small animals—were boarded while their owners left town. Shannon mostly followed the men around, enjoying the opportunity to see them interact. She was pleased to see that her husband and brother were quickly becoming comfortable with each other. They conversed without any awkwardness and often made each other laugh. Greg took an interest in the animals and liked the way Phillip knew them all by name and talked about them as if they were people.

"That's one of the reasons I fell in love with him," Shannon said to Greg, winking at Phillip. "And you haven't met Captain America yet."

"Oh yeah," Greg said. "That's your cat. I *haven't* met him yet." He said it as if he'd been denied something deeply important. "Why is that?"

"I think he's been hiding," Shannon said. "It's a big house, and he finds all kinds of places to hide when there's someone new around. But he'll warm up to you."

"And then you might wish he'd go hide," Phillip said with a little laugh. "Once he warms up to you he wants to lay on your head or sit on whatever you might be trying to read."

Shannon laughed too. "He actually sits right on the computer keyboard sometimes."

Greg said with a smile, "So it's a love-hate relationship you people have with Captain America."

"Something like that," Phillip said, and they continued their tour until Daphne found Phillip to tell him his next appointment had arrived; however, the patient's tardiness had given them a longer break.

Phillip kissed Shannon quickly before he hurried away, saying over his shoulder, "Lunch as usual?"

"We'll be ready," she said.

Alone with Greg, who was still admiring the animals in their individual kennels, she asked, "How are you doing?"

"I'm fine," he said. "I realize I've barely got my toe in the water of a normal life, but you really don't have to be worried about me every minute."

"I'm not worried," she said. "I just want to . . . well . . . I want to know how you are."

"Okay," he said. "I promise to tell you if I'm not fine."

"Fair enough," she said. "But you can't blame me for having some maternal instinct toward you."

"No," Greg admitted, focused on the way a small dog was licking his fingers through the bars of the kennel. "You always did." He turned to look at his sister, and at the risk of dampening the mood between them, he voiced his most prominent thought. "I can't count the times you put yourself between me and one or the other of our drunk parents who wanted someone to hit."

Shannon looked down, not wanting him to see how deeply the memory affected her. "You were just a kid," she said.

"*You* were just a kid," he countered. "Your being a few years older didn't make you any more capable of dealing with that kind of garbage."

"No, it didn't," she said and looked at him squarely. "But we survived it, and we've come a long way, and we're going to survive *this*. So forgive my maternal interference, but I know this is not easy. I can tell you're a lot more unsettled than you're letting on."

"Of course I'm unsettled," he said. "I feel like I'm sleepwalking. This life has absolutely no resemblance to what I've been living for years. I'm more grateful than I can say to finally be free, but I'm accustomed to being told what to do and being on a rigid schedule."

"Tell me what you need, Greg," she urged. "Talk to me."

"I don't know what to say," he insisted and moved on to the next kennel, where another dog was eager for his attention. "I guess I just . . . need something to do."

"Then it's time for us to talk about that and make a plan," she said.

"Yes, we need a plan," he said with a firmness that implied his relief that she'd brought it up. "I'm very grateful to be able to live with you and your family—to be with the kids and not cause any ripples in their lives—but I have to feel like I'm earning my keep. So . . . assign me some chores; put me in charge of something."

"We can do that," Shannon said.

"Good. And I need to find a job. I'm nervous about that. I don't want to fill out job applications and have to admit to my past. I realize that my having made peace with it all isn't going to change the way other people may see me."

"That's true."

"I know I just need to get out there and start looking for something . . . and start filling out those applications . . . so I can stop being afraid of it."

"Good plan," she said. "I know you've told me you're willing to do whatever might be available, and I've told you that this town doesn't necessarily offer a lot of employment opportunities because businesses are limited, but I actually started nosing around a little last week, and I know of a few possibilities."

"Good," he said, pleasantly surprised.

"How about this?" Shannon said. "Let's take the dogs for a walk, which means Phillip or someone who works for him won't have to do it. After that, we'll go sit in my office and make a list and talk about some ideas. Maybe you'll feel better if we have some things in writing."

"Always the attorney," he said, but he said it with a smile, and she knew he *would* feel better having some written guidelines in order to be better able to consider his job prospects.

Shannon was familiar with the routine of putting the visiting dogs on leashes and guiding them up the stairs and out the back door. She had helped Phillip do it hundreds of times. Daphne held the door open for them and told them to enjoy their outing. The day was warm, and the leaves on the trees in the park were starting to show the hint of changing colors. Shannon told Greg the story all over again of how she'd met Phillip in this very park when she'd first come to Sugar City with Neal and Jeanie, and Phillip had been walking dogs. They reminisced a little, focusing on what little good they had shared in their lives, and Shannon told him details about things the kids were doing that she'd never taken the time to write in letters.

After they returned the dogs to their kennels, Greg followed Shannon to her office. They both greeted Celia with a wave as they passed through the waiting room where she was working. Sitting across the desk from each other, Shannon asked Greg to tell her a little about his schedule in prison and the things he'd done there. He'd had work assignments in the laundry and kitchen, and he'd also worked in a vegetable garden. Shannon was thrilled to hear that he actually enjoyed pulling weeds since it didn't take much thought but felt productive; and Greg was thrilled when she admitted that keeping the yard looking good and managing the small vegetable garden were big challenges with everyone's busy schedules. Greg insisted that from that point on he would be in charge of both. And when winter weather made gardening and yard work unnecessary, he would be in charge of snow removal.

"Phillip will love you for this," Shannon said and laughed. "I mean . . . he already does, but . . . he will love you even more."

Shannon explained to Greg the chore schedule in the house for meals, cleaning, and grocery shopping, and they decided to talk with Marj later about how to best fit him into the routine. He couldn't drive until he got his license renewed, and his cooking skills were very limited, but he told her he was capable of cleaning anything and doing it well. Their conversation eased into the type of work he felt like he could do with the hope of getting a job.

"My skills are nothing to speak of," he admitted. "But I can work hard, and I can do the stuff nobody else wants to do. I'll take anything. As long as someone shows me what to do, I can learn fast."

"Okay, that's good," Shannon said. "And I think that attitude will go a long way with many people."

"Thanks to you letting me live with you, I don't need to make a lot of money right now. I just need to be able to pay my own way, take care of my own needs. You know? And eventually I want to be able to put some money away, and I want to start helping the kids more."

"Yes, I understand," Shannon said, respecting him even more than she had all these years through their letters and phone calls.

"I don't know how long it will take me to work up to being able to be on my own, but I've got to start somewhere."

"You shouldn't worry about that now." Shannon put her hand over his. "If being on your own means having any of us living away from Neal and Jeanie, maybe it's better if you don't—at least until they're off to college or something."

Greg hesitated and bit his bottom lip in a way that Shannon knew well as a sign of needing to say something he didn't want to say. She waited until he gained the courage. "But what if it doesn't work out? What if my being in your home causes problems or—"

"Greg, I honestly don't anticipate that being likely, especially if we are open with our communication. Don't worry about that now. Let's just . . . get you into a routine and try to find you a job. And let's not forget that the most important part is that you get to know your kids again, and I have some suggestions for that."

"Okay," Greg said easily, although she sensed he was showing more enthusiasm than he felt. But he was determined to be positive, and that was good. They talked about how he had done classes in prison to acquire his GED, so at least he had the equivalent of a high school diploma. "It's not much," he admitted, "but it's better than I had when I went in."

"I think it's great," she said and meant it.

When noon came, they met Phillip in the clinic waiting room so they could all go to lunch. Shannon invited Celia to join them, insisting they could close up the office, but she politely declined.

Shannon wondered if she felt nervous being around Greg, given her obvious attraction. Whatever the reason, Celia smiled and told them to have a good time.

Shannon and Phillip took Greg to the café where Shannon had taken Neal and Jeanie for their first breakfast in this town. Liv, the kind waitress who had helped them that very first day, was still working there and was thrilled to meet Shannon's brother. Her genuine warmth helped Greg seem more relaxed. Shannon felt grateful to Liv for her kindness now, just as she had felt years ago when Liv had been so good to Neal and Jeanie, even after they'd told her candidly that their father was in prison. Shannon believed that such kindness from people could go a long way in helping Greg heal and lead a normal life. Unfortunately, she knew people well enough to know that not all of them would look upon Greg's past so favorably.

Even though it was lunchtime, Greg asked Liv if he could still order pancakes, since he'd heard many times about how good they were, and he'd imagined for years how they might taste. Liv assured him that pancakes were available any time of day. Shannon found pleasure in how much Greg enjoyed his pancakes, mentioning three times how grateful he was to never have to eat prison food again. They discussed with Phillip some of the plans they'd made, and he agreed that it all sounded great— especially the idea of Greg taking over the bulk of the yard work and tending the garden, which he'd come to hate when life was so busy. Neal and Jeanie were each required to help in the yard every week, although it didn't end up amounting to much given their busy school schedule, prolific homework, and extracurricular activities. But it might give Greg an opportunity to connect with them while sharing work together.

"Oh, by the way," Phillip said, "until you get the driver's license thing straightened out, I wanted to mention that I have a pretty good bicycle that's just collecting dust in the garage. The town isn't terribly large, so it could get you wherever you need to go—for a job or whatever—until you can get yourself a car."

"That would be great," Greg said with genuine enthusiasm. It was clear he liked the idea of not having to rely on family members to give him a ride everywhere he went.

"Of course, if the weather is really bad or something," Phillip added, "we're always glad to help out."

"Thank you," Greg said, and Shannon felt proud of his natural attitude of appreciation and humility. He'd always been prone to that in his personality, but the difficulties of his life had suppressed it somewhat during the especially bad times. Looking at him now, she had to conclude that Celia had been right: her brother was *very* handsome and well built. But he was also sweet and kind and humble. On top of that he'd become a very spiritual man. He'd become everything she'd always hoped he could be. She only hoped the people he encountered would be able to see all the good in him and give him a fair chance to start a new life.

Chapter Five

GREG FOUND THAT HIS SECOND evening in his new home was far more relaxed than the first. He helped in the kitchen, and Phillip walked with him through the yard and the garden, talking about what needed to be done for upkeep. He also showed Greg where the lawnmower and all of the gardening tools were kept. Just the idea that he could go outside and pull weeds anytime he felt the need to be productive made Greg feel more at ease.

They got out the bicycle and discovered that it appeared to be in working order except for a flat tire, but Greg knew how to fix that. While he was working on it in the garage, he was pleased to have Neal come and ask what he was doing. Greg encouraged Neal to help him, and he found gratification in realizing that he'd just taught his son how to fix a bicycle tire. It was a simple thing, but it meant a lot to a man who'd never had a real relationship with his children.

The next day Captain America—the family's revered cat—came out of hiding, and he and Greg hit it off. Greg quickly realized that what he'd been told about the cat wanting attention was wholly accurate. The cat loved to crawl on Greg's lap and try to get between him and the book he was reading, but the children thought it was so funny that he didn't mind at all.

Grace and Evan quickly latched onto Greg's heart. He loved being an uncle and enjoyed helping keep the younger children occupied at times when others were busy and his doing so was actually helpful. Greg met Taylor the nanny and liked her as well. Noting how comfortable she was in the house and with the family helped Greg feel more relaxed about being able to follow her example. If Taylor—

who was no relation at all—could make herself completely at home, then Greg certainly could do the same.

Within a few days, Greg had acclimated himself to the household routine and felt more a part of it. Neal and Jeanie seemed comfortable with him, especially knowing that he had no intention of ever taking them away from Phillip and Shannon—even when a day came that he might legally have full custody again. They didn't talk about the children's mother at all. Greg felt sure the subject would come up eventually, but for now it seemed they all preferred to ignore the damage this woman had created in their lives.

On Saturday, Jeanie had a softball practice. She played on a city team and really enjoyed it. Ironically, Neal didn't care much for traditional sports; he preferred reading and anything to do with technology—which made him a typical nerd in every good way. But Greg's daughter loved sports, and he went to the practice just to watch. He was amazed at how good she was and how much she was enjoying herself. He was even more amazed to realize this was his daughter and she had grown up so much.

After Shannon picked them both up, she took them to the library, where she got Greg a library card, and he and Jeanie perused the shelves, talking about the kind of books they liked to read. She picked out something she thought Neal would like and a book for herself. Greg got a novel by an author who had written something else he'd read a few years earlier. During the drive home, Greg was able to note the location of the library in regard to other places he was becoming familiar with, and he felt certain he could find his way around town on his bike and easily get to the library, which was not far from the house.

On Sunday Greg was thrilled to be able to go to church with the family. Shannon had taken him to buy some slacks and shoes that were appropriate, as well as a white shirt and tie. He'd never owned such clothing before in his life. He promised to pay her back, but she was insistent that the clothes were a gift and she wouldn't have it any other way.

At church many people were friendly and kind, although he sensed a discreet avoidance from some and perhaps some vague stares and whispers. He knew it was to be expected, but he hoped that time would prove to everyone he encountered that he was not a man ruled by his past.

Celia came over for Sunday dinner, and Greg enjoyed seeing her dressed more casually than she'd been at the office. She was obviously very comfortable with everyone in the family, and she appeared to enjoy helping with Evan and Grace. He observed her with a strange fascination, as if he'd never really seen a woman before. More accurately, he'd never encountered a woman quite like Celia. He asked himself if his intrigue was simply a hangover from years in prison where he'd encountered no women at all, but he knew it was far more than that. He'd seen and spoken with many women since he'd walked out of those prison gates—even if most of those encounters had been brief. But Celia definitely sparked something in him that he'd not felt in a long time. With such thoughts, he couldn't help thinking of his ex-wife. He'd had girlfriends before her, but BK—as she'd always been known—was the only woman he'd ever considered himself to have truly loved. But looking back, he wasn't certain love ever had anything to do with it. He had been so messed up at the time, even more messed up than he. It had all been one disaster after another.

The bottom line was that he'd never had any kind of truly functional relationship with a woman, and while he had a strong desire to get to know Celia better, he had to conclude that he wasn't necessarily a good catch for a well-educated woman who actually had some class and refinement. So he tried to be polite and friendly and not get his hopes up. He had way too many bridges to cross in order to integrate himself fully back into the real world. Romance was something he'd be a fool to even consider until he at least had a job and a driver's license. Having neither, he felt more equal to his fifteen-year-old son. For the time being, he simply enjoyed having Celia around, and he found plealsure in their little snatches of conversation. Anything else he might feel or think in regard to her was simply pushed to the back of his mind to be looked at some time in the future.

As a new week began, Greg tried to keep himself occupied by either reading or working in the yard. Since the yard had already been fairly well groomed, it didn't take long to get it back into shape. He finished the book he'd gotten from the library and went back to get a couple more. During the days when Neal and Jeanie were at school and Phillip and Shannon at work, he felt a little out of place with Marj and Taylor doing things around the house and taking care of Grace and Evan. He tried to either stay in his room or outside, and he often rode his bike into town to meet Shannon and Phillip for lunch or a break.

He most enjoyed the time when the family was all together, which was usually only for dinner and breakfast, and much of the time Neal or Jeanie—or both—were rushing in or out with a variety of extracurricular activities. He had come to realize that the family's schedule was pretty crazy, especially with Grace and Evan almost always underfoot and having many needs. The problem was that he mostly felt on the outside of the orderly chaos, when he wanted to feel more involved. He figured that would just take time, so he reminded himself to be patient, and he watched for any opportunity to try to be useful.

Greg felt at home most of the time, but there were still moments of awkwardness when he felt out of place even if he couldn't quite pinpoint why. About a week into his new life, the awkwardness Greg was trying not to feel became suddenly impossible to ignore when Neal used the word *Dad,* and both Phillip and Greg responded simultaneously. Phillip and Greg exchanged a startled glance, and Greg saw nothing in Phillip's expression except compassion and uncertainty. Greg could only feel ashamed, finding no reason to deserve the title of father in Neal's and Jeanie's lives. A terrible silence filled the air. And since Marj and Shannon and Jeanie were all witnesses to the awkwardness, there was no hiding the fact that *everyone* felt uneasy and caught off guard.

No one knew what to say; that was obvious. Greg cleared his throat and said what he knew was most important. He looked directly at Neal and spoke with firm assurance, "It's okay. I understand." He turned to Jeanie to include her. "The last thing I want is to make anything difficult or uncomfortable for any of you. Let's just . . ." He realized he didn't know how to finish that sentence, but Shannon saved him.

"Obviously we have some things to work out," she said. "Let's just set this aside for the moment and give the matter some thought. We'll sit down and talk about it later. Is everyone free this evening right after we put Grace and Evan down for the night?"

Everyone either nodded or muttered a word of agreement. Greg just said, "I'll be there," and hurried out of the room, fearing he might exhibit some kind of childish behavior as the turmoil inside of him began to rumble out of control. He rushed up the stairs to his room and closed the door, leaning against it as he took in deep breaths. He'd feared moments like the one that had just happened. It was ridiculous to think that such things wouldn't occur, given the circumstances, but he hated the reality of it, and he wished that he knew how to solve it without creating more tension and awkwardness with the people he loved.

Greg feared that Shannon might come to his room and try to talk to him so he was relieved when she didn't. He wondered if she was just busy or if she sensed his need to be alone. Either way, he was glad for the time to think. He went down to supper—with the determination to behave normally and not contribute to the strain. He knew that the problem was his responsibility because it was his choices that had created it. He needed to act like a man and accept the consequences of his actions, exactly as he'd learned in the countless sessions of counseling he'd experienced during his years in prison.

Supper with the family went relatively well, mostly because Evan and Grace were both noisy and kept everyone entertained with their toddler antics. Greg insisted on doing the dishes after the meal was over, and no one said anything directly to him except for Shannon asking him quietly, "Are you okay?"

"I'm working on it," he said. "Don't worry about me." She looked worried anyway, and he firmly reassured her, "We knew stuff like this would happen. We'll deal with it. I'm fine."

"Okay," she said and hugged him before one of her children needed her and she left to deal with whatever the problem might be.

Later, after Evan and Grace had been put to bed, the rest of the family sat down together around the kitchen table. Greg felt only slightly nervous. He knew what he needed to say, and he felt relatively certain that everyone would be willing to hear him out and be reasonable about it. He was ready to just say it and get it over with, when Marj said, "Would it be all right if I say something first?"

"Of course," Phillip said.

"You all know this, but I think sometimes things need to be spoken out loud if only so we don't forget where things stand and how people feel. So I'm just going to speak my piece. When I contributed to the building of this home, it was with the agreement that it would always be my home for as long as I'm around. But I always knew that when Phillip married I would be more than happy to take my proper place. I'm grateful every day that Shannon and I have always gotten along well enough to share a home and never have any disagreement that can't be solved with some simple communication and compromise." She smiled at Shannon. "I am very blessed, and I feel blessed to be a part of my grandchildren's lives in such an active way. Having said that," Marj's focus turned to Greg, "I have loved Neal and Jeanie from the first time they helped make cookies in this kitchen. They are my grandchildren as much as Evan and Grace or any of the others who don't live so close. As strange as that might seem to you, dear, that makes you feel like a son to me. I know we only met very recently, but because of Shannon, I've gotten to know you through the years. And I just want to say that I consider it a privilege to have you here, and I don't think children can ever have too many people who love them. There." Marj pressed her hands down the front of her dress and then set them on the table as if to officially conclude her remarks. "That's what I wanted to say."

"Thank you, Mother," Phillip said and squeezed his mother's hand briefly. Greg observed one more piece of evidence of the love present in this home and marveled over it. But he forced himself to the issue at hand in order to say what he needed to say before anyone else had a chance to talk.

"I've been thinking about this," Greg said, "and there's something I would like to say because I want it to be perfectly clear where I stand and how I feel."

The other adults at the table nodded with expressions of encouragement. Neal and Jeanie just looked at him expectantly, as if they hoped he could ease the difficulty of this situation for them. He truly hoped that he could, and he looked directly at them while he spoke.

"In fact, this is something I've been thinking about ever since I knew that Shannon and Phillip had legal custody of you. I was so relieved to know they were taking care of you, and after your mother tried to get you back and failed—praise heaven—I was even more relieved. We have all been very blessed by what Shannon and Phillip and Marj have done for all of us. The situation here for the two of you is about as good as I think it could ever be for *any* kid. And I'm not here to change that or to do anything that might make things difficult or uncomfortable for you."

Greg could see a lessening of concern in his children's eyes, even though it was subtle. He took a deep breath and continued with what he needed to say. "Now, I want to talk to you a little bit about my place in your lives and why it is the way it is, and I'm glad that we're all here together because I want everyone to know what I have to say." He glanced quickly toward the other adults to be assured that they seemed okay with what he'd said so far. Then he turned his attention back to Neal and Jeanie.

"I've had a lot of time to think about what it means to be a father, and I've talked about it a lot with the counselors I saw in prison and even with the clergyman who took care of the church meetings there. I married your mother because, at the time, I really believed that I loved her and that it was a good decision. I look back and realize that my thinking was really messed up, mostly because I just didn't know any better. But I want you to know that in spite of all the grief your mother has caused for all of us, I do *not* regret marrying her for one reason—and that's because the two of you came out of that marriage. You wouldn't be who you are if I'd married anybody else, and being your father is the best thing that's ever happened to me."

Greg heard his own voice crack slightly at the same time he saw a hint of tears in Neal's eyes, and Jeanie wiped tears off her cheeks with a quick brush of her hand. He forged ahead before he lost track of his thoughts.

"But here's the thing," Greg said, realizing this was getting more difficult as he approached more sensitive issues. "I have not been there for you the way a father should be. I was there a lot when you were babies. I actually took care of you more than your mom did most of the time, and I loved doing that. I was pretty good at changing diapers and feeding you. I loved to give you baths and play with you and rock you. But you're both too young to remember that, I'm sure. And—"

"I remember that," Neal said. Since he was two years older than Jeanie, it stood to reason he was more likely to recall some of those early times. "I remember watching you taking care of Jeanie when she was a baby. I remember you playing with us on the floor. Jeanie and I have talked about that a lot."

Greg nodded and steadied his emotions, fearful of not being able to get through this without breaking down. He was glad to know that Neal remembered something good and glad that it meant enough to his children that they'd talked about it. But he also knew they both remembered other things that he deeply regretted. It was taking more courage now to press forward.

"I'm happy to know that," Greg said, "but I know the two of you weren't very old when things started getting really bad between me and your mom. When I think about how much we yelled at each other and the awful things we said—and how the two of you were there when it happened—I feel literally sick to my stomach. Even worse is how I feel when I think about how she made me leave and wouldn't let me see you at all. I've wondered a thousand times if I should have tried harder, but for the life of me I don't know what I could have done. If I'd known then what I know now, maybe it would have been different. But I didn't. One of my counselors told me that no one would ever be critical or judgmental toward a three-year-old who couldn't read. They simply haven't learned yet. It's the same way with people in this world who were simply never taught how to handle certain things in life. I just didn't know how to be a good husband and father, and when things got bad, I didn't know how to deal with how all of that made me feel. And that's why I made the worst possible decision—which was to turn to alcohol and drugs. And that's what eventually led to me going to prison. You know all of that, but what I want to say is that the situation now is a result of my bad decisions years ago. Even if I *didn't* know any better, I still have no one to blame but myself for the choices I made, and I have to accept the consequences of those choices."

"But," Jeanie protested, seeming confused and perhaps upset, "if you didn't know any better, then why should you have to be punished? Grace and Evan don't get punished for making messes and breaking things. They're just babies. You just said the same thing about a child who couldn't read."

"I hear what you're saying, sweetheart," Greg said. "But I broke the law. I had an addiction, and it was controlling me. It's not black and white, I know. But the law is the law. I had to serve time for what I did, whether it seemed fair or not. And that's why I couldn't be there for you all these years, even though I wanted to be. But you all know," he glanced at everyone quickly to include them, "that I firmly believe prison saved me. I became a better man because of facing up to the consequences."

"Because you made some really *good* choices while you were in prison," Shannon said. "The majority of inmates don't take advantage of the counseling and education opportunities that are available to them, and most of them don't attend church meetings or Bible study. You *chose* to do that."

"Yes, I did," Greg said, looking again at his children. "And my biggest reason for doing that was my desire to be the kind of man that deserved to be your father. If nothing else, I wanted my kids to be able to know that their dad was not a complete loser, that it was possible to change. But there's something else I need to say about consequences, and this is very important. I want to share an example a counselor shared with me. He had a close friend who did drugs a long time ago, and his life was pretty messed up. In time he got clean and turned everything around. He started helping homeless people and did a lot of good for other people. Then, years after he'd stopped doing drugs, he found out he had AIDS from using dirty needles. He suffered a lot from the disease and died, but he never felt bitter or angry over that because he knew that it was simply a consequence of his bad choices earlier in life. Do you understand what I'm saying? The AIDS was a result of his bad choices and it couldn't be changed, but that didn't mean that all the good choices he made weren't worth it or that they didn't count. Still, the consequences have to be faced no matter how much good we do."

"Did you ever use dirty needles?" Jeanie asked as if she feared he might be leading up to telling them he was sick and going to die.

"No, sweetheart," he assured her. "I never used needles at all. I just told you that story to make a point. What that story helped *me* understand is that—for all of my desires and good intentions—I have not been able to be involved in your lives during these years when you've needed a father. I have felt a lot of sadness over that, but I do not feel bitter. I have worked very hard to forgive the people that hurt me, and I've had to work even harder to forgive myself. I'm still working on that. The consequence of all that is the fact that I cannot come back into your lives now and *expect* to be your father. I mean . . . I *am* your father, and of course I always will be. I want to be a part of your lives as much as it's possible. But I just got out of prison. I'm not in a position to provide for your needs, and I don't know how to take care of teenagers because I stopped taking care of you when you were babies. And it's okay. The biggest reason it's okay is that you have . . ." Greg's voice broke, but he had no problem with everyone knowing that this was a point of deep gratitude for him. "You have . . . amazing people around you who have stepped up and given you a good life. You have a family and school and friends and church. You have everything you need right here, and I don't want that to change."

Greg sighed and realized that Jeanie and the women were all crying while Phillip and Neal were trying not to. He ignored that and tried to get to his point before he fell apart too. "So this is what I think about the situation, and I'm open to hearing what any of the rest of you think because I want us to work together to do what's best. There are lots of strange family situations in the world today. It's not that uncommon for kids to have two moms or two dads—or both. I want you to know that it doesn't hurt my feelings that you call Phillip your dad. He deserves it because he loves you and he's done so much to take care of you. So I don't want anyone to ever feel uncomfortable around me for that reason. You can call me Dad too if you want to, or you can call me Greg or dude or bud or . . . whatever you want. I will always be there for you as much as I can. I want to be a part of your lives, and I hope we can always be close. But I don't expect to come home and have things magically fall into place just because I'm your biological father. Eventually I will find my own place to live— when I can afford it—and when that happens I would like you to be comfortable there and always feel welcome. But I think *this* is your home, and that's the way it should be. I would like to be a part of the big decisions in your lives—or even the little ones. But Phillip and Shannon are the ones you need to look to for guidance. They decide your curfews and your chores and the rules you keep, and I expect you to always do what they ask of you because they deserve your greatest respect. Do you understand what I'm saying?"

Neal and Jeanie both nodded, and he sensed their growing relief. He felt grateful that he'd been able to say all of that, and that it seemed to be well received so far. Realizing he was finished, he added simply, "Okay, that's what I wanted to say. I would be very glad to hear what the rest of you think because this family stuff is all new to me."

Phillip said to Neal and Jeanie, "I just want to say that I think your dad is an amazing man, and I am honored to think of him as a brother, and I'm honored to be your *other* dad. Whatever challenges might occur, we're going to do what we've always done: we're going to talk it through and figure it out." Phillip turned to look directly at Greg. "I want you to know that I have never once felt like taking care of Neal and Jeanie was a burden. It's been nothing but a privilege."

"Amen," Marj interjected.

"I fell in love with them right along with falling in love with Shannon." Phillip took his wife's hand and looked at her as he added with a smile, "She's teased me about only marrying her so I could live under the same roof with Neal and Jeanie. That's not the *only* reason . . ." He chuckled and the mood in the room lightened a little.

"Thank you, Phillip," Greg said. "For everything. And thank you, Marj. Your kindness and acceptance have completely changed the way I see mothers, if you want to know the truth. I can understand why Phillip is such a good man. And I'm glad my kids have you for a grandma."

Marj smiled at him and dabbed at her eyes with a tissue. Greg reached for Shannon's other hand across the table and said to her, "And thank you, sis, for being the best sister a man could ever have. I am very blessed." Shannon squeezed his hand, and he turned again to look at his children. "And I want to thank the two of you for being such great kids. It makes me proud to know that you work hard to get good grades and to do what's right. That means a lot to me, and I want you to know that."

The kids both got out of their chairs at the same time and came around the table to hug Greg. He stood and put his arms around them both, and within a few seconds the others had stood up and joined the circle, creating the tightest, greatest group hug Greg had ever had.

Eventually they all sat back down and talked for a long while about their feelings regarding the things that had been said and clarifying some of the boundaries that seemed important in their unique family situation. When the conversation tapered off, they all knelt together for a family prayer, just as they did every evening—except that Greg felt more relaxed and a little more like a part of the family. They were making progress, and he was truly glad to be home.

* * * *

After being in Sugar City about two weeks, Greg got a job at the diner where Shannon had often taken the kids to eat when they'd first come to town. It was a solid establishment that had been around for many years, and the owner was also the manager. Bernie was someone Shannon knew only vaguely, but she told Greg he had a reputation for being fair and honest. She had heard a rumor that he was in need of some help at the diner, but it was a job that had previously been filled by high school students who never lasted long.

With Shannon's encouragement, Greg worked up the courage to go and talk to Bernie. He was glad for the use of Phillip's bike, which he'd been riding every day for exercise or to meet Shannon occasionally for a break or lunch. Bernie set up a time when the diner wouldn't be busy, and the two men shook hands and sat down across from each other at a booth. Bernie seemed pleased to meet Shannon's brother, but when Greg asked about the job, Bernie looked surprised and said, "Why would a grown man want to do the grunt work at a place like this?"

"I just got out of prison," Greg said, "and I'm willing to do anything that will give me something to do and even a little bit of income."

Greg was pleased that Bernie didn't seem put off by the mention of prison. He simply said, "May I ask why you served time? Was it anything violent?"

"You're welcome to ask me anything you like," Greg said. "I wouldn't expect someone to consider giving me a job without wanting to know more about the situation. I'm glad to say that I never did anything violent. I was a stupid, messed-up kid but never violent. I got into drugs, and that got me mixed up with some pretty crazy people. My time served was all in relation to drug charges, but that's all behind me now." Greg took a deep breath, assessed that

Bernie seemed interested, and decided to just say what he wanted to say, hoping it wouldn't sound like he was trying too hard. "I got my GED while I was in prison, and I turned my life around. I went to church and Bible classes. Now I'm living with my sister and her family; she took care of my kids for me."

"Oh, yeah," Bernie said, not seeming at all put off. "Neal and Jeanie. Good kids."

"Yeah," Greg said and smiled, "thanks to my sister. I'm just kind of getting to know them again. I think they have a lot to teach me."

Bernie sighed and said, "Well, the job is yours if you want it. Doesn't pay much, and it's nothing fun."

"That's okay," Greg said eagerly. "Tell me what you want me to do. I can start whenever you need me."

"Well, I'll tell you," Bernie went on and stood up, going around the counter and into the kitchen, motioning for Greg to follow him. "I've usually tried to hire two kids, each part time. It worked out best when I had someone out of high school who could come in during the lunch rush to wash dishes, take out the trash, stuff like that, and then clean up the kitchen when things slowed down." He motioned with his arm to indicate a fairly large, orderly kitchen, as if to introduce Greg to the potential work environment. Greg hoped that was a good sign, but he just listened while Bernie explained.

"I had another kid come in after the dinner rush to do the same thing in the evening. We close at nine, and things are usually cleaned up enough to get out of here before nine-thirty. Right now I don't have either shift filled. The kids I had working for me both quit. One went off to the city to work, and the other one had too much going on at school to keep working. So you can take either shift, or you can take them both."

"I'll take both," Greg said eagerly, resisting the urge to laugh loudly at the very idea of having a real job. "It sounds perfect, actually. If I have some hours between shifts, I can be there when my kids come home from school and have dinner with the family, then come back for the evening shift."

"Sounds great." Bernie held out his hand. "You've got a job, kid."

"Thank you!" Greg said and eagerly returned the handshake, unable to hold back a little laugh. "I'll work hard for you."

"I'm not worried about that," Bernie said. "And just so we're clear, I'm not worried about your record, kid. I just want you to know what I tell all my employees. I don't have much tolerance for messing up. So, you do things the way I want them done and you show up and do your work and don't cause any trouble. I don't care what you did before you went to prison. I just care what you're doing now. We clear?"

"Very clear, sir," Greg said.

"Great," Bernie said. "But don't call me sir. I'll see you tomorrow at eleven. Wear whatever you want. You won't be where the customers are going to see you."

"Sounds good," Greg said, actually liking the idea of avoiding interaction with people—at least at this point in his life.

Greg left the diner and rode the bike the short distance to where Shannon worked. He locked the bike to a stair rail behind the building and went in the back door and through the waiting room of the animal clinic, where Daphne greeted him warmly and insisted on giving him a hug. She was one of many people who had been extremely kind toward him, and he enjoyed her motherly attention.

Opening the door into the waiting room of Shannon's law office, Greg only caught a glimpse of Celia at her desk before his heart quickened. She was on the phone—which he knew now was typical for the work she did. But he felt relieved to not actually have to talk to her. He *wanted* to talk to her. He could have talked to her all day. But he didn't want her to see any hint of what he was feeling. He simply wasn't ready to address such things.

Celia waved at him, then motioned toward Shannon's office with a silent indication that it was okay for him to go in, which meant she wasn't in the middle of an appointment with a client.

"Hi," Shannon said brightly as he closed the door behind him. "How did it go?"

"I got the job," he said and couldn't hold back a little laugh. "It doesn't pay much, but it's a job and I'm grateful." He laughed again. "He usually hires teenagers, but I guess that's about where I am on the social scale."

"You have far too much life experience to make *that* comparison," she said as he sat down.

"Well, I was an irresponsible, self-absorbed teenager, and pretty much that way as an adult, too. So it seems fair that I have to start over."

"I never considered you self-absorbed," Shannon said in that big sister, slightly scolding tone she got sometimes. "Don't let your humility cross over into self-punishment."

Greg sighed. "I'll work on it," he said, "although I can't deny I feel very out of sorts here in the real world. The person I was before doesn't exist anymore. The man who went into prison is not the same man who came out."

"I know that," she said.

"So who am I?"

"Your personality is still the same. Your heart, your spirit. The changes you made were in your behavior, your beliefs. You grew up, became mature and responsible."

"And now I have to prove that to the world, which I have a feeling could be even more difficult than I imagined."

"Prove it to the world?" she asked. "Or to yourself?"

"Both, I guess." He sighed loudly. "But I have a job."

"We should celebrate," Shannon insisted and went on to tell him that the family was always eager for any excuse to celebrate—which usually meant ordering pizza or going out for ice cream.

That evening they ordered pizza for dinner *and* they all went out for ice cream. Greg enjoyed the celebration, and he'd come to feel entirely comfortable with his new family—most of the time anyway.

Later that night after the house was completely quiet, Greg simply couldn't fall asleep. He felt nervous but had trouble figuring out exactly why. He wasn't nervous about his job. He liked Bernie and felt confident about doing the work. His mind wandered as it frequently did to Celia. He thought about her far more than he considered wise under the circumstances. But his attraction to her just seemed to contradict every fact regarding his life and his situation. He forced thoughts of Celia away and finally concluded that his hovering anxiety was mostly a symptom of feeling like a fish out of water, of wondering what the next step might be toward a normal life and if he might be able to remain standing or trip and fall flat on his face.

Greg distracted his worry by turning to prayer and finally slept, having reached the conclusion that he was doing all he could do for the time being. He needed to trust that God would guide his path.

Chapter Six

IT TOOK ONLY A FEW days for Greg to feel comfortable with his job, and he quickly developed a routine for himself that allowed him to see his children as much as possible and to help around the house and yard as well. Even though he made every effort to be around when Neal and Jeanie came home from school and to share meals and activities with them, he still sometimes felt like an outsider in their lives. They were kind and polite toward him. They called him "Dad" and hugged him at least once a day. They also continued to call Phillip "Dad," but since they'd had their family meeting over that issue the awkwardness had lessened. He was glad for that, mostly for Neal's and Jeanie's sake; he didn't want his being here to cause any difficulty for them.

The more Greg observed this man with whom he shared the title *Dad,* the more Greg felt impressed by Phillip's character, and he wanted nothing more than to emulate him. Phillip was the most decent, upstanding man Greg had ever known. He could feel nothing but gratitude for the way this man had taken Neal and Jeanie into his home and his heart as if they were his own. Phillip had disciplined them, guided them, loved them, and helped them become the kind of teenagers that were expected to be polite and kind to their ex-convict father. Greg wanted his kids to come to him for advice or even just for comfort if they were struggling. But he knew he had to earn that place in their lives. He'd made choices that had denied him the right to be there for them, and the consequences were still very much a part of every facet of his life. He just had to keep Shannon's frequent advice in the forefront of his mind and take it one day at a time.

As required by law, Greg continued to check in with his parole officer. Shannon had taken him into the city twice to meet with Larry face-to-face, but generally a phone call was sufficient. Larry was tough but much kinder than most of the prison guards had been. He told Greg more than once that his job was to help ex-cons rehabilitate into a better life, but unfortunately many of them gravitated back to their old lives, which made Larry's job difficult.

"You're the kind that makes my job easy," Larry told him. "Just keep up the good work and I'll do everything I can to help you along the way."

Greg appreciated Larry's support, which made checking in with him mostly pleasant. Larry was pleased with the fact that Greg was working, that he had a stable home environment, and that his relationship with his kids was improving. And he was in Greg's corner with a sincere hope that it would all continue to get better.

Weeks passed with the routine of Greg's life becoming more comfortable. He was glad for the bike on which he'd already put many miles. It allowed him to get where he needed to go without having to rely on anyone else. He was in the process of getting a driver's license again, but he didn't feel in a big hurry. Even as the mornings and evenings began to grow colder with autumn easing toward winter, Greg just bundled up and pedaled to his destinations quickly and with ease. And he actually enjoyed the exercise and fresh air he wouldn't have gotten if he'd been driving a car.

Sundays were Greg's favorite day. The diner was closed, so he never worked Sundays, nor did anyone else in the family unless Phillip was called in for an emergency. They all went to church together and shared a nicer-than-usual dinner. Celia always came over for dinner, and he liked seeing her across the dinner table. They'd been able to share some casual conversation here and there while they helped clear the table or wash dishes or sometimes while she just hung around into the evening. Most often other people were around, but he was still glad to be getting to know her better, even if he hardly dared believe that anything romantic might ever evolve between them. The very idea of considering a romantic relationship felt like an item on his list of rehabilitation that was still too far away to even think about. And even then he couldn't help thinking that a woman like Celia deserved far better than anything he could ever give her.

The arrival of Halloween made Greg realize how seriously this family took holidays. He had a great time—even though his own children were teenagers and spent most of the evening with their friends. Once Halloween was over, the decor in the house was exchanged for all things that declared Thanksgiving was on the horizon. He looked forward to it with great anticipation, often thinking about how dreadful the holidays had been in prison. All that was cause for celebration when people could be with family and loved ones was exactly the opposite when walls and prison bars separated a person from those he cared about most. Although for him—and likely for many people in prison—holidays during his growing-up years held very few if any positive memories.

But being in the Meadows household was changing all that. Halloween had been delightful, but Thanksgiving was a more reverent holiday, focused on the emotion he experienced more than any other: gratitude. The idea of gathering for a feast with family made him feel like a child again—or perhaps for the first time. Even though he had no good memories of holidays from his childhood or youth, he'd always had the dream of being a part of such idyllic occurrences, and in Shannon's home he had already found the kind of family life he'd only dreamed of.

Greg felt a little disconcerted when he learned that all of Phillip's siblings and their families would be coming for Thanksgiving, but he was repeatedly assured that they were wonderful people and they would love him. He preferred to focus on the fact that Celia would be there as well. She would fly to her parents' home for Christmas, but she always shared Thanksgiving with Shannon's family.

The week prior to the anticipated event, the first snowstorm of the season came, but it wasn't so bad that Greg couldn't still manage to ride his bike back and forth to work. He returned from his evening shift in time to spend a few minutes with Neal and Jeanie before they went to bed or off to their rooms to read or do homework. He always asked what had become standard questions about how they were doing and what they had been up to. They generally gave him very brief answers, and he sometimes wondered if they would notice or care if he stopped the routine and disappeared. But he was determined to be tenacious if only to prove to them that he wasn't ever going to be absent from their lives again and he would never stop caring about what they were doing and how they were feeling.

Following these brief, shallow conversations with Neal and Jeanie, Greg went to his room and got comfortable on his bed to read for a while, which helped him relax and sleep better. He always left the door open until he was actually ready to turn out the lights and go to sleep. Shannon often popped in for a few minutes to tell him good night, and he always hoped that one of these days his kids might do the same.

Greg heard a light knocking on the open door and looked up expecting to see Shannon. He was not disappointed to see Jeanie.

"Hi," she said, seeming hesitant.

"Hello, sweetheart," he said, trying to express his enthusiasm without sounding as eager as he felt—which might scare her away. "What's up?" He set his book aside and leaned forward, motioning her into the room.

"Can I talk to you?"

"Of course," he said and patted the edge of the bed with his hand. He was relieved when she sat there. "What's up?" he asked again.

"You've said that I could talk to you about anything," she said, seeming mildly nervous.

"I *did* say that," he said, "but . . ."

"But?" she echoed, as if she was afraid he might renege now that she'd gathered her courage. He had no idea what she wanted to talk about, but he wanted so badly for this to go well that his heart was beating faster.

"*But,*" he quickly said, determined to make his communication clear and straightforward in order to avoid *any* misconceptions or assumptions. He'd learned a great deal from the hundreds of counseling sessions in which he'd participated. He was determined to apply what he'd learned for the sake of his children more than for any other reason. "I wasn't sure if you believed me or if you would trust me enough. And I wouldn't blame you a bit if you felt that way."

She looked a little confused and said, "It wasn't your fault that you were in prison . . . that you weren't here."

"Sweetheart," he said, taking her hand, relieved that she let him do so, "you and I both know that it *was* my fault. I made some very bad choices."

"Okay," Jeanie said with a maturity that exceeded her young life. He knew she'd been through a great deal that most kids never experienced. "I get that," she added. "I really do. But I also understand that with the way you were raised, you really didn't know how to make better choices."

"Wow," he said and laughed slightly. "That sounds like something my counselor in prison would have said. You're an amazing young woman, Jeanie, and I am so proud of you. It means a lot to me that you understand such things. Looking back, I often think that somehow I *should* have known better. Shannon made much better choices than I did. Still, for whatever reason, I made some bad choices, and my prison sentence was something that just had to happen. So whether or not it was my fault that I wasn't here for you and Neal might be debatable, the fact is that I *wasn't* there even though I wanted to be." He smiled at his daughter, hoping to lighten the mood. "I'm here now, and you *can* talk to me about anything. I don't know if I'll have the right answers, but I would love to talk to you about anything you want to talk about."

"Okay," Jeanie said and drew back her shoulders to imply she was gathering courage. "Can I ask why you married someone like BeeKee?"

Greg felt completely blindsided. He wondered why he'd never considered the possibility of his children wanting to know more about their mother and the fact that she *was* their mother. His ex-wife had always gone by BK, which were her initials and what she had always preferred. As a child she'd had the nickname BeeKee, which he'd occasionally called her. It was the name the children had picked up, and that was how they knew her. Shannon had told him in letters that Neal and Jeanie had stopped referring to BK as *mom* many years ago. They called her BeeKee, and they spoke of her rarely and with complete indifference—except for their adamant wish to never have to see her again. Greg shared their sentiments, but he also knew from counseling that it wasn't wise to speak ill of the other parent in your child's life. He quickly searched his memory for what he *had* learned about this very thing and prayed that he would handle it well enough to help strengthen the fragile bond he was gaining with his daughter.

Before Greg was able to respond, Jeanie said, "You know what? She's my mother, and I don't even know her real name. Aunt Shannon says that BK is the only name she's ever known, and she doesn't know what the letters stand for. How can she be my mother and I don't even know her name? But then . . . how can she be my mother and I don't have one good memory about her? Not one!"

Greg heard anger seeping into her tone and realized that Jeanie—and Neal too, he would guess—still had some healing to do in regard to their mother. For that matter, he likely did too. He took a deep breath and forced a calm voice that he hoped would diffuse her anger.

"First of all," he began, "her name is actually Bea Kay." He spelled it for her so she could understand that her mother's name actually sounded just like the initials. "Apparently she was named after two grandmothers, women she had never even known, and so she didn't like the name. She always preferred the initials. But that's her name."

"Okay," Jeanie said, taking that in.

Trying to remain practical about the conversation, he added, "To answer your original question, I married your mother because at the time I really loved her. At least I thought I did. Looking back, I'm not sure I had any comprehension of what love really was. I felt attracted to her, I enjoyed my time with her, and marrying her seemed like the right thing to do."

Jeanie blurted out yet another difficult question. "Does that mean you were sleeping with her and you thought marrying her would make it right?"

Greg chuckled in an attempt to cover his astonishment. "I'd been thinking you were a little shy. Silly me. Obviously you have no problem saying whatever you need to say." She looked concerned and he added, "That's a compliment, sweetheart. You *should* say whatever you feel like you need to say—as long as you do it appropriately."

"Yeah," she said, "it's all that counseling, I guess. After a while nothing feels embarrassing."

"That's true," he said, intrigued with the idea that he'd found a common bond with his daughter in the fact that they were both well experienced in emotional therapy. "So, I'm going to be completely honest with you. And I'm—"

"If it's none of my business, then—"

"If I thought something was none of your business, I would tell you so, I promise. But I think you have a right to ask that question. I would think every human being has a need to know where they came from and why. So I'll tell you. Yes, I was sleeping with her before I married her, but she didn't get pregnant with Neal until long after I'd married her. At *this* point in my life I would never do such a thing because now I know better. Now I know that it's not only offensive to God for a person to live that way, but it's not healthy psychologically. Saving intimacy for marriage is the way it should be. But when I met your mother, such things had never even occurred to me. I'd never had religion in my life, and you already know that my growing-up years were a mess. Your mother was among a group of friends I'd come to be involved with. I felt comfortable there, and I believed they were good friends even though they had bad habits. I know now that I felt comfortable because they were drinking and doing drugs and that's what I felt most comfortable doing myself. My perception of their being *good* people was simply that they were nicer to me than most people in my life had been. I learned the hard way that few if any of my so-called friends actually had any integrity. But that's another story."

Greg sighed and took mental note of Jeanie's expression, glad to see that she was interested and seemed to be keeping up so far. "When I started officially dating your mother, we made a pact to stop the drugs and cut down on the drinking. I really believed that she was inspiring me to be a better person. That's how it felt at the time. I believe her intentions were sincere, and so were mine. So we got married."

"Were you happy with her back then?" Jeanie asked, and he wondered if she wanted some evidence that her parents had ever loved each other. And why wouldn't a person want to know they were brought into this world as a result of love? Greg had wondered the same about himself, since his own parents were abusive alcoholics who had never exhibited any evidence of love for their children or each other.

"For a time I felt happy, yes. And I believe she felt the same. But we were both just two very messed-up people, and it didn't take long for the real problems to come back to the surface. I kept thinking we could do better, especially after you and Neal came along. A part of me wanted more than anything to be a good father and a good husband, but it seemed like no matter how hard I tried, I just kept messing up. I know now that I just didn't have the skills or knowledge to do it right. When your mom insisted I move out, I didn't have the strength to stand up to her."

Greg felt the sting of tears in his eyes and fought for only a moment to hold them back before it occurred to him that maybe his daughter needed to know how much these events still caused him pain. "I look back now," he said, as tears fell down his cheeks, "and I feel like I abandoned you and Neal." Jeanie looked surprised by the tears, and perhaps by the confession, but she just watched and listened as Greg continued. "I knew she was neglectful and treating you badly, but she wouldn't let me see you, and instead of trying harder to stand up to her, I just got more and more lost in the drugs and the drinking until I was in so deep that I ended up behind bars. You know the rest."

Greg sniffed and grabbed a tissue from the box on the bedside table. He hurried to explain something that he believed was important. "I don't want to speak ill of your mother, Jeanie, no matter how badly I think she behaved. I behaved badly too. I think there is a difference between bad-mouthing someone just to be mean and angry and discussing the facts of what happened in order to better understand how they impacted your life. Does that make sense?"

"Yes," Jeanie said. "I understand."

"I strongly disagree with so many things your mother did, most especially with the way she neglected you and Neal—and her anger toward the two of you. But I can't judge her behavior. Only God can do that. I don't know why she is the way she is. I've worked very hard to forgive her, even though I experience difficult feelings sometimes if I think about it too much. I try instead to think about how grateful I am for Shannon and Phillip—and Marj too—and how they've taken such good care of you, and all the excellent things they've taught you and your brother."

"I'm grateful for that too," Jeanie said, and Greg was surprised by the way she threw her arms around him with a tight hug. Easing back, she put her hand into his again. "Thank you for telling me. I just . . . wondered."

"You can ask me anything," he said, if only to remind her that he meant it.

"I think I'm good for now, but . . . I want to apologize for something."

"What?" Greg asked, genuinely confused. He couldn't think of anything she could possibly have to apologize for.

"I know you're my dad, and even though we talked about this and you said it was okay, I still think it probably feels weird for you when Neal and I call Phillip *Dad*. I probably should have said this when we had our meeting, but it kind of occurred to me later on. Anyway, I guess I want to say that . . . calling Phillip that just kind of happened. We weren't very old when Shannon and Phillip got married, and we started calling them *Mom* and *Dad*. But Neal and I talked about it since we had that meeting, and . . . we talked to Shannon and Phillip too. Now that you're here, we all agree that we need to remember that they're our aunt and uncle, and you're our dad. It's just a habit we need to change."

"Sweetheart," Greg said with all the love he felt. "You're so thoughtful, truly. I admit it's been a little weird, but I understand. I really do. It's okay for you to have two dads and two moms, or however you want to see it. Lots of people do. Whatever is comfortable for you and Neal is okay with me. I really mean that."

"Well, it's already been decided," she declared with a smile.

"And you're the instigator of this decision?" he asked lightly. "And the appointed spokesperson?"

"I guess I am," she said.

"Which shows how thoughtful you are." He kissed her cheek. "Thank you."

Jeanie kissed *his* cheek, stood up from the bed, and said, "Good night, Dad. Thanks for the talk."

"Anytime, sweetheart," he said.

She hesitated at the door and looked back. "I love you, Dad."

Greg cleared his throat to try and control a sudden burst of joy. He managed to speak with a steady voice. "I love you too, Jeanie."

"I'm glad you're back."

"I'm glad too. Now more than ever."

Greg contemplated their conversation for more than an hour before he could even force himself off the bed to go brush his teeth.

He marveled at his daughter's maturity and sensitivity. While he gave due credit to all the counseling and good parenting she'd been given the last six years or so, he knew that much of it was an indication of her personality, of characteristics that were simply indicative of the kind of person she was. He went to sleep feeling more gratified and more hopeful than he had since he'd come here to live under the same roof with his family.

* * * *

Greg was pleased when Neal came to his room a couple of days later to talk. Jeanie had obviously shared with him what had been said in her conversation with her dad. Neal had other questions about BK and about Greg's reasons for going to prison. He explained matter-of-factly that all of the charges had been drug related. He'd never done anything violent, and he'd never stolen anything. But the people he'd been hanging around with were much deeper into buying and selling drugs than he'd realized, and his naïveté had gotten him into horrible trouble. His supposed friends had let him take the fall for them by allowing it to appear that the large quantities of drugs that had been found in his possession had actually all belonged to him, when he hadn't even known they were there. He explained how the law made a distinction between having a small amount of drugs in your possession, which implied personal use, and having large amounts of drugs in your possession, which implied an intent to sell. And Greg had ended up being caught by the police with a very large amount of drugs.

Greg made it clear to Neal that he'd forgiven these people who had used him badly, that he'd served his time with an attempt to humbly accept the consequences for his bad choices, and that he'd become grateful for the way life in prison had changed him. He'd gotten an education, counseling, and an awakening to spiritual matters. He had found a deep connection to God and a desire to make his future positive and productive, based on living with integrity and gratitude.

Neal listened attentively, asked questions occasionally, and stayed in Greg's room talking far past when he should have been asleep. He too told Greg that he loved him, and Greg told Neal the same, grateful beyond words for the progress that was taking place with his children. He felt like his patience was paying off.

The Monday before Thanksgiving, Greg went home between work shifts as he always did and was there when Neal got home from school and when Jeanie came in a little while later. Since the ice had been broken with the kids the previous week, they had started telling him a few more details about their days at school, their friends, their church activities; sometimes they even admitted if they'd had a difficult day for one reason or another. After they had both gone to their rooms to do homework, Greg took advantage of the washer and dryer not being in use so he could wash a load of clothes. He was putting his wet clothes into the dryer when Jeanie found him there.

With no preamble or forewarning, she said, "It's all right if you start dating again, you know."

"What?" Greg asked, not because he hadn't heard her, but because he had absolutely no idea why she would say such a thing.

"I've just heard some kids who have divorced parents talk about how weird it is when their parents start dating other people. I just thought you should know that Neal and I both think it's fine. Not that you need our approval or anything. We just don't want you to not do it because you think we'd be weirded out by it or something."

Greg chuckled and focused on his task. "And once again you're the spokesperson. Just how much do you two talk about me?"

"Not *too* much," she said, her tone slightly teasing. But he liked that they had come to a place where they *could* tease each other. "We've got way less boring things to talk about than you."

"What a relief," he said with a hint of sarcasm.

"So if you want to go on a date or something . . ."

"I have your permission," Greg said. "Thank you for that. But I'm not sure it's a good idea for someone in my position to start thinking about stuff like that. I don't know if I could take care of a house plant."

"You take care of us," Jeanie declared.

"I'm around," he said. "I don't know if I actually *do* much to take care of you."

"You're missing the point, Dad," she said. "Just . . . go on a date."

Greg closed the dryer and turned it on. "You make it sound like I can just . . . decide to go on a date and the right woman will magically appear."

Jeanie's smile became utterly conspiratorial before she said, "Oh, come on, Dad. You can't be that blind."

"I have no idea what you're talking about."

"Celia?" Jeanie said, and Greg was glad she couldn't see how his heart quickened at just the mention of her name. But he couldn't believe that his daughter was saying this to him. *Was* he blind? Was he missing something that everybody else had seen?

"What about her?" he asked, pretending complete ignorance.

"She so has the hots for you," Jeanie said, and he felt like they were *both* in junior high.

"No," he protested. "No, no." He felt sure it couldn't be true. "She's been very kind to me, but . . ."

"Dad, I can see that spending years in prison with a bunch of ugly men has completely ruined you." She pointed a finger at him as if *she* were the parent. "You should take Celia on a date."

"I can't even drive," he hollered after her as she left the room.

"Excuses," she hollered back, and Greg stood like a statue in the laundry room for many minutes, considering the implications of what his daughter had considered an important issue to address with him.

Greg felt so completely out of sorts that he found Jeanie and asked if she would get his clothes out of the dryer for him and he'd return the favor sometime. She was glad to do so, and he left early in order to stop at Shannon's office before going in to work for his evening shift—even though it actually meant he would have to go back home to eat supper with the family and then back into town. That hadn't actually occurred to him until he was already on his way. But he felt a sudden need to talk to his sister, and he didn't want to do it where the kids might have any chance of overhearing them. As he approached the door to her office, he realized it also hadn't occurred to him that he had to pass by Celia before he could see his sister. Pretending indifference as he had trained himself to do, he waved and said hello to her. She did the same in return, and he asked, "Can I go in? Is she busy?"

"She might be busy," Celia said, "but she's not with anyone."

"Thanks," Greg said, and Celia quickly turned her eyes back to the work on her desk. He felt sure Jeanie had to be wrong.

"Hi," Shannon said, looking up from her desk.

Greg closed the door behind him and asked, "Is this a bad time?"

"Not at all," she said and leaned back in her chair and stretched as if she needed a break. "What's on your mind?"

"Jeanie just told me it was all right with her and Neal if I started dating."

Shannon let out a little burst of laughter. "So you have permission."

"She made a point to tell me I didn't *need* their permission but they wouldn't be weirded out by it. What kind of word is *weirded?*"

"It's a teenage word," Shannon said and chuckled again.

"Is this funny?" Greg asked.

"Kind of."

"Well, I don't feel ready to date. I live with my sister, and I have a job washing dishes and taking out the trash."

"And the right woman would appreciate your integrity, your spirituality, and your strong work ethic—no matter where you live or how much money you make."

"You mean how much money I *don't* make."

"Same difference," she said, then her eyes narrowed on him. "What *else* did Jeanie say? You look positively frazzled."

Greg felt like he'd been caught doing something wrong. The feeling was familiar from his preprison days. He hurried to give her an honest answer, if only to dispel the feeling. "She said," he lowered his voice to a whisper, "that I should ask Celia on a date. She told me I'm blind. She said that Celia has the hots for me. Is that teenage speak, too?"

Shannon laughed softly then bit her lip. "Maybe," she said.

"Maybe what?"

"I think adults talk like that too," Shannon said. She leaned over her desk and said in a dramatic whisper, "Truthfully, I've wondered myself if you're blind."

"What?" he gasped quietly. When Shannon only smiled, he muttered, "You mean . . ." He pointed toward the other room where Celia was working.

Shannon just nodded, wearing a silly grin that told him Jeanie's observation had been accurate—at least to some degree. So many thoughts and feelings assaulted him all at once that he slumped into one of the two chairs facing Shannon's desk.

"What's wrong?" Shannon asked and moved to the chair next to his, putting a hand over his arm.

Greg attempted to sort out his thoughts and put them into some kind of reasonable order. He looked at his sister and asked quietly,

"Am I blind? Am I so . . . out of practice with being around real people that I missed something?"

"First, why don't you tell me why you're so upset. You seem upset. Are you?"

"Yes, I suppose I am. But I'm not sure why; lots of reasons, I guess."

"Greg," Shannon said gently, "Celia has admitted to me that she finds you attractive, and more importantly, she thinks you're an amazing guy."

Greg sighed. "So I *did* miss something." He hung his head and sighed again.

"Why is this a problem?" Shannon asked. "If you're worried about her being pushy or making things awkward, she would never do that."

"I'm not worried about that," Greg said.

"Then what?" Shannon insisted with frustration. "Help me understand what's going on here."

Greg pushed a hand through his hair and messed it up as if doing so might help activate his brain cells. He reminded himself that he was talking to Shannon. His sister was completely worthy of his deepest trust, and she was sharp and wise. He took a deep breath and just admitted it. "I guess you could say . . . the feeling is mutual."

Shannon let out a little laugh of delight. "Seriously?"

"Do I look like I'm joking?" he asked, and she sobered her expression.

"Why didn't you tell me?"

"I'm not in a position to be feeling such things for *any* woman."

"Admitting to your attraction for a woman is not some violation of your parole."

"That doesn't mean it's smart."

"I wouldn't expect you to handle this or anything else without a lot of thought and careful consideration. That doesn't mean you should ignore it."

"I kept it to myself because . . . well, at first . . . it was just too soon. She was the first woman anywhere near my age that I'd spoken to since I got out of prison. My feelings haven't changed, but . . . I really had no idea she felt anything, and . . . if I missed what everyone else has seen, it makes me wonder what I might have inadvertently said or done to hurt her."

"*That's* what you're worried about?" Shannon asked, astonished. "You haven't hurt her, Greg. You've been nothing but kind and sincere toward her, the way you are with everyone; that's just who you are."

"But why didn't I see it?"

"Mostly because I don't think she wanted you to. She knows you're in the middle of a huge adjustment, and truthfully I think she believes the two of you aren't very well matched and she's better off keeping her feelings to herself."

Greg heard his worst fears implied in what his sister had just said, but he wanted to clarify. He wasn't about to have misunderstandings or assumptions flying around over anything that might cause difficulty for himself, for Shannon, or for the people they cared about.

"It's okay," Greg said. "I don't blame her a bit for recognizing that having an interest in someone like me is probably not a good idea. It's probably better if I just—"

"Wait," Shannon said. "Wait, wait. What are you saying?"

Greg looked right at her, surprised by her confusion. "I don't think I stuttered or anything."

"Greg," she said in a tone she might have used when he was a child and she was trying to console him following a horrible incident in their home, "it's not like that. It's not that at all."

"I don't understand."

"It's the other way around."

"What?" Greg asked, his heart quickening before his mind even grasped the implication.

Shannon leaned more toward him and tightened her hand on his arm. She lowered her voice even further and said, "I'm telling you this in strict confidence, but I think you need to know. It's not for any of us to know at this point if anything might come of this . . . attraction between the two of you. But she is my best friend; she's as good as family. And that means she'll always be around no matter what happens. I think she'd be okay with me telling you that she has her own issues. She grew up with all the appearances of a good, solid family. But they have their own brand of dysfunction—and a lot of it. Celia and

I are so close because we've helped each other learn how to get the voices of our parents out of our heads."

Greg felt the words sting his spirit. He was almost forty, and he could still hear his parents' voices in his head telling him how useless and stupid he was. He knew Shannon struggled with the same thing. But he never would have imagined that Celia might have a similar challenge. She came across so confident and genuinely kind and good. But then, so did Shannon. He scolded himself inwardly for being judgmental enough to assume that what others showed on the outside was an indicator of what might be going on inside. He ought to be able to look at himself in the mirror and realize the truth of the principle.

"She's so amazing," Shannon continued, her voice cracking, and Greg could feel the evidence of how deeply connected his sister felt to Celia. "But . . . she can't see it. She has developed a great deal of confidence in many respects, and she usually comes across that way, but deep inside she has a lot of personal doubts." Shannon focused directly on Greg, at the same time taking hold of his hand. "It's not for me to share any details, but she struggles a great deal with her self-image—among other things. And I am going to say that she *sincerely* believes she's not good enough for you." Greg let out an astonished gasp, and she hurried to add, "Don't tell me about your prison record and your minimum-wage job and that you're living with your sister. You have integrity, you're spiritual, and you're kind and generous. She hasn't encountered those traits with *any* man in her life. So don't sell yourself short, little brother. And just because you know she likes you—and you've admitted to me that you like *her*—doesn't mean that anything has to change. Just . . . be aware and . . . follow your instincts. And I'm here for you."

"Okay," Greg said, feeling like he wanted to talk about this for another hour—or two. But he honestly didn't know what to say next, and he also knew Shannon's workday was technically about over and it was time they both went home for supper before he went to work.

"Thanks, sis," Greg said and hugged her. On his way to the door he pointed a finger at her and said, "Don't you *dare* tell her *any* of this."

"I won't," she said. "I promise."

Greg opened the door, startled to see Celia about to knock on it. She gasped at being startled herself, then she started to laugh. "Oh, you really scared me," she said, still laughing.

"Sorry," he said and allowed himself to make eye contact with her, as if he might be able to see some evidence of what he'd been told about Celia's feelings for him. A fluttering in his stomach accompanied the realization that it was true. He *had* been blind!

Trying to remain nonchalant, he said, "You're looking lovely today, Celia."

"Thank you," she said and smiled brightly before she cleared her throat nervously and eased around him to say to Shannon, "I'm leaving now. I'm going to take home that stuff we talked about and search through those files."

"Thank you," Shannon said. "Have a good evening."

"You too," Celia said and waved at Shannon then at Greg, who was still standing in the waiting room, perhaps trying to let his brain catch up to everything he'd just learned. He felt most preoccupied at the moment with the very idea that Celia would struggle with feelings about her self-image. He thought she was beautiful. She almost sparkled with a light that just seemed to be a natural part of her. She had a flare in the way she dressed, and even with the unique jewelry she wore that wasn't gaudy or showy but always had a certain classiness to it. He tried not to stare as she turned off the lamp above her desk and flung her purse over her shoulder.

When Greg realized Celia was picking up a file box, he quickly took it from her, saying, "Here, let me."

"Thank you," she said. "So gallant!"

"It's just a box," Greg said and followed her to where her car was parked behind the building. She opened the trunk with the remote on her key ring, and he set the box inside.

"Thank you," she said again as he closed the trunk.

"Not a problem," he said and wished he had the nerve to ask her right now to just go out to dinner with him or something. But he needed more time to process all of this, so he just smiled and said, "Drive safely. I'll see you soon, I'm sure."

"Hope so," she said, giving him one more reason to believe he'd been blind.

Chapter Seven

ON SUNDAY, JUST BEFORE LEAVING the house to go to church, Greg asked Shannon, "Why doesn't Celia go to church with us? Does she go to a different church?"

"No," Shannon said, checking the contents of the large bag she took to church to keep Grace and Evan quietly entertained. "This is something you should ask *her* about . . . when you feel the time is right. I can tell you this much: Celia was raised in a home where religion was taken to the extreme. Her father is a very pious man who is far more concerned about outward appearances and what people think rather than actually behaving like a Christian."

"Oh, he would love *me,*" Greg said, sarcasm mixed with self-recrimination in his voice.

Shannon just scowled at him and added, "Celia is a very spiritual woman; she believes in God, she prays, and she's very conscious of trying to be a good person." Shannon zipped the bag closed. "The two of you have a lot in common that way. But she has a hard time with actually attending church because it stirs up painful memories. She's come with me a few times, and I think in time it might get easier for her. We attend a different denomination than she grew up with, and she likes this one much better. But . . . it's a work in progress."

"Okay," Greg said. "Thank you for telling me. I'll be discreet."

"I know you will." She smiled and kissed his cheek. "Now, why don't you see what's taking your children so long? We're going to be late if we don't get on our way."

Greg sat through the church meeting with Jeanie on one side of him and Neal on the other. He'd grown comfortable with the congregation and the different meetings he attended here. There were a few people who seemed to be ignoring him; he couldn't be sure if they were just not sociable or if they'd heard rumors about his history. But there were far more people who were kind and accepting in spite of knowing all of the reasons his sister had been raising his kids, and they respected that he was now trying to start his life over with practically nothing.

Greg pondered what Shannon had told him about Celia's upbringing in regard to religion. He found it ironic that he and Shannon had grown up with no exposure to religion at all, and Celia had been so overly saturated with it that she had negative feelings toward it. He thought of what Shannon had said about Celia being a very spiritual person but having trouble with religion. He'd never before thought of the differentiation between the two. For him they were very integrated; he considered himself both spiritual *and* religious. But he could certainly understand how religion could be used as an element for control or even abuse. The thought saddened him, but he was anything but naive about how messed up and cruel people could be. He felt a desire to talk to Celia about it, but as of now they'd talked about little more than the weather, their jobs, and his kids. He knew she would be coming over for dinner today. The thought thrilled him as much as it made him nervous. Knowing what he knew now, he wondered if he could be around her and not behave awkwardly—which made him wonder if it would be better to clear the air with her and admit to what he knew and how he felt, or if he should just give the matter more time while he tried to get to know her better. Either way, he hoped for an opportunity to share some real conversation with her, and he considered how he might be able to maneuver that later today.

As the church meeting continued, Greg tried to remain focused on what was being taught while at the same time offering up a prayer in his heart to be guided in regard to his feelings for Celia—and he offered a silent prayer on behalf of Celia herself. The depth of concern he felt for her made him wonder if what he felt was more than just attraction, more than a desire to share some companionship with a woman in his life. He felt more worried about her than he was about his own feelings. And he prayed that God would help him in both regards.

After church, Greg went up to his room to change his clothes and make his bed since he'd been rushed earlier and hadn't done it. When he came down to the kitchen to see what he could do to help with Sunday dinner, he was surprised to find only Celia there, standing at the counter peeling potatoes. Noises from the distance let him know that Shannon and Phillip were likely both engaged in trying to solve whatever problem was causing Grace and Evan to be screaming. He'd become accustomed to that particular type of cry from the toddlers; it was generally due to fighting over toys or something equally disastrous to a young child. Greg didn't know where Marj might be, but he couldn't help hoping that having even a few minutes alone in the kitchen with Celia could possibly be an answer to his prayers. He felt nervous but calmed himself with the reminder that he only had to be kind to her and share some conversation. Surely it wasn't that big of a deal.

"Hi," he said. She turned to look at him and smiled. So far so good.

"Hi," she said, seeming pleased to see him.

She continued with her task and he asked, "Is there something I can do to help?"

Celia laughed softly. "I have absolutely no idea," she said. "Marj left to take some food to a friend who is ill. She barely managed to tell me I could peel potatoes before she rushed out the door."

Greg had become familiar enough with the kitchen that he just washed his hands and found another peeler. "There," he said. "I *can* help." He started peeling too. "This family eats a lot of potatoes."

"Yes, they certainly do," Celia said, and Greg wondered how they could get off the topic of food. "How are you doing?" she asked, solving the dilemma, although he wasn't quite sure how to answer. She'd asked before, and he'd just considered it a polite inquiry to which he'd given a brief polite answer. But he decided that allowing himself to make this a little more personal might be a positive step toward a more personal conversation.

"I'm coming along," he said. "I can honestly say I'm doing a lot better than I was last month or the month before, so I guess that's good."

"That *is* good," she said with an enthusiasm that let him know she genuinely cared. Standing right next to her, Greg realized how short she was with bare feet. He estimated that her head came to the top of his shoulder. When he saw her at the office, she was usually either sitting or wearing high heels. He'd realized long ago that she liked shoes because she had many different pairs, and perhaps being shorter than average had made her like wearing shoes that made her taller. He glanced at her hands while they worked, and his stomach fluttered a little.

"How's the job going?" she asked.

"It's pretty straightforward," he said with a little laugh, well aware that she knew all about what he did and why. "But I like that. The work is simple. I like the people there, and they seem to like me." Preferring not to ignore what was most obvious in his life, he added lightly, "My parole officer is impressed, so that's something."

Celia laughed, which helped ease any possible tension over his circumstances. "And how are your kids?" she asked. "They're such great kids!"

"They *are* great kids," he said eagerly. "I think Shannon deserves most of the credit for that—and Phillip and Marj. We're so blessed to have them."

"I know that feeling," Celia said, and he realized that she really considered these people to be like family to her. He wanted to ask about her own family, but she repeated her original question. "So how are Neal and Jeanie doing?"

"They're good," he said, wanting to add what it meant to him that she cared about his kids. He and Celia were somewhere in the same age range—as far as he could tell from her appearance and what he knew about her life. But he doubted most women would be interested in a guy who had gotten married too young and had two teenaged children. "They're talking to me more," he said and smiled at the thought of his conversations with Neal and Jeanie and how they were becoming more frequent and comfortable. "And they're actually *really* talking to me."

"That's great," Celia said, seeming to understand what that meant to him. "I mean . . . isn't it? With teenagers I would think it's a very good sign that they're getting used to your being in their lives again."

"Yeah," Greg said, surprised by a warmth in his chest that came as a result of the way she'd summarized what was most important to him. He managed to keep his voice steady as he added, "It's the best."

He chuckled, then said, "They're even starting to give me advice and making it clear that in many ways they're a lot smarter than I am."

Before Greg fully realized what he'd just said, Celia asked, "Really? Like what?"

Greg thought about that for a long moment, realizing that the only actual *advice* he'd gotten had been in regard to Celia. Now what was he supposed to say? Words came to his mind as if to answer the question, and he decided to just go for it. Remaining fully focused on the potato he was peeling, Greg said, "Jeanie thinks I should start dating."

Celia didn't make a sound, but she stopped peeling abruptly. Greg pretended not to notice, taking in one tinier piece of evidence about his own obliviousness in regard to her. He could start talking hypothetically about all the reasons he didn't consider himself a good candidate for any reasonable woman, but she was Shannon's best friend, and he suspected she already knew—or could at least guess—most of that. He decided to just say the words hovering uncomfortably on his tongue, praying he wouldn't regret it.

"She thinks I should take *you* out on a date," he said.

Celia still didn't move; she let out a little gasp, but he had no idea why. For a moment he wondered how all of this might go down if Jeanie and Shannon had been wrong about Celia's interest in him. If she really *didn't* want to go out with him, this could be a disaster. His heart began to pound at the thought. He'd done it. He'd said it. He couldn't take it back.

Struggling desperately to know what to say next, he too stopped peeling potatoes, but he felt momentarily frozen. He was both relieved and a little startled when Celia asked, "And what do *you* think?"

Greg considered the best way to answer the question, and his relief deepened at the opportunity to be completely honest. He set down the peeler and put both hands on the counter, as if that might keep him standing, but he didn't take his eyes off the pile of potato peelings in front of him.

"I think," he drawled with a hint of drama, "that a woman as beautiful and smart and remarkable as you would probably be a fool to even consider going out with a guy who just got out of prison and lives with his sister and has a job that a teenager could do, when he actually has two teenaged kids himself. I think it's ridiculous to think of asking a woman out on a date when I don't even have a driver's license." He paused to measure the silence, hoping she might give some indication of her reaction. When she said nothing, he started rambling in a nervous attempt to fill the silence. "I've been studying the driver's handbook online, and I think I'm almost ready to take the test. I *do* know how to drive, but there wasn't much opportunity for that in prison. Imagine letting my driver's license expire? But truthfully it's just one more thing that makes me feel more like Neal and Jeanie's brother than their father. They're more mature than I am, and—"

"Can we back up just a little?" Celia said, interrupting his need to keep talking.

"That's probably a really good idea," he replied, recounting everything he'd just said and feeling like a fool.

Celia turned to look at him, and he returned her gaze, his heartbeat quickening so abruptly that he had to discreetly tighten his hold on the counter. "Can we go back to the part where you said all those nice things about me? Because I don't think *any* man has ever said *anything* like that to me in my entire life. And if you really meant it, I'd just like to hear it again."

Greg saw the vulnerability and childlike insecurity in her eyes that Shannon had hinted at. If not for Shannon's brief explanation, he would have been completely shocked. He'd only seen her as being completely confident and self-assured. But what he saw in her eyes now was something he understood. In that moment he felt like he *did* have something worthy to offer her, and he gave it with complete sincerity when he said, "I absolutely meant it, Celia. I don't say things I don't mean." He took a deep breath and kept his eyes focused on hers as he said, "I think you are beautiful and smart and remarkable."

She erupted with a delighted little laugh that contradicted the glimmer of moisture he saw in her eyes. She looked down, which he suspected was an attempt to hide her tears. But she looked up again quickly and said, "Well, in that case, I absolutely think you should take Jeanie's advice. If I'm half as smart as you think I am, then I would have the good sense to see the value in how hard a man works no matter what he's doing or how much he gets paid. And I would also be sensible enough to appreciate a man who has all of his priorities in the right order. Besides," she shrugged and turned more toward him, laughing softly as if she felt completely at ease, "a driver's license is overrated. In a town this size, who needs to drive to go on a date? If you *did* decide to ask me on a date, I could meet you anywhere."

Greg felt more than a little stunned at all the kind and complimentary things she'd just said to him—and her obvious sincerity. He realized she was waiting for him to speak, and she couldn't have made it any easier for him to just take the leap.

"Well, okay," he said, turning more directly toward her, finally able to let go of the support of the counter. "Celia Mae Lindley, will you go out with me?"

"I would love to, Gregory Evan Turney."

"Good," he said but didn't know what else to say. He hadn't thought it through beyond this point because he hadn't expected this to go so well.

Celia saved him when she said, "What time does your evening shift start?"

"Seven."

"Then . . . how about we meet at the café at five-thirty?"

"I'll be there," he said, and they heard Marj's car pull into the garage. He was glad she hadn't come home a few minutes earlier or he might have never been able to restart the conversation enough to get back to this point.

"Good," Celia said and smiled at him before she went back to peeling potatoes while he did the same.

"How did you know my middle name?" he asked.

"When your sister named her son Evan, she told me it was your middle name."

He stated the obvious. "I think you know a lot more about me than I know about you."

"Maybe," she said. "But since we're going on a date, we can work on that."

Greg smiled at her just before Marj came into the kitchen and Sunday dinner preparations swung into high gear. Shannon and

Phillip showed up a few minutes later to help, having left the little ones in the care of Neal and Jeanie—which was the typical routine. Greg felt almost giddy as he replayed his conversation with Celia over and over in his mind. By the time dinner was over and the kitchen was back in order, he had to conclude what should have been obvious a long time ago: he was falling in love with her. Or maybe he'd already fallen and he'd just been too afraid to even let himself think about such things. Maybe he was still afraid. No maybe about it. He *was* afraid. But again he concluded the obvious. Celia was a reasonable woman and easy to talk to. He just needed to be honest with her about his feelings and try not to scare her away.

Celia stayed into the evening, as she usually did on Sundays, comfortably involved with the family's "together time," as they called it. Greg had been around Celia enough that he felt at ease with having her around. Or at least he thought he had. Now that the ice was broken between them and their attraction for each other acknowledged—at least to some degree—he felt even more relaxed in her presence and sensed that she felt the same.

After the family shared prayer as they did every evening at bedtime, Greg hugged all the kids good night, then sat on the couch and watched them all hug Celia before she left. Everyone else went up the stairs at the same time that Celia smiled and waved comically at Greg. "I'll see you tomorrow." He considered getting up, but she was already walking toward the door that led from the kitchen into the garage.

"I'm looking forward to it," he said.

"Me too," she called over her shoulder, and he heard the door close.

Greg closed his eyes and took in a deep breath. Hearing the antics of Grace and Evan in the distance, he couldn't deny his gratitude that his children were old enough to get themselves ready for bed. He chose not to think about his regret for all the years he wasn't there to help them when they *did* need it.

"Hi again," he heard and opened his eyes to see Celia standing nearby.

"Hi," he said and moved to the edge of his seat to stand up, but she stopped him.

"You don't have to get up," she said, and he realized she was nervous. Was she going to renege on their date? He felt nervous himself. "I was going to tell you that I forgot my keys and I came back to get them, but I didn't forget my keys. And since I came back to clarify something with you and I really need you to be honest with me, I would feel like a hypocrite if I lied about the reason I came back, so . . ."

"What's wrong?" he asked and patted the couch beside him. "Sit down."

Celia sat down, but she was clearly tense.

"Just tell me," he said. "If you don't want to go out with me, or—"

"Oh, I do!" she said quickly. "I . . . guess I just have to say that . . . well, if Shannon hasn't already told you—and I really hope she did—I have some serious insecurity issues." She blew out a sharp breath as if her admission had taken great courage. "The last guy I could actually say was a boyfriend told me my insecurities were *extremely unattractive.* His words. So, to be completely honest, I'm torn between feeling the need to be honest about my insecurities, which might make me *extremely unattractive,* and the reality that I've come too far in my life to be anything but completely honest." She laughed nervously. "I guess I just have to say that I don't want you to go out with me because I'm your sister's friend who hasn't been on a date in years. Because . . . I don't even want to go there, and—"

"Celia," Greg said and put his hand over hers where it seemed to be keeping her balanced on the couch. She looked at his hand then his face. "I appreciate your honesty because I feel the same way. I told you that I don't say things I don't mean. I wouldn't have even mentioned our going out if I didn't want to spend time with you. As for your . . . insecurities . . . I find them extremely *validating.*"

She said nothing, but he saw what looked like confusion in her eyes. "You probably know every stupid and horrible thing about my life before I came here. If you are really okay with all of that, then . . ."

"I don't care about your past, Greg. I see who you are now, the kind of person you are." She let out a little burst of that nervous laughter again and looked away. "Hey, it's just a date, right? I'm sorry if I'm turning it into some kind of counseling session or something."

"I like your honesty," he said, and she looked at him again. He loved it when she looked at him. "It inspires me." She smiled and he added, "May I be completely honest about how I feel about all of this?"

"Please," she said as if nothing would ever mean more to her.

"If I put my foot in my mouth or make a fool of myself, I insist on a do-over."

"Absolutely!" she said. "I think everybody deserves a do-over now and then. I might be needing one myself any minute now."

"Celia," he leaned a little closer, "I'm scared. I'm scared out of my head. My life is a series of mess-ups and mistakes. I don't want to hurt you, and I would be a fool to think that I'm ready for any kind of serious relationship. I need to learn how to be a dad and to be an upstanding citizen. But at the same time, I can't deny that I think about you every hour of every day."

Celia gasped, and her eyes widened. Greg had said it now, so he had to keep going. He tightened his hand over hers, praying he wouldn't mess this up too badly—or that if he did she would really let him have a do-over. "Neither of us can predict where life will take us from here. I need to go slowly, and I would like to ask you to be patient with me and understand that my need for time is about me, not about you. I really think you're amazing. I want to get to know you better. But . . ." Now he was chuckling nervously, and he had to break eye contact in order to gather his thoughts. "I don't know, Celia." He looked at her again, not sure if she was in awe or horrified. "It just doesn't seem right for a man to be making any serious life decisions while he has to regularly report to a parole officer. So . . . in the meantime, I'm hoping you'll be my friend . . . that we can talk . . . like we're talking now. And maybe we can just . . . have some fun together and . . . see where it takes us."

Her smile alleviated his nervousness a great deal, and he felt an enormous burden lifted when she said with conviction, "I'm more than okay with that."

"Good," he said and felt more relaxed. "Then I'll see you tomorrow at the café—if not before—and we can talk about our insecurities."

"I'll be counting the hours," she said and stood up.

Greg stood as well and walked her out to her car, opening the door for her. Before she got in, she looked up at him and said, "You know, after I've spent time here, I always get a hug from everyone except you." She opened her arms. "Can I have a hug?"

"I thought you'd never ask," he said and chuckled. He had to lean over to hug her, which made him laugh again. "You are so adorably short," he said when the hug was done.

"And you," she pushed a finger against his chest for just a second, as if she could have pushed him over, "are so adorably tall."

She got into her car, and he shut the door right after he said, "Drive safely."

She nodded and waved through the window, and he stood in the driveway until she'd backed out and her car had gone around the corner. Greg looked up at the stars in the sky, loving the way that he could actually see them since he'd moved here. He felt more hope about his future than he'd felt in a long time—perhaps ever. Going into the house and up to his room, he considered how he might be feeling if his attempts at conversation with Celia had gone badly. But it had all been completely the opposite. Having real and honest conversation with her had only made him like her more. He had trouble going to sleep as everything they'd said to each other rolled around in his mind again and again. He focused instead on his anticipation at seeing her tomorrow, certain he had a smile on his face when he finally fell asleep.

* * * *

Celia went down the stairs to her basement apartment and turned the key in the lock. Once inside with the door locked behind her, she started to laugh and couldn't stop. She just felt so happy! She refused to consider the possibility of how it might feel if things didn't ever work out for her and Greg beyond friendship. For now, everything was perfect.

She plopped down on the couch, kicked off her shoes, and put her feet up before she pulled her cell phone out of her pocket and texted Shannon. It wasn't unusual for them to share little texts throughout the day, but she loved imagining the look on Shannon's face when she read this one.

I have a date tomorrow with your brother.

Less than a minute later Celia's phone chimed, and she looked at the screen, laughing as she read: *It's about time!*

They exchanged brief written messages of a promise to catch up more tomorrow, and good-night wishes whirled back and forth.

Celia got ready for bed and put on her bright-pink pajamas with cupcakes all over them—one of her favorite pairs. She climbed between the sheets but felt restless. She tried to read but couldn't focus. She ended up with the book spread over her lap, staring up at the ceiling, thinking that maybe—just maybe—her fears of ending up alone for the rest of her life might not actually come to pass.

* * * *

Celia was glad for a slow morning at work, which gave her an opportunity to talk with Shannon about this new turn in her life. After she'd repeated everything that had happened and all that she felt, just like any woman would share with her best friend, Celia asked, "Is this weird for me to be talking about all of this when I'm talking about your brother?"

"It doesn't feel weird to me," Shannon said. "And I'm not going to be offended over whatever either of you choose *not* to tell me. I respect your privacy—both of you. It might be a good idea for the two of you to establish a 'don't tell Shannon' boundary."

Celia laughed, even though she agreed it probably was a good idea. She just didn't know how she was going to get through the rest of the day with all the butterflies spontaneously fluttering around in her stomach.

Celia forced herself to get some work done, knowing that Shannon also had work to accomplish. She couldn't help hoping that Greg might drop by the office—as he often did. But when the day ended and he hadn't, she figured it was probably for the best. She most likely would have blushed at the sight of him, and there would be no concealing how thoroughly preoccupied she'd become over him. He'd frequently invaded her thoughts ever since she'd actually met him, but a lot had changed since they'd peeled potatoes together the previous day, and her mind hadn't quite caught up to those changes. She hoped their time together this evening would go well and that she could manage to not gush or make herself look foolish.

While Celia was organizing her desk in order to conclude her day's work and leave the office at five, her cell phone chimed, indicating a text had come in and she picked up the phone to look at it. The number was unfamiliar, but she was delighted to read: *Hi, it's Greg. Shannon gave me your number. I actually have a cell phone now. And now you have my number. Are we still on for five-thirty?*

Celia texted back: *How nice to hear from you! I'll be there.* Impulsively she added some humor: *Just watch for the really short woman with dark hair.*

Greg texted back a smiley face and the words he'd said the previous evening: *Adorably short.* And he added: *Can't wait!*

Celia added Greg's number to the contact list in her phone before she told Shannon she was off. After Shannon had teased her a little about her forthcoming date, Celia hurried home to change into something more casual and to make some attempt to breathe deeply and calm her nervous excitement. She arrived at the café at five-thirty, exactly. Given that she lived only a few minutes away, it wasn't difficult to time her arrival perfectly. She wondered if Greg was here yet as she walked through the door, then immediately saw him stand up from a booth across the room, as if he'd been watching closely for her. Their eyes met, and they exchanged a smile as she approached, but she was surprised when he greeted her with a hug, much like the one they'd shared at parting the night before. They'd graduated to hugging status; she liked that.

"It's good to see you," he said, motioning for her to sit down.

Once she was seated, he sat across from her, and she said, "It's good to see you too. How was your day?"

"Better now," he said. "I mean . . . it wasn't a bad day, it's just . . . better now."

Celia smiled. "I can certainly say the same." There was a long moment of silence that threatened to grow into something awkward until she added, "So you have a new cell phone."

"Yes," he said with exaggerated pride. "I'm a man with a job and a cell phone. I'm moving up in the world." Celia chuckled, and he went on to say, "Cell phone technology has changed a great deal since I lived in the real world. But my kids have given me some serious tutoring in the art of texting, and I've quickly discovered that it's a good way to keep track of them, and . . . well . . ." he shrugged slightly. "I like letting them know I'm thinking of them." He leaned forward a little and smiled. "And now I can let you know when I'm thinking of *you.*"

"And the other way around," she said, delighted by the prospect.

After the server brought them menus and glasses of ice water, Greg said, "I'm buying . . . in case you had any question about that." He smirked slightly. "I am a man with a job, and this *is* a date."

"Okay, I accept," she said. "Although, I have a job too, and it's a modern world. So I might buy next time, and you'll just have to live with it."

"As long as there's a next time," he said as if the idea meant as much to him as it did to her, "I think I can live with just about anything."

She smiled at him, then tried to focus on the menu, hating the way that the simple act of deciding what to order evoked so many ridiculous—and often painful—memories. Her childhood had been filled with passive-aggressive comments—mostly from her father—about how she ate too much and how fat she was. She'd dated men who had seemed to think they were doing her a great service to encourage her to order a salad while they would sit across the table and eat something covered in cheese and bacon.

Greg stole discreet glances at Celia over the top of his menu and felt like a hypocrite, recalling how he'd declared the need to take things slow between them, to be friends, to be able to talk and have fun together. What he wanted was to get down on one knee right here and now and beg her to always be a part of his life. She made everything that had always seemed wrong feel magically right—as if every stupid step he'd taken in his life had been worth it if only to end up here now, with her. She inspired him to be better and to do better. When she looked at him, he felt like she could see the real him and not be disappointed or disgusted.

He absolutely knew that all the practicality he'd presented to her last night was the way it needed to be. His life could only get on track one step at a time, and those steps had to be taken in the right order. But the logic and reasoning of his mind was battling with the absolute yearning in his heart that he felt for this woman. He just hoped he could keep up this balancing act between his heart and his head and not mess this up.

"So what sounds good to you?" he asked, if only to say something. "You've probably eaten here many times. Anything that you particularly recommend?"

Celia decided in an instant that this would be the perfect time to do something she'd been taught to do in one of her sessions with a therapist. When it had become evident through their many conversations in counseling just how badly Celia had handled most— if not all—of her dating experiences, the counselor had made some suggestions on how she could find out quickly how a man felt about certain things and what his attitude might be. She'd also learned a great deal about how to appropriately address any comments or behavior that might not sit well, or how to compliment or express appreciation for comments or behavior that made her feel more comfortable and respected. She'd been far too caught up in just enjoying the anticipation of this date to give a second thought to all she'd learned since she'd last been out with a man. But looking over the menu and being assaulted with all the negative memories of past dates gone bad, her training kicked in, and she decided to just try one of the tests the counselor had suggested. She folded her menu and set it down, saying, "You order for me. I want to try whatever you're in the mood for. As far as I know, it's all good."

Since one of Celia's big issues in growing up—and in dating— had been food, this was meant to let Celia know how a man might feel about the fact that she had a fuller figure than what was considered the ideal woman. To make certain that Greg didn't think this was some indication of her having no backbone or decision-making abilities, she added, "Next time, I'll choose."

"That sounds fair," Greg said and gave her a little crooked smile before he set down his own menu, as if he already knew exactly what to order. "You know," he said, "food in prison is not something to write home about . . . so to speak. One of the great things about being a free man is being able to eat all the things I craved for years and couldn't have. And there are some things I just can't get enough of."

"Hmm," Celia said, intrigued.

"Are you ready for this? Really?"

"Whatever you want," she said as if it were a challenge.

The server approached as if on cue, her notebook and pencil poised with anticipation.

Greg said boldly and without hesitation, "We'll have two bacon cheeseburgers with everything, and—"

"No onion on mine," Celia interjected.

"No onions," Greg said with a smile toward Celia. Then, to the server, "And two orders of fries."

"And to drink?" the server asked.

"Water is fine for me," Celia said.

"Me too," Greg added.

The server left the table with a smile and an enthusiastic, "Okey dokey."

Greg noticed Celia smiling and asked, "What?"

"I love bacon cheeseburgers and fries. How *did* you know?"

"I didn't." He chuckled. "But I'm glad you approve. Oh, and . . . I was thinking we could maybe do that thing where we order a big milkshake for dessert and share it with two straws. I *always* wanted to do that."

"Sounds delightful," she said. "Do you think we can agree on a flavor?"

"You choose," he said. "Anything you like is fine with me."

Greg didn't realize he'd reached across the table to take her hand until he saw her look at their clasped fingers. "Is that okay?" he asked. "If I hold your hand?"

"It's more than okay," she said. "And since we have agreed to be completely honest with each other, can I just say out loud that I wonder how it is that I like you more every time I talk to you, since we've shared little more than small talk before yesterday?"

"I don't have an answer," he said, "but I can say that the feeling is mutual."

Celia felt so completely comfortable that she didn't hesitate to say, "Now that we've ordered, can I make a serious confession?"

"Go for it," he said as if he would love to hear *anything* she had to say and her doing so only made him more comfortable about sharing his own confessions.

"Letting you order for me was a test," she said.

"Really?" he asked and laughed. "I was going to confess that *what* I ordered for you was a test."

"Really?" she said and laughed too. "How so?"

"Well, I really did order what *I* wanted to eat, but I was curious over how you would react. I wondered if you might renege on letting me order for you, or if you might try to tell me you shouldn't be eating all those carbs and calories."

"Would you have been put off if I said something like that?"

"Would you be put off if I said I'd been put off?" he countered.

"We agreed to be honest," she insisted.

"I want you to have a good time. And I want you to know that even though you asked me to order for you, I respect your right to make your own decisions about yourself. To tell you the truth, I guess you could say I'm put off by anyone—man or woman—who is too preoccupied with certain things to have a good time."

"Like what?" she asked, enjoying this more than she dared admit—even with the agreement for honesty.

Greg thought about that for a long moment and didn't like where the thought took him, but he had to tell her the truth. "You know what? In order for me to talk about this, I have to bring up my ex-wife. And I *really* hate talking about my ex-wife."

"But she *is* your ex-wife, right? She's the mother of your children, and a big part of your past. However much you're glad to have that part of your past behind you, we can't ignore her existence."

"I'd *like* to," he said, not too seriously. "But you're right. And the thing is . . . she's not the only woman I ever dated, but I married her when I was in my early twenties, and I never dated after the divorce before I ended up in prison. So it feels impossible to not look at you and find myself making comparisons in my mind. And the thing is . . . there's no comparison. You're everything she's not, and you can take that as a compliment, because coming from me that is the highest possible compliment."

"Then, thank you," she said. "And for the record, you realize I probably already know just about everything there is to know about BeeKee—at least from Shannon's perspective. I prefer calling her BeeKee because that's what the kids call her. You can tell me anything you want, or you don't have to tell me anything. But compare away if you have to. Don't think I haven't been making my own mental comparisons to past relationships."

"You have?" he asked, feeling added hope that this was not all too good to be true. Every little piece of evidence that they were thinking the same way just felt so great.

"Yes, but you first. I'm waiting to hear how BeeKee ties into you ordering my dinner."

"Okay, well . . . I'll just lay it all out. She would order a salad if we went out to eat, and she just had to say something—either to me or to the server or to anyone else who might be listening—about how she needed to watch her calories and avoid carbs in order to stick to her diet. The thing is, she was too skinny, in my opinion. Her comments were often like backhanded insults to the people around her—especially given the fact that it was all for show. At home she grazed on junk food, never exercised, and she sat in front of the TV and made critical comments about anything and everything she saw that she considered beneath her. All the while she's an alcoholic and a drug addict who wants people to believe that she's conscious of her health and therefore strict about her diet and exercise. Every time she used the words *diet* or *exercise,* I cringed. She was obsessed with her hair and her makeup and her nails, but she let my kids go hungry while I wasn't there to do anything about it."

Greg heard himself sounding a little too vehement as the anger he still felt over that rose too close to the surface. He looked down and checked himself before saying, "Sorry. That's not where I intended for this conversation to go."

"It's okay," she said and squeezed his hand. "I can't imagine how that must have been for you. I don't want you to ever think you can't talk about that stuff. Ever!"

"Thank you," he said and returned the gentle squeeze of her fingers. "Now, why don't you tell me how you were testing me by letting me order?"

"Oh!" she said with a histrionic drawl. "That's opening a can of worms. For now I'll just say that I've had food issues my entire life, so food can be a sensitive topic for me. Some other time when we're bored and we've run out of things to talk about, I'll tell you more about that. In a nutshell, the last guy I dated in what I would call a serious relationship was a man who thought that I should eat like a rodent and work toward a certain dress size in order to achieve the goal of being considered worthy of marriage to him, which apparently should have been considered a great prize for all my efforts. Eventually I figured out that I became involved with men like that because they had the same attitude about it that my father had."

"That is unbelievable," Greg said with all the astonishment he felt.

"What part?"

"All of it, but . . . I was thinking most about how *any* man could treat you like that and think it was okay."

"Well, I learned that I *allowed* men to treat me that way. So I guess I just wanted to see what you might order for me and if you might make any comment about it. I already knew you were the kind of guy who would show me respect, but I still had to know."

"I get that," he said. "And what would you have said if I'd ordered you a salad?"

"I would have told you that I'd changed my mind and I'd have a cheeseburger and fries because I'm on a date and I want to enjoy myself."

"Good for you." Greg smiled. "And for the record, I really do think you're beautiful—just the way you are. I want you to be healthy because I want you to live a really, really long time. So I don't think either of us should have a meal like this too often. But . . . that's it. I think you're beautiful."

"You're a one-in-a-million, Gregory Turney," she said. "And you should take that as a very high compliment."

He smiled but didn't have time to comment before their food was set on the table. Greg enjoyed the meal nearly as much as he enjoyed watching Celia while she ate and talked and laughed. She joked about how wide she had to open her mouth to get a bite of that burger, but she didn't exhibit the kind of self-consciousness he might have expected from other things she'd said. She was delightfully refreshing in so many ways that he doubted he could ever count them. He loved it when she started eating *his* fries to make certain they weren't better than hers; then she fed him a fry from her plate, laughing as she purposely got ketchup on his face. She wiped it off with her napkin and declared how much he needed her. He agreed with all of his heart.

Chapter Eight

AFTER THEY SHARED A STRAWBERRY milkshake with two straws, he looked at his watch to determine he still had a little while before he had to get to work for his evening shift. They talked until he had to go, and he walked her to her car, resisting the urge to kiss her. As much as his heart and head were battling over finding the correct pace for this relationship, he fought to keep his head in charge, responsibly rationing his desire to be with her every minute of the day and to let her know the true depth of his feelings.

"I had a really good time," she said, looking up at him.

"Me too," he said. "How long do you think I should wait before I ask you out again?"

"I don't think there's any protocol for that." She laughed softly. "Although . . . it's kind of a busy week for me." He felt disappointed until she added with a sly smile, "You see . . . I always spend Thanksgiving with my best friend and her family, and she ropes me into all these projects at her house. Homemade pies. Homemade stuffing. Making little turkeys out of gumdrops. It's insane." She laughed again. "So I'll be at her house this week . . . a lot."

"Then I must be the luckiest man alive," he said.

"Maybe you are," she said and got in her car.

"I'll see you tomorrow, then?" he asked, feeling it was so far away.

"You can count on it," she said.

Greg told her to drive safely and closed the car door. He watched her drive away before he hurried to get to work. He couldn't recall ever anticipating a holiday—and its preparations—quite so much in his entire life.

* * * *

Celia went home and could hardly do anything else the rest of the evening, due to the sensation she was floating. She mostly just sat on the couch and gazed out through the sliding glass doors toward the sloping backyard, lightly covered in snow, although she could only see what was visible in the scope of the patio light she'd turned on. She recounted her dating experiences in the past and how what she felt now was different in too many ways to count. Even this ongoing sensation of having a crush on a cute guy and having him like her back was more and more settling into an increasingly comfortable reality that there was nothing silly or immature about what was evolving between her and Greg. He *really* liked her. She could see it in the way he looked at her, hear it in the sincerity of his words. And she had learned a lot throughout her life about how to discern sincerity. And perhaps most amazing of all—given her history—he really liked *her*. For the first time in her life, she felt like she didn't have some reason to apologize or feel ashamed for the way she was built and the fact that her dress size had two digits instead of one. She found the irony truly sad—not only that the world in which she lived was so focused on appearances that she'd become indoctrinated in that culture, but also that she could be a woman in her midthirties and realize that for all of her efforts to find and feel self-respect, this was the first time she had ever felt truly beautiful. When Greg Turney looked at her, she *felt* beautiful. It was a miracle.

Celia laughed softly to herself, actually loving the irony as she thought of how her family would be absolutely shocked and appalled to know she was falling for a man like Greg with a such a tainted past. She found it especially ironic that the kindest, most decent, most functional man she'd ever known had come from a deplorable upbringing and had suffered so much because of it. Celia had strong feelings about both Shannon and Greg and how the difficulties of their youth had actually contributed to their becoming such amazing people. But she also knew it was just as likely for people to continue in a life of dysfunctional patterns as it was to break free and change. In fact, it was surely more difficult to create a new path than it was to just keep walking in the rut that had been created for them. She admired Greg and Shannon so much for rising above their past. But she marveled even more when she considered all the people she'd known who, despite being raised in good homes and given every advantage, elected to treat people badly in one way or another. She'd been the recipient of such deplorable treatment far too much in her life, which made her all the more appreciative of the way Greg treated her. She'd never felt so beautiful, and more importantly, she'd never felt so valued.

Celia finally went to bed feeling completely relaxed in spite of her anticipation of seeing Greg again—hopefully tomorrow. And with Thanksgiving only a few days away, this could be a very good week.

* * * *

Greg awoke Tuesday morning, well aware that Phillip's siblings and their families would begin arriving in town today. Some would be here today, others tomorrow, and they would all be staying until Sunday. He knew some were staying at a motel but would spend a great deal of time at the house; some were actually staying here. Greg couldn't keep track of their names or how many children there would be, even though he'd been told about them many times. Of course, not having met them it was impossible to connect names to faces. He'd been reassured that he shouldn't feel out of place, that they would all love him and that they were all going to have a wonderful time.

Marj had told him more than once that she considered him to be a part of her family, and he couldn't deny that he certainly felt that way about Marj. She was a remarkable woman, the kind of mother he'd always wished he'd had, and he'd grown to love her dearly. He just wasn't sure if he would feel that way about her children and grandchildren whom he'd never met. He had dreaded thoughts of this invasion and had determined that he would mostly just stay out of everybody's way and try to be invisible.

But his prior expectation to dread the coming week had changed. If Celia was going to be around more and if she was going to be in the middle of all the activities taking place, he wanted to be there too. He wanted to be *wherever* she might be. Everything felt easier and better and more right with thoughts of Celia.

When it occurred to him how easy it would be to see her before he went to work, he got out of bed with more enthusiasm than usual and was showered and dressed and in the kitchen before anyone else. Noting the time, he quickly found the package of instant pancake mix and had a pile of pancakes made before the family started showing up.

"Ooh, look who's cooking," Shannon said and kissed his cheek as soon as she set Evan down.

"I have a few skills," he said with a chuckle as he flipped a pancake.

"Good morning," Phillip said with a playful slap on the shoulder, which that had become a familiar brotherly greeting between them.

"Good morning, bro," Greg said and flipped another pancake. "How are the animals?"

The question had become somewhat of a joke between them, since Greg had quickly found it amusing to realize how well Phillip knew the silly names of many of his animal patients, as well as the animals that were being boarded at his clinic at any given time. Phillip had taken it a step further when the antics of his young children were a constant part of life in this family.

"Grace is still asleep," Phillip said, "and Evan appears to be fine." He chuckled and added, "No nighttime emergency calls, so I assume the others are all doing well."

"Good deal," Greg replied and put the freshly done pancakes on top of the growing stack. "Here's some hot ones," he said, and Shannon greedily reached for one.

Marj and Neal and Jeanie all drifted into the kitchen, giving Greg exaggerated praise for his cooking skills. And since they usually had cereal and toast for breakfast on weekdays, he knew they meant it when they all said that pancakes were a nice change. He asked his kids how they were doing as he always did at breakfast—even though this time of day was often rushed with everyone getting ready for work and school.

Following some routine conversation while they all ate, the inevitable question popped up, and he wasn't at all surprised when Jeanie was the first to ask. "How was your date, Dad?"

"Oh yeah," Phillip said with the glee of an older brother who might have something new to tease Greg about. "How *did* your date go?"

Greg had been expecting this and had told himself he could be a good enough actor to not let his true feelings show. But he only had to think of answering the question and he felt a smile force its way into his expression against his own will.

"Ohhhhh," Jeanie said with a chuckle before he'd said a word. "It must have been good!"

With that, Greg felt himself blush, and everyone laughed. But Greg didn't feel embarrassed as much as he felt loved. These people all loved him and wanted him to be happy. They were family and they'd become comfortable with sharing and teasing and communicating appropriately whether it was in jest or complete seriousness. He laughed with them and shook his head, finally managing to say, "Yeah, it was good."

He noticed that Shannon looked positively pleased with herself, and he wondered how long she might have been hoping he and Celia might at least attempt to share a relationship. He smiled at her with a silent promise that they would talk later, but he was startled from the thought when Neal asked, "Did you kiss her, Dad?"

Greg turned toward him and said with mock indignation, "No, I did not! A gentleman does not kiss a lady on the first date. Hasn't your Uncle Phillip taught you anything?"

They all laughed, since it had also become common for Phillip and Greg to joke about which good or bad behavior was the result of Greg being their father or Phillip having helped raise them.

"He's too young for talk like that!" Phillip said.

"You wish!" Neal countered with a chuckle.

"Is there something you want to tell us?" Shannon asked Neal.

"Yeah," Neal said. "I'm holding out for the hundred bucks Phillip said he'd give me if I didn't kiss a girl until I'm eighteen."

Phillip shrugged. "Bribery. I admit I resort to bribery."

"That's a good plan, buddy," Greg said.

"Wait a minute," Jeanie said to her father. "You changed the subject. How was your date?"

Greg looked directly at his daughter and said, "It went very well. We had a lot to talk about, and I really like her." He took a bite of pancake and chewed it while he noticed the smiles being passed around among his family. "With any luck," he added, "she likes me too."

Shannon took her empty plate to the sink to rinse it off and put it in the dishwasher. She muttered with light sarcasm, "It's too bad for you that she likes to spend nearly every waking moment here to get in on all the Thanksgiving celebrations."

"Or too bad for her," Greg said. "Hope I don't scare her away."

He wasn't worried, but he still liked it when Shannon said with a sly smile, "I don't think there's any danger of that."

After everyone was off to work and school, Greg helped Marj clean up the kitchen as he often did after breakfast. He declared that since he'd made most of the mess, he was happy to clean up after himself. While he was loading the dishwasher and she was wiping off the counter, she said earnestly, "I'm so glad to hear that you and Celia are spending time together. She's a wonderful girl, and she deserves someone like you."

Greg felt a little startled by the way she'd put that, but her words settled into him with warmth. "You're way too nice to me," he said and was surprised by the way she turned and put a hand on his arm.

"Gregory, my boy," she said as if he belonged to her and he always had, "you are such a fine young man. You deserve the best that life has to offer, and I say that with all my heart." She hugged him in that motherly way of hers that he'd come to love.

"Thanks, Mom," he said, and she laughed softly. He'd figured out weeks ago that she loved it when he called her Mom, and he loved it too. At the moment he felt so blessed he had trouble comprehending the depth of his gratitude. He figured that was a good way to feel when a holiday of thanks was on the horizon.

Greg told Marj he was going to leave early for work and stop at Shannon's office on his way. It was far from the first time he'd done so, but her smile let him know that she was onto to his reasons for doing so today.

"You have a good day," she said and focused her attention on Grace and Evan, who were in her care until the nanny arrived.

"You too." He kissed her forehead—another comfortable ritual he'd developed while living here—and bundled up to ride his bike into the center of town.

At the clinic, Greg pulled off his hat and gloves as he came through the back door, and he and Daphne exchanged familiar greetings. His heart quickened as he opened the door to the room where Celia worked. He was immediately disappointed to not see her there. It felt completely weird to even be in this room without her sitting behind the desk, and he realized it had never happened before. She obviously took breaks, but he'd just never been around when it had happened. Or she could be in Shannon's office, he thought. He took off his coat and threw it along with his hat and gloves into one of the few available chairs. He was debating whether to knock on Shannon's door or just sit down and wait when Celia came in through the door where he'd just entered.

"Hi," she said, indicating with the tone of that one word that she was thrilled to see him there.

"Hi," he said, hearing in his own voice some kind of exhale of relief, as if just seeing her and knowing she was real made everything feel better.

"Sorry," she said, closing the door behind her. "Potty break."

Greg chuckled. "You spend way too much time around my sister's kids."

"Never," she said with a smile. "Although," she pointed comically at him, "when I met *your* kids they were pretty young."

"Yes, I suppose they were," he said, trying not to sound sad. It was a familiar feeling when he was reminded of all he'd missed, but he didn't want to talk about that right now.

Celia proved how perceptive she was when she said, "I'm sorry. Was that insensitive?"

"Not at all," he said. "I missed a lot of their lives. It's a fact. I'm still working on trying to keep all of that in perspective."

She smiled as if she understood, then they both just stood there looking at each other as if something was supposed to happen but neither of them knew what. Greg didn't feel any awkwardness or discomfort over the silence. He just enjoyed watching her and finally said, "You're taller today." He glanced at her shoes, ones she typically wore for work.

"Yeah," she laughed, "I can only wear these when I spend most of my time sitting, which makes them fairly pointless, I suppose."

"Well . . ." he drawled, "not entirely pointless." He let his eyes wander from her red high heels to the black dress that hung just above her knees to the bright-red necklace and earrings that coordinated with the shoes. He finished his silent appraisal by looking into her eyes, saying, "You look really great."

She glanced away with a hint of shyness that he found endearing. "If you keep saying things like that you'll never get rid of me."

"Promise?" he said, and she glanced at him abruptly, seeming surprised that he was serious.

Celia walked to her desk and sat down. "For a man who declared that he wanted to take things slowly, you sound awfully . . ."

"Hypocritical?" he guessed.

"I couldn't think of the word, but it wasn't *that.*"

They were looking at each other again, and Greg didn't know what to say. Celia broke the silence by saying, "You came to see Shannon? She's free if—"

"No," he said and picked up a chair, setting it down right next to Celia's. He sat down to face her, and she swiveled in her chair to face him. "I saw her at breakfast," he added. "I came to see you. And if your boss gives you any grief for hanging out with your boyfriend in the office, I'll have it out with her."

Celia laughed, but her voice sounded serious when she asked, "Are you?"

"What?"

"My boyfriend?"

"I hope so," he said and took her hand. "Is that word too archaic for people our age? Am I sounding even more hypocritical now if I admit that—beyond my family—I don't want to spend my time with anyone else, and I don't want you going out with anyone but me?"

"No worries there," she said, seeming pleased, which eased his sudden nervousness as he realized what had just come out of his mouth. "Until last night I haven't been on a date in years."

"I don't know why there aren't a dozen men knocking at your door."

She squeezed his hand. "There are no dozen men in the world that would make me want to be spending my time with anyone but you."

Greg chuckled and glanced down as if looking anywhere but at her face might help him think more clearly. "I hadn't come here planning to say all that," he admitted. "And even though it makes me sound like a hypocrite, I'm glad I said it."

"Me too," she said, and he looked at her again.

Celia couldn't believe this was happening. She had to ask herself if she was simply getting caught up in the fact that an attractive man was being so kind and sweet to her. But in her heart she knew that wasn't the case. She'd learned to see through that kind of thing a long time ago; she'd learned to recognize the different voices in her own head, and she knew what her instincts were telling her. He was a good man with all of the most important qualities she knew she needed in a man. She'd be a fool to let any residue of her insecurities dampen this experience.

"Celia," he leaned closer, "my head is telling me I need to take it slow and be practical, but my heart is screaming that I'm tired of being alone . . . and that I will never find anyone or anything as perfect for me as you. So . . . somehow I've got to find a balance somewhere in the middle of that. Am I making any sense?"

"Yes, Greg. It makes perfect sense. And I think as long as we're honest with each other and communicate our feelings about what we're dealing with, we'll know what's right." He nodded, but she sensed some hesitancy in him. "Do you disagree with that?" she asked, wanting to establish right up front the fact that she would not allow feelings to go unvoiced in any kind of relationship.

"No, I don't disagree," he said. "It's just . . ."

"What?" she encouraged. "Tell me."

"I just keep thinking over and over that . . . that . . . you're smart; you're well educated and successful. And you're beautiful. I can't help thinking that you haven't really seen the real me, that you haven't really considered that I really am a man with nothing. *Nothing,* Celia."

Celia couldn't hold back a little laugh, but he looked mildly offended and asked, "Is that funny?"

"Not in the slightest. It's not funny, Greg. It's ironic. I keep thinking over and over that you're such an amazing man you can't possibly be interested in someone like me."

"Okay," he laughed softly, "you're right. It's ironic. Because I don't feel at all amazing."

"Well, you are," she said gently and reached up with her free hand to touch his face before she even thought about what she was doing. But she saw his eyes soften from her touch before he closed them as if to savor the feeling. The gesture alone added to her sense of awe in this moment.

They were both startled when Shannon's office door came open. Celia dropped her hand and Greg sat up straight, but he didn't let go of her other hand, which was out of Shannon's view.

"Am I interrupting something?" Shannon asked with a pleasant smirk.

Celia was trying to think of the right way to answer that question when Greg said, "Yes." She bit her lip to keep from laughing at the way he spoke to her as only a brother could.

"Fine," Shannon said, still smiling as she turned around, went back into her office, and closed the door.

Celia said, "I should probably get back to work."

"Probably," he said but tightened his hold on her hand as if he wouldn't let her go just yet. "But not until you answer my question."

"What question?"

"Will you be my girlfriend?" he asked, and a surge of pure delight lit up her entire nervous system with a tingling sensation. "And in case you're wondering exactly what I mean by that . . . I think we *do* need some time, or at least we have a great deal to talk about and figure out. But in the meantime I want something official between us. No lifetime commitments or anything irrevocable until we know a whole lot more about each other, but . . . I want to be able to hold your hand and see you as much as possible, and . . . so what do you think?"

"I think it's perfect," she said and leaned forward in her chair to hug him. For a split second she wondered if that was too forward, but he held to her tightly and pressed his face against her shoulder as if the closeness soothed him somehow.

"Okay," he said and eased away as he came to his feet. "I don't want your boss to be mad at you any more than I want my sister to be mad at me. I have to live with her, after all."

"That's true," Celia said and stood to face him. She was glad when he hugged her again, and given the height of her shoes, her forehead ended up against his cheek, which felt smooth from a recent shave. He smelled faintly of a mild shaving lotion that was so thoroughly masculine it felt intoxicating.

"Besides," he stepped back but took both her hands into his, "if I intend to keep visiting you at work, I don't want to wear out my welcome."

"I don't think that's possible," Celia said.

Greg smiled and squeezed her hands before he put his chair back where it belonged and opened Shannon's office door without knocking. "You can come out now."

"Oh, thank you," Shannon said lightly. "Only you could boss me around in my own office."

"I *am* your big brother," he said.

"Bigger," she said, "but younger."

"Fair enough."

"Are you going to tell me what's going on?" Shannon asked Greg while Celia could hear every word of their conversation and felt herself blushing.

Greg glanced over his shoulder and caught her at it, which made him smile before he turned back to look at his sister and declare, "I asked Celia to be my girlfriend, and she said yes."

"Well, isn't that nice," Shannon said as if she really meant it. Celia could hardly contain her delight. "How fortunate for you that she's already been invited to Thanksgiving dinner."

"So I heard," he said. "And *yes,* that *is* fortunate for me."

Greg said his good-byes and reluctantly left the office. Celia stared at the door through which he'd left until she heard Shannon say, "Wow. You look utterly smitten."

Celia sighed and couldn't deny it. "He's incredible."

"Yes, I would agree with that," Shannon said, sitting in one of the chairs meant for waiting clients. "Still . . . I never would have dreamed."

"What?" Celia asked, wanting to ignore her work and talk about this the rest of the day.

"I was just thinking of when you were assigned to be my assistant at that horrible, stuffy law firm, and since you would be taking my messages, I told you my brother was in prison and you promised not to tell anyone. And you were so great about it. Now look at us."

"Yes, look at us," Celia said, hearing the dreaminess in her own voice. Trying to be just a little bit practical, she added, "But if it doesn't work out it could make my hanging out with your family very awkward."

"I think the two of you are mature enough to be able to overcome that . . . *if* it doesn't work out. But I have a feeling it will."

Celia sighed loudly, unable to avoid sounding even dreamier. "Oh, I hope so!"

"I can't think of anything more wonderful," Shannon said, and Celia was glad to know that her best friend, who was also her boss, didn't have a problem with the possibility that being Greg's girlfriend might turn into something more permanent. If she *did* have a problem, things could *really* be awkward. "Although we do have some work that has to be tackled today."

"Of course," Celia said and tried not to think about Greg. It was more accurate that she managed to be productive in spite of thinking of him practically every moment. She hoped it wouldn't be too many hours before she saw him again.

* * * *

Greg's happiness hovered around and inside of him throughout the remainder of the day. He went home after his midday shift at work to find that some of Phillip's family had arrived. They were as kind as he'd been told they would be, but he still felt a desire to stick close to his room—until Jeanie came to tell him that Celia had arrived and was helping Shannon and Marj in the kitchen.

"Thank you," he said. "Don't tell anyone, but I think hanging out with the family suddenly sounds a lot more fun."

Jeanie giggled as if she were many years younger. "Is she your girlfriend, Dad?"

"Actually, yes," he said with a laugh and hugged his daughter tightly, lifting her briefly off the ground. "Do you have a problem with that?"

"I think it's great!" she said. "Celia is awesome!"

"Yes, she is," Greg said, and Jeanie ran off to do something Shannon had asked her to do.

Greg checked his appearance in the mirror and caught himself smiling. He told himself to try and look normal as he went downstairs, but he doubted he could hide how pleased he was to see Celia wearing one of Marj's aprons, up to her elbows in flour while she did something with pastry dough.

Before anyone had seen him there, Greg said with enthusiasm, "How many beautiful women can one kitchen handle?"

The implication in regard to Celia was apparently lost on Marj as she kissed his cheek and said, "I hope you're ready to get to work. We have a lot of food to prepare."

"I am your slave," he said, which made Marj giggle.

"Hello, little brother," Shannon said and also kissed his cheek before she went back to peeling apples, apparently for a pie.

The moment suddenly became a little awkward as Greg found himself there in the kitchen with Celia, as if he expected her to greet him the way the other women had. He smiled at her and said, "Hello," wondering if that was sufficient, but she went on her tiptoes to kiss his cheek.

"Hello to you," she said, her eyes sparkling. Then, with no warning, she put her other hand to his cheek, which for a moment seemed mildly romantic—until she laughed and he realized she'd just wiped flour on his face. Returning to her task, she said, "Now you look like you've been helping, Gregory Turney. Grab an apron and get busy."

"Yes, ma'am," he said lightly and did as he was told. He had no idea what he was doing, but the three women seemed to enjoy telling him what to do and were even a little bossy about it—all in good fun.

The next few days went by without a glitch—at least as far as Greg's experience in sharing Thanksgiving with the Meadows family. He was vaguely aware of some minor squabbling among the children of many ages, and he was proud of his kids for the way they helped supervise and referee the younger ones. It quickly became evident that they'd come to see these kids as their cousins over the years as they'd made their annual Thanksgiving visit. And that was fine. Greg was glad to see them being a part of such a great family. Phillip's siblings and their spouses were all very kind to him, although he figured that had more to do with how much they'd grown to love Shannon over the years.

Celia kept Greg more in the middle of everything than he might have been otherwise, but he found he enjoyed being more of a participant rather than an observer. Of course, he'd never experienced a Thanksgiving anything like this before. The entire production and execution of the grand feast was rather remarkable, especially with the evidence of so much love and respect among everyone involved. He even appreciated seeing hints that the family wasn't perfect and that even the adults occasionally disagreed over some minor issues, causing a couple of little spats. But they were resolved quickly and respectfully. He felt like he was learning something very important. It was one thing to read about how a functional family worked, and quite another to see it in action. There was no shouting or swearing; there were no derogatory or demeaning words spoken. And yet every person—young and old—was entitled to their own feelings and opinions.

Greg quickly became comfortable with his new status as Celia's boyfriend, and he was pleased when Shannon introduced him that way. "My brother and Celia's boyfriend," she said more than once as family members arrived. "Isn't that amazingly convenient?"

"If Celia had a different boyfriend," Phillip said once, "we'd have to find room for another chair at the table."

"And I'd have to challenge him to a duel," Greg had added.

Thanksgiving Day was full of activity and enjoyment. Although there was a lovely, reverent pause in all of that right after everyone was seated around the long tables that had been put together in the big common room to allow space for everyone to sit together for the meal. A beautiful prayer was spoken by Phillip's brother, and the sense of unity and gratitude was almost palpable. During the meal Greg occasionally took hold of Celia's hand beneath the table, and he loved the way she often smiled at him as if he really meant as much to her as she did to him.

It wasn't until late in the evening that Greg found an opportunity to be alone with Celia. They sat together on one of the couches in the common room, with a fire burning in the fireplace nearby. The house was quiet since all of the children and probably most of the adults had either left or gone to bed.

"I've enjoyed observing you through all of this, you know," he said.

"Well, I can say the same." She smiled when he took her hand.

"Seriously. You are so great with the kids. You're a marvelous cook. How did I get so lucky?"

"I can say the same about that, too," she said, and he resisted the urge to argue with her, knowing that was his ingrained insecurity trying to take over. He had no reason to believe that Celia wasn't completely sincere since she knew everything about the kind of man he was. He needed to try and believe her when she said things like that, the same way he wanted *her* to believe *him* when he expressed his feelings toward her.

Celia felt Greg squeeze her hand, a sensation that had become familiar. They shared a gaze that had also become familiar, but everything between them became very still and quiet. The silence suddenly felt very thick; even the hissing and crackling of the fire sounded distant and muffled. Celia's heart quickened, and her stomach fluttered as she felt something changing between them, even if there was no tangible evidence to support the theory.

Celia held her breath when Greg lifted his free hand to touch her face. He pushed his fingers into her hair, at the same time rubbing his thumb over her cheek, making her keenly aware of how large his hands were. She closed her eyes in order to more fully savor his touch and she let out her breath with a contented sigh. She gasped softly with pleasant surprise to feel his cheek against the other side of her face. The slight stubble that had grown there since he'd shaved this morning enhanced the masculine effect of his nearness.

"I can't stand it anymore, Celia," he whispered near her ear.

"You can't stand what?" she asked, keeping her eyes closed.

"Not knowing what it's like to kiss you," he said just before she felt his lips next to hers and then against them. She took his face into her hands, wanting their first kiss to never end but at the same time wanting it to remain brief and sweet and tender in order to forever preserve it in her memory.

Their lips parted, and she opened her eyes to find him watching her with a kind of fascination, wonder, and intrigue, as if he were a child looking at a star through a telescope. Celia felt so caught up in his gaze and the tingle of his kiss lingering on her lips that she was completely unprepared to hear him say, "I love you, Celia Mae."

Celia took in a sharp breath, then let it out slowly. She pressed her forehead to his and murmured, "Oh, I am so glad! Because *I* love *you*, Gregory Evan."

She felt more than heard a long sigh that seemed to exude deep relief just before he kissed her again.

"Wow," he said and relaxed his head against the back of the couch, still keeping his eyes on her. "I think that's one of the best things that's ever happened to me. Does that sound corny?"

"Not at all," she said. "It's just one more thing we agree on."

He smiled. "I wish I could explain it."

Celia *wanted* to try and explain it, but she felt sure her attempt to do so would only detract from the present experience. She wanted to tell him that every other time she'd been kissed in her life she'd been preoccupied with what the man's motives might really be, because surely he couldn't simply be attracted to *her* without ulterior motives. In the rare cases where she had gotten beyond *that* fear, she had eventually come to feel so badly treated in the relationship that every tender moment had become tainted in her memory. With Greg she had no fears or concerns on either count. The result was that she found nothing but sweetness and purity and a genuine expression of affection in his kiss. So she kept her thoughts to herself and simply said, "There is no need."

He put his arm around her, and she laid her head on his shoulder, feeling perfectly secure. Following a few minutes of silence, she said, "How would you feel about coming to my place and I'll cook you dinner?"

"What? Tonight?" he asked, not at all serious. "Haven't you kept track of everything I've eaten today?"

"Heavens, no. I was busy enjoying what I was eating." Looking up at him without moving her head, she said, "I've wanted to cook for you, but our evening schedules aren't very compatible, and I didn't want it to be rushed."

"Are you asking me on a date?"

"Yes, I believe I am."

"Good." He smiled. "I don't have to work tomorrow. Is there anything that conflicts with that?"

"Not that I know of."

"Then it's a date," he said and pressed a lingering kiss to her brow.

Celia sighed and uttered a silent prayer that this new beginning would never end.

Chapter Nine

THE FOLLOWING DAY GREG JOINED in the activities going on at the house. He enjoyed spending time with Neal and Jeanie, even though they were mostly spending time with their cousins. They were in no way related by blood, but that was how they referred to the children of Phillip's siblings, and Greg had already come to terms with all of that. He simply did his best to remain involved if only so his children would know he was there. It paid off when they all had a great deal of fun playing silly games and eating leftovers from yesterday's turkey feast. However, Greg was mostly preoccupied with thoughts of Celia and the opportunity he would have to spend time with her this evening. She had been invited to join the family for the day but had declined, telling Shannon she had other things to do. Greg felt thrilled to think that those things involved her desire to fix dinner for him. He was counting the hours.

Greg arrived at Celia's apartment right on time. He knew this was where Shannon had lived with Neal and Jeanie for a while prior to her marrying Phillip. It had been vacant when Celia had made the decision to move here and work for Shannon, and she'd been living here ever since. Just as it had done many times before, thinking of all that had happened in the lives of his sister and his children while he'd been absent left him feeling a little off balance. But he focused on the present and went down the outside steps that led to the basement apartment.

Celia answered the door; she was dressed casually while looking as beautiful as ever. Her feet were bare, and she went up on her tiptoes to kiss his cheek.

"Come in," she said, taking his hand. "It's freezing out there."

"It's awfully warm in here," he said and closed the door before he hugged her tightly, lifting her off the ground, which made her laugh.

"Dinner will be ready soon," she said. "I want to show you something first."

"Okay," he said, and she led him by the hand down the hall and flipped on a light switch just inside a doorway.

As if Celia had read his mind, she said, "This is the room where Neal and Jeanie slept when they lived here." He leaned his shoulder against the doorjamb and noted the bunk beds, the large dresser, and the cozy decor. "I'm sure Shannon told you how they didn't want to sleep in separate bedrooms even though there was another one available."

"Yes, she told me," he said.

"The apartment came furnished, so the beds go with it, and I don't have any need for this room, so I've just left it. Neal and Jeanie have stayed with me a few times for different reasons, so I keep the beds made up. I just thought you'd like to see."

"Yes, thank you," he said, recalling photographs that had been taken here. But this was different. He tried to imagine Neal and Jeanie here. He knew it had been a difficult time for them, but the transition had been from a hellish life into a good one. He could almost tangibly feel the security that they might have felt in this room, knowing they were safe and that they would be well cared for.

"You look so sad," Celia commented, bringing him out of his deep thoughts. "Should I not have shown you this or—"

"No, I'm glad you did," he said. "Thinking about all they went through—and my not being able to do anything about it—does make me sad. But it also makes me grateful. Few kids in their situation have ever been as blessed as mine. I shudder to think what their circumstances might be now if Shannon hadn't intervened. So, yes . . . it makes me sad. But I try very hard to focus on all that's positive." He flipped off the light switch and looked at her. "And there is a great deal of that."

"That attitude of yours—the way you try to keep things in perspective like that—it's one of the things I love about you."

Her words and her smile drew him completely away from any sadness. Impulsively he picked her up and carried her back to the living room, which made her shriek with surprised laughter.

While they shared a lovely meal with a menu that had no resemblance to the Thanksgiving leftovers he'd been eating at home, they talked and laughed and sometimes became very serious. Greg loved not being in public, which always brought the possibility of interruption along with a lack of privacy. He also loved not being at Shannon's house for the same reasons. It was nice to just be with Celia, and he became even more entranced with her as he realized how easy it was for them to talk to each other about their lives and their feelings in ways that were candidly honest and open. He felt no judgment from her about the ugliness in his life that he'd always felt so ashamed of, and he could almost literally feel himself healing inside as she offered genuine compassion and understanding. He found it amazing how easily she could make him feel better about himself, but he also found it surprising that she told him more than once he was doing the same for her. He wasn't *trying* to say the right things; he just said what he thought and how he felt. But apparently his indignation toward the dysfunctional behaviors in her family were hugely validating for her.

They lingered over their meal for a very long time, since they were far more focused on the conversation than the food—even though the food was excellent and Greg told her so more than once. He helped Celia clean up the kitchen and load the dishwasher while they kept talking. They'd intended to watch a movie together but both agreed they preferred to spend their time together continuing their conversation. When it seemed there was nothing more to say—most likely because it was getting late and they were both tired—Greg filled the silence by kissing her, not disappointed with the evidence that she enjoyed it at least as much as he did.

"So much for taking it slow," he said and pushed his fingers into her hair, amazed at how thick it was.

"Slow is relative," she said. "We've talked more tonight than I ever talked to a guy before in ten or twelve dates. Or ever."

"Good point."

"So . . ." she put a hand on his chest and looked up at him, "may I tell you what I think about that?"

"Of course," he insisted. "You never need my permission to tell me *anything* you think."

"How refreshing," she said with a seriousness that he found disturbing in regard to the way he'd come to realize her father had treated her. "So . . . I think that you and I need to use our heads and be practical, of course. I'm certainly not suggesting we rush into *anything*. But Greg . . . we're not getting any younger, and, well, it just feels like we've both lost so many years of our lives being alone and miserable. If being together makes us happy, we should be together. Forgive me if that sounds forward or presumptuous, but you told me I could say what I was thinking. And that's what I've been thinking."

Greg's stomach flip-flopped, and his heart beat faster as he realized Celia's implication. But it was still only an implication, and he felt the need for clarification. "It's not too forward or presumptuous," he said. "It's the twenty-first century, and I'm not archaic enough to think that it has to be the man who always initiates the next step. If you wait for me to figure things out, you could be waiting a long time, because I'm not very good at these things. But . . ."

"But what?" she asked when his hesitation grew into a long silence.

"My life is a mess, Celia. I . . ."

"Your life is *not* a mess, Greg. You're adjusting to life in the real world after being locked up for years, and you're doing rather well in my opinion. I don't care how much money you make or that you have a parole officer. I care about the kind of man you are. I care about the relationship you have with your kids and the way you treat me. I *don't* care what people think or if we're poor or—"

"I *do* care if we're poor, Celia," he said with vehemence.

"Listen to me." She tightened her hold on his hand and looked firmly into his eyes. "Of course we must always be sure we have the basic needs of life, and we will. I admire your ability and desire to work hard, and I know you would do whatever you had to do. Between us I have no doubt that we can always find a way to have everything we need. Those are all details we need to talk about. But there's something you need to understand because I don't ever want you to wonder over this. It was not poverty that created the circumstances of your childhood, Greg; it was alcoholism and abuse. And it is *vital* that you understand the difference."

Greg felt something hot beginning to smolder in his chest. He wondered why, in all the endless hours of counseling he'd experienced, no one had ever put it quite like that before. She was right. She was completely right. In his mind he had blamed it mostly on poverty. But it only took a few seconds now to think it through and recognize that many people existed on a very low income but still had happy, functional families. It wasn't at all about the money.

The heat in his chest shot through his nerves, and his eyes began to burn. He looked down, not wanting Celia to see his tears, but she touched his chin with her finger and lifted his face to her view, silently declaring that he should never hide his feelings from her. He squeezed his eyes closed and felt tears spill down his cheeks. But the next thing he felt was Celia's lips over his, and he felt more capable of creating a good and fulfilling life than he ever had.

It was very late when Greg finally returned home, and he found the house dark and everyone sleeping. He crept quietly to his room and got ready for bed, glad for the exhaustion that allowed him to sleep in spite of all the thoughts spinning in his head. He'd never felt so happy in his life.

* * * *

Greg woke late and actually had to hurry to get to work on time. The work was tedious, but he didn't mind it, especially with the way thoughts of Celia were almost constantly with him.

Work was long, with business being slower than usual due to the recent holiday. During a lull when there were no customers, Bernie asked Greg if they could talk. Greg felt a little nervous about the gravity of Bernie's countenance as they sat across from each other at one of the booths in the diner. Greg felt as if he were in some kind of trouble, even though he absolutely knew he hadn't done anything to warrant such a feeling.

"You are one of the best workers I have ever employed," Bernie began. "You do everything the way I want it done. You're never late. You stay after your shift ends if you see work that still needs to be done. You're polite and respectful."

"Thank you," Greg said, mostly because he couldn't think of anything else to say. Bernie's words were not congruent with his mood, and Greg still felt nervous.

"Which is why," Bernie said on the wave of a loud, heavy sigh, "having to let you go is so hard for me. And if it's hard for me, I know it has to be even more difficult for you."

Greg couldn't even get a sound out of his mouth. He wanted to ask why but felt sure Bernie would explain; he just didn't seem to want to. Greg had grown to really like Bernie—and he respected him. He was a good man, which meant that the dilemma over this decision must have been a heavy burden. But as Bernie explained the reasons, Greg found himself growing very angry—not at Bernie but at the circumstances that had put Bernie in such a deplorable position. Bernie explained everything very carefully and apologized multiple times. Greg assured him that he understood and that he didn't blame Bernie at all. And he didn't. He thanked Bernie for being so kind and giving him a chance, and then he left, knowing he would likely never step foot in this diner ever again—for Bernie's sake if for no other reason.

Once outside, Greg felt his anger rising, and he fought to keep it from consuming him. He texted Celia and asked: *Are you home?* Since it was a Saturday, he knew she wouldn't be at work.

He was relieved when her answer came seconds later: *I'm at your house with Shannon.*

He wrote: *Can we talk or are you busy?*

Celia responded: *Yes, we can talk.*

He concluded: *I'll be there soon.*

Throughout his brisk bike ride home, Greg felt his anger settle into sorrow—and perhaps fear—as he considered its source. He saw the garage door open as he approached and Celia standing there waiting for him. He rode the bike into the garage and left it in its usual spot while she closed the garage door and met him with a hug. He held to her tightly for a long moment before she stated the obvious, "Something's wrong."

"Yes, something's wrong," he said, and the sounds of a houseful of people wafted through the door that had been left open between the kitchen and the garage. "Can we go for a drive? Please."

"Of course," she said. "Let me grab my stuff and tell Shannon I'm going."

"Thank you," he said and didn't follow her. He wanted to talk to Celia before he told Shannon. He found it ironic how quickly he'd come to rely on Celia more than his sister, who had been his rock throughout his entire life.

Greg met Celia at her car just a couple of minutes later. He opened the driver's side door for her before he got into the passenger seat.

"Did you tell Shannon I was leaving with you?" he asked.

"No," she said, glancing back and forth between him and the road ahead. "I didn't know if you wanted me to."

Greg took out his phone and texted his sister, not wanting her to wonder where he was. *I'm with Celia,* he wrote and put the phone back in his pocket.

"Where do you want to go?" she asked.

He thought about it a moment and said, "I'd rather have you holding my hand than the steering wheel, but it's too cold to sit in the car without leaving the engine on."

Greg thought of public places they might go in order to talk, and he hated the way this town suddenly felt stifling and anything but private. He was more relieved than he could ever say when Celia suggested exactly what he'd been hoping. "Do you want to just go back to my place?"

"That would be great," he said. "I promise to be a gentleman."

"I'm not worried about that," she said and tossed him a quick, concerned expression that made it clear she had fully grasped the severity of his mood.

"I know," he said, looking out the window. "But I had to say it anyway."

They said nothing more until they were inside the apartment. "It takes a while for the place to heat up," she said, adjusting the thermostat. "I'd suggest leaving your coat on until it does. Have a seat and I'll be right back."

Greg sat on the couch, wondering how to tell her. He'd felt a desperate need to talk to her, but now he didn't know where to begin. She came back and tucked a blanket over his lap as if she were his mother and didn't want him to get cold. He couldn't deny that he loved the way she made him feel cared for in such simple ways—ways that had rarely if ever happened in his life. She sat at the other end of the couch and wrapped a different blanket over her lap as she lifted her stockinged feet up beneath her and turned toward him.

"I can tell you're upset," she said, "so just get on with it."

Greg preferred looking out the window toward the snow-covered yard. "I am now unemployed," he stated, getting directly to the point. "Bernie let me go."

"Why?" she gasped. Her astonishment felt somewhat validating to his own hovering shock. "I thought Bernie *loved* having you there."

"This isn't about Bernie," he said, still not wanting to look at Celia. He felt ashamed and embarrassed even if he knew there was no logical reason for it. "Bernie told me I was one of the best employees he'd ever had and he would gladly give me a letter of recommendation, but he just couldn't keep me on."

"I don't understand," Celia said, and that too was validating. "Why would Bernie do such a—"

"It's not his fault," Greg said and looked down, clasping his hands together. "I think having that conversation with me was very difficult for him." Greg sighed and told himself to just say it. "He had to let me go because he has some very influential customers who will boycott his establishment if he has an ex-con working for him."

Greg heard Celia gasp and turned to look at her just in time to see her put a hand over her mouth as if it might keep her from screaming or saying something unseemly. That's what *he* felt like doing. "He doesn't know how people found out, which really doesn't matter. I've never tried to hide it. He wouldn't tell me who, which is fine; I don't want to know—and I probably wouldn't know who they are, anyway. Bernie said himself how ridiculous it was because I don't even interact with customers; I'm never even out of the kitchen until the place is empty. All he would tell me is that someone in town who has a great deal of influence in the community came to talk to him and—"

"Influence being synonymous with a great deal of wealth, I assume?" Celia said, sounding angry.

"I would assume," Greg said, surprised at how calm he sounded. But he knew being angry wouldn't solve this. "The way Bernie tells it, this guy was apparently the spokesman for several people who are also very influential, and their refusal to ever eat at the diner—and the other people they could tell about the situation who would follow their lead—would create a far too dramatic drop in business for Bernie. He has no choice, and I understand that. He's got a family to provide for, and other employees who need their jobs. It's not his fault. It's mine."

"No, it is *not!*" Celia said with such vehemence that it almost startled him. "You have done *nothing* wrong. *Nothing!*"

"I went to prison, Celia," he said, as if she didn't already know.

"And do these people—most of whom attend one of the Christian denominations in this town—have any comprehension of forgiveness? Of giving people a second chance? Of brotherly love and all that stuff?"

"That's not for me to judge," Greg said, feeling far more sad than angry.

Celia stood up and began to pace in front of the couch, and he realized she was angry enough for both of them. "Do these people even care *what* you went to prison for? I could understand some concern if you had been guilty of something violent or heinous, but even *then* I would think some caution could be in order, but not this kind of exclusion and condemnation. They might as well have lit a cross on fire in front of Bernie's home. This is the twenty-first century, for the love of heaven. What next? A lynching?"

"Not literally, anyway," Greg said, realizing the word felt appropriate. He *felt* like he'd been lynched—emotionally at least. Recalling Bernie's kind attitude while he'd apologized over the position he was in, it *did* feel like he'd had a burning cross put on his lawn as some kind of threat to the security of his business and his loved ones.

Aware that Celia was still pacing and growing more agitated, he held out his hand and said, "Sit down. There's no reason to get so worked up. It's not going to change anything."

"It might not change anything," she said, taking his hand and sitting beside him, "but I can't help how I feel . . . and for the moment I just have to . . . feel it."

"Okay," he said and saw tears in her eyes. "Hey." He wiped a thumb over her cheeks after the tears fell. "There's nothing to worry about. Everything will be okay. I'll find another job; I'll figure something out."

"I'm not worried about you being able and willing to work, Greg. I just . . . feel horrible that people would be that way when they have no idea what life is really like outside of their little bubble. These people, who have probably always had *everything* they ever needed or wanted have no right to judge you this way, and—"

Greg put his fingers over her lips to stop her. "And what do you propose we do? Call a town meeting and publicly declare my indignation?" She sighed at the obvious ridiculousness of such a proposition and put her head on his shoulder, where he knew she was still crying. Greg put a hand to the back of her head and pressed a kiss into her hair. He admitted quietly, "I didn't think you would be this upset."

"Why *wouldn't* I be upset?" she asked and sniffled.

"Truthfully . . . knowing you care this much—and that you understand—well, it feels good, but it feels strange. No one besides Shannon—and I mean *no one*—has *ever* expressed so much compassion or indignation on my behalf."

Celia lifted her head to look at him, her eyes betraying sorrow and perhaps astonishment.

"What?" he asked, hating the way his confession was left hanging out there.

"I'm just . . . so sorry it's been that way. I wish I could make it better."

"Celia, my love," he said as he wiped away her tears, "you make it better for me every day, but . . ."

"But what?"

Greg looked down long enough to gather his thoughts. He had to say what he was thinking; they were committed to honesty, and it was too big of an issue to try and ignore. He had to say it. He looked back up, cleared his throat, and said, "Celia, I do not in any way question your feelings for me or your commitment, but . . . I fear this kind of thing could happen a great deal in my life, and I hate the thought of how such things could affect *you.*"

She smiled and touched his face. "You think I'm going to be frightened off by some judgmental snobs and a little unemployment?"

"Maybe you should be," he said severely.

"No, Greg," she said and gave him a kiss that had a soothing effect on his spirit. "I know your heart, and I know you're not going to let something like this keep you from striving to move forward. I know you'll keep working at making your life better, no matter what anyone else says or does. If I thought this would turn you into a couch potato or make you start drinking again, I would most definitely be concerned. But I'm not worried about that. I know you better than that."

Greg couldn't hold back a smile, and she asked, "What's funny?"

"Not funny," he said. "It's just that . . . for years I've been trying to imagine how my future might be. All I could see was just this . . . obscure reality of living a clean life, keeping a job, going to church, and trying to be there for my kids. That's it. I never even allowed myself to think of the possibility of anything romantic in my future. It didn't seem possible. The kind of women who are generally drawn toward men with a life history like mine are exactly the kind of women I don't want anything to do with; they're the kind of women who would drag me right back to the gutter I've fought so hard to climb out of. And I just couldn't imagine that any woman with all the qualities I might want to emulate would want anything to do with me. And yet . . . here you are. To me it's a miracle, Celia. *You* are a miracle."

"It's *totally* the other way around," she said and wrapped her arms around him, setting the side of her face against his chest. He hugged her tightly, then indulged in his recent fascination with the thickness and softness of her hair.

Following many minutes of soothing silence, Greg felt the need to ask, "So what do I do now, Celia Mae? What if I can't find work in this town? What if Bernie isn't the only one who will face trouble if they hire me? I have to live *here* because nothing is more important than being a part of my kids' lives. They need to be with Shannon and Phillip; that's where they can have the stability and structure I can't give them, and that's what's best for them—plain and simple. But I need to be around; I need to be easily accessible to them, emotionally and physically. I'm their father, and that has to be my highest priority."

Celia sat up straight so she could look at him. "You're always telling me we need to be practical, so may I just say what I think . . . practically speaking?"

"Of course. I would welcome it." He noticed hesitancy in her expression and asked, "Why would you think I wouldn't want to hear what you're thinking?"

"Truthfully, expressing my thoughts and opinions never went well in my family, and as a result I think I tended to date men who treated me the same way. For all of my truly believing that I *can* speak freely with you—and even if I say something you disagree with it would be okay—I suppose I just get this emotional trigger that makes me afraid to do it."

"Well, don't be," he said.

"Then promise me that if I say something that's too bold . . . or obnoxious . . . or *anything* that doesn't sit well with you, you'll be honest with me and we can talk about it."

"I promise," he said.

She was quiet for another long moment and added, "I guess if I'm really trying to define how I feel, I think I'm also afraid of disagreements being filled with passive-aggressiveness and mixed messages, because that's always how it has been previously. I just want us both to be able to be honest and not hurt each other by being that way."

"Listen to me, Celia." He leaned toward her. "I can't promise I won't behave dysfunctionally in a conversation, but I'm very teachable. If I do or say something that feels hurtful or confusing to you, just tell me so we can figure out why and talk it through. We'll work on it together, okay?"

"Okay," she said, seeming more relaxed.

"Now, tell me what you think. Please! I need someone to help me think past this."

"Okay, well . . . first of all, I know you have just a few technicalities to take care of before you can drive again. Point being, the majority of people in this town commute one direction or another to go to work. If you can't find something here where you can be treated respectfully, then you can live here and be close to your kids and still find work."

"Okay," he said, liking the sound of that. His present limitations had kept him from even considering what now appeared to be such an obvious possibility. He needed a license and he needed a car, but he and Shannon had discussed a plan for that. The situation was temporary.

"The commute is less convenient, yes; but it's not really that big of a deal, all things considered."

"Okay," he said again, motioning with his hand for her to continue.

"Also, I just want to say . . . because I've thought it a thousand times . . . I admire you so much for the way your children are so important to you. Your attitude about that in itself speaks volumes as to the kind of man you are. And I want you to know that I will always give my full support in making them the highest priority—whatever may happen between us."

Greg felt choked up, but he cleared his throat and spoke firmly. "You can't know what that means to me."

"Maybe not," she said. "But I think I can imagine. If it were the other way around, I wouldn't go out with a guy twice if he had no interest or concern for my kids—if I had kids." She smiled and added, "That's one of the biggest reasons I think Shannon was initially so attracted to Phillip."

"What?" he asked, not grasping the connection.

"He was so great with Neal and Jeanie. He was genuinely interested in them and *wanted* to be a part of their lives." Celia made a disagreeable noise and added with some disdain, "Technically I didn't come from a broken home; my parents have been married for over forty years, and they've always had a moderate but steady income. But they were never united in their concern for their children, and I never felt like my well-being was much of a priority. So in some respects it *feels* like I came from a broken home."

"There are surely many definitions to that term."

"Yes, there are," she said and added with zeal, "and it gives me some experience in knowing how important it is that your kids know you love them and you're there for them. The dynamics of your family situation might not be considered normal, but Neal and Jeanie know they're loved by a great many people—not the least of which is you. Your determination to allow the situation to go on as it is for their benefit is evidence of your selflessness on their behalf. At least that's how I see it. Some men would let their pride or their ego be more important than what's best for the kids." Celia sighed and let out a nervous laugh. "I'm talking too much. I just had to say that."

"I'm glad you did," he said and meant it. "I've tried to tell myself that I'm doing what's best for them and that it will take time to feel like I'm really a part of their lives, but . . . most of the time it just feels strange, and . . . hearing you say that and knowing you support me that way . . . well, it means a lot."

"Now," she said, and with that one word she was all practicality again. Greg could imagine her this way in the work she did for Shannon. "Another thing I've been thinking is that maybe you should consider the possibility of getting more education. Surely there are some grants available for people in your situation or at least some good deals on student loans."

Greg blew out a lengthy sigh, which gave him a moment to consider why that made him uncomfortable. "Shannon has mentioned the possibility," he said, "and I believe there are some options for financing, but . . ."

"But?" she pressed, as if there wasn't anything he could say that would diminish her opinion of him.

"Truthfully, Celia, I don't know if I'm capable of something like that."

"Of what? Learning?"

"Exactly," he said. "It might sound silly, but that's how I feel. I got my GED in prison, and some of it was really a challenge for me. I always hated school—what little I went once I was old enough to figure out how to avoid it. I've wondered if it's just some psychological mess in my head, because a day doesn't go by when I don't recall all of the times my parents screamed at me and told me I was stupid and wouldn't amount to anything."

"That can be tough to overcome," she said, and he liked the way she could express compassion and validation rather than trying to talk him out of his feelings—even when they didn't make sense. "However, in my personal opinion, the best way to counteract their voices in your head is to prove them wrong. I'm certain you can always find work doing manual labor in one way or another, but I sincerely believe you can find something you *enjoy* doing, something that can give your life some meaning."

Greg thought about that and was most surprised to realize that he had never considered looking at it like that before. He and Shannon had been talking for years about overcoming the false beliefs their parents—and many of their foster parents—had instilled in them. But he'd never heard it put quite that way before. The idea of proving them wrong by actually accomplishing something he didn't feel capable of accomplishing felt suddenly like a challenge he wanted to take on. He voiced what he considered the most obvious problem:

"I have absolutely no idea what I might pursue that would give my life some meaning; it feels like a completely foreign concept. But I certainly like the idea."

"Okay, so . . . give it some time and thought. And pray about it; I know you're a praying man."

"Yes, I am," he said, then he asked something he'd wondered many times but hadn't felt he knew her well enough to ask. "Are *you?*" Shannon had told him that Celia was very spiritual, but he and Celia had never actually talked about it.

"I'm a woman, not a man," she said facetiously.

"Oh, I am well aware of that," he said in the same tone. More seriously, he asked, "Do you pray, Celia? I know you won't tell me what you think I want to hear. You know how I feel about having a relationship with God. I want to know how *you* feel about it."

Celia looked like she didn't want to talk about it, but she wasn't put off by his asking. "I'm relatively sure Shannon has given you at least some idea of the reasons I don't go to church. Truthfully, it's something I've thought about rectifying, especially after seeing what a positive effect it has on Shannon and her family. I suppose they have shown me an example of the beneficial aspects of religion, whereas the home I grew up in seemed to be an example of all the damage that can be done by extreme piousness and self-righteousness. So . . . I admit to having some trouble with organized religion, but I'm working on it. As for my personal relationship with God, I've never had a problem with that. Yes, I *am* a praying woman. I always have been. So we'll both pray that you can find a meaningful path to follow, and perhaps that in the meantime you can find some work that will help you get by."

"Sounds like a good plan," he said and kissed her forehead.

"Just out of curiosity . . . what would you do if I told you that I didn't pray . . . or didn't believe in God?"

"I would pray for you," he said with a smile that she mirrored back at him. He kissed her brow again and added, "And I would not love you any less."

He heard her sigh and felt her arms come around him. Holding her close with his chin on top of her head, he silently thanked God for all the compassion and perspective that Celia had offered him. He felt better. In fact, he felt far better than he'd thought possible considering his reasons for wanting to talk to her. With Celia in his life he truly believed he could face any challenge and overcome it. He prayed that she would always be there.

Chapter Ten

WHEN GREG RETURNED TO THE house, he walked inside, and Shannon asked, "Everything okay?"

He needed to tell her what had happened, but more than one of Phillip's family members was within hearing range. "Yeah," he said, feeling sincere about his answer. Talking things through with Celia had helped his outlook immensely.

"How long until you have to go back to work?" she asked. "We were going to work on some Christmas projects, but the kids wanted to do some of it with you, so—"

"I don't have to go back," he said cheerily. Being able to spend time with his kids—especially doing something related to Christmas—made the prospect of not having a job feel a little less unfavorable. In response to Shannon's questioning gaze, he added, "I have tonight off." He knew she sensed there was more to that story, but his discreet glance toward the other people in the house let her know they would talk later. He saw that she understood, and he went to find Neal and Jeanie, glad to know that they *wanted* to do their projects—whatever they were—with him around.

Greg was glad to find his children together in Neal's room, with none of their cousins present. They were both sitting on the floor, each writing in separate notebooks.

"What have you got there?" he asked, sitting on the floor nearby.

Jeanie explained, "Shannon has us make wish lists for Christmas. She says the longer the better, because it gives her more to choose from when she buys presents, and she wants us to be surprised. But we already told you about that in letters."

"Yes, I seem to recall that," Greg said.

Neal added, "Phillip says it's what they did when he was a kid. It's kind of like a more grown-up version of a letter to Santa, I guess."

"Makes sense," Greg said, thinking it should be *him* buying gifts for his kids for Christmas. He made a mental note to discuss this with Shannon. He wanted to get them *something*, but they all knew he wasn't making enough money to buy much. And now he was unemployed. For the millionth time he forced his mind away from all he hadn't been able to do for his kids and focused on the gratitude he felt for the good things they had in their lives as a result of Shannon being such an exceptional aunt to them and marrying into such a great family.

"Can I see?" Greg asked. "Or is it a secret?"

"No secret," Jeanie said and showed him her list, explaining what some things were, since he honestly had no idea. He was impressed to realize that Shannon and Phillip had taught the children not to ask for expensive gifts because it was more fun to open lots of inexpensive presents—which helped preserve the intended spirit of the holiday. He recalled that she'd explained this as well to him in letters, but he'd forgotten. Perhaps he *could* help get them some of the things on their wish list. At least he'd been able to put away most of the money he'd made while he *had* been working.

Greg looked at Neal's list too, loving every conversation he had with his kids and the opportunity it gave him to continue getting to know them a little better. It was Jeanie's idea that Greg make a wish list, and she turned the page in her notebook and handed it to him. He looked at the blank page and chuckled. "I have everything I need or want," he said and meant it.

Preferring to change the subject, he said, "Guess what? I don't have to go back to work tonight. I heard we're doing some Christmas stuff."

Neal and Jeanie were both pleased, and he followed them back downstairs where a cookie-making project had begun. It was fun, even though it turned into a huge production that got very noisy with so many people there. Greg was relieved when Phillip nudged him and said, "Are you up to helping me with something outside?"

"Sure," Greg said and followed Phillip to the garage, grabbing his coat, hat, and gloves on the way. The task turned out to be hanging

Christmas lights along every edge of the roof of the house. Phillip had a system but declared it went much faster with some help, and Greg was glad to give it. The night was cold but beautiful with a partial moon and scattered stars shining above them.

"You're pretty good at this," Phillip said. "We have some neighbors who would probably appreciate some help with their lights, and they'd probably be willing to pay for it."

Greg stopped what he was doing and felt almost eerie—in a good way—from the very idea. "Are you psychic or something?" he asked his brother-in-law.

"What do you mean?" Phillip asked while they both crept carefully across the roof, unrolling lights as they went.

"I haven't told Shannon or the kids yet, only Celia. But I'm now unemployed. Maybe I could get a little work putting up Christmas lights."

"What happened?" Phillip asked, sounding genuinely concerned, with no hint of accusation in his voice, which Greg appreciated more than he could ever express.

Greg explained it as briefly as possible. Phillip got a little worked up, but Greg assured him he was okay. He told him what Celia had said about considering the option of going back to school, and Phillip was all for it.

It was late by the time they finished the lights, but everyone who was still awake came out to appreciate the results when they were turned on. A short while later the house was quiet, and Greg was able to talk to Shannon and catch her up on what had happened and how he felt about it. He felt grateful to have the support and encouragement of his family. And he told Shannon—not for the first time, "And at least I don't have to worry about whether or not I'll have a roof over my head or if my kids will have what they need. I'm more grateful than I can say."

"You will never have to wonder or worry about any of that," Shannon said and kissed his cheek. "We're family."

He smiled and kissed *her* cheek before he told her about his conversation earlier with Celia and how she'd helped him consider possible options for the future. Shannon was pleased with Celia's support as well as the idea of him going to school, but she seemed more interested in his blossoming relationship with Celia. "You really like her, don't you," she said as if it were a foregone conclusion.

"No, Shannon, I do not," he said, feigning severity to the point that she looked alarmed, which made it impossible for him to not laugh. "Actually," he leaned closer and whispered loudly, "I'm very much in love with her, and I told her so."

"Really?" Shannon asked and laughed before she hugged him. He might as well have told her she'd won a trip to Hawaii.

"Really," he said, taking his sister's hand. "She's amazing."

"She is. And I don't have to ask if the feeling is mutual."

"Don't you?"

"She's been smitten with you ever since you got here," Shannon stated.

Greg had heard her say something to that effect before, but he still found it hard to believe. "I want to be what she deserves, Shannon. I'm not sure that I am."

Shannon took on her firm, big-sister tone and said, "You need to stop putting your value as a human being on such worldly, shallow things. It's your character and strength of spirit that she's attracted to." She grinned. "Well . . . and she tells me you're pretty good-looking. I can't argue, even though you *are* my baby brother."

Greg ignored the compliment. "Well, Celia is gorgeous, and *I'm* the one who is smitten."

They talked for another hour about Celia and Christmas and Neal and Jeanie. He felt grateful for how easy it was to talk to Shannon and for how uncomplicated she made everything that could have been *terribly* complicated. She had already talked to Phillip about how to handle Christmas for the kids now that Greg was here, and she assured him that they considered it a privilege to get Neal and Jeanie some gifts and carry on their traditions as they had been doing for years—which meant that most of the gifts would be from Santa. Phillip had suggested that Greg should get something for Neal and Jeanie that was personal and perhaps sentimental, and Shannon had some ideas, for which Greg was grateful. He was glad to have her there to help coach him on his role as a father—even if he often felt that his role was minimal.

The following morning, Greg was pleasantly surprised to receive a text from Celia asking if she could go to church with him. She sat next to him and held his hand throughout the service, and he could honestly say he'd never enjoyed church more. She hung around the rest of the day—as she usually did on Sundays—and when they had a quiet moment, they both marveled at how far they'd come in a week.

With Phillip's siblings and their families having now left to return home, everything quickly got back to normal. Sunday evening after Celia had gone, Greg sat down with Neal and Jeanie and talked to them about losing his job and the reasons for it. They both expressed indignation on his behalf, but he reminded them that it wasn't right to be judgmental toward other people—even when *they* were being judgmental. "We need to not let this make us angry. Things like this could always be a part of my life, and I need to learn to deal with it. Like it or not, that's who your father is."

"But it's not fair," Jeanie insisted.

"No, it's not," Greg said, wanting to validate her feelings. "But there is a lot in life that isn't fair. So we just have to always try to do the right thing and do the best we can. I'll find another job, and everything will be okay."

He distracted them with questions about plans for Christmas, and they asked him questions about how things were going with Celia. He was honest with them about his feelings, and he was rather amazed at their maturity in having a conversation about such things. Both Neal and Jeanie seemed pleased, and since they already knew Celia very well, it was likely easier for them to be enthused about their father dating her.

The following day, Celia let him know that she'd talked to her landlords, who lived in the house above her basement apartment. Bruce and Ida were thrilled with the prospect of having Greg put up their Christmas lights and were happy to pay him to do it. Bruce had usually done it in the past, but he was getting older and the cold bothered his arthritis more than it used to. The house was big and there were a lot of lights, but Greg got it done in a couple of days and was paid generously. He haggled with them, insisting it was too much, but Bruce wouldn't back down, and in the end Greg just graciously thanked them and said the price included his taking the lights down after the holidays.

"We'd love to have you take them down," Bruce said, "but as for the price, we'll quibble about that come January."

Phillip lined up two more jobs for Greg, involving two other large houses that needed to be decorated with lots of lights. By the end of the week he'd made more money than he'd made in a month working at Bernie's, and he liked working daylight hours, which left his evenings free to spend time with Celia and the family. They made Christmas goodies, and he went tree shopping to help get a tree for the Meadows' home, as well as one for Celia's apartment. He helped decorate them both, and so did Neal and Jeanie. Apparently it wasn't the first time his children had helped Celia decorate her tree, and he loved the unusualness of that as they all sat together drinking hot chocolate while admiring their work.

The following week he did lights on two more houses, knowing that would likely be the last of it. By now everyone who put lights on their homes already had them in place. But he'd made enough money to get him through the holidays, put some more into savings, and still be able to buy gifts for the people he loved. And he didn't feel pressure to look too hard for a job until after the first of the year—especially since he'd promised to take down all the lights he'd put up. When that was done he'd get serious about finding another job. In the meantime, he'd been looking into the possibilities of attending college. When he had his usual weekly phone call with Larry, the parole officer was clearly thrilled with Greg's desire to get more education. Larry told him about some possibilities for financial aid, and he offered to help guide him through the process. Greg felt encouraged with the idea of school in general, but he honestly had no idea what profession he might want to pursue. Celia and Shannon both kept reminding him that with time the right path would present itself.

Celia took a day off work and drove Greg into the city, where he was able to finally get his driver's license. It was one more step that made him feel closer to being a part of the human race again, even though he didn't actually own a car. But since Phillip, Shannon, and Marj all had vehicles, they had already told him repeatedly that it was rare when one of them wouldn't be available for him to borrow when he needed to get somewhere. He was grateful for the option but looked forward to when he could get a car of his own.

Greg took Celia out to lunch, then they did some Christmas shopping, and she helped him pick out the right gifts for Neal and Jeanie and everyone else in the family. He was disappointed to realize she would be going home to Kansas for Christmas, but they agreed to have a private celebration before she left, with Christmas dinner and the exchange of simple gifts. In the meantime, she spent a great deal of time with the family, comfortably involved with baking and decorating and wrapping gifts. They watched Christmas movies together and took Neal and Jeanie to the city a couple of times— once for some shopping and a movie, and once to go ice skating. Greg loved seeing how comfortable Celia was with his children, and every day that passed made it more difficult to imagine living his life without her.

* * * *

Greg thoroughly enjoyed his private Christmas celebration with Celia, even though he couldn't stop dreading her departure. He told her more than once that he wished he was going with her, to which she replied, "I don't want to be away from you, Greg, but I'm not sure you would enjoy spending time with my family. I'm not looking forward to it, to be truthful. I go home for Christmas more out of a feeling of obligation." She smiled at him. "Maybe next year I'll just stay here."

"Maybe we should plan on that," he said, liking the implications. "However," he added, "eventually I need to meet your family, don't I?"

"Ooh," she said with a sparkle in her eyes. "That sounds serious, Gregory."

"Does it? Good. Shouldn't I meet your family?"

"Quite frankly," she said. "I don't care if you ever do."

He had to say what was obvious. "That's pretty extreme."

"Yeah, I suppose it is," Celia said, obviously not liking the topic. "But that's how I feel."

"So . . . I have to ask: Is it because they won't approve of me?"

She looked astonished. "I don't care *what* they think of you, Greg. I am proud of you and proud to have you in my life. That is not it at all. I just know they will be unkind to you, and I don't want that to happen. They *will* be judgmental and cruel. I know because they are cruel and judgmental to me. Why would I want to expose you to that? Why would that be worth the price of a plane ticket?"

Greg considered the way she'd put that and asked, "Then why do you feel like you have to go home for Christmas?"

"Truthfully?"

"Of course."

"For my mother," Celia said. "My mother is a kind, dear woman . . . even if she has absolutely no backbone. I go home for her, and I put up with the rest for the same reason."

"Okay, that's a worthy reason, I admit. But I'm still going to miss you. And if only to meet your mother, we might just have to get me a plane ticket one of these days."

Celia sighed. "I really like the sound of that," she said. "And I dare say you're probably tough enough to handle whatever the rest of them can dish out."

"Yeah," he said and kissed her. "Having dealt with prison bullies, I think I could probably handle it."

"We'll see," she said and laughed.

* * * *

Three days before Christmas, Greg drove Celia to the airport. She'd asked him to drive even though it was her car, and she'd asked him to take charge of it while she was gone, which meant he wouldn't have to borrow anyone else's car. Throughout the drive they had little to say, and he hated how deeply he was dreading this separation. Knowing it would be less than a week before he saw her again wasn't helping at the moment.

Celia broke the silence by asking, "What are you thinking about so seriously? You haven't said a word for miles."

"Neither have you. What are *you* thinking?"

"I asked first."

Greg sighed. "When I was arrested and being taken to jail to wait for my hearing, I had this horrible dread in the pit of my stomach." He glanced at her. "This is reminding me of that."

Celia took in the deeper meaning of his words, combined with the gravity of his countenance, and she felt freshly astounded. *He really does love me*, she thought, wondering if a day would ever come when it would stop surprising her.

"The time will go quickly," she said, even though she'd said it before. Then she added an original thought. "It will probably go more quickly for you than for me. At least being in a houseful of kids will keep all the celebrations lively."

"But that's just it," Greg said. "Maybe if it was any other week, it wouldn't seem quite so bad. It's Christmas . . . and I don't want to spend it without you."

"I don't want to spend it without you, either," she said and kissed his cheek.

"Then don't go," he said. "Or let me go with you."

"You know you couldn't not be with your kids for Christmas, and I have to go."

"I know," he admitted.

"Next Christmas will be different; we'll be together wherever we are."

Greg squeezed her hand before he forced himself past his fears enough to ask, "Do you really believe we'll be together?"

Celia returned the squeeze of his fingers and couldn't keep her voice from cracking when she said, "I certainly hope so; I can't even imagine it being any other way." Sensing his relief, she asked, "Are you worried that we *won't?*"

"Maybe," he admitted. "I'm not going to pretend that I don't hope and pray this will last forever. Maybe it was growing up being shuffled around from one foster home to another that makes me afraid that nothing good will last."

"Well, I'm not going anywhere," she said with all the conviction she felt.

"Yes, you are," he said lightly. "You're going to Kansas and leaving me here to face Christmas without you."

"But I'll be back," she promised and squeezed his hand again.

After Greg parked the car at the curb of the airport unloading zone, he got out and opened the door for Celia. He got her suitcase out of the trunk while she was double-checking in her purse to make certain she had her ID and her ticket. She looked up to find him facing her, and she went on her tiptoes to wrap her arms around his neck, loving the way it had become so comfortable and easy to do so. She also loved how tightly he held her and the way he kissed her as if she were going off to war.

"I love you," he whispered.

"I love you too," she said, and he kissed her again. "Text me—a lot."

"I will if you will. And call when you can. I want to hear your voice every day."

"I promise," she said.

"Merry Christmas," he said and kissed her once more.

"Merry Christmas," she said and hurried into the building with her suitcase rolling behind her so as not to drag this out any longer.

* * * * *

Throughout the flight Celia felt a deepening dread and wondered if Greg's mood had rubbed off on her, or maybe he'd had a sense that this trip wasn't going to go well. Practically speaking, she'd told him a great deal about the dynamics of her family, and he was simply concerned. But something occurred to Celia after she'd arrived in Kansas, rented a car, and driven for nearly two hours. She was not the same woman who had come home for Christmas the previous year. She considered herself to have been evolving emotionally over the course of many years, and she had gradually learned to recognize the dysfunctional behaviors of her family members. But something inside her had changed dramatically. It was as if all the things she'd learned in theory many times over finally applied to her own life in a very real way. She only had to recall the way Greg looked at her—and the way he spoke to her and believed in her—to feel more valuable as a human being. And the closer she got to home, the more that new person inside her began to squirm and feel uncomfortable. She sincerely missed her mother and wanted to see her, but she felt sad to realize that she had no such feelings toward her father or her brother or sister. She *should* have cancelled the trip. She could have talked to her mother on the phone and gone to see her next month when holiday celebrations would not provide a front-and-center forum for her dysfunctional family. But it was too late now, Celia concluded. She was here, and she had to make the most of it.

Celia parked her rented car in front of the farmhouse where she'd grown up. She looked at it for a few minutes, considering how few of her memories were good. She turned to take in the wide, flat stretches of farmland covered in snow, knowing that her father's land was now leased, which made him a retired farmer. Just thinking of her father's tall, thin frame and his almost constant stern expression made her shudder a little. She had to fight back tears to realize she couldn't find a single really good memory with her father.

"How sad," she said aloud to no one, and her sadness deepened as she steeled herself to go inside, knowing that people weren't supposed to dread going home for Christmas. She wondered what Greg was doing now. And Shannon and Phillip and Marj and the kids. She missed them all and wanted to go back. The temptation became great, but her mother came out onto the front porch, wrapped in a big sweater, waving at her with excitement. She'd obviously seen the car and had probably wondered why Celia was taking so long to come in.

Genuinely glad to see her mother, Celia got out of the car and ran up to the porch, where they shared a long, tight embrace. Celia was actually glad to have this moment *outside* of the house and away from the view of anyone else in the family.

"Oh, you look so beautiful!" Betty Lindley said with a glimmer of tears in her eyes.

"You're always so sweet, Mama," Celia said. "And you always look beautiful."

"Oh, hush now," Betty said with a familiar tone that made it evident she saw no beauty whatsoever in herself—or value for that matter—and she probably never had. Celia thought it was no wonder she had trouble believing Greg when he told her she was beautiful; she'd gotten it from her mother.

"Let's go in," Betty said. "It's freezing out here."

"Let me get my bag," Celia said and hurried back to the car.

Betty held open the front door for Celia to go into the house. While closing the door, Betty hollered, "She's here, Melvin. Our baby is here."

Celia smiled at her mother. Since she was the youngest child, Betty had always called Celia her baby.

Melvin rose from his recliner and looked mildly happy to see Celia. They exchanged a hug that felt like an obligation for Celia more than anything else. Worse than that was how she felt like her father only hugged her out of some kind of obligation. He was taller than Greg, which made Celia's shortness all the more evident, and since he was extremely thin, she always felt fat standing next to him. The fact that he'd called her that since she was a child didn't help.

Celia smiled at her father and pretended not to remember all of the derogatory remarks he'd made to her throughout her life. She was met with mutually obligatory hugs from her sister, Tawnia—who was built very much like their father—and her brother, MJ—who was built more like Betty and Celia, but since he was male she'd never once heard him get any grief over it.

They all sat down together in the familiar front room. Everyone except Betty seemed to be present only out of some sense of duty. Betty was thrilled to have all of her children together and said so more than once, but Celia felt sure her mother's sentiments stemmed from a belief that having the family together would result in something positive.

It only took ten minutes for Celia to start feeling that temptation to leave again or at the very least to be alone with her mother so they could actually talk about something worthwhile. Tawnia was twice divorced, childless, and bitter. She lived and worked in the closest town, which was nearly an hour's drive, so she would be staying in her old bedroom tonight and again on Christmas Eve. MJ—an abbreviation of Melvin Junior—had moved back in with his parents the previous spring after his wife had kicked him out, and he was now divorced as well. Celia noted that MJ's normally large build had expanded immensely, but then she knew from phone calls with her mother that MJ was unemployed and lazy and ate way too much. Betty had never put it that way, but Celia knew the truth of the matter. He'd regressed to being a child in his parents' home, and since the farm was being leased, Melvin required no work of him; and sadly enough, Betty would forever be enabling her husband and children. As long as she did—as if anything less would make her a bad wife and mother—they would take advantage of her and let her wait on them hand and foot. Celia had tried to explain to her mother how unfair this was, but Betty held a lifetime of such beliefs, and things were not likely to ever change.

No one had anything to talk about except complaining over stupid things. By the time supper was over, Celia felt like she needed a shower just to wash off all of the negativity. Betty was so desensitized that she didn't even feel it anymore. When they were done eating, Celia offered to help her mother with the dishes, and the others went their separate ways. Celia enjoyed time with her mother, and they were able to visit while they worked together. When the kitchen was clean, Betty helped Celia unpack her suitcase and move temporarily back into the bedroom that she'd used as a child. With the door closed, they talked about Celia's job and her friends and the community that she had grown to love. When they were sitting together on the bed, Celia took her mother's hand and told her something she'd wanted to tell her face-to-face.

"I've met someone, Mama. I think he may be the one for me."

"Oh," Betty drawled with glee. "Tell me all about him."

Celia told her everything great about Greg before she told the truth about what his upbringing had been like and that he was divorced with two teenagers. Betty seemed mildly concerned but only said, "He must have been through such a great deal."

"Yes, he has," Celia said. "But he's one of those really special guys who has turned it all around and made his life into something good—in spite of everything." Celia took a deep breath and said what needed to be said, "And Mama, he spent some years in prison."

Betty gasped and said exactly what Celia had predicted, "Oh, I think it would be better if we just don't tell your father that."

"Mama, why are you so afraid of him?"

"I'm not afraid of him," Betty said defensively. "I've just learned how to avoid talking about things that upset him."

Celia wanted to point out that it amounted to the same thing, but she bit her lip, knowing it wouldn't help. She steered the conversation back to Greg's good qualities, but Celia didn't like the way that was how it had always been: ignore anything uncomfortable and just pretend that everything was rosy and ideal.

Once Betty had gone off to bed, Celia called Greg and felt better just hearing his voice. She'd sent him a number of texts to keep him apprised of her travel progress, and he'd known she'd arrived safely. But it felt so good to talk to him. She told him what she'd been feeling and about Betty's reaction. They talked it through in a way that had become easy between them and finally said good night when it got very late—especially for him since he was in a different time zone.

The following day Celia helped her mother with Christmas preparations. They drove into town to do some shopping, and she was deeply relieved when Tawnia declared she wasn't feeling well and declined to go along. Back at the house, Celia helped her mother make an apple cake and caramel sauce that was a Christmas tradition, and they also made two kinds of candy. Suppertime was the most miserable time of the day while Melvin asked Celia abrasive questions and made passive-aggressive remarks about her job, her living in another state, her line of work, and, of course, her weight. Celia spoke up much less than she wanted to, mostly because she knew how upset her father would become if she stood up to him and how upset that would make her mother. She was glad to have supper over so she could spend more time with her mother. After the kitchen was cleaned up, they wrapped some gifts before bedtime.

Again Celia talked to Greg on the phone, hating the fact that tomorrow was Christmas Eve and they were so far away from each other. It was truly the first time in her life she'd really wanted to spend Christmas with a particular man, and she had to admit, "You were right. I should have stayed. Being here feels all wrong, so much more wrong than it's ever felt before."

"We'll make up for it when you get back," he promised, and she liked the sound of that.

The following day Celia tried very hard to focus on helping her mother create the holiday illusion that meant so much to Betty. Celia appreciated the texts and pictures that kept coming to her phone from Sugar City. Most of them were from Greg and Shannon, but she also got a few from Neal and Jeanie. Jeanie especially seemed to like sending her pictures of Greg and adding funny comments about what he was doing. Remaining connected even in this small way helped Celia get through the day, dreading the actual Christmas celebrations, knowing there would be no avoiding her father and siblings.

In the afternoon a ridiculous argument broke out between Tawnia and MJ After listening to it for nearly an hour, Celia declared, "You two sound exactly like you did when you were teenagers. Have you not matured at all since then?" She then said to her mother, "I thought of something I need in town. I'll see you later."

"But that's such a long drive," Betty protested.

"I know, Mother," Celia said. "I grew up here."

She walked out of the house, grateful beyond words for just how long of a drive it would be. Hopefully by the time she drove into town, did a little bit of shopping for something that she would figure out she needed, and then drove back, the contention would have died down and she would feel better prepared to get through the next twenty-four hours of family fun.

Celia was able to talk to Greg after she arrived in town, which helped build up her resilience to get through the somewhat forced traditions of the evening. She was glad to finally be able to escape and go to bed, wishing she could be in her childhood bedroom and feel warm memories of Christmases gone by. She found some good moments in the dusty chambers of her memory, but almost all of them were tainted by something negative.

Christmas day went relatively well, with gift opening and a big brunch—even though Celia and Betty did all of the work in the kitchen. Following brunch, they kept working to prepare a big Christmas dinner while MJ played video games in the basement, Melvin watched TV, and Tawnia declared the need for a nap. The only good thing was that Celia far preferred to be alone with her mother; what she hated was seeing how much work her mother was going to in order to try and make everything perfect for their great Christmas feast. And no one else really seemed to even care.

When the feast was barely underway, Melvin said to Betty—as if it were a joke, "Don't be eating too much now, dear. Christmas or not, you need to watch what you put in your mouth."

Celia saw her mother's countenance falter into shame. The entire thing was so horrifically familiar that Celia felt her appetite waning.

Since Celia was built very much like her mother, the comment also seemed indirectly aimed at her.

"You don't look like you've lost any weight since you were here last," Melvin said to Celia just as she was lifting a forkful of potatoes and gravy toward her mouth. Celia set the fork down loudly on her plate with the food still on it. "You'll never catch yourself a husband if you don't learn to control your appetite."

Celia knew she couldn't stay silent any longer, but she was still measuring what words she might say when Betty interjected, "Oh, Celia's got a boyfriend! He's very nice from what she says."

"There must be something wrong with him," MJ said as if it were hilarious, the implication being that no *decent* man would be interested in someone like Celia.

Celia swallowed hard and counted to ten before she looked at her father and said, "Is it really necessary to ruin every nice meal with cruel comments about weight and food and eating?" She heard her mother gasp but pressed on. "I don't eat any more than you do, and neither does Mother. Your ignorance on matters of metabolism and genetics is appalling, but not nearly as appalling as your need to use this issue as an excuse to be cruel to your wife and daughter. It's amazing how you make no such comments about Tawnia being such an arrogant little snot that she can't find or keep a decent man."

Tawnia's gasp was accompanied by another gasp from her mother. Melvin and MJ just stared at Celia in astonishment, but she used the silence to finish this tirade. Now that she'd started, she had no desire to stop before she'd said everything she'd wanted to say for years.

"It's also amazing," Celia said, "how you never say a negative word to or about MJ Is it okay to be fat if you're a man? Is it okay to be fat and lazy and spouseless as long as you're male? Apparently it's okay to say whatever you want as long as you're male—at least in this house. And apparently it's okay to be unmarried as long as you're skinny."

Celia tossed a brief glare at her sister, then turned to face her dumbstruck father once again. "Well, I'm done." She stood up and flung her napkin onto the table. "I'm done being treated this way. I'm done feeling less valuable in this house because my dress size has two digits and I don't look like the women on TV who represent a very tiny percentage of the population of this country. I exercise, I use balance and discretion in what I eat, and I have a good life. I don't need this. I'm done. I will never allow you—any of you—to speak down to me again or use me as an emotional punching bag to make you feel better about your own messed-up lives."

Celia was beginning to feel her knees shake as her own words echoed back to her. It was only the stunned silence of her family that kept her from having a complete meltdown. If they started telling her what they thought about her outburst, she would never survive it. She had to get out of there.

With a calm control that felt almost superhuman, she turned to her mother and said, "I'm sorry, Mother. I know you put a lot of work into making Christmas nice for the family, and I'm sorry they don't appreciate it more or treat you with the respect you deserve. I really wish I understood why you feel like you have to put up with it." She turned again to her father. "She deserves a purple heart for living with you all these years. If she chooses to do so, that's up to her. As for me, I'm never coming back here. You know my address if any of you ever want to write a letter or visit. But just know that your negativity and criticism will not be tolerated in my life, no matter where or how you think you can dish it out."

Chapter Eleven

CELIA LEFT THE ROOM BEFORE her knees had a chance to give out on her. She felt a deep sadness burning in her chest. She'd just told her family she was never coming back, and she meant it. She was leaving. She'd made her declarations, and she couldn't back down. She wanted to believe that her mother might come to see her in New York someday, but she knew it would never happen. And she felt deeply troubled by the fact that she didn't care if she ever saw the rest of them again—ever.

The next twenty minutes felt to Celia like something out of a movie. She hurriedly but carefully packed up her things, not wanting to forget anything. She was aware of her mother in the room, crying and begging her to stay. But Betty was also asking her to apologize to the rest of the family. Celia tried to explain why she couldn't do that, but Betty didn't understand, and Celia knew she simply wasn't capable of seeing beyond the way she'd always lived. Betty's own father had been much like her husband, so she didn't know anything different was possible. But Celia knew that it was. Celia felt the strength of Greg's love helping her ignore her mother's weeping while she packed and carried her bag down the stairs. She wasn't surprised to be met by her father, who had now gotten over his shock and was furious. He started yelling at her, calling her disrespectful and rude and cruel. He told her she would go to hell for not honoring her father. Celia resisted pointing out that the commandment in the Bible said to honor father *and* mother, and Melvin had *never* honored Celia's mother in any way.

Celia ignored her father's tirade while she hugged her sobbing mother and whispered a quiet, "I love you; I'll call."

On her way out the door, Melvin yelled, "If you leave now, don't ever come back." Celia said nothing. He shouted more loudly, "If you do this you're dead to me. I won't have a daughter who treats me this way."

Celia thought of a thousand possible retorts, but she knew there were no words that could fix problems so deeply ingrained. She put her bag in the trunk of the car and drove away as quickly as she could, barely looking back once to catch a glimpse of her parents on the porch where there was a light next to the door. Her mother was weeping; her father was yelling. And Celia was never going back.

Once she'd started the long drive into the nearest town, Celia allowed her own emotion to bubble up. She was glad for the long stretch of road with absolutely no other vehicle in sight while she sobbed and kept her hands firmly gripping the wheel. Once in town she got a motel room and curled up on the bed, feeling as if a loved one had died.

After she'd cried for more than an hour, unable to believe this was actually Christmas day, it occurred to her that sometimes the bad had to die in order for something good to be born. Perhaps she truly needed this kind of a break with her family. Her only regret was in regard to her mother. But Betty was strong. She *had* lived with Melvin for more than forty years. Celia only wished it would be possible to keep in touch with her mother without the fear of her father's intervention. Since he'd retired, he hardly left the house unless Betty was with him. The inevitable separation from her mother hit Celia the hardest, and the grief burned inside of her, provoking her tears to flow without pause.

Celia fell asleep and woke up in the night to realize she was still in her clothes and she hadn't brushed her teeth. She changed and got ready for bed, going back to sleep at about four in the morning. When she woke up hours later, there were several missed calls and texts from both Greg and Shannon. She realized that ignoring her phone was causing them concern, but she felt so utterly depleted that she just turned the phone off again, hoping they would understand.

Celia arranged for a flight home that evening and managed to get her ticket changed without too much extra expense. She drove back to the airport, turned in her rental car, and forced herself to eat something once she'd checked in. She felt numb throughout the flight and even more so when she got back to New York in the middle of the night. She had to wait for over an hour before an airport shuttle service was available that could take her home, which cost much less than a taxi. She knew she could call Greg or Shannon—even in the middle of the night—and either one of them would come to get her. But she wasn't up to facing them right now. She only wanted to be alone and absorb her grief and sorrow. Once in her apartment, she did manage to get into pajamas and brush her teeth before she crawled into bed and once again cried herself to sleep, not even bothering to turn on her phone.

* * * *

Greg enjoyed Christmas more than he ever had—in spite of Celia's absence. Their regular exchange of text messages and photos helped immensely, and he still felt like they were able to participate in sharing Christmas to some extent.

Late in the afternoon on Christmas day, after all of the excitement had died down and the messes were cleaned up, Greg realized he hadn't heard from Celia for hours. His attempts to contact her with no response initially just made him think she was caught up in family activities and she would text or call at any time. When she didn't, he tried calling her and was surprised to have the call go immediately to voice mail, which meant her phone was likely turned off. He felt deeply uneasy but didn't know what to do about it.

He asked Shannon if she'd heard from Celia, and she simply said, "No, she's probably just busy. It is Christmas day, after all."

Greg didn't bring it up again; he didn't want to mar Shannon's Christmas with his concerns, but his worry increased with every hour of not hearing from Celia. He realized he was more concerned about her emotional well-being than he was about her physical safety. He knew what her family could be like and what holidays generally entailed. But to think of things getting bad enough for her to completely cut him off felt disconcerting. He wondered if she'd lost her phone charger or something. But surely she could pick up the land line in her parents' home and call him or Shannon to let them know.

When bedtime came, Greg hugged everyone good night as he always did. He tried to focus on how great it had been to share Christmas with Neal and Jeanie, and he told them so more than once. He had a quiet moment with Shannon and expressed his gratitude once again for all she'd done for him and his children. She just hugged him tightly and told him how much she loved him and how grateful she was to have him there. He said nothing about his concern for Celia, figuring it was best to just leave their tender moment on a good note.

Greg tried to sleep but only drifted in and out of restless dozing, always coming awake to realize not much time had passed, and still there was no message from Celia. He fell asleep around dawn and awoke midmorning only to find that there was still no message. He was beginning to feel frantic, and his minimal sleep wasn't helping. He found Shannon in the kitchen and was glad she was alone.

"Something's wrong," he said to his sister before she even realized he had come into the room.

She looked at him in alarm, taking a few seconds to figure out what he meant. "You still haven't heard from her?"

"No, have you?"

"No," Shannon said. "I'm ashamed to say I forgot about it. But then . . . she's never kept in touch as closely with me as she does with you." She looked a little dazed while she thought about it a long moment, then asked, "When did you last hear from her?"

"A text yesterday, early afternoon. She said it was time to help her mother fix Christmas dinner." Greg sighed loudly. "Shannon, listen to me. She has not gone more than a couple of hours without texting or calling me since Thanksgiving—unless she was sleeping. Something is wrong. But what can I do?"

"I will call her mother," Shannon said, and Greg wished he'd thought of that.

"Yes!" he said. "Do you think we can find the number online or call the operator to get it or—"

"We probably could, but we don't need to." She reached into her pocket for her phone. "Celia gave me the number a long time ago; I don't even remember why. I've never met Celia's mother, but I've spoken to her on the phone."

Greg's heart began to pound when Shannon quickly found the number and pressed the button on her phone to dial it. He started pacing while she waited for the call to go through, and he was grateful when she switched it to the speaker option and set the phone on the counter.

A woman answered, and Shannon said, "Mrs. Lindley?"

"Yes," the woman said. "Who is this?"

"This is Shannon . . . Celia's friend." Shannon hesitated, but they heard nothing so she went on to explain, "We haven't heard from Celia, and we just wanted to make sure she's all right. Do you—"

"Oh, dear!" Mrs. Lindley exclaimed and started to cry. Greg's stomach tightened, and Shannon shot him an alarmed gaze. Maybe something *had* happened to her. Had she been in an accident? Had something gone wrong medically? He imagined her in ICU with a burst appendix or broken bones and internal injuries. But Celia's mother quickly put those concerns to rest in a way that didn't ease the knots in his stomach at all. "She got so upset." Mrs. Lindley cried, sounding as if she'd been crying when she'd answered the phone, barely maintaining her composure long enough to do so. "She just . . . got so upset."

When no further explanation was offered while Mrs. Lindley continued to cry, Shannon asked, "Can you tell me *why* she got so upset?"

"I don't know," the older woman said and sniffled loudly. "I still can't figure it out. But she got upset . . . and she left. She just left. I've tried to call her. I've tried and tried." She sniffled again. "I just don't understand why she got so upset."

Shannon said some kind words to Celia's mother to try and calm her down, assuring her that everything would be all right. She ended the call graciously by promising to let her know when she heard from Celia. The moment Shannon pushed the button on the phone to disconnect the call, Greg said angrily, "I bet I know *exactly* why she got so upset."

Shannon sat down, looking a little queasy. "It doesn't take much imagination, does it? She's been disgusted for years by the way they treat her—especially her father. I'm guessing she just . . . decided she'd had enough."

"I wish I'd been there to see it," Greg said, overcome with indignation on Celia's behalf. But worry for Celia quickly drowned out every other emotion. "So where is she?"

"My guess is that she's either in a motel in Kansas, or she's working her way toward home—which will take some time. If she's turned off her phone, then it's apparent she just needs some space. And until she gets home, there is absolutely nothing we can do about it."

Greg sighed and resisted the urge to curse. He didn't want Celia going through this alone. He wanted to be there for her, to help her through it. He wanted to tell her he was proud of her for standing up for herself. However the drama might have gone, he knew she wouldn't have left the house on Christmas day without having stood up for herself.

"Hey," Shannon said and came to her feet to hug him, "I know you're worried, but there really isn't anything we can do. I'll call Bruce and Ida and ask them to let us know when they have any indication that she might be there—although she could sneak in and they might never know. In the meantime, we will pray for her—and I think we need to try and stay distracted."

"Easier said than done," Greg admitted.

Shannon examined his face as if she might be searching for evidence of some kind of illness. She then declared, "You really love her."

Greg felt surprised, mostly because he figured that should have been obvious for weeks now. Having no need or desire to hide anything from Shannon, he just said, "Yes," with all of the confidence he felt. Shannon smiled as if she was pleased, but he still felt the need to ask, "Am I crazy?"

"For loving Celia? Never."

"No, not for that. But maybe for . . ."

"For what, Greg?"

"For hoping that I could be good enough for her."

"Oh, Greg," she said with compassion and put a hand on his arm. "I wish you could see yourself the way I see you—the way *she* sees you."

"Well, apparently I can't," Greg said. "I know that I try to be a good man, and I would do anything for her. But the fact is that I am unemployed, and I have nothing. What little money I've saved up doesn't amount to much. She deserves the best, Shannon."

"Yes, she does," Shannon said. "And you are the best thing that's ever happened to her. I have never seen her so happy. You need to stop trying to measure your value as a human being by standards of money and belongings and education. You're moving in the right direction. She loves you for who you are, and that's the best kind of love."

Greg inhaled her words, wanting to believe them—to really and truly believe them in his deepest self. Just like he wanted Celia to see herself as the amazing woman he knew her to be.

"You know what I think?" Shannon said, and he looked at her to see her smiling. "I think it's highly likely that Celia felt strong enough to get up and walk out on Christmas Day because of *you*. I think she finally found the courage to do what she's told me for years she wanted to do. It's just a guess, but I'd bet on it—if I were a betting woman, that is."

Greg felt intrigued by the idea but didn't know what to say. At the moment, he just wanted to know where she was and be able to talk to her.

"And if that's the case," Shannon went on, "this is one of those times where things have to get worse before they can get better. If whatever happened has upset her mother that much, then Celia is surely upset as well. Celia loves her mother so dearly that she's held her tongue for years mostly out of concern for her; she hasn't wanted her mother to have to deal with the fallout."

"Yes, she's told me as much."

"But I've always believed it was inevitable and that eventually Celia would just have to say what needed to be said in order to make peace with herself. Maybe she finally did it. And if she did, I think it's because you've helped her feel strong enough and valuable enough to do it."

Greg hugged his sister again but couldn't think of anything else to say.

* * * *

Greg pondered Shannon's remarks throughout the day, frequently offering up silent prayers on Celia's behalf while he waited and wondered. He was grateful for the distraction of spending some time with Neal and Jeanie and took them into the city so Jeanie could exchange a new blouse she'd gotten for Christmas, since she needed a different size. They went out to lunch and went ice skating together. Greg enjoyed it, but he missed Celia and he was worried about her. He did well at not letting on that anything was wrong, just wanting to appreciate this time with his kids.

They returned home to find Marj overseeing some kind of cooking extravaganza in the kitchen, which she often did so the family could share a nice meal—having the preparations serve the purpose of spending time together. She quickly assigned each of them a task, and Greg couldn't deny that he enjoyed such activities. He'd learned a lot about parenting from Marj and from observing all she had taught Phillip and Shannon. Greg also appreciated the distraction from his worries, especially when Shannon reported that she'd talked to Bruce and he was absolutely certain that Celia hadn't come home.

Given his desire to not be alone—which only enhanced his concern for Celia—Greg was glad when dinner merged into family game time, and that went on until it got very late and everyone was tired. He personally felt exhausted, especially given his lack of sleep the previous night. He prayed fervently on Celia's behalf and went to sleep, surprised to wake up to daylight—and disappointed to find nothing on his phone from her. He called her to leave yet another pleading voice mail.

Greg showered and got dressed; he cleaned up his personal living space and made his bed, feeling as if he'd go mad. He went down to the kitchen, where the whole family was already gathered, eating the standard fix-it-yourself breakfast. There was toast and bagels and cold cereal aplenty, but everyone old enough to fix their own was expected to get what they wanted. It was rare that anyone cooked breakfast, but breakfast time was still most often shared as a family, and he liked it. Although today he really wanted a minute alone with Shannon. She apparently read his mind and took him by the arm before he even had a chance to say good morning.

Shannon led him into the nearby laundry room and said quietly, "Bruce called me a few minutes ago. He said that Celia got home sometime in the night. There are motion sensor lights in the driveway, and Ida got up to use the bathroom and noticed they were on, and she saw a van backing out of the driveway. And they've been able to hear water being used in the basement; you know those plumbing sounds that go through the whole house."

Greg breathed in some relief to know she was all right—physically, at least. Still, he said, "Then why hasn't she so much as sent two words of a text to either of us?"

"Are you angry?" Shannon asked.

"Yes, actually. If she needs space, fine. She could text and let me know she needs space."

"I agree. So, when you *do* talk to her, you can *appropriately* let her know how you've felt not knowing what was going on. Establish an agreement between the two of you to prevent something like this from ever happening again. It usually takes something difficult to make people realize what needs to be worked out." Shannon hugged him and added, "She's home safely. Just give her a little time."

"Okay," he said grudgingly. "Thank you."

By late afternoon he had still heard nothing, and Celia still wasn't answering her phone. By evening he was fed up. He talked to Shannon, and she admonished him to remember that his anger was rooted in worry and frustration and that when he was finally able to talk to her, the last thing Celia needed was anger from him.

"You're right," he admitted.

"We've talked about this," she said, "but sometimes it takes having something happen to be able to actually realize what all the talking about it means."

"I don't understand."

"We only saw our parents respond to a problem in one way, and that was to get angry. As much as we might have learned over the years that it wasn't right or appropriate, it's still programmed into our brains. Sometimes it takes some real conscious effort to remember the *right* way to handle something, as opposed to just reacting. But until you actually *feel* angry with someone you love, you can't really try out what you've learned."

"Okay," he said, "I hear you. Point taken." He sighed and closed his eyes as echoes of all the yelling and shouting from his childhood popped effortlessly into his brain, followed closely by all of the yelling and shouting he'd experienced in his marriage. Shannon was right. He'd learned how to speak appropriately to his children, but they had never really made him angry since he'd come back into their lives. And a romantic relationship was entirely different. If he wanted to be the kind of man Celia deserved, he needed to never speak to her the way he'd spoken to his ex-wife—or the way he'd heard his parents speak to each other. He needed to never just react to his emotions; he needed to be man enough to remain self-disciplined no matter how he felt.

"Good," she said and put a key in his hand that was attached to a key ring with a silly stuffed cat.

"What is this?"

"It's the *just-in-case* key," she said. "Celia and I are best friends. We have *just-in-case* keys to each other's houses. You never know when you might need a friend to go to your house and take care of something for you." She nodded toward the key. "I trust you'll use it wisely and with discretion."

As her meaning settled in, Greg gasped and hugged Shannon tightly. "Oh, thank you!" he said.

"This might keep you from going over there and beating down the door," Shannon said with a little laugh.

"Yes, actually," he said without a trace of humor.

"Hey." Shannon put a hand to his face. "Just . . . be there for her; let her know you love her. And the rest will work out. Talk about the anger *later.*"

"What would I ever do without you?" he asked and hugged her again.

"Back at you," she said. "Now hurry up. I'll tell the kids where you went."

"Thank you," he said and grabbed his coat.

Greg prayed all through the short drive to Celia's apartment. He prayed that his own emotions would be calmed and that he could say and do what was in Celia's best interest. He prayed that whatever difficulties were behind this, the outcome would be favorable—especially for Celia. He also prayed for Celia's family—especially her mother—with the hope that their hearts would be softened and healing could take place. He knew Celia well enough to know that she wouldn't have been cruel to them, but he also knew that dysfunction could distort thinking enough that they might *believe* she had been cruel.

Greg pulled into the large driveway and uttered another quick prayer as he hurried down the stairs to the door. He knocked loudly and waited. He knocked again and shouted, "Celia, it's me. Open the door." Again he waited. "Celia, I don't care what you look like. Open the door. I'm not going away." Still he waited. He took a deep breath and shouted, "I have Shannon's key, and I'm coming in. If you can hear me you'd better make yourself decent because I'm opening this door."

Still Greg heard nothing but silence, and he wondered if she was asleep back in her bedroom. Not with all the pounding on the door and shouting, he thought. He wondered if she was in the shower. If so, he would hear the water running once he got inside and deal with that appropriately. If she was just ignoring him, he was going to end it right now.

Greg turned the key in the lock and opened the door, calling more softly, "Celia? Are you here?"

"Yes," he heard her say out of the darkness. Her voice sounded hoarse and strained. "But you should just go away and come back when I can be reasonable and I'm not such a horrible mess."

Greg closed the door and leaned against it. "Sorry," he said. "I'm not leaving until I know you're all right—however long that might take."

As his eyes adjusted to the darkness, he could see now that she was lying on the couch, huddled underneath a blanket. She reached up to turn on a lamp within her reach, then her hand disappeared beneath the blanket, which she'd pulled up over her head.

"You must be furious with me," she said.

"I've had my moments," he admitted. "But mostly I'm worried." He sat down at the other end of the couch from where her head was. He could see from the way the blanket was settled over her that she was practically in the fetal position, and he felt a sudden temptation to cry. Now that he was with her, his anger and frustration completely melted away and all he could feel was love and concern. He set a hand on what he knew was somewhere in the vicinity of her ankle. "I've been so worried about you, Celia. Whatever is going on, I want to help you get through it. I want to be here for you. I can't do that if you won't talk to me." She said nothing, and he added, "If it was the other way around, I dare say you would feel the same way."

"If it was the other way around, I would be *furious* with you," she said with a feistiness that made him chuckle.

"Okay . . . well, I guess we understand each other. Now, why don't you come out from under that blanket and talk to me?"

"I look horrible."

"I don't care."

"I haven't showered for two days; I haven't even washed my face or—"

"I don't care," he repeated.

Greg offered a minute or two of silence, hoping she would come out and look at him or at least start to speak. When she didn't, he sat on the floor near the other end of the couch and carefully pulled the blanket from over her face. She looked up at him with eyes that were as red and swollen as if she'd been mourning the death of a loved one. What little makeup was left around her eyes was smeared.

"I don't want you to see me like this," she said with an expression that contradicted her words. She was as glad to see him as he was to see her.

"Since my biggest goal in life is to spend it with you, hiding from each other when we look less than our best isn't very practical, Celia Mae." He touched her face, so grateful to be with her and not be wondering and worrying. "Did you really believe I'd think less of you to see you looking human and real?"

"When you put it that way . . . no, I would never think that of you."

"Good, because I love you . . . and I've missed you . . . and I've been so worried."

He saw the glimmer of fresh tears in her eyes just before she reached her arms out from under the blanket, and he bent over enough to embrace her. She was wearing an adult version of what looked like a child's Christmas pajamas—bright red and covered with snowmen—which was so like her.

"I'm so sorry," she cried while holding tightly to him. "I've just been so . . . confused and upset with my family . . . and with myself. I don't know if I did the right thing, and . . ."

"Are you ready to talk about it? Truthfully, I'm dying to know why you just left on Christmas day and—"

"How did you know that?" she asked, looking at him.

"Shannon called your mother." Celia put a hand over her eyes as if the mere mention of her mother brought on some kind of shame. Greg wanted to address that, but for now he just went on. "She told Shannon you were upset and had left but she didn't know why. That's all I know. That and the fact that you have been on complete radio silence. But I'm here now, and I'm not letting you go through this— whatever *this* is—alone. I'm not leaving until we talk about it or at least get started talking about it. I need to know you're okay, and I need you to promise me you'll never do that again."

"Do what?"

"Cut me off like that," he said. "You just admitted you would be furious with me if I did the same to you. If you ever need space or time I completely respect that. But I have been losing my mind with worry over you. So . . . just text me and tell me you're upset and need some space but you're safe. Just . . . check in once in a while so I know you're all right. Promise me."

"I promise," she said immediately. "And I'm sorry. I really am. I wasn't thinking clearly."

"Okay," he said and touched her face mostly because he wanted to so badly. "I'm just glad you're home and you're okay . . . physically at least." He paused and asked, "Are you ready to tell me what happened? Or do you need more time?"

"I think I need to talk about it," she admitted. "I've had more than enough time crying and feeling sorry for myself. I need somebody who is thinking clearly to help me figure all of this out and to know what to do now."

"So let's talk, but it's freezing in here. Is something wrong with the heat?"

"I don't think I turned the thermostat up after I got home. I just crawled into bed, and at some point I made it out to the couch to eat a bowl of cereal."

"Where's the thermostat?" he asked, and she told him.

Greg went to turn up the heat and returned to the couch to find Celia sitting up wrapped in her blanket. He sat beside her and decided to keep his coat on until the room warmed up a little. She reached out from beneath the blanket to take his hand.

"Thank you," Celia said.

"For what?"

"For worrying. For caring. For coming over here and making me come out of my shell." She touched his face. "I really missed you. I just . . . didn't know what to say."

"Just start at the beginning. I think I have enough history to have a pretty good idea of what *might* have happened and why. So . . . tell me what happened."

Celia looked at Greg, seeing the unmistakable evidence of his concern and sincerity. She felt like bursting into tears again, but at the same time she was sick to death of crying. "Okay," she said. "Just give me a minute."

She left the blanket behind and hurried to the bathroom, needing to use the facilities as much as she needed a couple of minutes to collect herself. She groaned when she looked in the mirror, even though she knew Greg was right. If they were hoping for their relationship to last, it was ridiculous to think they wouldn't see each other at their worst far more than at their best. Still, she grabbed a washcloth and soaked it with warm water to quickly wipe away what little residue of makeup was left. She also brushed her teeth and pushed a brush through her hair, which she determined was hopeless, but at least she felt a little better. Letting him see her in her pajamas didn't bother her, since she would have worn them to Shannon's house if she'd been around for Christmas. She knew that Shannon always wore silly Christmas pajamas for the holiday—and she also got plenty of good out of them the rest of the year.

Celia returned to the couch and wrapped the blanket around her shoulders before she sat beside Greg and took his hand.

"I texted Shannon," he said, "to let her know you're all right and that I'm staying a while. And she's going to call your mother and let her know you're safe. I hope that's okay. Your mother was worried, and Shannon told her she'd let her know."

"Yes, of course. I should talk to my mother, but I don't know what to say. And I don't know if I can ever call her without wondering if my father would be around; there's a high possibility that he would be."

"Maybe you should write her a letter," Greg suggested. "I learned the art of letter writing while I was in prison. Phone calls were rare and brief. But letters are great, and something of a lost art. In a letter you can say exactly what you want and not worry about your emotions getting in the way—which often happens in a conversation."

Celia said, "I like that idea. There is a great deal I want to say to her—mostly that I love her and respect her and I never wanted to hurt her, but I had to do what I did. I know she will never stop catering to my father, no matter how badly he behaves. But I still want to tell her that she deserves better. It might not make a difference in her life, but I would like to think that something inside of her might find some comfort in knowing I believe that."

"I agree," he said. "So you should write her a letter."

Celia thought about it a long moment. "My father always picks up the mail. I'm not sure he'd give it to her or that he wouldn't read it first."

"First of all," Greg had to say, "that's terrible. Screening mail is the kind of thing that happens in prison. It shouldn't happen in a marriage."

"No, it shouldn't, but there are a lot of things in their marriage that shouldn't be the way they are."

"Does she have a friend you could mail it to? Someone you can trust?"

"Yes," Celia said, brightening at the idea. "She does. I could do that." Her mind briefly worked through how good it would feel to write down all of her feelings to her mother and to be able to explain her behavior and to know that the letter would get safely delivered through the hands of a dear woman who had been her mother's friend since they were children.

"That's a brilliant idea, Gregory Turney," Celia said. "You're a genius. I think I feel better already. I've just . . ." her voice cracked, "felt the worst about how I ruined my mother's Christmas . . . when she puts so much effort into making everything perfect. She is so guileless, Greg. She deserves much better."

"Yes, she does. Like you said, you might not be able to change anything in her life. She's lived for decades seeing things a certain way. But you can let her know how you feel and explain yourself. I think it will make both of you feel better."

"And maybe with the help of her friend, I can keep in touch with her," Celia said. "Because I think it's rare that I could call her and not have my father answer the phone. He's retired and hardly leaves the house without her. And I was worried that if I even *tried* to call, he would be angry with her *and* with me. And I don't want her to get any more grief over this. But if I can keep in touch with her through letters that my father never knows about, I can live with that."

"Good," Greg said and allowed her the silence to think and share with him whatever she felt inclined to share.

"I'm never going back there," Celia said with a firm determination that had replaced all evidence of sorrow. "It's like that house is . . . toxic. And I've never been able to see it as clearly as I did on this visit. It was like every passive-aggressive, judgmental, unkind thing that happened just stood out in neon and I could hardly breathe. I was holding it together and just trying to bite my tongue and keep peace for my mother's sake. I had some time alone with her, which was nice. But there we were—at Christmas dinner—and I felt like I was looking at the whole thing through someone else's eyes, and I just couldn't take it another minute."

Greg saw indignation and perhaps some anger cross Celia's countenance as she repeated the things her father had said and the way her mother and siblings had responded. Her mother had been hurt and ashamed but tried to pretend everything was all right— as she always had. And Celia's brother and sister had seemed to be completely comfortable with their father's emotionally abusive comments—because none of his words were directed at them.

Greg felt indescribably proud of Celia for what she'd said to her father and the courage it had taken. His heart ached for her as she described packing up and leaving the house while her mother was weeping and her father was shouting and heaping abuse upon Celia.

Celia became distant and silent, and Greg just tightened his hold on her hand, sensing there was something important she needed to say. She looked at him firmly and said, "My father told me if I left like that not to ever come back. He told me I was dead to him. He said I would go to hell for not honoring my father." Greg gasped but said nothing, wanting her to continue. "He said he wouldn't have a daughter who treated him this way." Huge tears rose in Celia's eyes, then fell. "After thirty-something years of allowing my father to treat me like a lesser human being, I finally stand up for myself and that's what I get. It's not a surprise, really. I never expected him to be capable of being able to see the truth, but it still . . ."

"Hurts?" Greg guessed.

Celia nodded and scooted close enough to put her head on his shoulder. He put his arms around her and let her cry. "I don't think I'll ever see any of them again. With the exception of my mother, I'm not terribly upset over that—which is pathetically sad."

"Yes, it is."

"But . . . just the idea that I can never go home again . . . that I can never have the hope of something positive with my own father, my brother and sister, simply because I am trying to become a stronger, better person, more emotionally healthy . . ."

"I know," he said, rubbing the back of her head. "It *is* pathetically sad, Celia. And I'm so sorry. But I'm proud of you. I really am."

She looked up. "You are?"

"Oh yes!" he said. "I wonder if I ever could have done such a thing. I was just wondering what it might have been like if Shannon and I hadn't been taken away from our parents at a young age. At what point—if ever—would I have been able to stand up to them the way you did? As it was, I just had to reach a point where I accepted that my parents were selfish, dysfunctional people who never would have been able to change—and that had nothing to do with me."

"And they're both dead now, I know," Celia said and sniffled. "Shannon's told me."

"Yeah," Greg said. "It's been years. People who live that way don't tend to live very long. It still makes me sick if I think about it, though. My mother died of a drug overdose; she was found in one of those filthy drug lairs where homeless junkies go to get stoned and hide from the police."

"That's so horrible," Celia said. She'd heard it before, but it felt different hearing it from Greg. Shannon was her best friend, but Greg was the man she loved. His heartache felt similar to her own, even if their circumstances varied greatly.

"And my father died of alcohol poisoning; he was found in an alley. Alone and filthy." He let out a weighted sigh. "I've often wondered how much alcohol someone has to drink to die from it."

"I'm so sorry," Celia said and wrapped her arms around him, settling her head more comfortably onto his shoulder.

"We both have our pathetic stories, don't we," he stated, then brightened his tone. "But your mother is alive and well, and she loves you. In spite of all the things you *can't* fix or change, you can do your best to let her know the kind of woman you've become and how you feel." He kissed the top of her head. "And we have the ability to do better than our parents did. We will always make certain our children feel safe and secure—emotionally *and* physically. And they will always feel loved."

Celia lifted her head to look at him, and Greg realized what he'd just said. He'd come to think about such things so comfortably that it had slipped out. He held her gaze, wondering what she might say. She sat up straighter as if it might allow her to look at him more clearly and therefore assess his words more carefully. His heart began to pound. What if he'd offended her? Was he being pushy? Presumptuous?

"By *our* children do you mean *your* children as hypothetically separate from *my* children? Or do you mean *our* children . . . as in . . . children that belong to both of us?"

Greg pondered exactly how to answer that question, and his conclusion was quick and firm. He could only be completely honest, and there was no reason not to. He leaned slightly closer and said, "Would this be a bad time to tell you that I want to marry you?"

Once again he saw tears in her eyes just before she asked, "Are you proposing to me?"

Greg chuckled. "Do you want to tell our children that I proposed while you were wearing silly Christmas pajamas and we were talking about how dysfunctional our families are?" Before she could answer he leaned closer still and answered his own question. "No, I think you deserve a better proposal story than that. Right now I'm telling you that I am planning my life around the goal of proposing to you, and as soon as I feel like I have my life in some form of working order, I intend to ask you to marry me, and as long as you keep hanging around with me, I'm going to keep hoping you'll say yes. How does that sound?"

"It sounds perfect," she said, smiling through a rush of tears.

She hugged him, and he returned her embrace, saying close to her ear, "Good, because if I had any doubt whatsoever—which I didn't—it all went away when I was wondering if something awful might have happened to you. I need you in my life, Celia, and I'll do whatever it takes to make that happen."

Chapter Twelve

CELIA LOOKED AT GREG WITH their noses almost touching. She took his face into her hands and laughed softly. "Oh, I like this plan. I like it very much."

"Good," he said and kissed her. "But I have one stipulation."

"Anything," she agreed and kissed him again.

"I am *not* asking your father for his blessing," he said, and Celia laughed. He was glad she could laugh over it, which he considered enormous progress. But he was serious when he said, "I don't respect him, Celia. I can't judge the reasons that motivate him to behave the way he does, but I could never trust such a man to have your best interests at heart. So this is between you and me. The only other people that really matter have already made it clear they're on our side." He chuckled. "In fact, I don't think anyone will be happier about this than Neal and Jeanie."

"Shannon would probably be in close running."

"True," he said. "You want her for a sister?" he asked in mock dread, and she laughed.

"Best sister ever," she said. "And being officially a part of Neal's and Jeanie's lives just . . . well, it's great. I love them, Greg."

"I know you do," he said. "I couldn't marry someone who didn't."

He kissed her again before she settled her head on his shoulder once more, and he cradled her in his embrace. Following a few minutes of silence while they both reflected on everything they had discussed, Celia said, "A thought has come to me a number of times while I've been traveling and crying my guts out and—"

"And eating a bowl of cereal."

"And that," she said. "I did eat something at the airport in Kansas, although I can't remember what it was."

"You need to eat something half decent," he declared.

"In a minute," she said. "I was telling you something."

"Right. Sorry. Go ahead."

"I realized something as I kept replaying that ugly scene at the dinner table . . . how I felt . . . and what I said. You know how I said it felt like I was looking at the whole thing through someone else's eyes?"

"Yes."

"I just kept thinking of how that felt, and . . . at some point I figured it out. It just came to me so clearly, and I knew."

"What? You knew what?"

She looked at him intensely. "It was *your* eyes, Greg. Without even realizing it, I was seeing the whole thing through *your* eyes. It was as if I could see it all so much more clearly because I saw it from the perspective of someone who loves me and thinks I'm beautiful and valuable. And I could see how pathetic it all was. It's as if I could feel how angry you would have felt if you'd been there. I could imagine what *you* would have said on my behalf. I wasn't consciously thinking all of that at the time, but looking back I know it was all there in my mind—and in my heart—and that's what made everything different. *You* are the reason it was different. You're the reason I did what I did. I've known for years that I *should* stand up to them, but I could never bring myself to do it until now. As upset as I've been, a part of me has known that it needed to happen. I don't regret what I did or what I said, especially now that you've helped me see how I can explain myself to my mother. I think what I've been feeling is grief—plain and simple. I have cut the cord, so to speak, between myself and my home and family. So grief is . . . understandable."

"Yes, it is," he said and touched her face.

"I just wanted you to know that even though you weren't there, I couldn't have done it without you."

Greg felt warmed by the thought, and he couldn't help but recall that Shannon had speculated over this very thing. However, he was quick to point out, "It was *your* courage, Celia. Your words. Your strength. That's not me."

"So it was a joint project," she conceded. "I still couldn't have done it without you."

"I can't imagine doing anything without you ever again," he said and kissed her. As always, her kiss was sweet, and he kissed her again. Realizing they were alone and both enjoying this far too much for two people who weren't yet married, he stood up and took off his coat, glad to feel the apartment warming up.

"What are you doing?" she asked as he walked toward the kitchen area on the other side of the room.

"I'm going to fix you something to eat," he declared.

"I doubt there's much available. I left town, remember? And I didn't leave anything in the fridge that would spoil."

"I'll figure something out," he said. "Or I'll go buy you something."

"In this town this late in the evening, your options are limited."

"Limited, but it's not like I can't find food late at night."

He opened the fridge and found nothing but eggs and some orange juice, along with basic condiments and some different flavors of salad dressing. But in the freezer he found some English muffins.

"You don't have to do this," she said, coming into the kitchen.

"My cooking skills don't amount to much," he said, "so I'm sure I won't exert too much energy. Why don't you just . . . sit down or something. You're making me nervous. What little I can cook could easily become a disaster if I have an audience."

"Okay," she drawled. "I think I'll take a really quick shower."

"You do that," he said, and she left the room.

By the time Celia was out of the shower and wearing a *different* pair of silly Christmas pajamas, Greg had cooked scrambled eggs and had set the table for both of them with the dishes he'd found in the cupboard. The eggs were in a covered dish to keep them warm, and there were toasted English muffins on a plate, with butter, honey, and jam on the table. He'd poured orange juice into two glasses and was waiting for her when she emerged with her hair wet and her countenance much brighter than it had been when he'd arrived. He watched as she approached the table and expressed excitement over his simple efforts. He wanted his whole life to be like this. Just sharing ordinary day-to-day life with her seemed the best gift that life could possibly offer, and he prayed that she would never change her mind about wanting to share her future with him.

After sharing their late-night breakfast, Greg helped Celia put the kitchen in order before he kissed her good night and made her promise to turn her phone on and answer the messages. He kissed her once more and forced himself to leave, feeling both grateful and gratified—especially in contrast to how he'd felt before he'd come here earlier this evening.

Back home, he did his best to come in quietly, knowing how late it was and that everyone would be in bed. But he knew the garage door opening and closing could be heard through most of the house. It wasn't loud enough to wake anyone, but if they were still awake they would know he'd come in. Still, he was surprised to find Shannon sitting in the kitchen, reading.

"Waiting up for me?" he asked.

"Yes and no," she said. "I took a nap, so I was a little restless when bedtime came. I thought I'd read until I got sleepy. And I thought I'd do it where I could run into you on the chance that you came home before I got sleepy."

Greg sat down, and she asked, "So how did it go?"

"I asked her to marry me," he said, wanting to get that out of the way up front.

Shannon chuckled. "Well, *that's* not what I expected to come out of your mouth."

"Well . . . I didn't actually propose. I just . . . told her I intended to when I get my life in order. Obviously I have things to work out, but I don't want to lose her in the meantime." He looked at his sister to gauge her reaction. "You're smiling."

"Did you expect me to be unhappy over the possibility of you two ending up together? I think it's wonderful."

"It *is* wonderful, isn't it," Greg said, realizing he'd gotten past many of his own doubts about being good enough for Celia. He loved her, and he would take good care of her. Perhaps it helped to see how much more capable he was of doing that than her own father.

Greg filled Shannon in on what had happened, knowing that Celia wouldn't mind if he did, since they had firmly agreed to clarify if there was ever anything said that one of them didn't want repeated.

Shannon was a best friend to both of them, and her interest in their lives and their relationship was a fringe benefit for all of them. However, Greg stuck to the basics, figuring Celia could fill Shannon in on the details the way he knew they enjoyed doing.

"I'm glad she finally told her father what he needed to hear," Shannon said. "I've been wanting her to do exactly that for years. I think we can both understand how difficult it must be to feel severed from home and family—but when people are toxic, you can't maintain relationships without getting radiation poisoning."

"Hey, that's a good analogy," he said lightly, even though he really meant it. Most of the people in his life—at least prior to prison—had all been toxic, and he'd been very, very sick as a result. It had taken years of counseling and spiritual guidance to heal, and he was still healing. But he would never go back to living in the proximity of that kind of toxic waste. And he could never bear to see Celia do the same.

After he and Shannon had said good night, Greg went up to bed, feeling calm and completely at peace. He didn't have a job, and he had no idea what he might do in regard to his education or profession. But the important things were heading in the right direction, and that's all that mattered. He recalled talking with Celia about their hypothetical children and smiled. He wondered what Neal and Jeanie would think of getting younger siblings at this point in their lives, and he believed they'd be fine with it. When the time was right he would talk to them about his plans to marry Celia and have her become a more permanent part of their lives. For now, he just relished the thought of one day making Celia his wife—and with any luck and God's blessings, that day might not be too far in the future.

* * * *

The following morning Greg was glad to wake up and find two text messages from Celia. One was to tell him that she loved him and how grateful she was for his help and intervention the previous evening. The other was to tell him she was planning to spend the day drafting a letter to her mother so that she could work through her feelings and know that she had done everything she could to help her mother understand what had happened. Since it was standard procedure for Shannon's legal office to be closed between Christmas and New Year's, Celia wanted to take on this essential task while she had the time off work. Greg texted back to tell her he loved her and would come by to bring her some much-needed groceries so she could focus on the letter and not have to go out.

Laden with grocery bags, Greg arrived at Celia's apartment to find her dressed casually and her computer set up on the kitchen table. He made her a good breakfast and sat with her to make sure she ate it while they talked about the importance of this letter. She had decided to write letters to her other family members as well, although she doubted she would ever mail them. Celia felt a need to explain her actions to her mother so there would be no hard feelings between them and they could carry on a relationship as far as it was possible. She knew that her father and siblings had no interest in hearing what she had to say; repairing their relationships was highly unlikely if not impossible, mostly because she knew from vast and past experience they had no interest in anyone's views but their own. But for Celia, articulating her feelings in writing could be very cleansing and help her let go. She considered herself on a mission to move beyond the dysfunctional behaviors of her life prior to standing up to her father, and until this project was completed, she would stay in and work on it. Greg was glad to be her support and assured her he would bring her anything she needed. He also assured her that he'd be happy to come over if she needed a break or needed to talk something through, but he would keep his distance if she needed to focus. He left her well supplied with food that was healthy and easy to prepare, and promised to see her later.

Greg took advantage of having a day with his kids while they were out of school for Christmas break, even if that simply meant hanging around the house to be there as they came and went to their friends' houses and sharing meals with them. He helped Shannon with Grace and Evan so she could get some laundry done and balance her checking account. Phillip technically had the week off as well, although he was on call, which meant he had to deal with any emergencies that might arise. He left to make a house call for a sick horse and came back just before lunch. The little ones had just gone down for naps and the adults were lingering over their lunch when Phillip's cell phone rang, and it was evident he had to leave for another emergency.

"What is it?" Shannon asked as he hung up, looking concerned.

"A dog hit by a car," he said grimly. "The owner is a widow—one of those cases where the pet is the center of her life. I hope we can save him."

Phillip was making a call as he walked out of the room, and Greg knew the standard procedure was to get one of his assistants to meet him at the clinic. Greg was surprised when Phillip came back into the kitchen and said to Greg, "Are you free? Do you think you could come and help me?"

"Sure," Greg said, wondering what he might be getting himself into. "But I have no idea what I'm doing."

"All you have to do is be a second pair of hands," Phillip said. "I can tell you what to do. But no one else is available at the moment."

"I've done it before," Shannon said. "I was a little squeamish over the blood, but I survived."

"I've done it too," Marj said, barely lifting her head out of the book she was reading.

"Okay," Greg said and followed Phillip out to the garage. They both grabbed their coats on the way without breaking their stride; they were obviously in a hurry.

At the clinic a car was waiting in the parking lot. The dog's owner was sitting in the backseat with the injured animal; a friend of the owner had driven them to the clinic. Greg watched as Phillip calmly reassured the frantic women while carefully assessing the injuries of a medium-sized gray dog that was not moving much and appeared to be in pain. Phillip handed Greg the keys to the clinic and carefully picked up the dog. Greg hurried to get the door open and hold it for Phillip, who told the women to make themselves comfortable in the waiting room and assured them he would come and talk to them as soon as he had assessed the damage and had any information he could share.

In a room that was used for animal surgeries, Phillip carefully laid the dog down, and Greg heard some mild whimpering. "Hey there, Felix," Phillip said soothingly, as if he and the patient were close friends, "I'm going to do everything I can. You just take it easy."

Phillip turned to Greg and said, "Wash your hands and put on some of those sterile gloves."

Greg hurried to do so as Phillip did the same. While Phillip carefully inserted an IV line so that he could give the dog medication,

Greg helped hold the dog still by placing his hands gently where Phillip instructed. Once the dog was sedated and no longer in pain, Phillip worked quickly to assess the injuries, then went to the waiting room to tell the anxious owner and her supportive friend that it appeared Felix didn't have any internal injuries, which he said was miraculous considering that in most cases, animals hit by moving vehicles were injured internally, and there was usually nothing that could be done. But Felix *did* have a badly broken leg that would require surgery.

Greg was deeply impressed with Phillip's tender bedside manner as he gently explained to Felix's owner that it would be all right if she made the decision to let the dog go peacefully, which was an option. Or he could perform the surgery on Felix's leg, which would mean some difficult recovery time for the dog and a great deal of extra work in caring for him; however, there was no reason to believe he couldn't make a full recovery. The distraught woman cried with relief and insisted the surgery be done. Phillip tactfully explained the expenses involved but assured her that payments could be set up if necessary. She assured him that the money wouldn't be a problem and told him to go ahead. Greg wondered how it would feel to be so attached to an animal and genuinely *not* be able to afford such an expensive procedure. Having grown up poor, his mind always went to such things. He figured that in some cases, the issue might fall under the category of it being all right to let go of the animal and have it put to sleep peacefully.

Phillip encouraged the two women to go home since the surgery would take a long while, and he assured them he would call if there was any need for them to come back, implying that if something went wrong, they would be the first to know and they could be back at the clinic in minutes. But there was no point in them hanging around an impersonal waiting room.

"Okay, let's get started," Phillip said to Greg once the ladies had left.

"Okay."

"Are you up for this?" Phillip asked, his tone more teasing than serious.

"If I feel like I'm going to faint or something, I'll let you know."

Greg was surprised by how much he actually enjoyed assisting Phillip, and rather than feeling uncomfortable or squeamish while observing a fairly intense surgical procedure, he was nothing but fascinated. One of Phillip's assistants showed up when they were nearly finished, apologizing for her delay. But since one of her kids had become unexpectedly ill, it obviously couldn't be helped. Phillip assured her everything was under control, and even if Felix had needed to wait for surgery, he would have been fine.

"But Greg is a pretty good assistant," Phillip said to her. "He might be sorry to be living under my roof when I start dragging him out to do more of this kind of stuff."

"Glad to help," Greg said and meant it.

Felix came through the surgery fine, and Phillip arranged for his assistant to get the dog cleaned up after he was moved to a recovery area. Phillip called Felix's owner to report the positive results of the surgery and told her his assistant would be staying with Felix and she was welcome to come and be with him when he woke up.

On the drive back to the house, Phillip said to Greg, "I meant what I said. You were good. Have you ever done anything like that before?"

"Does administering first aid following a prison brawl count?" Greg asked.

"Maybe," Phillip chuckled. "Anyway . . . thank you. I'll pay you for your time, of course, and—"

"No, you will not!" Greg insisted. "I live in your home and you've been feeding me for months. I'm glad to help."

"Fine," Phillip drawled with a sideways smile. "But for the record . . . it's been great having you in our home. I know I can now admit that none of us had any idea how it would go, but it's actually been great."

"Well, for the record," Greg said, "I'm grateful."

Phillip just smiled, and Greg was relieved to drop the subject.

That evening he took Celia a plate of the dinner that Marj had prepared. He heated it up for her in the microwave, and she asked if he would read through the letter she'd written. He did so while Celia ate, and more than once he felt the sting of tears in his eyes. It was the perfect combination of expressing love and compassion for her mother while at the same time explaining Celia's own hurt and her need to set boundaries for the sake of her own self-respect and well-being.

When he'd finished reading he looked at Celia, feeling his love and admiration for her deepening. "It's perfect," he said.

"Really?"

"Really. I mean . . . really. It's incredible. Make sure you keep a copy. Whenever you struggle with wondering what's important and why, you should read this and remember that the *real* Celia Mae wrote this and that every word is true."

Celia became emotional and had to interrupt her dinner to hug him tightly, which was certainly fine with him. While she continued to eat, he read a much more roughly written letter that she'd been working on for her father and siblings.

"Basically," she explained, "the letter applies to all of them—and anyone else for that matter—because no one but you and I and Shannon will ever read it. This letter is more of a firm and therapeutic statement of where I stand. And yes, I need to keep a copy of this one, too. But I think I'm going to burn a copy, just for the sake of symbolism or something."

"That's a great idea," he said as he read yet another remarkable expression of all that Celia had risen above as she'd come to understand the emotional abuse that had always been present in the home in which she'd grown up. He finished reading, looked at her, and said, "It's no wonder I love you so much. You're amazing." She smiled somewhat shyly, and he added, "I mean it. I am so deeply impressed. With any luck you can help me believe all of this kind of stuff about myself."

"We'll keep working on it together," she said and took his hand across the table.

"I like the sound of that." He stood up and leaned over to kiss her.

* * * *

Greg had trouble sleeping that night. His brain felt like some kind of pinball machine, with ideas and thoughts bouncing around sporadically. He thought of all he'd learned over the last several years that had helped him put his ugly past behind him. Combining his own learning with all that Celia was teaching him from her own experiences felt overwhelming but so incredibly right. He felt as if together they could be truly capable of something great—even if it meant nothing more than raising a family in a way that was everything they'd both wished they'd had in their own lives.

Mixed into these thoughts was his experience of assisting Phillip with surgery on Felix's broken leg. It had awakened a fascination in him, and he wondered what it might mean. When his inability to sleep got worse instead of better, Greg got up and went quietly downstairs to the family computer, which Shannon had told him he was welcome to use at any time. He started doing searches and reading bits and pieces of information, not even certain what he was looking for. One idea led to another as he used the mouse to click on key words that stood out to him. He lost track of the time while he kept reading a chain of ideas that was seemingly meaningless until he found himself looking at something that actually made him gasp. He read and read and searched some more. Finally feeling tired, he printed some information, turned off the computer, and went up to bed after he left a note for Shannon on the kitchen counter to let her know he might sleep late but to wake him if he was needed.

Before attempting to sleep he sent a text to Celia, knowing it wouldn't wake her but would be there when she woke up. He then drifted off to sleep, feeling for the first time in his life like there was a clear path before him and he could see something worthwhile and meaningful in his future.

Greg woke up late morning to realize he'd slept soundly in the hours since he'd finally been able to relax. He reached for his phone, glad to find a text from Celia. He texted back to ask if he could bring lunch over in a while and talk to her. She was available and wrote: *Can't wait!*

As soon as Greg was showered and dressed, he checked in on Neal and talked to him for a few minutes, then he found Jeanie and caught up with her a little. However, he said nothing to either of his children about his plans; he wanted to run them by Shannon and Celia first if only to make certain that he wasn't simply caught up in some ridiculous notion that was the product of a sleepless night.

Greg found Shannon in the kitchen making a grocery list. He put a small stack of papers in front of her that he'd printed off the night before and simply said, "I want to be an EMT. I qualify for financial aid, and I can start the preliminary classes soon."

Shannon looked at the paper on the top of the stack, then at Greg, intrigue sparkling in her eyes. "Does this have something to do with you helping Phillip yesterday?"

"That started it, yes," Greg said and sat on a barstool. "It just felt easy. And right. But it didn't take much thinking to realize that I prefer helping people over animals; I'll leave the animals to Phillip. But I know I'm good at staying calm under pressure. And the icky stuff didn't faze me at all. It just feels so . . . right. Please tell me I'm not crazy."

"I don't think it's crazy at all," Shannon said with enthusiasm, and he already felt better. "Maybe being exposed to so much icky stuff in your life could actually pay off."

"That was my thought exactly," Greg said, hearing an excitement in his own voice that added credibility to his decision. "This is something I believe I can learn to do and be good at, and I can make a positive difference in people's lives. This kind of work will always be needed, and I'm sure it doesn't appeal to most people. It will never make me rich, but it's good, steady work. And that's what I want, what I need. I can do this. I know I can."

"I think it's great," Shannon said with a laugh and walked around the counter to hug him.

Greg hugged her back, so grateful for her never-ending support. He glanced at the clock and said, "Oh, I've got to go. I'm taking lunch to Celia. Obviously I need to talk to her about this."

"Obviously," Shannon said, looking as pleased about his excitement to see Celia as she was over his newly discovered goals in life. The two seemed to naturally go together.

A short while later, he lightly kicked Celia's door because his hands were full. She opened it with a smile that made her glow. He could honestly say that the progress she'd made in dealing with her family issues had brightened her countenance. That alone gave him added incentive in regard to his own life. For the moment he just gave in to the urge to kiss her before either of them said a word. She went on her tiptoes to make it easier for him, but he had trouble embracing her the way he wanted to, given that his hands were still holding everything he'd brought with him.

Celia stepped back and laughed, closing the door. "Hi," she said.

"Hello," he replied, and she took the bag of food that he'd picked up at a local deli.

He set everything down and took her in his arms to kiss her again. She laughed and said, "You're certainly in a good mood."

"Yes, I am," he said. "So are you . . . which is a big improvement over the past few days."

"It's quite miraculous, really," she said.

While they shared lunch, she told him how liberated she felt now that she had gotten beyond the shock of separating herself from her family. Writing the letters had helped her put everything into perspective, and since she'd mailed the letter off to her mother—in care of her lifelong friend—she felt as if she could put the matter to rest for now and know that no matter how her family responded or behaved in the future, she had come to terms with her own life.

Greg listened eagerly and said, "You're an inspiration to me, Celia Mae. In fact, I think you're like some kind of good-luck charm or something."

She laughed, and he could only think how much he'd grown to love her. Evidence of her feeling happy and at peace contributed to his desire to be a better man, and he told her so. When he shared his idea about wanting to become an EMT, she was so enthusiastic and encouraging that he felt all the more capable of actually following through with his plans.

Since Greg was supposed to check in with his parole officer today anyway, he called Larry and left a message. Larry called back a while later and was pleased with Greg's ideas for an education and his enthusiasm over them. Greg felt dismayed when Larry pointed out that some professions were more difficult to pursue with a criminal record, and since being an EMT meant being involved in many emergency situations—including things that were a result of crime—it could be more difficult to get accepted into school and to get hired. "Difficult but not impossible," Larry said. "And if you really feel good about it, then I think you should go for it. Given that everything else in your life is far better than many ex-cons, I think that with some glowing letters of recommendation from family members and other associates, I can help you get past that hurdle."

"Thank you," Greg said, "for your help *and* your encouragement. I really hope we can make this work."

Larry reminded Greg of opportunities for financial aid, which they had previously discussed, and explained where to find pertinent information online. He also told Greg that he could probably help speed the process along, since he had some experience with this kind of thing.

"When someone sincerely wants to take steps toward a better life," Larry said, "I'm all for doing everything I can to make that happen before you might change your mind." He chuckled comfortably and they talked a while longer. Greg had grown accustomed to answering Larry's detailed questions about what was going on in his life, but he liked and respected Larry, and he was grateful to have a parole officer who actually cared about him.

After Greg was off the phone, Celia used her computer to help him look up the websites to which Larry had directed him. Greg expected it to take days to figure out exactly what to do and how to do it, but with Celia's computer skills, she helped him with the first steps of applying online for the program and applying for some financial aid. It took a fair amount of time and they got hungry again, so they took a break to make some sandwiches. But Celia urged him to quickly get back to figuring things out, guiding him through the process efficiently. Even when glitches occurred, she knew how to figure them out eventually, and he learned a great deal about using a computer just from watching her and having her walk him through some of the steps himself.

"There!" she said when they were done.

"Wow," he said. "That would have taken me ten times longer. Technology definitely left me behind."

"I'm glad to help," she said. "And I'll be glad to help all I can . . . with whatever you need."

"Then I just might get through," he said and took her hand to kiss it.

"Of course you will!" she said as if she had no doubt.

"It could get crazy," he said. "I've still got to find a job, and hopefully I can find something that will work with the school schedule. I don't want you or the kids to feel neglected while I get through this."

"Listen to me," Celia said and kissed *his* hand. "You are doing all the right things for the right reasons. That doesn't mean it will be easy, but I do believe it means that God will be with you. And I know you believe that, too."

"I *do* believe that," Greg said. "I believe He guided me to this. And I believe He put *you* into my life, the same way He brought Phillip into Shannon's life—which has been a blessing to all of us."

"I agree," she said. "So we need to trust that God will be there for us as we move forward. I worked my way through school and struggled to find a decent job. I know what that's like, and I'll always be in your corner. Shannon and Phillip both worked hard to get through school too. They'll know what it's like, and I think they'll be nothing but proud of you."

Greg breathed in her words of encouragement and what they meant to him. In that moment the possibility of a truly good life felt more tangible to him than it ever had. Looking into Celia's loving eyes, he actually believed he could do it.

* * * *

Greg felt some letdown after the holidays were officially over. Shannon and Celia went back to work, Phillip's clinic went back to normal hours, and Neal and Jeanie went back to school. Greg filled some time with taking down all of the Christmas lights that he'd put up the previous month. The work gave him a little more money to put in the bank, which was where most of what he made went except for his minor contributions to Neal and Jeanie. Unless there was an absolute need—which occasionally included taking Celia on a real date—he saved all that he could, knowing he had a long list of things on which to spend it: first and foremost getting his own car.

Weeks passed, and Greg still hadn't been able to find any work that could actually be called a job. Occasionally he was able to help Phillip here and there, but the clinic was well staffed, so there was generally little for him to do. He was always watching for extra things he could do to help around the house and yard—although the cold weather and minimal snowfall didn't leave him much to do outside. He also looked for ways that he could help make Celia's life easier. When she wasn't working they were almost always together, either at Shannon's home or Celia's apartment—unless they went out. Greg couldn't help thinking every day that she fit so comfortably into the family that marrying her felt like the most natural step for both of them. But he couldn't get over believing that he had a long way to go before he would be ready to take on marriage and be able to do it right.

Greg was thrilled but also nervous when everything fell into place for him to start the training program to become an EMT. There was an opening that made it possible for him to start right away. Overwhelmed with all he would need to learn, he found it difficult to believe the first stage of the program was less than six months. He would have more stages of training after that in order to achieve the level he wanted, but having the program divided into smaller sections gave him the hope of being able to make some progress with a time frame that didn't seem quite so daunting. With any luck, he could manage to pass all of his classes and reach the first stage of certification about the same time he would be eligible to no longer have to report to a parole officer. Maybe by then he would feel ready to make a serious commitment in his life. But that felt difficult to imagine under the present circumstances, especially when he didn't even have a job. As much as he and Celia had become very close and enjoyed spending almost all of their time together, he still often felt like they were in high school—or at least *he* was; he lived with his sister, had very little money in the bank, and was unemployed.

A couple of weeks after Greg started classes, Phillip came home from work and handed Greg a sticky note with a name and phone number on it.

"What's this?"

"The answer to your prayers, I'm hoping," Phillip said, seeming pleased. "If Onion the cat hadn't gotten into a fight with another cat, which caused an infection that needed medical attention, we would have never known that Onion's owner—Rob Wright—is a successful contractor who is building houses in a new subdivision on the edge of town, and he's frustrated by his lack of reliable employees. He told me that most of the people who live around here commute to the cities for work, and very few want to commute *from* the cities to do construction. He just needs someone to do very basic work, and the hours are flexible so you can work it around classes." Phillip nodded toward the paper in Greg's hand. "Call him. He wants to meet with you, but I think the job is yours if you want it."

"Amazing," Greg said and impulsively hugged Phillip. "Thank you."

"Don't thank me," Phillip said lightly. "Thank Onion. He's been through a lot today."

"If I meet Onion, I'll be sure to express my gratitude," Greg said with enthusiasm.

He called Rob right away and quickly felt no need to be nervous when this man sounded happier to hear from Greg than Greg was with the possibility of getting a job. Rob told him the address of the construction site and asked if Greg could meet him there the following morning at ten. Greg assumed it would be for an interview, but Rob said, "Bring some good gloves and dress warm. The weather should be clear tomorrow, so we might actually get something accomplished."

"Sounds good," Greg said, glad he didn't have classes tomorrow. He was also glad that Shannon had been so gracious about loaning him her SUV. Since Marj rarely used her car and Shannon and Phillip both worked at the same place—which was only minutes away from home—they were able to manage some simple adjustments that made it possible for Greg to have a vehicle when he needed one.

As soon as Greg finished his call with Rob Wright, he called Celia to tell her the news, and she was thrilled. At supper he told the rest of the family, and they too were happy for him. He just hoped that it would go well, not certain if his first day of work might be some kind of test or probation. But he knew he could use a hammer; he was a fast learner when it came to hands-on tasks, and he was willing to do whatever needed to be done. He just needed to go to the hardware store before his interview with Rob and get himself a decent pair of work gloves. Even that made him feel more productive as he imagined wearing them out.

Chapter Thirteen

GREG LIKED ROB THE MOMENT he met him, and he liked him even more after he'd followed him around the construction site for an hour while Rob gave him some basic instructions and discussed his expectations. Greg knew he had to say, "Did my brother-in-law tell you about my situation?"

"That you were in prison?" Rob asked. "Yeah, he told me. He also told me you're an honest man and I can trust you. His word is good enough for me. I believe in second chances." Greg wanted to thank him or say *something* appropriately gracious, but Rob hurried on. "No need for you to fill out an application or anything, but I'll need your social security number before I can pay you."

"Of course," Greg said, then talked to him about his class schedule; Rob was fine with him putting in whatever hours he could manage. "As long as it's daylight, you can work whenever it fits your schedule; just punch in and out at the office." He motioned toward the trailer that served as a portable office for his construction company. "Except for Sundays, if I'm not here, one of the supervisors is, so the trailer is always open while we have enough sunlight to work."

Rob then told Greg what he paid per hour for basic labor, and Greg held back a gasp; it was more than double what he'd been making at the diner. He really *did* think it was a miracle that Onion the cat had gotten into a fight. His feelings regarding that settled in more comfortably as he spent the day doing the work Rob had assigned him. He had no trouble carrying lumber or other supplies to where they were needed, and with very little instruction, he was able to hammer those pieces of lumber into place to help erect the framework of one of the many homes that was being built at this site. There was always someone nearby who knew what to do if Greg had a question, and he quickly felt confident and capable. That, combined with simply being employed, helped him feel better about himself in many respects.

He'd texted Celia as soon as he knew he'd gotten the job, and had asked her to let Shannon know. She'd texted back to tell him she loved him and she would bring him some lunch. When he saw her car arriving, he felt a familiar lightness in his heart that always occurred whenever he saw her. He told Bill—the guy working close by—that his lunch had just arrived and he was going to take his break.

Bill glanced toward the woman getting out of the car and smiled. "Lunch always tastes better when you get personal delivery."

"Yeah, I'm sure it does," Greg said and hurried to greet Celia with a kiss.

They sat together in her car to eat the food she'd picked up for both of them.

"So how's it going?" she asked.

"Great," he said with enthusiasm and told her all there was to tell. "It feels good to be working, Celia."

She smiled. "That is one of many things I love about you."

"What?"

"That working is so vital to you. I never have to worry about you turning into a couch potato because it makes you crazy when you don't have any work to."

"No, I don't think you have to worry about *that*," he said with a chuckle.

* * * *

Celia felt a growing contentment in her life as winter merged into spring. She loved working with Shannon—just as she always had. And she loved being a part of Shannon's family, even more so now that she and Greg were becoming more and more a part of each other's lives. She felt a sense of belonging she'd never found in her own family, and she basked in the difference this was making in how she felt about herself. Here in Sugar City she had found love and acceptance for who and what she was. And with the passing of time, the difficult declarations she'd made at Christmastime were settling into her spirit as new parameters in her life were being established. She was exchanging regular letters with her mother via the friend that could be trusted, and occasionally Celia could talk to her mother on the phone when Betty was at her friend's home. Celia found it ridiculous that her mother had to hide their communication from Celia's father, but Melvin had not budged even a tiny bit on having disowned Celia for her disrespect. To him she was rebellious and arrogant, and he had set her dysfunctional siblings on pedestals as examples of what he believed she should be. For Celia, that implied she would be acceptable to her father if she was skinny, selfish, and unkind. Unless she'd had the privilege of being born male, and then it would have been admirable to be steadily gaining weight due to eating way too much of all the wrong foods and never exerting herself physically. Being unemployed—and blatantly lazy—also seemed acceptable when it came to Celia's brother. She marveled at the contrast between her shiftless brother and how hard Greg was working to better himself and his life. For her, there was no contest regarding who was the best and most decent man.

Celia knew all about the attitudes of her father and siblings from her conversations with her mother. Betty agreed that their views were distorted and unfair, but Celia knew she would never be capable of standing against them, and she had to accept that it was okay. She was grateful to at least have a relationship with her mother, and Betty was thrilled to hear about the details of Celia's life and especially about her evolving relationship with Greg.

Celia's love for Greg kept growing with every passing week, and she felt continually amazed at the evidence of his love for her. She found her love for Neal and Jeanie growing as well. She'd cared about them as soon as Shannon had taken them in, and over the years she'd grown to love them, feeling as if she were an honorary aunt of some kind. But now her feelings for them had become more personal. Coming to love Greg the way she did, it was impossible to observe his love for his children and not grow to share it. And she couldn't help being pleased with the way Neal and Jeanie seemed more drawn to her. It was as if they sensed the growing possibility that she might become a permanent part of their family, and they made it clear they were more than all right with that. She wondered how it might have been for Greg if he'd brought a woman into their lives they hadn't known previously. Neal and Jeanie were great kids, and they would have surely been gracious about any decision their father made, but as it was, the present situation seemed ideal. When the family was gathered together for Sunday dinner, they often joked about what an unusual family they were, and it was most commonly Marj who settled it with some kind of pronouncement that the most important ingredients in a family were love and respect, and they all had plenty of that.

Celia had grown to love Sundays. Since she'd started going to church with Greg—which meant going with the whole family—she had come to see religion through completely different eyes. The entire spirit of worship in this congregation and with this family was the complete opposite of what she'd grown up with. Between her father's pompous piousness and verbal abuse, she had come to see religion as something restrictive and even destructive. She now knew that religion in its proper form was a structure of good principles and a sense of community, where people came together to love and support each other in living good lives. Of course, there were all kinds of people in the congregation, and some were stuffy and even judgmental. But Celia had come to see that it was her own relationship with God that mattered, and that was something she'd never let go of. It felt good to express her devotion to God by being part of a religious body and to share that belonging with the people she loved most.

She also enjoyed Sundays because no one had to go to school or work—unless Phillip was called away for an emergency. Greg had firmly declared when he'd begun his journey of education that he was not going to study or do homework on Sundays, believing that if he kept the basic commandment of honoring the Sabbath, he would be blessed in being able to better accomplish all he needed to do during the other six days of the week. This often meant many late nights of studying, and Celia didn't see much of him during the week. But on

Sundays he set all of that aside, and they were able to spend some relaxing time together and with the family. She saw evidence of those blessings Greg was seeking if only in the way it helped keep balance in his life. She felt sure his stress would be more intense if he were preoccupied with his studies on Sunday, and it would have put more of a strain on his relationships with her and his children. As it was, everything was going relatively well in spite of how busy he'd become and how little they saw each of other.

With the passing of time, Celia wanted nothing more than to be married to Greg so that they could share their lives more closely, and at least he would be studying while they lived under the same roof. But she understood and respected his desire to progress to a certain point in his life before he took that step. The fact that they had come to talk about marriage very matter-of-factly as a part of their future gave her comfort in having every reason to believe that this relationship was not temporary. She'd come to rely on him so completely that she couldn't even imagine how it would break her heart to lose him, and he often made it clear he felt the same way about her.

As they got to know each other better and feel more comfortable in the relationship, they both naturally relaxed and became less conscious of being on their best behavior with each other. Of course Celia knew that was one of the reasons it was considered wise to know someone a decent length of time before getting into a committed relationship. But she wasn't surprised at how minimally things changed between her and Greg over time, since neither of them had ever been anything but completely honest with each other. She took careful notice of the times when they had disagreements and of how they both behaved as they settled them. She loved the way he taught her through the course of dozens of interactions that he was not like her father or her brother, nor was he like her previous boyfriends, who had behaved much the same. And she was equally gratified with how teachable and humble Greg was when his own false beliefs about relationships surfaced. He had learned communication and problem-solving skills in theory through much counseling, but he struggled at times to apply what he'd learned; however, they were always able to talk things through and keep learning together.

In looking back over the months since they'd been dating, she felt quite amazed to realize that the majority of their disagreements were a result of one or the other of them getting down on themselves. She knew from extensive research on human behavior that many people with deep insecurities unconsciously attempted to feel better about themselves by putting down their partner. She'd seen plenty of evidence of that with her parents. But with her and Greg, it was the opposite. While he never got *angry* with her, he expressed great frustration and even some level of scolding whenever she got into one of her self-demeaning moods and made derogatory comments about her weight or how terrible she thought she looked in a particular outfit. He was always quick to tell her she was beautiful and perfect just the way she was. And she usually argued with him, as if she might be trying to convince him that there was something wrong with her and he could do better.

Greg firmly settled the matter late on a Sunday evening in April when he said, "Are you trying to tell me that you really believe there is something wrong with you because you aren't built like the women on TV and in the movies?" He didn't give her a chance to answer. "Because that is just *wrong*. Do you know what percentage of men and women in this country actually look that way?"

"*You* look that way," she said, hating the way she seemed to have regressed to a snotty teenager, as she probably had in that moment.

"That is not fair," he insisted. "You eat healthier than I do, and I don't exercise any more than you do. Whatever body type we are, just is what it is. And if you're trying to tell me that this relationship is based on physical appearances, as opposed to who and what we are inside, then I want to know exactly what that means. If I get in an accident and become covered with burn scars, are you going to love me less?"

"Of course not!" she declared hotly.

"So what's the difference?" he asked and again didn't give her time to answer the question. "I'll tell you the difference. In some cases it might take some effort to look past scars or deformity to see what a person is inside. But that is *not* the case with you. *You* are beautiful!"

Celia was overcome with tears at his analogy *and* conviction, but she managed to hold them back. Still unconvinced and overcome with a particularly foul mood, she said something that had haunted her for years, something she'd wanted to say to him but had never dared. "And what happens when I have babies and gain weight the way all women do? What if I can't lose the extra weight? What if I blimp out and—"

"Do you hear yourself?" Greg asked, sounding as close to angry as she'd ever heard. "I defer to my last point on that count. And I'll tell you what I've told you a hundred times: I want you to be healthy. I will always love you no matter what. And *you* need to learn to believe me. If you lived in another time or a different culture, you would be considered the ultimate example of feminine beauty. So get over yourself and stop hearing your father's voice in your head. He doesn't have the right to be there anymore. And I need you to believe that I'm not just saying what I say to make you feel better. I'm telling you how I really feel."

Celia melted into his arms and cried, but her tears were cleansing. She knew he was right. The biggest problem was the way she still heard the derogatory things her father had said to her throughout her upbringing and how it had been perpetuated by other people in her life because she hadn't had the confidence to recognize and ward off such things. But she was a different person now, and she had the privilege of being loved by a man who understood.

A couple of weeks later the tables turned when Greg hit an especially difficult stage in his studies. He told Celia he felt stupid and completely incapable of ever making anything worthwhile of himself. She just followed his example of reminding him boldly of all that was good in him, of all his qualities that she loved and admired and that were so important to her. And she was able to tell *him* to stop hearing the voices of his parents in his head. He became emotional as she struck this sore point and the true source of the problem. And they were able to conclude with even more certainty that they were perfectly matched because at the core they understood each other perfectly—even if their issues were dramatically different.

Moving beyond these strong discussions, Celia felt her own self-confidence growing in proportion to the love Greg gave her. But she knew it wasn't her reliance on knowing he loved her that was making the greatest change in her, but rather it was the way he was teaching her that she didn't need anyone to validate her worth and value as a human being. She only needed to have that knowledge within herself, and little by little she could feel it happening and becoming more of a solid belief. As much as she loved Greg and couldn't imagine life without him, she also knew that with or without him, she was strong and whole and beautiful in her own right. Realizing the depth and breadth of how his love was teaching her to feel that way about herself, she could only love him more.

Celia could also see Greg's self-confidence growing, and she could easily imagine a day when he would be so comfortable with his new life that prison—and all that had happened before that—would be impossible to comprehend. He enjoyed his construction job and felt like he was getting pretty good at it while acquiring new skills as well—skills he knew he could always use for future employment if the need should arise. He was also enjoying his education, and in spite of some difficult patches when he'd felt overwhelmed with how much there was to learn, he was becoming comfortable with the prospect of being an EMT. He could humbly admit that he could look around at his classmates and recognize he had a knack for handling the stress and pressure of an emergency situation, all the while remaining calmer than others in his same situation. This too gave him confidence, and he began counting the weeks until he would be able to at least achieve this first level of certification and know he was moving toward having the potential of a job in that profession. Until that day came, he had the security of working for Rob.

When Greg was finally able to get his own car and also contribute a little more to the needs of Neal and Jeanie, his confidence grew in other respects as well. He was still required to check in with his parole officer but not nearly as often. In fact, Larry had told him more than once that he'd never seen anyone do so well in their transition back into society. Greg attributed that to the support of a good family, but Celia often reminded him of all the appropriate choices he'd made and his own personal convictions about doing the right thing.

* * * *

Spring became summer seemingly overnight, with a sharp rise in temperatures and a sudden increase in Greg's stress level over getting everything done for school and work, and also maintaining balance in his personal life. But Celia took careful note of how his increased stress never made him sharp or unkind to her or to anyone else. She just kept encouraging him and tried to be helpful wherever she could. They both started talking about how great it would be when he was able to finish school, although that felt so far away. After he achieved the first stage of certification, he would have a bit of a break, but then more education would follow. Still, they both knew that this education phase was temporary. Celia eagerly looked forward to the day when classes and study were no longer a part of Greg's life, but even more so she hoped for the day when Greg would feel ready to settle into his life and get married. Living under separate roofs felt more and more challenging to her, and she knew her feelings for him would never change. She also knew that he was every bit as good a man as she'd wanted to believe at the beginning. He talked about marrying her, but it was always in a someday hypothetical kind of way. She often wondered if she should say something to him about her growing impatience, but instinctively she held back. She knew they were both traditional enough that it felt more seemly for a man to initiate an official proposal. And she certainly didn't want to set a precedent in their relationship of her always being the one to initiate important decisions.

Given how much the matter had come to preoccupy her thoughts, Celia felt frustrated over the fact that her best friend was Greg's sister. If Shannon and Greg weren't related, she would have felt comfortable sharing her feelings with Shannon. As it was, she didn't feel comfortable going to Shannon with this. She'd certainly shared her feelings with Shannon since she'd been dating Greg, but never over something this big. Shannon had asked her a few times over the course of a week or more if everything was all right, and Celia had assured her that it was, but she was well aware that Shannon had known her long enough to know she wasn't being completely truthful. For that reason she wasn't at all surprised when Shannon stopped in the middle of a work conversation and asked, "Is there something going on with you and Greg that you don't want to talk to me about because you don't think that's fair to Greg?"

"If I say yes can we drop it?" Celia asked.

Shannon looked deeply concerned. "I completely respect what you're doing, Celia. I agree that I shouldn't be in the middle of things that should be left between the two of you, but I just . . . hate the thought of anything going wrong."

"Nothing is *wrong,*" Celia assured her. "I love him more than ever, and he's never been anything but perfectly good to me."

"Then what is it?" Shannon asked, then immediately added, "Oh, sorry. None of my business."

Celia went back to the work topic they'd been discussing, thinking how glad she would be when all of this resolved itself. And she felt certain that with time it would.

* * * *

Greg enjoyed a particularly relaxing Sunday, with summer weather making it possible to use the barbecue grill on the patio to cook much of their Sunday dinner. That evening after Celia left a little earlier than usual, saying that she was tired, Greg was surprised to have Shannon ask if they could talk.

"Sure," he said and followed her out to the patio, where they sat in two of the comfortable outdoor chairs. He realized then that no one else was outside, and she had apparently left Phillip in charge of the children. She'd planned this. "What's going on?" he asked.

"I'm your big sister," she said. "Can I not just check in once in a while and see how you're doing? We haven't really talked for a long time."

"Okay," he said, wondering if his closeness to Celia had left Shannon feeling excluded, although she had a very busy life, and she had Phillip.

"So how are you?" she asked.

"I'm fine," he said. "How are you?"

"I'm fine," she said. "But we're talking about you."

"And why is that?"

"I know you've been under a lot of stress; I want to know how you're doing."

"I'll be glad to get a break from school," he said. "And I'll be really glad when school is done."

"That will be a while, though. And then what?" she asked.

"Then . . . hopefully I can get a job doing what I'm growing to love. That's the goal, right?"

"Right."

"I know it will be shift work, so that could be challenging at times, but at least I won't be pulled between work and school."

"Yes, of course," Shannon said. "And what about your personal life?"

Greg turned slightly in his chair and focused more intently on his sister. "Is that what this is getting to? My personal life?"

"How *is* your personal life?"

"I would think you'd know," Greg said, not bothering to hide his growing irritation with this conversation.

"As far as I have observed, everything is fine with you and your kids. But if you're thinking Celia would keep me updated on your relationship with her, she tells me practically nothing."

"Is that the problem?" he asked. "That she tells you practically nothing?"

"I have absolutely no problem with the two of you keeping your personal issues between the two of you. I don't *want* to ever be caught in the middle of anything. But I do have some observations . . . if you're interested in hearing them. You've told me many times that you don't have much practice with relationships. I just wondered if you might want some sisterly advice. But maybe you don't need any—or want any. That's why I asked how it's going. You don't have to tell me; I just wondered."

Greg felt less irritated now. "As far as I know, it's fine," he said, "but if you've observed something I've missed, then maybe it's not as fine as I think it is."

"Well, as I said, Celia hasn't told me anything. But I think part of the problem might be that if her best friend wasn't your sister, she might have. The point being that I'm thinking she might want advice from a friend, but she isn't comfortable talking to me about anything that involves you."

Greg sighed, feeling deeply sad to think that he might have unwittingly put Celia in such a position. And he wondered what he might have missed that could be causing her distress. She'd seemed all right, but he'd been so preoccupied that maybe he wasn't paying attention as closely as he should have been. Now that he thought about it, she had been a little quieter and a little less chipper than usual.

"So," Shannon continued, "I don't actually *know* anything, but I can tell that something is bothering her. She assured me that she loves you more than ever, so you don't have to even wonder if that's the problem."

Greg nodded, more relieved than he could say over *that* clarification. "Do you know what it might be?" he asked.

"I'm thinking you should discuss this with her. I just . . . know you've been overwhelmed, and I thought I should point out that I can tell something's bothering her."

Greg pushed a hand through his hair, then wiped his face. "Okay," he drawled before he admitted, "I have no idea what I'm doing, sis. I am open to any advice you're willing to give me. I *will* talk to Celia, but I don't think it's out of line for you to at least tell me what you think."

"Okay . . . well . . . I assume you intend to marry her."

"Of course," he said, figuring that should have been obvious to anyone who knew them as well as Shannon did.

"May I ask when?"

"When I get my life straightened out," he said firmly, figuring she should have known that as well.

"Greg," she took his hand as if he were a child, "your life *is* straightened out. It's not perfect; it's never going to be perfect. Would I be way off base to guess that maybe you have some fear of taking that step, given the way your first marriage went, along with other things you've struggled with?"

Greg needed a few minutes to take that in, and Shannon allowed him the silence to do so. He finally had to say, "Maybe I do."

"And do you really think that your life now has any resemblance *at all* to the life you were living when you got married the first time?"

Greg only had to think about that for a moment before he answered resolutely. "No, it does not!"

"Then why would you believe at any level that you are not in a position to make better decisions and do what is right by Celia?"

Greg couldn't answer, mostly because the answer seemed obvious, but he had trouble accepting it into his spirit.

"I'm going out on a limb here, Greg, so let me say that it's not my intention to be nosy or intrusive, and I certainly don't want to be offensive, but there's something I feel like I need to say."

"So say it," he said. "After the way we grew up, I can't imagine you saying anything that would offend me."

"We're not the same people we were back then. We've learned how to treat certain aspects of life with more respect."

"True," he said and nodded toward her, encouraging her to go on.

"I know the two of you want children; you've both talked about it."

"Yes," Greg said.

"Well, you're not getting any younger," Shannon said. "And I'm going to say again that you are not the same man you were when you became a father the first time around. I know you have a lot of regret over not being the kind of father to Neal and Jeanie that you now know you should have been. But that's the point. Now you know the difference. Many children are born into less-than-ideal circumstances, and they do just fine because they're loved and cared for. But you and Celia have everything going for you. The thing is . . . *you* have had the experience of getting married and becoming a father—however far from ideal it might have been, you *have* had those experiences. But Celia has not."

Shannon paused as if to allow Greg the opportunity to speak, but he couldn't disagree with anything she was saying. And yet it all felt overwhelming.

"For as long as I've known Celia, she's wanted to be a mother. For most women that instinct and desire can be very strong, and she's not so many years away from the age when it starts to become more complicated physically. You're a practical man; surely you can understand the logic of that."

Greg nodded but still couldn't speak.

"The two of you aren't college kids," Shannon went on, "and you've been dating for several months now."

"Yes," Greg said, wondering what *that* was supposed to mean, since it felt like she was changing the subject.

"I know you both have strong convictions about saving intimacy for marriage."

"Yes," Greg said again, hoping she didn't think he was taking advantage of Celia in such a way.

"So it must be difficult for two mature adults to be so in love with each other and not be sharing that kind of relationship—especially when so much time has passed since you both knew that marriage was highly probable."

Greg felt a little startled by how accurately she had pegged something he thought about a great deal, but he always fought to push the thoughts away, believing there was nothing to be done about it at this point in his life. He simply said, "I just try not to think about it. I'm usually too busy to think about it."

"And do you think Celia is too busy to think about it?" Shannon asked.

Greg looked at her in surprise as her meaning began to sink in. He didn't feel embarrassed by the topic, but he felt a little stupid over the way he hadn't connected the attraction he and Celia felt for each other to her obvious desire to be married and become a mother.

"As I told you," Shannon added, "she hasn't said anything to me, so I'm just guessing. Maybe I'm wrong. But I know her pretty well. It's my guess that she really loves you and she wants to get married and start a family, but she's too much of a lady to bring up what should be obvious. And if I were to take my speculations a step further, I would bet that if she's wondering why you haven't proposed, she's probably wondering if it has something to do with the things that she feels most insecure about."

Greg nearly gasped aloud as Shannon's meaning fully struck him, and he felt something painful at the very idea that his getting caught up in his own fears and issues had allowed him to miss the possibility that his hesitancy might be hurtful to Celia.

"It's something to think about," Shannon said. "Whether I'm right or wrong doesn't matter. I still think you should get over whatever it is that's holding you back and just marry her. I bet you can't tell me one good reason why you shouldn't."

Greg thought of a few reasons immediately, but even before he could get them to his lips, he could hear in his mind how Shannon would come back with far more logical reasoning as to why they were ridiculous. In that moment, he knew the reasons he'd been telling himself were nothing more than excuses. It was time for him to deal with his issues and get on with his life.

"It's something to think about," Shannon repeated and stood up to go into the house, leaving him alone on the patio. He stayed there while the sun went down and long after it became completely dark, praying and pondering and considering every facet of the situation. He'd unofficially proposed to Celia right after Christmas. And now it was August. He'd told her he needed time, but he could see now that he was being a fool. It was time for him to put the past behind and truly be the man Celia deserved, and that meant stepping forward and giving her all he had to give. In worldly terms that wasn't much, but he knew now that it was enough. He loved her and would devote his life to taking care of her and making her happy. She'd made it clear over and over that that was all she wanted or needed. It was time he took the hint.

Chapter Fourteen

GREG LEANED HIS FOREARMS ON his thighs and prayed silently for a long while. A quiet peace settled into him, and he knew that the steps he'd been reluctant to take were the right steps for his life—and for Celia's. Shannon had been right—about everything. The situation wasn't perfect, but life wasn't like that. If he waited for everything to be perfect, they would both grow old and never get on with their lives.

Greg felt snapped out of a stupor as his need to move forward became suddenly urgent. Now that he knew it was right, he didn't want to waste a moment. The busy week ahead stretched out before him in his mind, and he wanted to talk to Celia tonight. He pushed a button on his cell phone so it would light up and show him the time. It wasn't as late as he thought it might be. He wondered if Celia had gone to bed, but she usually texted to tell him good night before she went to sleep. He hurriedly sent her a text: *Are you awake?*

Within seconds he got the reply: *Yes, why?*

I know it's late, he wrote back. *But I need to talk to you. Can I come over?*

Of course, she replied, and Greg was on his way to his car. He imagined Shannon lying in her bed and smiling with self-satisfaction when she heard him drive away. But that was fine. What would he ever do without her? He wondered how long he might have gone on in a stupor without her gentle intervention.

Celia answered the door of her apartment wearing silly pajamas with fluffy sheep patterned all over them that looked like clouds with legs and heads.

"Hello," he said and kissed her.

"Is everything all right?" she asked and closed the door after he came in.

"I hope so," he said and sat down at one end of the couch. "I just . . . came to some realizations, and . . . it's going to be another crazy week. I didn't want to wait to talk to you."

"Okay," she said and sat at the other end of the couch, tucking her feet up beneath her and turning toward him. "May I ask what brought this on—whatever it is?"

Greg looked at the expectancy in her eyes and felt sure that Shannon had been right—about everything. "I wish I could say that I was sharp enough to notice that something wasn't right and I had a great epiphany completely on my own. The truth is that I've been so wrapped up in work and school that I have been completely oblivious to the fact that something isn't right, and I needed my big sister to slap me in the face—not literally, of course."

"What did she say?" Celia asked as if she might be unhappy with Shannon for talking about her.

"Nothing she didn't have the right to say," Greg said. "She told me you hadn't said anything, but she could tell you were struggling. The rest of what she said was her own guessing and speculating, and she made that very clear. However, given that she knows both of us better than anyone else, I'm fairly certain she knew what she was talking about."

Celia didn't comment, and Greg turned more toward her, determined to just get to the point and not make this any more complicated than it needed to be. "It doesn't matter what she said, Celia. What matters is that I've been thinking about what she said, and I've been praying. So I want to tell you what *I* think."

"Okay," she said, her voice soft, her countenance open and accepting.

Greg looked directly into her eyes, not wanting her to have any question over his sincerity. "I've known for months that being with you forever is not only the best possible thing I could do with my life but it's what I want more than anything. I told you I needed time to get my life in order, and that was true. My life is in much better order now than it was then. The thing is that I think I had some idea in my mind of how my life needed to be before I even considered marriage."

Greg saw her eyes react to the word, and he saw her shoulders shift as if to disguise the change in her breathing. He hurried on before he lost the words that he'd been struggling to put together in his head.

"I can see now that I'm probably putting off what's most important, more out of fear than any practicality. Shannon pointed out that my life now is nothing like it was when I got married before, and I am not the same man. She's right. What she didn't say but I know is true is that . . . well . . . I need to give myself credit for how far I've come and recognize that I *am* capable of being a good husband and father." He saw tears forming in her eyes but forged ahead. "I know in my heart I would do anything to make you happy and take care good care of you. What I've been overlooking is that we would both probably be a lot happier if we were married."

Greg paused to gauge her reaction, but she'd squeezed her eyes closed and he honestly couldn't tell. "If I'm off base here, all you have to do is say so and—"

"Oh, I think you're hitting pretty close to the mark," she said and opened her eyes. A sound came out of her mouth that was something between laughter and a sob.

Greg reached for her hand and squeezed it while she wiped her tears with her other hand. "I've really been blind, haven't I," he stated.

"You've been very busy," she said.

"But it's not just about being busy," he pointed out. "I've been oblivious to what you were feeling, and I don't ever want to be that way." He eased a little closer and wiped her tears for her. "Why didn't you say something?" As soon as he asked, he recalled something else Shannon had said, and he hurried to answer his own question. "Let me guess: because a man should love a woman enough to notice when something's not right, and he shouldn't have to be told."

"Yes and no," she said. "What you just said is true, but rest assured I'm not afraid to express my needs and feelings when it's necessary. I would never expect you to read my mind. I just thought we would talk about it when you have a break from school; it's only a few more weeks."

"Yes," he said, "but that's too long for you to be wondering where we stand."

Celia nodded but was suddenly crying so hard that he knew she'd been holding in a great deal of sorrow and concern. "I'm so sorry, Celia," he said and eased close enough to wrap her in his arms and allow her to cry against his shoulder.

"It's all right," she muttered. "I'm all right. I just . . ." She kept crying, and he knew she just needed to get it out of her system without having to talk about it.

Greg let her cry and kept holding her long after she'd become still and silent. He didn't want to analyze the situation any more right now. They had their whole lives to talk about anything and everything. The best thing he could do now was just get to the point.

"You can *never* throw away these pajamas," he said.

"Why?" she asked, looking up at him so genuinely puzzled that he couldn't help feeling pleased with himself.

"Because someday you're going to show them to our children and tell them this is what you were wearing when I proposed."

Celia gasped softly before Greg slid off the couch to his knees and took both her hands into his. "You can tell them it was a simple moment—no big fanfare or extravagance—but you knew beyond any doubt that my proposal came with all the sincerity of my heart and with all the conviction a man should have when he makes the biggest commitment of his life."

Celia had tears on her face again, but she made no attempt to let go of his hands in order to wipe them away.

"I love you, Celia Mae. Will you marry me?"

"Yes," she said on a wave of delighted laughter. "And you can tell our children I answered the question with all the sincerity and conviction of my heart." She wrapped her arms around his neck and whispered, "I love you too."

They sat close together, holding hands while they discussed their plans until it became late and they both knew they needed some sleep. Greg hated to say good night and leave, but now that they had set a date to be married—a during his upcoming break from school—he could start counting the days until they could live under the same roof. Now that they'd talked about their plans for a wedding and honeymoon, Greg felt lighter in spirit, and he realized the matter had been weighing heavily on him, but he hadn't stopped to notice.

He knew now that this was right, and in fact the timing was perfect. It was far better to take time for a honeymoon and get settled into life before he began the next busy stretch of his education.

The following morning, Greg went early to Neal's room, just a few minutes after he knew his son's alarm clock was set to ring. He found Neal awake but still in bed, which was just what he'd hoped for.

"I wanted to tell you something," Greg said, "but I know mornings are busy."

"Okay," Neal said and sat up.

Greg sat on the edge of the bed. "I wanted you and Jeanie to be the first to know, but you wake up earlier than she does." He chuckled at the thought of just saying it, and he loved the way the words felt as he spoke them. "Celia and I are getting married."

"That's awesome, Dad!" Neal said and hugged him.

"Yes, it is," Greg said. "And I'm glad to know you're okay with it."

"I think it's great," Neal said. "I really do. When?"

Neal didn't seem surprised when Greg told him the wedding would be in about a month. Neal reminded Greg that when Shannon and Phillip had decided to get married, they carried out the wedding even faster than that.

Greg left Neal to get ready for school, and a short while later he knocked at Jeanie's bedroom door and also found her awake but not out of bed. He repeated the news to her just as he'd given it to Neal, and her reaction was much the same except that, in a typically female fashion, she expressed even more enthusiasm. He truly was glad that his children loved Celia and that they were fine with the arrangement. He felt sure it would be difficult to take such a step if it caused difficulties or big changes for the children. As it was, he wouldn't be living in the same house with Neal and Jeanie anymore, but he would see them nearly every day and continue to be involved in their lives. They had discussed the matter more than once already, knowing this would be a possibility.

At breakfast Greg told the others the good news. Shannon let out a squeal that even outdid Jeanie's enthusiasm. She hugged him and whispered, "I guess you know how to take a hint."

"I'm not *completely* stupid," he said facetiously, and she hugged him again.

Phillip and Marj were also very pleased, and the conversation over breakfast mostly consisted of the women talking about food and flowers and cake for the wedding. Greg didn't care about any of that. He wanted Celia to have whatever made her happy. He just wanted to get married.

* * * *

Even though Greg remained very busy, he couldn't help but be well aware of Celia's happiness and contentment, which felt perfectly synchronized with his own. During the snatches of time they were able to share with each other, she kept him apprised of the ongoing wedding plans, and he loved hearing all of the details but not as much as he loved observing her enthusiasm. They would have a simple church wedding, elegant but not extravagant—with a fairly small guest list—and an open house afterward at the Meadows home. Marj was in her element with overseeing the party, and both she and Shannon were helping Celia make all of the arrangements.

Celia expressed some regret over knowing that none of her family would be present, although she admitted her only real regret was the absence of her mother through this entire process and knowing she wouldn't be there to see Celia get married. Celia felt no true sorrow over the inevitable absence of her father and siblings, knowing they would only dampen the mood for her and thus mar the experience.

Celia *did* talk to her mother on the phone about her wedding plans, and she promised to send Betty pictures and video following the event. Betty expressed her sorrow in not being able to come, but she completely resisted Celia's efforts to talk her into just getting on a plane and making the journey. Celia had even offered to pay all of her expenses, and Shannon was more than willing to let Betty stay in her home. But Betty wouldn't do it; her fear of upsetting her husband was far greater than her desire to be present at her daughter's wedding. Celia shed some tears over that, and she and Greg talked through her feelings more than once. But she made peace with the situation and was determined to not let anything stand in the way of their wedding being everything it should be.

Greg wanted to get Celia an engagement ring; however, he'd preferred that she pick it out herself. They both knew he couldn't afford anything too extravagant, but he wanted Celia to have what she wanted, and he knew that the ring was something a woman treasured for a lifetime. Celia, however, made it clear that she'd never wanted a fancy ring. In spite of regularly wearing necklaces and earrings that were fashion accessories coordinating with her wardrobe, she didn't like wearing rings that got in the way. She insisted that she preferred to just have matching wedding bands, and she didn't need anything on her hand to prove that she was engaged during the short time left before they actually got married. So the Saturday following Greg's proposal, they went into the city to pick out rings and take care of several wedding-related errands. Celia had organized the plans carefully, and they used Greg's free time to accomplish the things that he absolutely had to be involved in.

On a night less than two weeks before the big day, Greg was able to fall asleep feeling sweet anticipation for the way his life was about to change. Celia had assured him that everything had been ordered and arranged, and she'd never felt happier. Celia's happiness added to his own, and he could now look beyond the last little stretch of school he had to get through in order to get to his wedding day.

Greg came abruptly awake in the darkness with his heart pounding. It took him a few seconds to realize that Jeanie was sitting on the edge of his bed, crying.

"Daddy, wake up," she said, sounding like a little girl.

"What's wrong?" he asked and sat up, reaching over to turn on the lamp on the bedside table. She looked even more upset than she sounded, and he put his arms around her, urging her face to his chest. She clung to him and cried, muttering a few words here and there that made no sense. He kept assuring her that everything was all right until she finally calmed down and relaxed with his arms still around her.

"Tell me what's wrong, sweetheart," he encouraged.

"I had a nightmare," she said, which explained why she was so upset in the middle of the night. But he felt a little sick just trying to imagine what might have induced so many tears. He knew from the regular letters and phone calls during his years in prison that Jeanie had gone through a period where she had been prone to terrible nightmares resulting from the neglect and verbal abuse she'd been subjected to while in the care of her mother. As far as Greg knew, such dreams had stopped a long time ago, and he wondered what might have brought this on. He was glad she had come to him instead of Shannon or Neal, which would have been the case in the past. While he was grateful she had come to feel at ease enough with him to seek his comfort, he wondered if he might somehow be the cause—directly or indirectly.

"Tell me," he said, instinctively knowing she wouldn't have come to him if she hadn't felt the need to share with him whatever was causing such anxiousness.

"It was just like that day in court," she said, "when BeeKee was trying to take us away from Shannon." Jeanie clung to him more tightly, as if he literally represented the guarantee that such a thing would never happen again. Maybe he did.

Greg hated to hear any reference at all to his ex-wife—which was the only way he'd personally referred to her either mentally or verbally in many years; he preferred this more generic, impersonal term. In the same respect, it seemed appropriate that the children would refer to her as BeeKee. In his opinion the name suited her well; she was shallow and selfish and completely preoccupied with her own appearance and pleasure. He far preferred to hear his children call her that as opposed to referring to her as their mother. They hadn't used any form of the word *mother* in regard to BeeKee in many years. As far as he could see, she had done nothing to earn that title beyond actually giving birth to them. Even when the children had been babies, BeeKee had shown very little interest in them—especially when they needed care and attention.

Greg had worked very hard to forgive his ex-wife for all the damage she'd done to their children. He'd long ago gotten over any hurt she'd inflicted on his own life. It was the way she'd treated Neal and Jeanie that upset him deeply, and thoughts of it still had the power to upset him. But he'd learned to breathe deeply and pray for the ability to forgive her and let go of what he couldn't change. Now, with Jeanie so upset by memories and fears in regard to this woman, Greg found it more difficult to not feel angry.

Reminding himself that he was the adult and he needed to be strong and rational for his daughter, he kept his voice calm and said,

"Tell me about the dream, sweetheart. Tell me everything so we can talk about it."

"It was just like that day, but it's like I could see everything that happened—even the parts when I hadn't been in the courtroom but I heard about later. In my dream I saw it all, and I was so afraid I would have to go back home with her." Jeanie started to cry again. "I was afraid of the horrible people she would bring into the house and how I would have to hide in the closet when they were there. I was afraid of feeling hungry and not being able to find anything to eat."

Greg squeezed his eyes closed against the sting of tears. He'd known about all of that, but to hear Jeanie tell him herself—and with such emotion—threatened to crack his heart right down the middle. He told himself that he'd been in prison; he couldn't have done any more than he did. But he still felt responsible. Once again he felt inexpressibly grateful that he'd had a sister like Shannon, someone he could call on and beg for help once he'd realized the situation was critical. Shannon had gotten them away from their pathetic excuse of a mother, and she'd fought for them in every way necessary to keep them safe and secure. But the emotional impact of all that had happened was obviously far from being healed.

"Was there more?" Greg asked, wanting to understand why this nightmare had come up for Jeanie now.

"Just . . . a feeling . . . a horrible feeling that . . . I had to go home with her . . . that I had to go back." Jeanie looked up at him with pleading eyes. "Please don't make me ever go back there. Promise me!"

"You *never* have to go back!" he declared quietly. "I promise!"

"But maybe it's not up to you," Jeanie said, sobbing again. "Shannon told us last time that it had to be up to the judge, and sometimes things didn't work out the way we want them to."

"That's true," Greg said, "but it was all settled a long time ago, and—"

"No, that was temporary!" Jeanie snapped and practically jumped out of his embrace, as if she were suddenly angry with him. "The judge said Shannon would have custody until our father was out of prison and became capable of taking care of us. That's happening now. You're capable of taking care of us, so that means BeeKee could sue for custody again, and she can lie to the judge and pretend that she's changed, and because she's our mother she'll have the right to . . . the right to . . ." Jeanie was practically hyperventilating now, and Greg felt too astonished to speak. He wanted to go wake Shannon up right now and ask for a clarification of what Jeanie had just said. Was it true? Could the custody agreement be amended now that he was in a position to care for the children? Was it really possible that this ugly battle could begin all over again? Regardless of whether the odds might fall in his favor—given that he would allow the children to remain in their comfortable and safe environment—the stress and grief that could be stirred up made him so sick that he actually felt nauseated.

Trying to focus on the drama of the moment, Greg took Jeanie in his arms again and hugged her the way he'd wanted to during all the years when he was separated from his children. She clung to him again while she cried. He wanted to promise her that no legal battle over her well-being or that of her brother would ever happen again. But he wasn't sure he could make that promise. He wanted to promise that her mother could never have any legal power in their lives again, but without understanding the details Jeanie had shared, he couldn't promise that either without talking to Shannon first. He prayed silently for strength and guidance and for his daughter to be comforted. He *did* promise her that everything would be all right and he would do everything in his power to keep her safe. She seemed reassured and gradually calmed down, but she was still crying when Shannon pushed open the bedroom door that he now realized had been left partially open—which meant the noise of Jeanie's outburst would have surely been heard down the hall.

"What's wrong?" Shannon asked, her concern readily evident. Greg thought of all the times she'd been there through the years to soothe Jeanie following the onset of her nightmares. Not only could she answer the questions that were pounding through his mind, she also had a great deal of experience in dealing with Jeanie's fears.

"She had a nightmare," Greg explained when Jeanie said nothing.

Shannon sat on the other side of Jeanie and asked, "Have you been having bad dreams you haven't told us about?"

"No," Jeanie said and turned toward Shannon, who wrapped her in a motherly embrace. "Not until tonight."

"Will you tell me what you dreamed?" Shannon asked, looking at Greg over the top of Jeanie's head. Greg did his best to silently express all of the concern he felt while Jeanie repeated the essence of the dream, focusing mostly on her feelings of fear that she'd have to go back and live with BeeKee.

"Is that true?" Greg asked Shannon.

"Is *what* true?" Shannon countered.

"Can the custody agreement be amended now that I'm in a position to take care of them?"

"What?" Shannon exclaimed. "No!"

"But that's what the judge said!" Jeanie said to Shannon, pulling away from her. "That's what you told us. It was settled until Dad got out of prison and was able to take care of us. And he can do that now. BeeKee would remember that. She would! She doesn't love us. She doesn't want to take care of us. She's just angry and embarrassed because she made such a fool of herself, and she wants to use us to get even with you for taking us away. She'll try to get us again! I know she will!"

Jeanie was getting hysterical again, and Greg was extremely glad to have Shannon here. His heart actually pounded while he waited to hear how she would respond to Jeanie's concerns that had now become his own. When she hesitated, he said, "You're the attorney. You were there. What's the reality of the situation, Shannon? Is there some truth to what Jeanie is saying?"

Shannon replied calmly but with a mild defensiveness in her tone. "Do you think I wouldn't have thought that through? Do you think I wouldn't have talked to you about any potential problem if I believed that *anything* could go wrong?"

"No, I wouldn't think so," Greg said. "But obviously Jeanie believes there is cause for concern, and that makes me realize that I don't have any idea what exactly my legal rights are with my children in regard to their mother. If there is *any* chance she could try and get them back again, I need to know."

"She could try, but she would *never* succeed," Shannon said.

"If she could try," Greg countered, "that implies she has enough leverage to convince an attorney to represent her, and if she has that, then—"

"Listen to me," Shannon said, reaching for his hand, at the same time taking hold of one of Jeanie's hands with the other. She looked at Jeanie, then Greg, then Jeanie again, including them both in what she had to say. "Any attorney who would choose to represent her after what happened last time would be a fool. Every word that was said in the last hearing is in a permanent court record. And *you,*" she nodded toward Greg, "are their father, and you have everything in your favor in regard to your conduct and your relationship with the children. We also have in our favor the fact that judges put a high priority on keeping children in their present situation if it's well established and they are thriving there. Not only that, Neal and Jeanie are both old enough now that any judge would also put a high priority on allowing the children to have some say in where they want to live. Even *if* BeeKee was living a perfectly exemplary life—which we know she is not—she would not be able to take the children away from their present situation. The most she could ever get is some minimal visitation, but even with that, the kids would have some say in the matter. If she so much as sneezed wrong in their presence, they would not have to stay for even an hour."

Greg took that in with a deep breath and silently echoed Jeanie when she asked Shannon, "Are you sure?"

"Yes, Jeanie," Shannon said with confidence. "I'm sure. We all know what she's like, and I'm not saying she couldn't try and stir up some trouble, and none of us want to deal with that. But she will not be able to get you and Neal back—not ever! Your dad getting married is actually one more thing in our favor. For him to be in a stable relationship with a woman who is steady and successful and has no criminal record shows that he is in a far better position to be the parent who determines what's best for you and your brother."

Jeanie nodded and started to cry again, this time with relief. Shannon held her, and Greg put a hand on her shoulder, again exchanging an intense look of concern with his sister.

"Forgive me," Greg said, "but I have to say it . . . I have to be sure." Jeanie looked toward him anxiously as he asked Shannon, "How can we *know* she isn't living an exemplary life? What if she *has* changed?"

Jeanie looked at Shannon as if her life depended on the answer. But Shannon kept her focus on Greg, saying firmly, "Do you really believe that's possible?"

"I believe people can change. *I* changed."

"You always had a good heart. But to answer your question: even *if* she had everything good going for her, the most she would get is some visitation rights, because no decent judge is going to uproot the kids at this stage of their lives when everything is good for them. And if she *had* changed, there wouldn't be any fear about having the kids spend time with her, because she wouldn't behave the way she did before. *However,*" Shannon added firmly, "I know for a fact that *nothing* has changed in her life."

"How can you know that?" Greg demanded.

"Let's just say that she's not very bright about using good privacy settings on her social media."

"What?" Greg asked. He knew what she meant; he was just surprised at what she'd just admitted to. "You've been spying on her?"

"I've been checking up on her occasionally in a way that anyone with access to a computer could." Shannon looked at Jeanie firmly. "And I don't want *you* to do that! Trust me when I tell you it's far better that you don't."

"It's not like I didn't know I could do that," Jeanie said. "I have no desire to do any such thing."

"Good," Shannon said and turned her attention back to Greg. "Without going into any details, let me assure you that she has not changed at all. Social media has given her one more way to express her selfishness and to be shockingly crude and vulgar. And don't think that a judge or attorney couldn't do a Google search if they have a case where a person's character comes into question. No attorney in their right mind would represent someone in a custody battle who is posting almost daily the kind of stuff she is posting. Enough said."

"Okay," Greg said, feeling better. "Thank you, sis. Sorry for getting so grouchy. I just—"

"You weren't grouchy," she said. "You need to know the kids are going to stay safe. I understand. We're all in this together."

"Dad?" Jeanie said, again sounding like a little girl.

"Yes, sweetheart."

"I'm so glad Shannon is your sister."

"Me too," Greg said, kissing the top of his daughter's head while squeezing his sister's hand. "I shudder to think where we would be without her."

* * * *

After they had talked a while longer, Shannon took Jeanie back to her room, and Greg tried to sleep—with little success. Through the course of a very busy day following this trauma, Greg tried to keep his mind from wandering back to Jeanie's nightmare and its deeper implications. He felt reassured by all that Shannon had said, but he still felt uneasy.

During his lunch break he talked to Celia about what had happened. She listened and offered reassurance. But still he felt uneasy. Late that evening, he arranged for Shannon and himself to sit down with Neal and Jeanie and make certain that both children knew exactly where the situation stood so they would have no cause for concern or anxiety. Neal asked some questions that made it evident he'd been having some of the same thoughts as Jeanie; however, her concerns had resulted in a terrible nightmare, which they all hoped would not be repeated.

Days later, Greg still found himself preoccupied with the situation regarding his ex-wife and the fear his children felt regarding her. He prayed about it night and morning and many times in between, feeling like he needed to do something specific to help ensure they had nothing to worry about. He just didn't want to go about it the wrong way and stir up a hornet's nest. For all he knew, BK still believed he was in prison. He'd gotten out much sooner than he'd expected due to his good behavior and the education he'd received in prison. But she didn't know that. Or did she? Did she know he was out of prison? Had she been planning and scheming, waiting for the right moment to sue for custody again? Or what if she tried something that had nothing to do with the law? She'd done that before as well. When the children had been in Shannon's care prior to her marrying Phillip, one of BK's despicable friends had actually attempted to kidnap the children. Thanks to Shannon's quick thinking and Phillip's timely assistance, the guy had been arrested and BK had been warned that if anything untoward happened again in regard to the children, she would face legal repercussions. But BK was known for having a short memory when it came to what was legal or ethical. Something deep inside Greg feared that one of these days Jeanie would remember the attempted kidnapping and start having nightmares about the possibility of it happening again. And there was no legal information Shannon could give to assure any of them that it wouldn't happen. Greg had made the decision to marry a woman like BK He felt certain it was up to him to make sure she never caused any more grief for his children—ever again.

By the time Sunday came around again, Greg knew what he needed to do; he just wasn't exactly certain how to go about it. He was grateful to have two women in his life who were well-educated concerning the law and already knew the situation inside and out. Knowing that church and the usual Sunday dinner routine would be keeping all of them busy for several hours, Greg texted Celia early and was glad to learn she was awake and had some free time to talk. He arrived at her apartment to find her ready to go to church; since he was too, they could talk until it was time to leave.

"Good morning," she said, greeting him with a kiss.

"Good morning," he replied and kissed her again.

Celia motioned him inside and closed the door, saying, "I am going to assume this has something to do with your ex-wife."

"Why would you assume that?" he asked.

"Because the situation with her has been bugging you ever since it came up with Jeanie, and I suspected you hadn't put it to rest just yet."

"How is it that you know me so well?" he asked as they took their usual seats on the couch where they always sat when they shared any kind of serious conversation.

"You tell me *everything*," she said. "Why wouldn't I know?"

"And you have very good intuition," he said and took her hand. "Because you're right. I've realized that I need to do something about this situation, not just wait and hope that nothing develops. I divorced her officially many years ago, but I feel like I need to do something that will demonstrate my complete emotional separation from her—and more importantly, a complete separation between her and the kids. I need to do something that will let them know I'm in their corner, that I will protect them. I have somewhat of an idea, but I need to know what I can do legally."

"Okay," she drawled, sounding mildly concerned.

"I'm not proposing anything dangerous or reckless," he assured her. "I just feel like I need to face her, and I need to say some things that need to be said. I've thought a thousand times that I hoped to never actually see her again, but now I realize that until I do I will always fear how it might feel if I were to see her. This way, it will be over and done and I don't have to dread it. I don't need her to be cooperative or to say anything in return; in other words, I don't have any expectation or need about how she might respond. There are just some things I have to say."

"Not unlike my need to say what I did to my father," she said, and he felt completely validated, even though the comparison hadn't occurred to him before now. "It didn't take long and I didn't say much, but it had to be said, and it had to be said to his face."

"Yes," he said. "I think it's very much like that."

"So . . . what? You're just going to show up at her door?"

"Exactly," he said. "Shannon said that according to her social media, it's obvious BK is living in the same house; her address isn't posted anywhere, but there are recent pictures that show her in the same house. Her work schedule and habits are also very obvious."

"Doesn't she realize how stupid—and even dangerous—that can be?"

"I could ask that question about almost everything she has ever done," Greg said with disdain. "I can't even comprehend that I was ever married to her or that I was part of the same crowd. If it weren't for the children, I would think it had all been a dream."

"Yeah," Celia chuckled, "they are pretty valid evidence that you didn't imagine it." She pointed at him comically. "And I've seen their birth certificates. Your signature is on them."

"Why have you—"

"I've helped register them for school—among other things. I do anything Shannon asks me to do."

"Anything?" he asked lightly, interrupting their conversation long enough to lean over and kiss her.

"If she asked me not to marry you, I would tell her to forget it. But not to worry; she would never ask that of me."

"Because she knows you're the best thing that ever happened to me," Greg said and put some distance between himself and Celia, needing to get through this conversation in the short amount of time they had.

"Back to the point," he said. "I also need to do something that will help the kids feel safer and more secure." He took a deep breath and asked, "Can I get their mother to sign over her parental rights—for good?"

"I don't know, *can* you?" Celia asked, and the question surprised him. "If you're asking me if it can be done legally, the answer is yes. What I'm wondering is *how* you would convince her to do that when she's not known for being agreeable to giving up her control in any given situation."

"Because I know where the bodies are buried," he said with conviction.

"What?" she gasped as if she suddenly feared he wasn't the man he'd been pretending to be all this time.

Greg chuckled. "Not literally; I mean . . . there are not literally any bodies. I promise." She looked so relieved that he chuckled again. "What I mean is that I know her, and I know many of the people who are still her friends. And I know that many of them were involved in a great deal of illegal activity—most of it pertaining to drugs. When I went to prison I took the fall for more than I was guilty of because I thought I was protecting my kids by protecting people I had believed were my friends. Either way, I knew that BK would continue to associate with them. Well, she knows I paid the price for some of their crimes; and those people know it too. Truthfully, I don't have much to hold over them, but I can be very convincing in making them believe that I do."

"Them?" she asked fearfully. "You can't go have conversations with drug dealers. Not only is it dangerous, it's a violation of your parole, and—"

"Let me clarify," Greg said. "I'm not going to talk to anyone but my ex-wife. But I know what to say and how to say it to make her believe that I would and could cause trouble for her and her friends. And she's probably embarrassed enough by her own lack of ethics that she would do just about anything to be reassured that I wouldn't act on what I know. Knowing her as I do, she has probably been less than honest with almost everyone she knows, which means she wouldn't want one friend knowing the truth about a different friend—if that makes sense."

"Yes, I think it does," Celia said and became thoughtful. She finally looked at Greg and said, "I can draft up the document you need her to sign, and I'll run it by Shannon to make sure it's sound. I assume you want me to do that."

"Yes, thank you," he said.

"I have one condition."

"Anything," he said, knowing she wouldn't be unreasonable.

"I'm going with you," she said, and he wondered if he had spoken too soon. He wasn't sure he wanted Celia to actually meet his ex-wife and get a real glimpse into the life he'd once lived. "If you have to face her, I think that maybe I do too. You don't have to tell her I'm your fiancée if you think that's a wiser tactic, but I want to meet her. Besides you're going to need a notary."

"A what?"

"When you get her to sign the paper, you need it witnessed and notarized. I'm certified to do that. Then there won't ever be any question over the validity of the document."

Greg let that settle in and said, "Okay, but I have a condition on your condition."

"What?"

"I know you *wouldn't* do this, but I still have to say it."

"Go ahead."

"I don't have any desire to step back into that part of my life. I'm only doing it because I believe it's necessary. Having *you* step into that part of my life feels . . ." He couldn't find the words.

"Do you think I will see you differently if I actually meet your ex-wife and see where you used to live with her?"

"Maybe. It might not be reasonable, but that's how I feel."

"And I understand," she said and squeezed his hand. "Once again, our situations are very different, but the emotions are much the same. I have no desire for you to ever meet my father; the very idea makes me a little nauseous. But if it ever happens, I'm certain you'll know how to handle the situation, and since you're already well aware of what he's like, I need to trust that it wouldn't change anything between us. I think you need to give me the same consideration."

Greg sighed. "Okay. Point taken." He looked at her intently. "Do you think this is the right thing?"

"I can't answer that," she said. "You have to decide whether or not it's right. I will support you either way. But I think you already know it's right or you wouldn't have come here to make such a strong case for it. You're allowed to change your mind if your feelings don't stay the same, but I can pull the document together and get it ready just in case."

"Okay," he said. "Thank you." He sighed again. "I *do* feel like I need to do it. And I need to tell Neal and Jeanie what I'm doing and why. I'm afraid they'll want to go with me . . . that they'll want to face her too."

"Why should you be afraid of that?" Celia asked. "So what if they do? They're strong and smart. They've already faced her in court. Personally, I think you should *ask* them if they want to go. We'll have a family road trip."

Greg actually liked that idea, even if he didn't like thinking of having the kids anywhere near the woman who gave birth to them.

"It'll have to be quick," Greg said. "Next weekend, I guess. It's the only time I could do it before the wedding. And I don't want *anything* to get in the way of having the perfect wedding."

"Amen," she said and stood up. "It'll be a fun little getaway. Well, other than, say . . . a certain twenty minutes or so; hopefully it won't take longer than that. The rest will be fun."

"With you along, I think it will be," he said, grateful now at the thought that she was going to accompany him and the children on this difficult errand. He felt sure if she didn't, he would be wishing she was with him.

Chapter Fifteen

THAT AFTERNOON GREG MANAGED TO get some time alone with Shannon, and he told her what he'd told Celia. He was surprised at how supportive she was, and he wondered why he'd believed she might want to talk him out of it. He was also surprised at how eagerly she agreed that Neal and Jeanie should be given the option to also face BK if only so she could see how strong and confident and grown-up they had become.

With Shannon and Celia fully backing him, Greg sat down with Neal and Jeanie later that evening and explained his plan and his reasons for it. They were both insistent upon going, so much so that he was glad Celia had suggested he be prepared to give them that option. Otherwise, he might have been trying to talk them out of it, and he could see they had their own reasons for wanting to be a part of this ceremony of sorts that would hopefully free them from BK and her influence once and for all.

* * * *

The week was busy for everyone, but Greg remained almost continually mindful of the upcoming road trip and its purpose. He did a great deal of praying that it would all go well, and in spite of busy schedules, he found time to check in with Neal and Jeanie and make certain they were doing okay with the pending visit to their mother. He assured them repeatedly that it was their decision whether or not they went and they could change their mind. They were both equally determined to go, even though neither of them had anything in particular that they wanted to say to BK He talked to them a little about how they might be emotionally prepared for what was most likely to take place, but he wasn't sure if he was good at talking to teenagers about such things, especially when he was struggling with it himself.

The closer it got to the day they were to leave, the more grateful Greg became that Celia was going with them. She would help him maintain perspective, and she always had a way of keeping the mood light when challenges were underfoot. While they were getting ready and making plans, she focused on the fun they would have and jokingly called the visit with BK *that little errand* they had to take care of.

Greg finished all of his finals and did well, surprised to realize that he was done with this initial portion of his education. He'd been so preoccupied with other matters that he'd just mechanically gotten through it. Now he could put all of his focus on the little weekend trip he was taking with Celia and the kids, and once that was behind them, the wedding would be only a few days away.

They set out very early Saturday morning in Shannon's SUV, since it had a lot more space and was more comfortable for a long drive. She had suggested the idea, glad to trade cars with Greg for a couple of days. While he drove, Greg was fascinated with the way that Celia kept conversation going with Neal and Jeanie. She had a gift for connecting with them and meeting them at their level of thinking. They took turns choosing songs from their iPods to listen to, and he was surprised to learn that Celia was familiar with the majority of the music his kids liked, while he'd never even paid attention to it. If he'd handpicked a woman simply on the merits of what kind of stepmother she would be to his children, he couldn't have picked anyone better than Celia, and he told her so when they stopped at a service station to put gas in the car and take a restroom break. She just smiled and kissed him as if her being so great with Neal and Jeanie took no effort on her part whatsoever.

The drive across the state of New York didn't feel too cumbersome with good company and good music and conversation. Even with making a few stops to eat and take breaks, they still arrived at the edge of the city in time to check into their motel rooms before going to find some supper. Greg had called days earlier to make a

reservation for two rooms—one for the boys and one for the girls—
with an adjoining door between them that could be opened when
they desired.

They all settled quickly into their rooms and freshened up before
they went out to eat at a place where Greg had gone occasionally prior
to going to prison. He admitted he had no good memories of the place
other than the fact that they had the best Chinese food he'd ever eaten,
and he'd often wondered whether it was as good as he'd remembered.
He was happy to say that it completely met his expectations.

"Are you nervous about tomorrow?" Celia asked Neal and Jeanie
when they were almost finished eating.

"A little, maybe," Jeanie said at the same time Neal just shrugged.

"Well, I am," Greg admitted, not only wanting to be honest but
also hoping to get the kids to talk about any possible concerns. He
wanted them to be prepared for any potential scenario, but perhaps
they'd already done that and he needed to just stop worrying and take
it as it came.

Back at the motel, Neal sat on his bed with the remote control
and started flipping through channels while Greg perused a travel
book that had been left on the bedside table. The door between the
two rooms was open, and he could hear Celia and Jeanie laughing,
which made him smile. When they laughed again, Neal said with
light sarcasm, "They are having *way* too much fun in there."

"Yeah, I think we're pretty boring."

"No, we're good," Neal said, still looking for something interesting on
TV. "Girls just have to talk and giggle."

"And guys just . . . what?" Greg asked. "We grunt and pass the
popcorn while we watch a game?"

"That works for me," Neal said, "but I'd prefer a good science-
fiction flick."

Greg chuckled and pretended to be looking at the book in his
hands while he was actually more interested in trying to hear what
Celia and Jeanie were laughing about. He couldn't hear with the TV
on and he felt tempted to join them. But he thought it best to allow
them to have their girl time.

Before settling down for the night they shared a prayer and hugs
all around.

"I'll see you in the morning, handsome," Celia said to Greg as she kissed him.

"I'll be looking forward to it," he said, wishing he wasn't dreading the morning.

As if she'd read his mind, she added, "By lunchtime tomorrow, it will all be over."

"Provided she doesn't decide to not be home for the first Sunday morning in twenty years."

"We've all been praying," Celia said. "Everything will be fine."

Celia and Jeanie went to their room, and Greg felt sure he wouldn't be able to sleep.

He woke up to daylight, surprised at how long he'd slept. A quick glance showed him that Neal wasn't in his bed, and he could hear quiet conversation. He realized the door between the two rooms was open, and Celia and the kids were in the other room talking. He went quietly closer to the door, curious about what they might be saying but not wanting to intrude. He figured if it was private they would have closed the door.

He heard Celia saying, "It's like there's some kind of homing beacon planted in every human being that makes us want to be connected to who and what we came from. You hear about it with people who have been adopted, and even if they've had a good life with an outstanding family, most of them still eventually want to find their birth parents and know the story of where they came from and why."

Neal talked briefly about a friend he knew at school who was adopted and had talked about those very feelings. He concluded by saying, "I told him that Jeanie and I had talked about how we have felt like we were adopted. The difference was that we could remember our birth mother and we wished that we couldn't."

"It's not fair, is it," Celia stated. "Parents are supposed to be the people who take care of you and keep you safe. You're supposed to be able to trust them and look up to them."

Greg heard Neal and Jeanie agreeing with her. Celia then told them a condensed version of her experience with her father, of what it had been like to grow up with him being so pious and verbally abusive. She told them how she'd stood up to him the previous Christmas and that he'd told her she was dead to him.

Neal said vehemently, "But if he treats you like that, it's better that you never see him again, isn't it?"

"I believe it is," Celia said. "I wished for years that my father would be able to see how much he'd hurt me and would apologize and try to do better, but a time came when I had to accept that my wish wasn't realistic, and I had to let go of hoping for something that was out of my control. I believe some people are toxic. They simply don't know how to be kind or positive, and their attitudes and their words can be very harmful when we are exposed to all that. It's a healthy decision to draw a boundary with people like that and to choose to keep your distance. We want to believe people can change, that they will become the way we want them to be. The sad fact is that most people don't change because they don't want to or don't know how. And even if they knew how, they probably wouldn't because it's a lot more difficult to change than it is to just stay the way you are."

Jeanie said, "I know BeeKee will never change. I'm not expecting her to. I guess I just want her to know that I don't care."

"I can understand that," Celia said.

"Dad talks about how much he's changed," Jeanie went on, and Greg's heart quickened as he became the subject of the conversation. He wondered if they might talk about how he'd disappointed them.

"He seems the same to me," she added, and Greg felt confused.

"Yeah, me too," Neal said. "I mean . . . he stopped doing drugs and stuff, and he started going to church in prison and reading the Bible, and I know that made him happier, but he doesn't act much different as far as I can remember."

Jeanie agreed, and Celia said, "Do you know what I think? I believe your father was always a good man, and he always had a good heart. But with the way he was raised—lots of different foster homes and all that—he just didn't know how to deal with his environment or his circumstances. So he made some bad choices, but he's worked very hard to make all of that right. I agree with you. He's the same man he's always been; he's just learned how to handle life better."

"He's the best dad ever," Jeanie said, and Greg was glad to be out of sight when tears immediately filled his eyes.

Neal agreed, and Greg had to put a hand over his mouth to keep from making any sound.

"Well, I kind of like him," Celia said, and the children laughed.

"I'm glad you're going to be our mom," Jeanie said, and Neal made a noise of agreement.

"Oh, I'm glad for that too," Celia said. "We're all going to be a very happy family, I think."

"And a lot happier in a few hours," Neal commented.

"Yes, indeed," Celia said. "Once we get *that little errand* taken care of, we can all just focus on keeping our distance from the family members who have hurt us and making a better family for the future."

Now that Greg had his emotions under control, he decided this would be a good time to intrude on their conversation. He stepped into the room, glad to see that his children seemed fairly relaxed and calm. He certainly had Celia to thank for that.

Everyone was apparently in good spirits while they shared breakfast, but on the drive to BK's house, they all became very quiet.

"You guys nervous?" Greg asked with a quick glance toward the backseat.

"I don't feel nervous," Neal said. "It's just . . . weird. We used to live in this house, but the memories aren't very good."

"It *is* weird," Greg said. "Jeanie? How are you?"

"I'm okay," she said. "My clearest memory is the night that Shannon came and took us away. *That's* a good memory."

"Yeah," Neal agreed, and they became quiet again.

Celia reached for Greg's hand and offered a reassuring squeeze and a comforting smile. What had he ever done without her?

When Greg drove into the neighborhood where he'd once lived, he felt a huge increase in that weirdness Neal had mentioned. It was like some kind of time warp. It was a fairly poor neighborhood, but he noticed some stark contrasts. Some houses were small and old but the yards were well kept and showed evidence of people living there who actually cared about their lives. And then there were other houses bordered with dead grass where weeds flourished and where garbage was carelessly strewn about—which was exactly how the house looked where he and his children had once lived.

"Wow," Neal said as Greg stopped the car in front of the house. "I remember it being bigger."

"You were smaller," Greg said.

"Her car is here," Jeanie said, and Greg marveled that the kids seemed so calm when he felt intensely nervous. Maybe they'd had more counseling than he had. "She still has the same car. Weird."

"Yeah," Greg agreed. He put the car in park but left it on to keep the air conditioning running. "I'm not going to think about it; I'm just going to do what I have to do." He took a deep breath and exchanged a glance with each of the others. "All according to plan, right?"

"Right," they all said together.

"We'll be right here until you give us the signal," Celia said and gave him a quick kiss.

"Go, Dad!" Neal said with a chuckle that seemed not quite in keeping with the situation, but Greg considered it far better than an indication that his children were on the verge of some kind of PTSD episode.

"If it goes bad, we'll come save you," Jeanie said and let out a brief laugh.

"Yeah," Greg said more seriously, "I might need that."

"It'll be fine," Celia said, and he got out of the car, hurrying to the front door with a burst of courage. He knocked but got no response after waiting nearly a minute. Oh, how he prayed she was home! And not stoned. He'd been praying for that for days. He knocked again, turning to look at Celia and the kids, who were watching him with expressions that reassured him this was the right thing to do.

Greg heard noises indicating that someone was home, and his heart quickened just before the door came open. He'd considered the possibility that someone else might be here, since it hadn't been uncommon in the past, but he prayed that wouldn't be the case.

When BK opened the door, he felt an eerie sensation as his brain attempted to connect the present with the last time he'd seen her, which had been months before he'd gone to prison. The lines in her face made her look twenty years older than Greg, which was sad considering that she was actually a little younger than he was. That was what long-term drinking and smoking and drugs did to a person, he thought. She was far too thin, and her hair was colored a platinum-blonde that looked ridiculously phony. She was wearing too much makeup, which had obviously been applied the day before, and her clothes were typically skimpy. He couldn't help comparing her to Celia, and he couldn't wait to tell his fiancée how she outshone his ex-wife in every way.

"I don't believe it!" BK said, seeming happy to see him. At least she was sober enough to recognize him and converse. So far so good.

"Hi," he said, and she surprised him with a hug, which he quickly returned, then eased away, not wanting to be too close to her. He thought of Celia's description of certain people being toxic, and he felt as if BK might contaminate him with some kind of emotional radiation poisoning.

She motioned him inside and closed the door, not taking any notice that there were people in the car parked at the curb. He preferred it that way.

"What are you doing here?" she asked as if they were long-lost friends and they should both be thrilled to see each other. For whatever reason she might be pleased to see *him,* he had no pleasure in seeing her except to get this over with. And he didn't trust her. and the house was a mess and smelled stale. That hadn't changed either. When he'd lived here, he'd done most of the cleaning. After he'd left he'd hated what he'd seen on the rare occasions she had let him come to pick up the kids for a visit.

"I won't stay long," he said. "I just thought you should know I'm out of prison, and it would be good to clarify where we stand with the kids."

"Okay," she said, sounding mildly irritated at the mention of the kids, as if they were a matter of distasteful business. Or perhaps she'd been hoping that he might have returned to once again become a part of her social circle. The very idea made him sick.

"How are they?" she asked, her tone indicating more resentment than any kind of real concern.

"They're great," he said. "Shannon's taken very good care of them; they couldn't ask for a better situation." He decided to just jump straight to the point. "That's why I thought it was important for us to make sure that nothing disrupts that. I think the most responsible thing we can do as parents is to let their lives go on as they are. They have good friends, and they like their schools and neighborhood."

"Is that why you came? To talk about the kids?"

"Yeah, that's why I came."

She let out a disappointed sigh and folded her arms. "Are the kids living with *you?*" she asked, and he could sense her competitive nature in the question. Even though he hadn't ever thought of it this way, he was glad to be able to say, "They're living with Shannon and her family, and that's where they're going to stay. I've been living there, but I'm moving out next week. I think it's best to leave Neal and Jeanie where they are. Shannon can give them what you and I could *never* give them." She said nothing, and he hurried on to say what he needed to say, wanting to have this over with. "It will only be a couple of years before Neal is an adult, and then he can choose if he wants to see you. And Jeanie is just a couple of years behind him. Maybe when they're adults you can keep in touch with them." He wanted to point out that she knew their mailing address but hadn't sent so much as a birthday card in all the years since they'd been taken away from her.

"Okay," BK said, sounding indifferent.

"And just to make that legal so it doesn't cause any problems for the kids, I hope you'll be willing to sign a document." She looked skeptical, perhaps on the verge of anger, but she didn't speak. "It's just a formality, really, because they're old enough that a judge would let them choose who they want to live with as long as their needs are being met."

"Have you *asked* them?" she countered like a snotty child, as if she thought they might actually *want* to come and live with her if they'd been given a fair choice. And her assumption of course was that they *hadn't* been consulted.

"Would you like to ask them yourself?" Greg asked. "Because they're in the car."

"They're here?" she asked and unconsciously straightened her hair, which only made it look more like she'd just gotten out of bed.

"Yes, they wanted to see you. I also brought my fiancée. She'd like to meet you, although I'm not sure why."

"You're getting *married?*" she asked as if it were a dirty word.

"I am," he said proudly.

"Is that why you're doing this?" she asked with suspicion.

"I'm trying to move forward with my life. I thought it would be good for us to have some closure and to clarify the custody of the children. My fiancée also happens to be a notary, so she can witness the signing of the document. Again, let me say that signing the document isn't going to really change anything, but the kids don't want to worry about ever having to leave their home and their friends. This might help them feel better. I would assume a responsible mother would want to do what's best for her children."

She glared at him, but he knew he had her—almost, anyway. There was still a glimmer of something devious in her eyes, which immediately leaped forward when she asked, "And why should I? Why would I give up my kids?"

"First of all, you're not giving up anything that you haven't already been legally denied—twice. And secondly, you don't want to mess with me in any way for any reason."

"Are you threatening me?" she hissed, and he hated her in that moment as he remembered hearing her say things just like that a thousand times during their years together.

Greg remained completely calm and said what he'd come prepared to say. "Look at it this way. I know a *lot* about you and your friends and what you do and who you go to when you need a fix. I took the fall for a couple of them. Let's just say it would be wise for you to just do the right thing and avoid any possible . . . complications."

"Fine, I'll sign it," she said so quickly it almost startled him. "Can I see the kids?"

"For a minute," he said and opened the door. "Try to be nice."

"Of course I'll be nice," she said, as if she couldn't imagine him thinking she'd behave any other way.

Greg stepped onto the porch and motioned with his arm for the others to come in. He knew Celia would bring the document, a pen, and her notary stamp. He held the door open while they filed into the house, where BK was standing some distance back in the tiny front room, her arms folded. He saw her eyes widen when she realized how much Neal and Jeanie had changed, and she visibly scrutinized Celia from head to toe, as if she was surveying the *other woman*.

Turning her focus back to the kids, who appeared to be doing okay so far, BK said, "Wow. You guys have grown up."

"Yep, that happens," Neal said as if he were talking to a cashier at the grocery store.

"Are you doing okay?" BK asked, and both kids responded firmly that they were. "So you want to stay with . . . Shannon?" The name came through her lips as if it were a foul word.

"Yes, we do," Jeanie said firmly.

"Will you sign the paper?" Neal asked.

"Sure, why not?" BK said. "If that's what you want."

"Hi," Celia said, stepping forward to set the paper and pen on the coffee table, after she'd slid aside the junk piled there. "I'm Celia. We finally meet."

"Hi," BK said and sat down on the couch.

Celia sat beside her, handed her the pen, and pointed to places on the paper. "Just sign here and initial here."

B.K. did so, and Celia stamped it and signed her own name as a witness. The two women stood, and an awkward silence descended over the room.

"You can write to us if you want," Jeanie said to her mother.

"You *do* know our address," Neal added as if to remind her that she'd known ever since she'd sued for custody of them years ago.

"Maybe," BK said, adding nervously, "You be good, now." It seemed the total sum of mothering she could muster.

"Sure thing," Neal said and led the way out the door.

"Bye," Jeanie said with obvious indifference.

"Nice to meet you," Celia said as if she truly meant it before she followed the kids outside.

"Okay, I guess that's all," Greg said. Feeling a sudden surge of concern, he asked, "Are you doing all right? Do you need anything?"

"Yeah, I'm fine," she said with a stubborn pride that he recognized, which was a strong contradiction to his knowing that she would gladly take anything and everything from him if it suited her and she thought she could get away with it.

"Okay," he said, taking her comment at face value. "Well . . . take care of yourself."

"You too," she said, and he hurried out the door, closing it behind him while letting out a huge sigh of relief. It was over.

Greg had to make himself walk to the car when he wanted to run. Once inside with the door closed, he couldn't drive away fast enough.

"Mission accomplished," he said. After he turned the corner and gained some distance, he asked, "You guys okay?"

"Yep," Neal said at the same time Jeanie said, "Sure am."

"I'm great," Celia said, and he looked over to see her grinning. She waved the signed document as if it were the deed to a priceless estate. Maybe it was. "And for the record, I have never felt *less* intimidated by any woman in my life! With everything I've heard, she was exactly what I'd expected."

"Oh, you are so awesome compared to her," Neal said.

Greg chuckled. "That is the greatest understatement of the twenty-first century."

"And you are *so* much prettier," Jeanie said. "I wish I could grow up to look like *you.*"

"You're so sweet," Celia said, reaching for Jeanie's hand to give it a squeeze.

"It's true," Jeanie said.

"You're beautiful, sweetheart," Greg said to his daughter.

"Because she looks like you," Celia said to Greg. "They both look a lot like you. I used to think they looked like Shannon, but that's only because she's your sister and *she* looks a lot like you." Celia peered into the backseat. "I think you both got the very best of your parents."

"Amen," Neal said and changed the subject by asking, "What are we going to eat for lunch? I'm hungry."

"Me too," Jeanie said.

Greg smiled at Celia, more gratified than he could say to see how smoothly his children had just faced a woman who had caused them unspeakable grief. In that moment he truly felt as if his life was starting over.

* * * *

The days remaining until the wedding passed by quickly and with a noticeable absence of stress. Everything was organized and under control, and Greg truly felt ready to take this step, as he knew that Celia did. He loved her so much that the very idea of making her his wife sometimes made his heart actually feel hot inside his chest, and he feared at moments that it might burst.

Greg wanted to spend every waking minute with Celia, but two days before the big event, it became evident that she had a great deal to do, and Shannon discreetly told Greg that she and Marj would take very good care of the bride and he could have her all to himself after they were married and went on their honeymoon. She suggested that in the meantime he spend his free time with his children, but she gave him a list of things to do for the wedding that made it evident he wouldn't have very much *free* time. He enlisted Neal and Jeanie to go with him on some of his assigned errands, and they had fun while they were out, which he declared to be the best bachelor party ever.

Celia could hardly believe that she was finally getting married and that she was now close enough to the event to start counting hours instead of weeks or days. Given her insecurities and the countless times her father had told her she'd never get a husband unless she lost weight—as if that were an automatically assumed prerequisite—she had spent many years wondering if she would end up alone, participating in family life on the outskirts of Shannon's family. But a miracle had happened, and she would now be officially a part of the most wonderful family she'd ever known. She loved Greg more every day, and the thought of spending a lifetime with him filled her with perfect happiness. To have Shannon as a sister-in-law—and Neal and Jeanie as her children—were the greatest fringe benefits she could possibly imagine.

Celia was grateful beyond words for the way Shannon had decided to just close down the office for a couple of days, which meant that Shannon stayed almost constantly at her side the day before the wedding, making certain everything was under control, and helping keep Celia's nervousness from overtaking her. She wasn't worried about any of their celebration plans going awry; if that happened, they would laugh about it and move on. And she certainly wasn't worried about whether or not she was doing the right thing or that Greg might change his mind or back out. She was as sure of his love and commitment to her as she was of hers to him. But she felt an almost constant rush of nervous adrenaline that made her stomach flutter and her heart often beat too quickly. She had trouble sitting still—or sitting at all. And she could hardly eat a thing, which

Shannon cautioned would only make the situation worse if she had a sudden blood sugar crash.

Celia basically moved into a guest room at Shannon's home so that Shannon could help Marj as food and flowers and such were delivered to the house, and the women could still be close by to remind Celia to eat and to stay calm. She was glad that Greg had taken Neal and Jeanie into the city. Every time she came face-to-face with him her nervous excitement skyrocketed and she almost feared she would faint, or at the very least hyperventilate.

Celia had a moment in the afternoon when it fully and finally sank in that her mother would not be there for the wedding. She cried to the point of having a brief meltdown, but Marj and Shannon sat with her and said all the right things to remind her of the reasons for the situation and that she'd done everything she could. Once Celia had a good cry over it, she gratefully accepted Marj's lengthy, motherly embrace—and Shannon's sisterly one—and she couldn't deny how blessed she was.

When bedtime finally came and everything was all set, Celia feared she wouldn't be able to sleep at all and she'd be even more of a mess the next day. But Shannon gave her a mild over-the-counter sleep aid and promised to make certain she would wake her up in plenty of time to get ready. Celia ended up sleeping well and she awoke feeling completely calm and nothing but happy.

When the moment finally came to exchange sacred vows with Greg, Celia felt as perfectly beautiful as any bride should. Her biggest reason for that was not the exquisite dress she wore, or the extra care that had been put into her hairdo and makeup. She felt beautiful because of the way Greg looked at her throughout the ceremony while everything else became distant and almost nonexistent. Looking into his eyes during the course of those life-altering minutes, Celia saw a reflection of herself that at one time she would have never imagined possible. The love they shared had changed her for the better in too many ways to count, and she knew it had changed him too. They were helping each other become their best selves, and she knew that surely had to be the meaning of real love.

Throughout the remainder of their wedding festivities, Celia loved the way Greg would hardly let go of her hand. He kept looking at her as if most of what was going on around him meant very little.

The sparkle in his eyes let her know that he was every bit as happy as she, and that whatever life might bring in the future, they were in it together in every possible good way.

Epilogue

WITHIN DAYS AFTER RETURNING FROM her honeymoon, Celia felt so comfortably settled into her life with Greg that she couldn't even imagine what it had been like to live without him. School soon began again for him, and of course their jobs both continued, which kept them incredibly busy. But living under the same roof made everything easier and more gratifying. He was always there beside her when she went to sleep and when she woke up, and the passion they shared privately as husband and wife enhanced everything else that was good in their relationship.

Celia's bond with Neal and Jeanie settled in more deeply. It was as if knowing she would always be there made them want to be around her even more, and they became more comfortable in the apartment where Greg and Celia now lived together. They usually stayed over at least one night a week, and Celia loved the way they truly felt like a family—albeit a unique one. The family bonds she felt with Shannon and Phillip and Marj—and Grace and Evan, too—also deepened, and she often just looked around at family gatherings and basked in the warmth she'd not even known existed throughout the majority of her life.

Just a few months after Greg and Celia were married, Celia discovered she was pregnant. Contending with nausea and excessive fatigue, she was more grateful than ever to be working for Shannon. Not only were they close as sisters and friends, but Shannon had empathy for dealing with pregnancy and trying to work. Celia was able to put in fewer hours at the office on days when she felt particularly awful, and she made up for it by doing paperwork and making phone calls from home. Together they made plans for Celia to take a maternity leave, when Shannon would take on a lighter schedule at work or perhaps hire a part-time temp if necessary. Since Shannon had kept her babies at the office with her a great deal when they were little, she made it clear that not only was Celia welcome to do the same, but Shannon truly hoped she would so they could all spend more time with the baby when it came. For Shannon, the prospect of becoming an aunt to a new niece or nephew made her almost as excited as Celia was to become a mother.

As Celia's pregnancy progressed, she marveled at the miracle of a new life growing inside of her that was a tangible representation of the love she and Greg shared. He was so tender and solicitous that even when he was busy and overwhelmed, she never felt neglected or unloved. While she was sometimes lonely for his company, she never doubted his convictions and commitment.

With her pregnancy making her more hormonal, Celia was often overcome with an increased tendency to cry over the absence of her mother in her life. They talked on the phone regularly—still with the aid of Betty's friend—and Betty was thrilled to hear every detail of Celia's pregnancy and of all the plans being made for the baby's arrival. But Celia felt like she had to grieve all over again for the dysfunction in her family that made it impossible to have her mother more involved with this part of her life. Marj helped make up for Betty's absence a great deal. She checked in with Celia every day and was always eager to help in any way she could. She also planned a baby shower for Celia that rivaled the wedding open house she'd had. Celia couldn't feel more loved or cared for, but she still missed her mother, even if she had accepted that it was simply a part of her life she couldn't change.

Along with going to school, Greg continued to do construction work for Rob. The two men became good friends, and Greg and Celia sometimes had a double date with Rob and his wife. It was Rob's idea to help Greg and Celia start working toward building a home. He told them about his long-established terms of offering discounts to all of his employees and how there was an available lot in the subdivision he was working on that he believed would be perfect. It turned out that with both Greg and Celia's incomes—and the amount of money they had in the bank that would make a significant down payment—they could actually qualify for a home loan and be able to manage just fine. Payments on the house wouldn't begin until it was done and they could actually move in, at which time they would no longer need to pay rent on the apartment. The month before the baby was born, construction on their new home began.

For all of Celia's discomfort and nausea throughout the pregnancy, her health remained good and the baby grew at a normal and healthy rate. Labor commenced four days before the due date and proved to be a long, exhausting ordeal. It took several hours for Celia to reach the point when she could start pushing, and then for more than three long hours, she pushed with each contraction. The blessing of modern medicine prevented her from feeling the pain as intensely, but the pressure was still readily evident, and she still had to endure labor without being able to rest at all. Greg remained by her side almost every moment, holding her hand, encouraging her, and continually expressing his love for her either verbally or simply by the way he was so obviously concerned and every bit as engaged in the process as she was.

When their new son was finally born—perfect and healthy and strong—Celia had never felt so happy, and she knew that Greg felt the same. While she laughed and cried with relief and joy, there was no missing the sparkle of tears in her husband's eyes that magnified the adoration and intrigue he felt for this child they had brought into the world together.

"I love you so much, Celia Mae," Greg said, kissing the top of her head while they both admired the baby in her arms. "More every day."

"Oh, I love you too," she said and looked up at him. He kissed her and they exchanged a long gaze that silently expressed all that words never could.

Their eyes were both drawn back to the wiggling infant, who made a grunting noise that provoked them both to laughter. Celia barely noticed the door coming open, surrounded as she was by nurses who were still putting things in order and making certain all was well. She glanced up and felt such a deep, sudden shock that she could hardly breathe. With great care but hurried urgency, she shifted the baby into Greg's arms and began to sob as her mother moved to the edge of the bed and wrapped her in a careful embrace.

"Oh, Mama," Celia cried, and the two women looked at each other, laughing through their tears. "I can't believe it. You're here. You're really here."

"Shannon called to let me know you were in labor," Betty said, taking hold of Celia's hand. "She told me if I wanted to come she would help me make the arrangements and that I could stay with her for as long as I wanted."

"Oh!" was all Celia could say as her tears overtook her again and she hugged her mother tightly.

Greg observed Celia's reunion with her mother and felt overcome. While he had a difficult time taking his eyes off his new son, he also wanted to just savor Celia's obvious joy at having her mother there. And the glow on Betty's face was unmistakable. Greg just took it all in and silently thanked God for all he'd been blessed with. Looking back over his life, most of it just felt like a bad dream. He remembered it enough to retain all he'd learned, but abuse and neglect and prison all felt like something that had happened to someone else. Now he was a man with what seemed the perfect life, and he could feel nothing but eager to just savor every minute of it—whatever joys and challenges it might bring. For the moment, he found perfect joy in becoming acquainted with the newest member of the family and the opportunity to finally meet his mother-in-law.

After some brief, official introductions, Greg hugged Betty tightly and said, "I can't tell you how happy I am that you came."

Betty smiled at him through a fresh wave of tears that continued while she held her first grandchild and beamed with visible joy.

"Oh, I'm so glad Shannon talked me into coming," Betty said, her focus completely on the baby. "Shannon and Marj are in the waiting room, by the way. Such wonderful ladies! They picked me up at the airport. Oh," she repeated, "I'm *so* glad Shannon talked me into coming. Although she didn't have to talk very hard. I've been stewing over this for months, and I finally decided I wasn't going to let Melvin keep me from being with my baby girl at a time when a girl needs her mother most. And I certainly couldn't miss spending time with my grandchild."

"What did you say to him?" Celia asked, astonished.

Betty looked up at her daughter. "Nothing," she said, seeming pleased with herself. "I left him a note, and I just . . . left." She laughed and looked again at the baby in her arms. "I told him where I was going and why and that I didn't know when I'd be back. I told him that when I came back there would be some new house rules." Betty laughed again while the baby tightly gripped her finger with his tiny hand. "I don't know if he'll be up to living with my new rules. But that's all right."

"Is it?" Celia asked, exchanging a quick glance of amazement with Greg at the same moment he took her hand and squeezed it.

"Oh yes," Betty said with triumph in her voice. She looked at Celia and said with strength and courage in her voice, "If he doesn't like it, he'll just have to figure out how to get by without me—if that's even possible." She laughed again and added, "Shannon told me if she had her way, I would just move into Greg's old room and Marj and I could grow old together, and we would enjoy being one big happy family."

"How delightful," Celia said with a little laugh that perfectly expressed her joy.

"Amen," Greg said and kissed the mother of his child. Looking into her sparkling eyes, he added, "How delightful, indeed!"

About the Author

ANITA STANSFIELD HAS MORE THAN fifty published books and is the recipient of many awards, including two lifetime achievement awards. Her books go far beyond being an enjoyable, memorable story. Anita resonates particularly well with a broad range of devoted readers because of her sensitive and insightful examination of contemporary issues that are faced by many of those readers; readers come away from her compelling stories equipped with new ideas about how to enrich their own lives, regardless of their circumstances.

Anita was born and raised in Provo, Utah. She is the mother of five and has a growing number of grandchildren. She also writes for the general trade market under the name Elizabeth D. Michaels.

For more information and a complete list of her publications, go to anitastansfield.blogspot.com or anitastansfield.com, where you can sign up to receive e-mail updates. You can also follow her on Facebook and Twitter.